"In her d____ _____ _____ Souls, Anne Lyle creates an alternate Eliza_____an England done right. A world where history meets fantasy in the streets, and where neither emerges unscathed. With a twisting plot, endearing characters, fast-paced action, and truly unique and alien 'fey', Lyle steps up and gives notice to the genre. No wilting faerie queens and tortured knights here: this is how historical fantasy gets dirty. A great first instalment in a promising new series."

Douglas Hulick, author of AMONG THIEVES

"With an effective mix of espionage, backstage drama, and mystery, Lyle provides compelling drama in an intriguing setting."

Publishers Weekly

"Anne Lyle's fluid writing brilliantly evokes the heady and gritty atmosphere of her alternate Shakespearean London – from the day-to-day life of theatre troupes to the pomp of official ceremonies."

Aliette de Bodard, author of SERVANT OF THE UNDERWORLD

"Anne Lyle's *The Alchemist of Souls* teems with intrigue and magic worthy of the Bard himself, all set against the backdrop of Elizabethan London. The attention to historical detail brings the time and place alive and peoples it with characters I could instantly empathize with. An outstanding debut!"

Lynn Flewelling, author of the Nightrunner series

"Murder, mayhem and intrigue at the court of Elizabeth I. All this and magic too makes for a great ____."

Mike She____

ANNE LYLE

The Alchemist
of Souls

Night's Masque vol. I

ANGRY
ROBOT

ANGRY ROBOT
A member of the Osprey Group

Lace Market House,
54-56 High Pavement,
Nottingham,
NG1 1HW, UK

www.angryrobotbooks.com
'Cross the sea

An Angry Robot paperback original 2012
1

A catalogue record for this book is available
from the British Library.

ISBN: 978-0-85766-213-2
EBook ISBN: 978-0-85766-215-6

Set in Meridien by THL Design

Printed and bound by CPI Group (UK) Ltd, Croydon, CR0 4YY

"They say this town is full of cozenage,
As, nimble jugglers that deceive the eye,
Dark-working sorcerers that change the mind,
Soul-killing witches that deform the body,
Disguised cheaters, prating mountebanks,
And many such-like liberties of sin."

William Shakespeare, THE COMEDY OF ERRORS

CHAPTER I

Darkness came early to the streets of Southwark, even in summer. The jettied upper storeys of inns shadowed the great thoroughfares and turned its alleys into foetid rat-runs that hadn't known sunlight since King Henry's time. Mal kept his hand on his dagger hilt, scanning every doorway and alley mouth out of habit, though his thoughts were elsewhere. By his side, his companion continued his own side of the conversation unheeded.

"Hmm?" Mal said at last, looking round as Ned clutched at his elbow.

The younger man's features were indistinct in the gloom, but the irritation in his voice was plain enough.

"I said, it's worth a try. Isn't it?"

"No." Mal quickened his pace, forcing Ned to break into a jog-trot to keep up.

"Fifty shillings, Mal–"

"Fifty-two."

"All right, fifty-two. Makes no odds if it's fifty or a hundred. Where else are you going to find that sort of money by Midsummer Day?"

"The answer's still no."

They walked on in silence for a while, Ned trailing at Mal's heels like a terrier after a deerhound. Despite the lateness of the hour, the streets teemed with Londoners determined to wring the last drop of pleasure from the evening. Dukes and bishops rubbed shoulders – and more – with sailors, whores, apprentices and players. The noise and stench were enough to deprive a newcomer of his wits, and the suburb's denizens ever ready to deprive him of his money.

"But you'd be good at it," Ned went on, when Mal halted to let a finely dressed woman and her maidservant cross the street. "You've got such an honest face."

"And I'd like to keep it that way," Mal replied in a low voice. "Getting branded in the ear isn't good for business."

The woman smiled at Mal and fingered the lace around her neckline. His eyes lingered for a moment on the curve of her breasts, then he shook his head regretfully. She pouted and walked off down the street, hips swaying.

"What business? You haven't had a job since Easter–"

Mal stopped dead in his tracks and Ned ran into the back of him.

"What–?"

"Shut up," Mal hissed, clenching his fist, thumb between first and middle fingers in the sign called "the fig". An ancient protection against evil, as well as a sign of contempt.

The crowds parted to reveal a group of man-like creatures, the tallest of them no bigger than Ned. They wore tunics of undyed wool, cream and dark brown woven in complicated geometric patterns, over breeches tucked into low boots. Silver-streaked hair hung loose about their shoulders or was braided like a girl's and threaded with beads. Most outlandish of all were their faces, painted in whorls of blue lines that disguised their not-quite-human features.

As the skraylings walked past, Mal thought he saw one of

them turn and look up at him with slit-pupilled eyes. The skrayling's patterned face was somehow familiar, though his hair was more silver than – No, he was imagining things; these foreigners all looked alike, didn't they? He raised his hand to make the sign of the cross and his vision shifted; the skrayling was not looking at him at all, was staring straight ahead in fact. Mal finished the protective gesture and shoved his trembling hand into his pocket.

"What was all that about?" Ned asked as the crowds closed behind the skraylings.

"Nothing," Mal lied.

"They're not demons, you know, whatever the Puritans say."

"You think they're wondrous faery folk of the New World?"

Ned shrugged. "Why not? You've seen their camp; tell me that's not magic."

Mal had no answer to that. He well remembered his first glimpse of the skraylings' stockade at night, lit by lamps of cold blue, violet and yellow that never flickered despite the gusts of icy wind blowing in off the Essex marshes.

"You should be grateful to 'em," Ned said as they set off again. "Since they set a bounty on rats, there's been scarcely a hint of plague in the city."

"You think killing rats made the difference?"

"Something did. Why else would they be paying a penny a tail?"

Because they want everyone to forget that skraylings don't get the plague? He added aloud, "Perhaps they're fond of rat-tail soup."

Ned pulled a face. "Even I'm not that desperate. Hey, that gives me an idea!"

"Another one?"

"We could buy us a terrier and set ourselves up as rat-catchers. They say a good ratter can kill twenty a minute."

"And where would we get the money to buy a dog?" Mal said. "Tom at the White Hart wanted ten-and-six for that scrawny pup the other day."

"It was a little runt," Ned admitted. "My money would have been on the rat. So, where to? The Bull's Head?"

Mal ignored him. He was trying to decide whether or not to pawn his rapier. Not an attractive option, since his livelihood depended on it.

"Bull it is, then." Ned grinned and rubbed his hands together.

Mal glowered at his friend, cursing himself for letting his mind wander. He had been idle too long. In a fight, carelessness like that would get him killed.

"Anywhere but the Bull, I beg you!" he said. "I have no desire to spend another evening listening to your actor friends reciting interminable speeches and slandering their rivals. I'm for the Catherine Wheel." He set off down the street again.

"And I've no wish to spend another evening listening to your old comrades' tales of death and glory," Ned shouted after him. "At least at the Bull I might earn a shilling or two on my own account."

"Please yourself, but you go alone. I'll not be your pander."

Ned groaned. "All right, all right, you win. But you're buying."

The Catherine Wheel was as busy as a brothel mattress, and twice as pungent. The only difference was, the fleas here had steel teeth. Tucked away in a courtyard off the high street, the Wheel saw few outsiders venturing through its low door. Even if they did, one look told them to step back outside and seek somewhere more congenial. Somewhere the patrons still had the usual complement of eyes and limbs, for a start.

The first empty seats Mal came to were opposite a lone man who was muttering an endless stream of oaths into his beer, mostly about the French and their filthy sexual practices. Ned rolled his eyes in protest so they moved on, Mal nodding to various acquaintances who inclined their heads in response but failed to beckon him over. They found themselves a table near the back door; the stink of the jakes wafted in whenever someone went in or out, but at least it was unoccupied. Ned said something that was drowned by the sudden roar from a group of dice-players nearby, and stamped off. He returned a couple of minutes later with two jacks of beer, grumbling under his breath.

"Right, you owe me a penny," he said, sliding one of the beers across the uneven tabletop.

Mal forced a smile. Ned's remark was too near the knuckle. He needed to earn silver, and soon. The fellow at the next table looked more respectable than most; he was apparently un-maimed and wore a well-cut frieze jerkin. Private armies might have been outlawed, but in a city where the watch was poorly paid and often infirm, a man with money and property to de-fend always had need of a few stout fellows who knew how to handle themselves in a fight. Mal tried to catch the man's eye, but he was deep in conversation with his companions.

Ned leaned across the beer-damp table. "Any prospects?"

"None so far."

"Well we need something to tide us over. And this time of year the city's full of fools just waiting to be parted from their money."

"You know what I think of your… devisings."

"Look." Ned lowered his voice. "I'll deal the cards and do all the talking. All you have to do is bet against the gull, and feign drunkenness."

"How can I bet when I have no money?" Mal asked. He took a sip. The beer was no worse than usual. No better either.

"So you'll do it, then?"

"No. And don't try it alone, either." He glanced meaningfully towards the bar, where a man with a belly like a pregnant mare was wiping tankards with a rag. "Sideways Jack has no love for coney-catchers; he'll skin you alive if you ply your tricks in here."

"As if I would," Ned replied, all injured innocence. "Credit me with *some* wits, mate."

The door of the tavern opened, and the taproom fell silent. Four men came in, wearing dark blue livery, scarlet cloaks and steel breastplates and helmets, and bearing pole arms with long blades that glinted in the candlelight. The foremost of the guardsmen, a man of about thirty-five with a broken nose and the bearing of a professional soldier, cleared his throat.

"I am Captain Edward Monkton of the Tower Guard. I seek one Maliverny Catlyn, lately of the parish of St Mary Overie–"

"No one 'ere by that name," Sideways Jack said. "Sir."

Monkton scanned the room. Mal forced himself to sit still and neither try to hide nor catch the man's eye. Long moments passed in which Monkton's gaze alighted on first one patron of the tavern, then another. All were youngish men with dark hair.

The captain advanced into the taproom, peering into the shadows. Then he looked back at one of his men, who nodded. Mal exchanged glances with Ned. As one they leapt from their seats and ran for the blessedly near back door.

"What in Christ's name–?" Ned gasped as they raced across the back yard, slipping in puddles of piss left by customers who hadn't made it as far as the jakes.

"Damned if I know!" Mal replied. "Come on!"

The back gate was padlocked. He rattled it in frustration. Any moment now the guards would come bursting through the back door.

"You go over the fence." Ned crouched with his hands laced together, ready to give Mal a boost. "I'll hinder them."

"Are you sure?"

"Yes, yes! God's teeth, get out of here!"

Mal scrambled over the rough wooden paling, wincing as a splinter dug into his thigh, and dropped down into the alley. He could hear the shouts of the guardsmen as they slithered around in the muddy yard, and Ned protesting his innocence. No time to hang around. He jogged off down the alley as fast as he dared in the near-darkness, hand on his dagger hilt.

"Hold, sirrah!"

Mal skidded to a halt. A helmeted figure was silhouetted in the lamplight at the end of the alley. "Goddamn beefeaters!" he muttered.

He turned and ran back the way he'd come, looking for a side turning, but there was none. As he passed the back gate of the Catherine Wheel, it crashed open and two of the other guardsmen cannoned into him, crushing him against the brick wall opposite. He ducked slightly, elbowed the nearest man in the belly and pulled himself free of the mêlée. A moment later a fist like a half-brick impacted with his temple and he slumped against the wall, head reeling.

Someone grabbed him by the scruff of the neck and hauled him to his feet. His arms were pinned behind his back, none too gently.

"Maliverny Catlyn?" The captain held up a lantern and shone it in Mal's face.

"No, I just happen to look like him."

That earned him a fist in the guts. He gritted his teeth, forcing back the urge to puke up his beer.

"That's him, all right," said one of the other guards. "I've seen him in the Wheel a few times. When I was off-duty, of course, sir."

The captain grinned unpleasantly at Mal. "Right, boys, let's go."

They stripped Mal of his dagger and escorted him through the streets of Southwark to the down-river side of London Bridge. A sleek skiff bobbed amongst the wherries, with six men at the oars. Mal was pushed into the boat and the captain waved for him to sit.

"What are you arresting me for?" Mal asked, hoping they wouldn't risk upsetting the skiff by laying into him here.

"How should I know?" Monkton replied. "I was just told to bring you in."

Mal opened his mouth to protest again, but the captain shoved him onto the thwart. The skiff rocked alarmingly, and the soldiers laughed as he clutched at the gunwales.

"Enough!" The captain glowered at his men, then turned to Mal. "You, my friend, can squeal all you like once we get to the Tower."

The skiff cast off, and the rowers bent their backs, making slow headway against the incoming tide that threatened to drive it into the treacherous channel between the piers of the bridge. At last they broke free of the eddies and made their slow way downstream, bearing northwards towards the dark bulk of the Tower.

Crouched on the lower slopes of a hill on the eastern edge of the city, the Tower of London dominated the approach to the capital from the sea. Formerly the principal royal residence, the ancient fortress now housed Queen Elizabeth's chief enemies, detained at Her Majesty's pleasure in a style befitting their status. The Queen herself preferred the comforts of her father's palace of Nonsuch in Surrey, to which she had retreated in mourning for her late husband, Robert Dudley.

On the south bank of the Thames, opposite the Tower, a much smaller fortress squatted by the waterside. Though naught but a wooden palisade surrounded by ditches, it was no less forbidding than its ancient rival. Coloured lamps floated amongst the trees within and eerie piping sounds, like dying seabirds, echoed across the water. The skrayling colony. Mal made the sign of the cross and looked away.

The skiff lurched against the current as they turned sharply towards the water gate. Mal clutched the plank he was sitting on, hoping he didn't look as anxious as he felt. The severed heads of traitors, mercifully no more than silhouettes in the twilight, gave grim testimony to the fate awaiting those who defied their Queen. The splash of oars echoed from the stonework as they passed through a narrow tunnel under the wharf, then the skiff crossed the castle moat and entered the larger archway under St Thomas's Tower, emerging in a dank, shadow-hung pool where a flight of stone stairs led up to the outer ward. Mal was hurried up the steps and four of the guards closed in around him before he could so much as get his bearings.

A yeoman warder in scarlet livery beckoned to the captain, and Mal was taken a short way along the ward, through a sheltered rose garden and thence into a great courtyard with a tower at each corner. The warder unlocked a low door at the base of one of the towers, and Mal was escorted up the spiral stair and through another low door. It thudded shut behind him, and the key grated in the lock.

It was no filthy cell they had brought him to, but an octagonal chamber perhaps twenty feet across. Opposite him a blackened stone fireplace gaped like a bear's maw, and glazed windows to either side of it let in the last of the dim evening light. A second door, to the right of the one he had just come through, proved to be locked also.

The chamber was plainly furnished with a bedstead curtained in plain woollen stuff, a table and bench, and a padded leather prie-dieu under the eastern window. Only the walls betrayed this place as a prison. His fingers traced the shapes carved painstakingly into the stone: names of former inhabitants, several Jesuitical inscriptions, and an E within a heart. Both Catholics and Protestants had been held here over the years.

He knelt at the prie-dieu and began to pray that whatever mistake had been made in bringing him here, Our Lady would see fit to right it before his captors resorted to torture.

He spent a sleepless night alternately pacing his cell and praying. This was worse than the eve of battle. Death at the hands of the enemy was quick and clean compared to the punishment meted out to traitors. The fact that he had not to his knowledge committed treason was no comfort – why else would they drag him in off the streets and throw him in the Tower without charge? He tried not to think about what it must feel like to be disembowelled alive, and failed dismally.

Some time after dawn the sound of a key scraping in the lock roused him from his contemplations and he leapt up from the prie-dieu, groping at his side for the absent rapier. A yeoman warder peered into the chamber, bleary-eyed and drunk judging by the smell of cheap wine that preceded him into the room. Mal wondered if he should rush the man and try to make his escape, but without planning or accomplices he doubted he would get far.

The warder limped across the room, burdened by a heavy basket. From it he produced a battered pewter tankard and plate, an earthenware bottle and a loaf of bread. After setting these out on the table the warder left, locking the door behind him.

Mal went over to the table and sat down to eat. The fear of the night before had subsided into a numb determination to face whatever cruelties his captors were planning. A man weakened by hunger would not resist torment for long.

He had not managed more than a few mouthfuls of the dry bread, washed down with a small ale, when the warder returned.

"You're wanted." The man beckoned him through the door.

Mal's stomach flipped over. So soon?

He was taken back along the narrow outer ward, still deep in shadow at this time of day, and through a tunnel that pierced one of the inner towers. A steep cobbled road led upwards between high walls, with the vast bulk of the Norman keep looming to their right. The warder turned left at the top of the slope and directed Mal across the green towards a handsome timber-framed house built into the angle of the south and west walls. The L-shaped building looked incongruously domestic against the Herculean masonry all around it.

He was shown into a wood-panelled antechamber. Benches stood against the wall opposite the fireplace; above them, portraits of middle-aged men in elaborate armour or outdated clothing stared down at him with the indifference of the long-dead. Mal distracted himself by going from one to another and reading the inscriptions below each: Thomas Grey Marquess of Dorset, Edward Lord Clinton, Sir John Gage.

"My illustrious predecessors."

The man in the doorway was forty or so, well built and a little above middle height, with fair curly hair and beard and a ruddy complexion. His doublet and hose were of sherry-coloured velvet, and his ruff was dyed with saffron. As if on cue, a lion roared in the Tower menagerie, and Mal had to keep his head down as he bowed, to hide a smile. A lion of a man indeed.

"My lord?"

"Master Catlyn." The steel in the man's voice belied his courtier's finery.

"Yessir." Mal didn't quite snap to attention, but his back straightened of its own accord. Old habits died hard.

"I am Sir James Leland, Lieutenant of the Tower. No doubt you are wondering why I invited you here?"

Invited? Well, that was one word for it.

"Yes, sir." Mal swallowed, anticipating the worst.

Leland walked around him in a slow circle, eyeing him up and down as if he were a horse for sale. Mal stared straight ahead. If Leland thought to intimidate him, let him think again.

"Not exactly what I expected," the lieutenant muttered. "But I suppose you'll have to do." He paced some more. "Maliverny. French name, isn't it?"

"My father's second wife – my mother – was Béatrice de Maliverny, from Aix-en-Provence. Being her first-born son, I was named in her family's honour."

"You are half French, then?" Leland frowned at him.

"By blood only, sir. I am an Englishman born and bred." Mal could not help adding, "The French *are* our friends, sir."

Leland muttered something under his breath, then turned to face Mal again. "How old are you?"

"Sir?"

"It's a simple enough question, surely?"

"I am five-and-twenty, sir."

"That dagger you were carrying is of fine workmanship. I fancy it is part of a matched set, a mate to a rapier?"

"Yes, sir." Was that what this was all about? Surely they wouldn't haul him into the Tower over an illegal duel. "I've had lessons from Saviolo himself."

"Hmm. Italian swordplay is all very well, but what about real fighting? I have been told you served under the Earl of Devon."

"I was at the siege of Bergen-op-Zoom, and afterwards I fought in Italy against the Turk."

The lieutenant nodded approvingly. Mal kept his features impassive, trying to follow the course of this interrogation to its logical conclusion. There was none he could see, or none that made any sense.

Leland cleared his throat noisily. "I have a commission for you, Catlyn. From Her Majesty the Queen, no less."

Mal stared at him.

"Have you nothing to say for yourself, man?"

"I – Thank you, sir." Mal began to laugh, near drunk with relief, then fell silent. Leland did not look amused. "Forgive me, sir, I... Well, after last night I thought for certain I had been arrested for treason."

"Arrested? I sent Captain Monkton to find you, certainly, since no one knew your whereabouts. If there has been any misunderstanding, well, that is very regrettable."

Mal went over the previous evening's events in his mind. He was the one who had bolted like a guilty thing and thus begun the chase. On the other hand, this Captain Monkton had taken great delight in letting him think he was under arrest. Had the captain misunderstood his instructions, or was he merely brutal and malicious?

"Now, about this commission," Leland said. "You are to guard a foreign ambassador who will be visiting England later this summer."

"An ambassador? Of where?"

"Vinland."

"Vinland? But–"

"He is a skrayling, yes. You have an objection to that?"

"N-no, sir," Mal said. His thoughts were racing. Bodyguard to a skrayling? Why had he of all people been chosen for such a task? And how could he get out of it? "I was merely surprised. I didn't know they had an ambassador."

"The savages seem to have taken a while to grasp the idea, but it pleases their fancy to have one now. And of course he must be treated with all the courtesy due a foreign ally."

"Of course."

"The pay is four shillings a day," Leland went on, "also board, lodgings and a suit of livery. You will report here on the twentieth day of August and learn your way around the Tower and the ambassador's quarters."

Four shillings a day. Twenty-four shillings a *week*. That was not a sum he could turn down easily, not the way things were going. But August was a long way off. Too long. He cursed under his breath in frustration.

"Well, what is it?" Leland asked.

Mal swallowed. It was a gamble, but if they really wanted him for this job... "I am, as you undoubtedly know, sir, out of work at the moment. How I shall shift for myself in the next few weeks, I know not, but I doubt I can find a position for so short a while..."

"You are asking for a retainer?"

Mal lowered his gaze. "Yes, sir."

"Very well," Leland said after a pause for consideration. "Half pay until you start – and of course no board or lodgings."

Two shillings a day – and now it was barely two weeks until Midsummer Day. Nowhere near enough to pay off what he owed.

Leland sighed. "Come on, man, out with it."

Mal could not meet the lieutenant's eye. He feared this was a step too far. "I have some small but pressing debts. I–"

"How much?"

"Three pounds, sir." Or thereabouts. He prayed the lieutenant would not ask what the money was for.

After a long moment Leland began to laugh. "Three pounds. Well, we cannot have His Excellency's bodyguard thrown in the Clink for so paltry a sum. Here." He took out a purse and counted out six gold angels.

"Thank you, sir," Mal said, pocketing the coins. "I am in your debt."

"You are in the Queen's debt, not mine. I'll instruct the purser to take it out of your pay."

"Of course, sir."

"Someone will be along presently to see you out, and return your blade. Until August, Master Catlyn."

The moment Leland left, Mal sank down onto a nearby bench, shaking with relief. He had been so certain he was condemned to die – and dammit, Monkton had let him stew here all night in that belief. Did the captain know more than he was letting on, or was he judging Mal by his elder brother's reputation? And then there were the skraylings. If Leland found out why the very sight of the foreigners chilled his heart, he would be back in that cell faster than a sixpence into a whore's bodice.

He wondered again why he had been chosen. It had not been Leland's decision, that was clear enough. So whose was it? With the Queen herself in seclusion, any orders most likely came from her advisors, the shadowy members of the Privy Council: Puckering, Cecil, Suffolk, Walsingham, Oxford, Pembroke and Effingham. Mal had the uncomfortable feeling he was being used as a pawn in a game where he could see neither board nor pieces, still less the players making their moves.

CHAPTER II

The cockerel's cry split the cool damp air, heralding the end of another all-too-brief night. Ned groaned and buried his head under the bolster. How much had they drunk last night? Next time he would stick to beer, regardless of who was paying. Speaking of which…

He slid out of bed, wincing at the bruises: a parting gift the other night from a pair of disgruntled Tower guards. Rummaging around in Mal's discarded clothes, he found a familiar pair of worn slops, and in the pocket a purse heavy with gold. He counted the coins out slowly to avoid clinking them together. Almost three pounds, less the few shillings Mal had spent on wine and oysters by way of an apology. Where did he get hold of so much money, and so quickly?

Ned's chest tightened. With that much money Mal could have spent the night with the best whore in Bankside, and yet here he was, back home with Ned. Was it only caution and a desire to be certain of repaying his debts, or had his feelings changed? Best not to dwell on it. Hope was a treacherous mistress.

Mal muttered something in his sleep. Ned eased back into bed and propped himself up on one elbow, the better to admire his companion's profile in the fragile dawn light. A half-grown-out military crop curled above a smooth tanned brow that led his gaze down to a chiselled nose as perfect as an Italian statue. Black lashes fluttered as Mal's eyes twitched beneath closed lids.

"No! Leave him alone!" Mal tossed his head from side to side, struggling as if pinned to the bed by invisible hands.

"Hush, my lamb," Ned whispered.

His reward was a soft moan and a furrowing of that dark brow. He leant over and kissed the sleeping man's shoulder, savouring the salt sting of sweat – and nearly got his lip split open a second time when Mal sat bolt upright with a cry of fear.

"What is it?" Ned asked softly.

Mal rubbed his face, then swung his legs out of bed and sat with his head in his hands, breathing ragged as if he had been running. Ned reached out a hand to comfort him, then thought better of it. After a moment Mal got to his feet, stretched as best he could under the low rafters, and scratched his groin.

"I can't do this," he muttered, picking up his shirt.

"That's not what you said last night." The words were out of Ned's mouth before he could stop them.

"What?" Mal popped his head through the neck of the shirt and frowned at him.

"Er, nothing." Ned wriggled sideways into the warm hollow Mal had just abandoned, and watched him dress. Play of muscles under milky skin, tantalising glimpses of tight arse as the hip-length shirt rose and fell with each movement… He sighed. What was the point of an early rising if you didn't get to use it?

"Going somewhere?" he asked as Mal pulled on his boots.

"Just down to the garden. I need to think." He took his rapier down from its peg.

Ah, that kind of thinking. "Can I watch?"

"If you will."

Mal threaded the rapier's scabbard onto his belt. The matching dagger joined it, then he cinched the belt around his hips.

Ned ducked as Mal turned to leave. The long, slender blade was meant for the lofty halls and galleries of noblemen's mansions, not cramped attics in the backstreets of Southwark.

After Mal had gone, Ned lifted the bed-sheet and peered into its musky depths.

"Never mind, mate. Maybe next time."

Was that a nod or a shake? With a grunt of effort he climbed out of bed.

"First sign of madness," he muttered to himself. "Talking to your… self."

He cast about the room for his own discarded clothing, and remembered the purse. Whatever Mal was up to, he was determined to get to the bottom of it.

Mal drew his rapier and held it up to the light. The rising sun gilded the elegant curves of the hilt and shimmered along the blade. Forty inches of finest Solingen steel, exquisite and deadly.

Mandritta, reversa, fendente, tonda… His fencing master's voice echoed in his memory as he adopted the *terza guardia* stance, blade dipping towards the grass.

He moved through the familiar drills, emptying his mind, becoming the blade. Stepping back and forth along the garden path, the tip of his rapier wove a pattern of glittering arcs above the rows of dew-spangled cabbages, sending butterflies spiralling up like scraps of torn paper.

"Hey, what are you doing?" Ned cried out as the rapier snicked the head off a flowering onion.

"Sorry," Mal muttered.

He wiped the blade on his cuff and sheathed it. Ned looked at him expectantly.

"Yesterday," Mal said, "I was offered – no, *given* – a job."

"But… that's marvellous news!" Ned leapt off the upturned barrel he'd been sitting on. "It is marvellous, isn't it?"

When Mal did not answer, Ned went on: "Are you... Are you leaving London?"

"No." Mal looked north and east, towards the dark smudge of the city on the opposite bank of the Thames. "No, you'll have to put up with me for a while yet."

"Then what's the matter?"

Mal picked up a stone and threw it at a pigeon that was eyeing the cabbages with interest.

"The job is to guard the skrayling ambassador."

"Oh. I didn't know they had an ambassador."

"Neither did I, until now."

"So, what are you going to do?"

"What I should have done a long time ago." He walked back towards the house. "Put on your Sunday best. We're going to Court."

A young Englishman of noble birth could generally be found in one of two places: on campaign in Ireland, or at Court. Fortunately for Mal, Blaise Grey had managed to avoid the former, so he and Ned made their way to Whitehall Palace, on the Thames west of London.

Two enormous gatehouses straddled King Street, guarding the east and west entrances to the palace and its gardens. A constant stream of people flowed in and out under the watchful eyes of the royal guard.

"If anyone asks," Mal told Ned as they neared the gate," you're my manservant. Keep your mouth shut and your eyes down, even if you recognise someone; this isn't the Bull's Head on a Saturday night."

Whitehall swarmed with courtiers, servants and petitioners, though this hive no longer centred on a queen. Prince Robert took care of much of the kingdom's business, sitting at the head of his mother's Privy Council as *de facto* regent. On the

riverward side of King Street lay the prince's lodging and private gardens. Even if Blaise were there, Mal knew he stood
little chance of gaining admittance. In any case, his quarry was
far more likely to be found on the other side of the street, in
the maze of tennis courts and bowling alleys where the young
bloods idled away their hours.

After making several enquiries of servants and getting lost
twice, they found Grey in the larger of the palace's two tennis
courts. The game was still in progress, so Mal and Ned joined the
press of spectators in the mesh-covered galleries running down
one side of the court. There was little to be seen without pushing
through the throng, though judging by the cries of triumph and
anguish from the crowd, the game was reaching its climax.

Mal glimpsed Blaise's dark blond curls for an instant over
the heads of the spectators, then the whole court erupted in
deafening cheers that echoed off the white stone walls. Money
changed hands, and the crowd began to disperse.

Signalling for Ned to hang back, Mal moved forwards, letting the departing courtiers flow past him. Amongst the
stragglers was a slight red-headed figure, face flushed, his fine
linen shirt soaked in sweat. Prince Arthur, the younger of the
Queen's two sons. As the prince passed, laughing at a jest from
one of his companions, Mal swept a low bow.

"Catlyn, isn't it?"

Mal looked up to see Grey staring at him. "My lord."

"Come for a game?" Grey asked, wiping his brow with a towel.

"I– Yes, why not?"

He removed his sword belt and doublet and tossed them to Ned,
who frowned at being treated in such a peremptory manner.

"Manservant, remember?" Mal hissed.

Someone handed him a racquet and he followed Grey through
a side door onto the tennis court. A few of the departing courtiers
drifted back, curious to see how long the newcomer would last.

Mal was out of practice and Grey had a good four inches on him, but he managed to hold his ground, at least to begin with. He's playing with me, he realised after a poor shot gained him a point. He feigned clumsiness on his next return. Grey, falling for the feint, tapped the ball into what should have been empty space – to find Mal there.

"Thirty all!" the umpire announced.

Surprised murmurs echoed around the gallery, and by the sounds of it, bets were placed.

On the far side of the drooping net, Grey twirled his racquet in one hand and shifted his weight from foot to foot. Mal smiled. Impatience: that would be his opponent's weakness. He strung out the moment as long as he dared then served, sending the leather ball bouncing off the left-hand wall and onto the sloping penthouse above the galleries.

It teetered on the penthouse edge for a moment before falling into the hazard end of the court, and Grey flicked it straight back over the net. Mal returned the ball in a high arc that sent the other man running sideways until he all but collided with the tambour wall. The spectators roared with laughter, and Grey flushed. He scooped his racquet under the ball as it bounced heavily on the wooden floor and sent it flying back to the service end. Mal stopped it with a neat backhand – too neat. Grey watched, grinning in anticipation, as the ball hopped over the net and bounced once, twice–

"Hazard chase, second gallery!" the umpire announced.

The spectators clapped or jeered according to their allegiance and placed further bets.

"Got money on this one yourself, Catlyn?" Grey asked. "Or perhaps you're not your father's son after all?"

Mal bit back a retort. This is no different from duelling, he told himself. Better to keep silent and let the other man's ill temper work in your favour. He served again, focusing all his attention on the flight of the little leather ball.

"So," Grey said, "what have you been doing with yourself since you were sent down?"

Mal froze. "I was not sent down, I left."

The tennis ball whistled past his head, hit the wall with a crack like a pistol shot and ricocheted into the *dedans*.

"Forty–thirty!" Grey smiled. "Change ends, Catlyn."

From his vantage point halfway along the court, Ned was paying more attention to the players than to the game, of which he knew little and cared less. Mal so rarely talked about his past, it was easy to forget he was the son of a diplomat, as far above a mere scrivener as Prince Arthur was above a gentleman commoner like Mal. This was a rare window on a part of his friend's life he seldom got to see.

"That's merely what I was told," Grey said, preparing to serve.

"What else did you hear?"

"Nothing." Grey wiped his hand on his damp shirt, which clung to his tall, muscular frame. He was handsome enough, Ned had to admit. If you liked cold-eyed arrogant bastards.

A heavily built young man in a gaudy scarlet doublet slashed with yellow silk pushed in front of Ned, blocking his view of the game. Ned was about to push back when he remembered where he was. Muttering under his breath he stepped backwards until he could go no further. He leant against the condensation-damp wall of the tennis court, eyes closed, wishing he was somewhere else, somewhere he didn't feel like a stranger in his own city.

When he opened his eyes he saw another courtier leaning against the wall not far away, watching him slyly from under lowered lids. The youth was no more than sixteen, thin and with a sickly complexion like something found under a stone. Eyes down, mouth shut, Mal had said. But if he was approached, surely it would be rude to say no? Not that he wanted to say yes to anything this creature might propose.

"You. Fellow."

Ned bridled at being so addressed by a mere boy, but ducked his head anyway.

"My lord?"

The youth detached himself from the wall.

"You are Catlyn's man?"

That was one way of putting it. "Yes, sir."

"He is the swarthy fellow playing against Grey?"

"Well, I wouldn't call him swarthy–"

A well-manicured hand slapped him backhanded, rings scraping his cheek.

"Do not talk back to your betters, sirrah," the youth hissed, lifting a silver pomander to his nose.

Ned ducked his head again, not daring to reply. The crowd applauded: Mal had won another point. When Ned looked back, the boy with the pomander was gone.

It was not hard to let Grey win. Mal's pride would not allow him to give in without a fight, but the other man's superior height and reach made him a tough opponent by any standard. Mal hoped he would never have to face him in a duel.

Afterwards they wandered out into St James's Park, where servants brought flagons of chilled Rhenish wine for their refreshment. Young ladies strolled arm-in-arm under the watchful eyes of chaperones or sat on cushions in the shade of beech trees, fussing over lapdogs and pretending not to make eyes at the young men as they passed. The stink and crowds of London might as well be a hundred miles away.

Mal gestured for Ned to wait at a discreet distance. The last thing he wanted was for his friend to overhear anything about his not-so-glorious past.

"So," Grey said at last, putting down his silver goblet, "what is this matter you are so anxious to discuss in private?"

Mal told him about the commission, leaving out the ignominious nature of his arrival at the Tower.

"And you want me to get you out of it?"

Mal hesitated, wondering how best to put it.

"I know we were not close acquaintances at Cambridge, but we have certain... sympathies in common."

"Go on."

"I also know you and your father are not close. But – he has the ear of Prince Robert. If there is anything you can do, I would be eternally grateful."

"We were never the best of friends, I'll grant you that, Catlyn, but one Peterhouse man looks out for another." Grey leant forward. "I'll see what I can do. And since you are looking for work, I have something that might suit you very well."

"You do?" Mal said, trying to keep the eagerness out of his voice. There was no point getting out of Leland's commission if he could not pay back the advance.

"After you left Cambridge, I fell in with some fellows from Corpus Christi. Tradesmen's sons, mostly, but money poured from their purses like Cam water from a drowned drunk. Well, one that I know of has come home to London and is minded to become a gentleman. I can hardly introduce him at Court, but noblesse oblige..."

"What do you need from me?"

"The fellow needs to be seen in the company of gentlemen, learn a few graces – perhaps the art of the sword?"

"Why does he not hire a fencing-master, if he is so rich?"

Grey shook his head. "I urged him to, but he would have none of it. 'Filthy swiving Italians', he called them, and refused to have them in his house. But a stout Englishman like yourself... Shall I write you a letter of introduction?"

Mal was inclined to refuse. It was bad enough that he had to crawl to the likes of Grey; he had no wish to renew his acquaintance with the sort of men Grey favoured as friends. But it appeared he had little choice.

"Thank you," he said at last. "That would be most generous."

"'Tis trifling. What are friends for?" He waved away the servant offering to refill his goblet. "Where shall I send it?"

"Address it to Deadman's Place, Southwark; first house past Maid Lane. I will be lodging there for the summer."

"You're living in Southwark? God's bones, Catlyn, no wonder you're going nowhere. The sooner you remember who you are and where you belong, the better. I'll have that letter to you by morning. Swear to me you'll take the job, and get yourself some decent lodgings."

Mal made a vague, noncommittal noise. No work for months, then two jobs come along at once – and both of them an uncomfortable link to his past. The Fates were conspiring against him, of that he was certain.

"All right," he said at last. "I'll see this shopkeeper of yours. But I make no promises. I owe no loyalty to you or your friends."

"Oh I think you do," Grey said. "You can wash the blood away, Catlyn, but the stain will always be there. Always."

Contrary to Grey's promises, no letter arrived the next day, nor the day after. Mal was by turns relieved and annoyed. He considered seeking Grey out, but did not want to appear too desperate. In any case, one did not press a duke's son to hurry with his favours.

A week passed, and the matter of the fifty-two shillings still had to be dealt with. So it was that on Midsummer Day, Mal walked up to the gates of Bethlem Hospital with a heavy heart. Every time he came here, he swore it would be the last. Every time…

He rapped on the door set into the tall wooden gates and waited. After several minutes it opened a crack, and the stubble-jawed porter poked his head out.

"What is it?"

"I have your money," Mal said, tapping his pocket.

The porter's eyebrows lifted, and his sneer twisted into an ingratiating smile.

"Come in, sir, come in."

He unbolted the gate and Mal went through into the courtyard, wrinkling his nose at the smell from the nearby cesspit. It was a wonder the patients hadn't all died of plague long ago. Judging by the screams coming from the nearby Abraham Ward, however, they were still very much alive.

"You go right on in, sir," the porter said. "Mistress Cooke will see to you."

He looked expectantly at Mal. who grimaced but gave the man thruppence from his purse, "to oil the hinges of the gate" as the fellow liked to put it. Much as Mal disliked the fact, he would need to come back here at least once more.

"I have to ask for your blade as well, sir," the porter added. "New rules, sir."

"He has become dangerous of late?"

"Lord bless us, no, sir! He's been gentle as a lamb since you was last here." He shook his head. "There was this young gallant, see, showing off to his lady in the Abraham Ward, and one of the inmates got hold of his rapier. Nasty mess, it was, sir. We don't want any more trouble like that."

Mal drew his dagger and handed it to the porter. He was tempted to point out that anyone who thought taunting the insane was a pleasant way to spend a Sunday afternoon deserved everything he got.

"I trust such visitors are not allowed into my brother's lodgings," he said. "I pay you well to keep him secluded."

"Of course not, sir." The man grinned nervously.

He was lying, of course. The occasional visitors paid for the little luxuries that made the keepers' lives bearable in this vile place. He hoped Sandy had afforded them little entertainment.

The western gatehouse provided accommodation for patients whose families were willing to spend a little extra on their keep. Like the eastern gatehouse it had rooms on the ground floor which opened into the gateway itself, and several chambers above. Originally interconnecting, these had been subdivided to create a corridor with locked doors to either side and a narrow window at each end. The lodgings were a little more comfortable than the main ward where the meaner inmates were kept, but it was a melancholy place nonetheless.

After a few moments Mal's eyes adjusted to the gloom and he spotted a woman of middle years coming out of one of the rooms, accompanied by a pale-faced girl of about fourteen. Their aprons were smeared with filth, and the girl carried a brimming chamber-pot.

"Mistress Cooke?" he called out. "I'm here to see my brother."

"O' course, sir." She fumbled through the bunch of keys hanging from her belt. "I was just in there a few minutes ago, happily for you. All cleaned up, he is, sir."

The chamber was about the size of the one in which Mal had been shut up at the Tower, though without the luxury of a fireplace or glazed windows. The only furnishings were a narrow cot bed against one wooden side-wall and a rickety table bearing a small pile of books. The rushes on the floor had long since been trampled into a layer of matted filth that stuck to the soles of Mal's boots.

"Sandy?"

The pale figure curled up on the cot bed did not move.

"Sandy, it's me, Mal."

He went over to the bed. Mistress Cooke's idea of "clean" was a sweat-soaked shirt which clearly had not been changed in days, and the same breeches her patient was wearing last time Mal visited. Sandy's feet were bare and filthy, the toenails grown long, and his black shoulder-length hair was matted into elf-locks. Well, all of that could be remedied, at least. Having expected no better treatment in his absence, Mal had brought some of his own spare clothes and shoes this time.

"Bring me hot water and towels," he told Mistress Cooke. "And a pair of shears."

The matron looked offended but eventually complied. Neither the towels nor the water turned out to be particularly clean.

"Before you go," he said, "I would also like the keys to my brother's shackles. I cannot change his clothing as he is."

"Oh, you mustn't unchain him, sir. Master Charles was quite insistent about that."

"Charles gave him into my care. I pay the bills now, I will do with him as I see fit. And you will give me the keys."

Grumbling, Mistress Cooke removed a small iron key from the ring and handed it over.

"On yer own head be it, sir," she said and hurried out, locking the door behind her.

"Sandy?" Mal put the bucket of water down by the bed. "Sandy? They've gone now."

"I'm not here," Sandy whispered. "You can't see me."

He was right, then. The warders had been allowing paying customers in here.

"It's all right, Sandy," he said, "there's no one here but me. It's Mal, your brother."

"Brother?" Sandy sat up suddenly. The chains joining the iron manacles slithered into his lap.

"Yes, your brother, Mal."

He took up the shears and began trimming his brother's hair and beard, taking care to keep the blades well away from Sandy's eyes. One sudden seizure and... He drew a deep breath and forced himself to continue. At last it was done. He ruffled Sandy's hair, sending a last few severed curls tumbling into the rushes.

"There, now you look yourself again."

Sandy smiled back, his features a gaunt mirror-image of Mal's own. Same black hair, same straight nose and narrow jaw, same dark eyes – no, not the same. Not any more. It was as if a stranger looked out at him, a stranger who wore his twin's shape like an ill-fitting suit of clothes. But if he were possessed, it was by no demon any priest had been able to drive out.

Mal unlocked the shackles around Sandy's wrists and ankles, wincing at the sight of the chafed and blistered flesh. He bound the wounds with clean bandages then set about stripping off his brother's filthy clothes. Sandy began to shiver.

"Come on, you big baby, it's not that cold," Mal said with a smile, and dipped a bit of flannel into the tepid water.

"My brother is coming," Sandy moaned, staring past Mal and pointing. "He is coming for me."

"Yes, I'm coming for you soon, to take you away from here." He took the thin, cold hand in his own. "But there's something I have to do first. A job."

"I was all alone." Sandy's eyes focused on him at last. "You're not him. I see him in my dreams. Old, so old..."

"Father?" Their father was dead. If he were still alive, none of them would be in this mess.

"No. I told you." Sandy pulled his hand away. "My brother."

Mal frowned. Their elder half-brother Charles had been no more than thirty when they last saw him. Sandy must be thinking back to his childhood.

"Charlie's gone, Sandy, he left us here in London." You in this hell-hole and me in whatever job will earn me enough to keep you from dying in here. "He's not coming back."

"Not coming back?"

"No. There's just me now."

He helped Sandy dress, then gently replaced the shackles. Sandy whimpered as the metal closed around his limbs and Mal feared he would struggle, but after a moment Sandy fell silent and lay down on the bed once more.

Mal sat with him until the bell of nearby St Botolph's tolled the hour. Sandy seemed to take comfort from his presence, and Mal could think of nothing to say that would not spoil that. If only... He cursed his stupidity. Now he had money again, he could redeem his lute. Sandy always found his playing soothing. Well, there was always next time.

A key grated in the lock, and the cell door opened. Mal got to his feet.

"Goodness me," said Mistress Cooke, "I can scarce tell the two of you gentlemen apart now. I hope I lets the right one out!" She laughed at her own joke, chins quivering.

Mal was not amused. He counted out the fifty-two shillings under her avaricious gaze.

"That is for this quarter. I will be back every week, to ensure you are keeping my brother in the comfort I am paying for."

"Of course, sir. Everything will be done as you wish, sir."

CHAPTER III

Coby brushed the dust from her hands and wiped her brow with the back of her cuff. There, that was the last of the chests from the wagon. Most people assumed a life in the theatre was a life of idleness; indeed she had thought the same, once upon a time. Now she had arm muscles like a washerwoman and more blisters on her feet than a Bedlam beggar.

Realising she was alone for the first time in a month, she bolted the door to guarantee herself a few moments' privacy. She stripped off her doublet, lifted up her shirt, and loosened the upper lacing of her corset, wrinkling her nose at the ripe smell of unwashed flesh. She had managed to keep a couple of spares hidden in the costume trunks, but changing into them – and washing the used ones and herself – was not so easy. Fortunately all the company smelt at least as bad after a warm spring on the road, so no one had noticed. Yet.

She exchanged the foetid garment for a clean one she had left amongst her tailoring supplies, pressing her breasts downwards as she laced it so they were flattened to boyish proportions rather than plumped up like a whore's. No time for a wash, but most of the stink was in the corset anyway.

She put on a clean shirt for good measure, then donned her doublet once more and unbolted the door.

At least she had not started her monthly flows yet. She knew from eavesdropping on the maids' gossip that she ought to expect it very soon, indeed it ought to have happened by now. She was relieved, of course, since keeping her sex a secret was hard enough already, but the waiting was an agony. Without a mother or sister to advise her, she had no idea how women dealt with the business.

No time for gloomy thoughts – there was still work to be done. She unlocked the nearest chest and lifted out the gown that lay inside. She had meant to check all the costumes back in Sheffield before they were packed, but everything had been a great rush as usual. There, the lace around one cuff was loose. She held the gown up to the light, scanning the ornate fabric for other damage.

She wondered, not for the first time, what it would be like to wear skirts again. It had been – what? – five years now. Would she feel awkward and foolish, like the apprentice actors when they first put on a woman's costume? Or would it be like going home?

An appreciative noise from the doorway made her turn. Gabriel Parrish was leaning on the door post, toying with the fashionable blond love-lock that hung over his left shoulder. At barely twenty he was the youngest adult actor in the company, a former boy player who – unlike most of his kind – had successfully made the transition to male roles.

"Aren't you a bit old for such ambitions, Jacob?"

"Sir?"

"An apprenticeship. A little late to make a lady of you, I fear."

"Y-you mistake me, sir. I have no desire to be a player, nor ever did."

"Really? Why not?"

"I have not the art for it, sir. Pretending to be someone else… I cannot imagine how it is done."

She looked away, afraid he would see the lie in her eyes, but she could not tell him the real reason: that if once she put on women's clothes, walked and talked in her true nature, everyone would see she was Jacomina Hendricksdochter, not Jacob Hendricks as she had long pretended.

"A pity," he said. "You have the fairness of complexion for women's roles, even at your age."

That was true enough. Though not as fair as Parrish, she had long been able to rely on her pale colouring to explain her lack of a beard. All the disguising in the world could not put hair on her cheeks, at least none that would bear close examination. Actors, of all people, knew what false whiskers looked like.

He stepped closer and put a hand under her chin, lifting it until her eyes met his own. His breath smelt of violet comfits.

"How old are you?" he asked.

"S-s-seventeen, sir."

His eyes narrowed. "Are you sure? Perhaps your mother miscounted."

"I d-don't know, sir." She blinked back tears. "I have not seen her this past five years. Nor my father neither."

"I'm sorry." He released her. "Think yourself lucky. I never knew my parents."

Coby didn't know what to say. Was he flirting with her, trying to use this similarity between them to forge some connection? Before Parrish joined the company a few months ago, his name had been a byword for the beautiful boy player adored by men and women alike, indulged and showered with gifts and flattery. He also had a well-deserved reputation for preferring the attentions of his male admirers. For both reasons she had avoided his company as much as possible.

"Parrish!" Master Naismith's voice echoed up the stairs like cannon fire.

The actor froze, and Coby took advantage of the moment to slip past him and out onto the landing.

"Hendricks!" Master Naismith shouted up. "Have you seen Parrish?"

"He is with me, sir," she replied, leaning over the banister, "unpacking the costumes."

"Well tell him to get his pretty arse down here. We have a play to read through before the morrow."

Parrish materialised at her shoulder.

"I come, sir, I come!" He patted her on the shoulder and headed downstairs.

Coby went back inside. She would have to be more careful than ever around him now. As long as he believed her to be younger than her years, he might think her merely a late bloomer. As for his other interest, the only way to put him off completely would be to tell him her secret, but that she could not do. In a foreign land full of sin and wickedness, a poor, friendless girl had no other way to guard her virtue but deceit.

"Lord Jesu, forgive me," she whispered.

"Come on, boy!"

"Sir?"

Master Naismith glared at her.

"I have a meeting with Master Cutsnail at noon – or have you forgotten?"

"No, sir, of course not, sir," she replied, hurrying after him.

"Cutsnail" was not the skrayling's real name, of course, but most Londoners found the foreigners' language almost impossible to pronounce, so they warped their names into something more familiar; preferably something bawdy, or at least humorous. Merchant Qathsnijeel was one of the lucky ones.

They walked in silence along Thames Street. Between the houses, Coby caught a glimpse of the river, spangles of sunlight dancing on the green waters. She trudged along behind her employer, wishing they could take a wherry downriver. Behind his back, the actors often said Naismith's purse-strings were tighter than a nun's lips.

At last they came to London Bridge, where the traffic condensed into a solid mass of humanity flowing even more sluggishly than the river beneath their feet. Coby could see little of the shops and houses on either side, only the towers of the gatehouses that blocked the thoroughfare at intervals. Master Naismith shouldered his way through the press, leaving her to slip along in his wake.

After what felt like half the morning, they reached the far end and passed through the Great Stone Gate into Southwark. Before them stood the wide road leading south-eastwards towards Canterbury, but Master Naismith turned left along St Olave's Street, parallel to the river. They continued at a quickening pace, and as they neared the far end, the church bells began to toll the hour. Master Naismith broke into a trot.

The last house in the street was a large timber-framed building, much like any other guild-house in the city. The only thing that distinguished this one, at least from the outside, was the sign hanging over the door. The rectangle of wood was carved with a design of dots, triangles and curving lines, all picked out in gold leaf. The abstract symbols meant nothing to Coby, but their very alienness made their meaning clear: here was the Distinguished Company of Skrayling Merchant Venturers.

The actor-manager paused for a moment, hands on thighs, panting like a hound. Sweat ran down his forehead into his bushy eyebrows. Coby pulled a handkerchief from her pocket and he mopped his face gratefully.

"Never get old, lad," he told her, wheezing. "'Tis a most grievous business."

He straightened up, grimacing, and walked up to the front door of the guild house. Coby trailed behind, nervousness at meeting the senior merchant warring with avid curiosity. The skraylings kept to themselves for the most part, and though she had been able to learn their pidgin easily enough in the marketplaces of Southwark, the foreigners were still something of a mystery to her.

Just inside the front door stood two skrayling guards armed with heavy staves, ready to eject anyone not on legitimate business. They seemed to know Master Naismith, however, and waved him inside with but a passing glance at Coby.

The main hall was packed with skraylings hurrying to and fro between the tables that lined the walls. At each table sat a merchant, a painted sign before him. The clack of counting blocks and the sibilant growl of the skraylings' native tongue filled the air. It was all disappointingly mundane: no invisible servants, no heaps of enchanted gold, no one suddenly appearing out of thin air or disappearing into it.

Master Naismith led her away from the dealing room through a side door and up a flight of stairs to a long corridor lined with identical-looking doors. Naismith turned left and went down to the far end. Pausing before the last door on the right, he knocked gently.

The door was opened by a young skrayling wearing horn-rimmed spectacles. His silver-streaked hair was tied back in a neat queue and he wore a clerk's plain brown tunic and breeches rather than the patterned garb of a merchant. The tattooed lines on his forehead gathered into a frown.

"Naismith," the actor-manager said. "Cutsnail and I talk trade."

The clerk gestured for them to enter, saying something to his master in Vinlandic.

Master Cutsnail's chamber took up the whole of the upper floor of one side-wing of the building. Three large glazed windows looked across the gardens to an identical wing opposite; the other three walls were lined with tapestries from floor to ceiling. Some were European in design, others bore similar patterns to the merchants' garments. The chamber was stiflingly hot despite its size, and the air was heavy with the musky scent of the foreigners.

The clerk gestured to their feet.

"Take your shoes off," Master Naismith told Coby in a low voice.

"I have a hole in my stocking toe, sir," she whispered back.

"No matter." He cast a meaningful glance at the expensive carpets covering the floor.

Cutsnail was sitting cross-legged behind a low table. He stood as they approached and greeted them in the skrayling fashion, head turned to the right and palms displayed. Master Naismith bowed English-style, and Coby followed suit.

"Sorry us late," the actor-manager said. Tradetalk was not the most elegant of languages, but it got straight to the point.

Cutsnail grinned, fangs half-bared in an expression that meant he accepted the apology out of courtesy but was still displeased. He gestured for them to sit, and the clerk brought over a pitcher full of *aniig*, a herbal infusion which was as popular with the skraylings as beer was with the English. The liquid clinked and splashed as the clerk poured it into three elegant Venetian drinking glasses, and Coby realised with a start that there were small chunks of ice in it. Ice in June? Now that was real magic, and of a most welcome kind. She thought guiltily of Pastor Jan's sermons on the subject of witchcraft. Surely there could be no harm in such a useful practice?

Cutsnail raised his glass, and Coby followed his lead, sipping the cold liquid. She knew better than to drink it too quickly. It might not make a man drunk like beer, but it had a potency of its own which might equally lead to incautious behaviour. She did not want to shame her master in front of this powerful foreigner.

Master Naismith's Tradetalk extended only to the common courtesies and he relied on Coby to translate for him in matters of business. After the obligatory exchange of pleasantries about the latest trade fleet and the state of the Queen's health, Cutsnail got down to business.

"The theatre building progresses well?" he asked, eyeing Naismith across his glass of *aniig*.

"Very well. The timbers are all in place and the labourers begin work on the walls this week. And I have the plans you asked to see."

Naismith passed a leather document-tube to the skrayling, who shook out the roll of paper and spread it on the desk, weighting the corners with sea-polished stones.

"This is to make things rise up from underground, yes?"

"Indeed," Naismith said. "This is for the trapdoor under the stage; a similar device is used to lower players from above."

He gestured for Coby to explain further. She gathered her thoughts; this was going to push her grasp of Tradetalk to its limits.

"It uses weights, as you see here," she said, pointing to the diagram's counterweight mechanism. "All I do is pull this handle, and the trapdoor slides to one side and the platform rises up to replace it."

"And this?" Cutsnail stabbed a thick grey fingernail at another part of the diagram, where the rope connected to the counterweight spiralled around a groove cut into a tapered spindle.

"Ah, that is the cunning part," she replied, suppressing a grin of pride. "The teeth on the wheel make it turn at a constant speed, but because the drum is like so –" she formed a tapering shape with her hands "– it lets out less and less rope as it turns, slowing it down so the platform comes to a gentle stop."

"And you made this?"

"I designed it, yes. There is none other like it in all London."

She did not add that the mechanism had been inspired by memories of learning to spin wool at her mother's knee. Boys were not expected to know such things.

Cutsnail made an approving sound. "How soon will the theatre be ready?"

Master Naismith gazed at the ceiling. "There's still all the plastering and thatching, and the painter can't start work on the stage until that's finished, because of the dust, so I'm afraid it won't be until September at the very earliest."

Cutsnail bared his teeth.

"It must be done for August."

Naismith frowned at Coby and she nodded in confirmation.

"August?" Naismith shook his head. "That will not be easy."

"It must be done."

"May I ask why?"

Cutsnail hesitated. "It is not yet widely known, but my people are sending an ambassador to England, and your Prince Arthur has proposed a contest of plays in his honour."

"A contest?" Naismith smiled. "Then you are indeed in luck, sir. Are not my men the best actors in London?"

Coby rephrased the question as a statement. She did not think her employer would appreciate her issuing a formal challenge to his business partner.

"That is why I wished to invest in your new theatre," the skrayling replied. "But it must be ready for the ambassador's visit."

"Surely performances of such grandeur will be played at one of the royal palaces?"

"That is not our custom. I am certain the ambassador will wish to see the plays in their rightful setting."

"Still, August…" Naismith shook his head. "If I had known sooner–"

"If the theatre is not ready, it will hurt my standing in the guild. I will have to increase my share of the theatre's profits to four-fifths to compensate for any losses I will make elsewhere."

"Four-fifths?" Naismith looked faint.

Coby suppressed a smile.

"That is fair recompense," she told the skrayling.

"I will do everything in my power to ensure the theatre is ready in time," Naismith said when he had recovered his composure.

Cutsnail smiled, showing off his long eye teeth to full advantage.

"I am certain you will," he said.

The purse of crowns weighed heavy in Coby's pocket as she walked to Goody Watson's. She could not have felt more conspicuous if she had been wearing girl's clothes, or none at all. Surely a sharp-eyed cozener had already spotted the tempting bulge or heard the muffled clink of coins? She scanned the crowded streets, but nothing seemed amiss. A few minutes later she reached the house of the tailor's wife without incident, and slipped through the open front door with a sigh of relief.

She paused on the threshold, sneezing at the dust that filled the air. Gowns, jackets and cloaks of every colour hung from pegs along one wall, whilst doublets, breeches and various linen items were folded in neat piles on shelves or scattered across trestle tables. A variety of hats, most of them black, occupied another set of pegs, and pairs of boots and shoes lurked under the tables alongside boxes of small household goods such as candlesticks and pewter dishes. Goody Watson sat by the window with her mending basket, half an eye on her work and the other half on a portly gentleman who was swaggering up and down, trying out the hang of a hip-length cloak that did nothing for his figure.

"Mistress Watson?"

The pawnbroker peered up at her, pressing her spectacles against the bridge of her nose with a work-reddened forefinger.

"Ah, Naismith's lad!" She put down her work and got to her feet stiffly. "The minute I heard you were back in London, I thought, 'Naismith'll be by any day now'." She looked around, frowning. "Your master ain't sick, is he?"

"No, just very busy. He sent me–"

"I'll take it," the portly gentleman said, elbowing Coby aside. "Ten shillings, did you say?"

Whilst Goody Watson haggled with her customer, Coby wandered around the shop examining the goods on offer. Buying costumes was one thing, but Master Naismith had insisted she get some new clothes for herself too, if she was to be his deputy. What to choose? She picked up a dark green doublet that looked about her own size.

"I put a few things by for you," Goody Watson said, when the man had gone. "I know what Master Naismith likes. Here."

She hauled a chest out from under the table and opened it.

"There, what do you think of that?" she asked, laying out a pair of scarlet velvet trunk hose trimmed with silver braid, complete with matching codpiece. "Belonged to Sir Walter Raleigh when he first came to court. Handed down a couple of times since then, o' course."

"Very… handsome." She doubted the provenance, but the hose were perfect for the stage. The more eye-catching the better. "I'm sure we can find use for such… striking apparel."

The tailor's wife produced a succession of fine garments, each with its sad tale of an impoverished gentleman desperate for a few shillings. Coby selected those few that fitted both their requirements and her master's purse, and was about to pay when she remembered her own needs.

"May I try this on?" she asked, returning to the green suit.

Goody Watson gestured for her to go ahead, and went back to her mending. Coby turned her back and began unbuttoning her doublet, grateful for the shopkeeper's poor eyesight. She pulled on the garment and was pleased to discover it was not too wide in the shoulders nor yet too long in the sleeve. The waist was a little loose, but she knew a few tailoring tricks to make that less obvious. The matching slops looked as though they might be a reasonable fit, and in any case she wasn't going to try them on in here.

She was in the middle of changing back into her own clothes when a shadow darkened the doorway. Suddenly aware she was half undressed, Coby shrank into the corner clutching the doublet to her chest like a child with a cradle blanket.

A man entered the shop, tall and rangy, with black hair and a neatly trimmed beard. He looked familiar, but Coby couldn't place him.

"Mistress Watson." He inclined his head towards the proprietress. "I'm here to redeem my pledge."

"Back in work at last, eh, Master Catlyn?"

She got up from her stool and began rummaging around under one of the trestle tables. The man gazed idly around the shop, and seemed to notice Coby for the first time.

"Don't I know you?" he said, staring at her.

"Er…"

"The Bull's Head." He pointed a finger at her, as if in accusation.

"Er, yes." Now she knew where she recognised him from. She had seen him several times with Gabriel Parrish's former… companion, Ned Faulkner. "I'm with Suffolk's Men."

"A player." He didn't sound impressed.

"N-no, I'm the tireman."

"Really?"

"Really." His cockiness was starting to irritate her. "I'm here buying costumes for the company."

The tailor's wife emerged from under the table, holding up a lute in a dusty leather case.

"Here we go." She held out her free hand. "Four shillings."

"I think you'll find it was two," Catlyn replied.

"Two-and-six, then. You was late last month."

A jingle of coins changed hands and he took the instrument, cradling it in the crook of his arm with absentminded affection.

"Mistress Watson," Coby said, "can you bundle those clothes up for me? And I'll take this green suit as well."

She turned away and hurriedly put her own doublet back on, feeling sure his eyes were boring through her shirt to the corset. Her fingers fumbled over the buttons. If he was one of Faulkner's friends, he might be more interested in the lie than the truth.

"Good day to you, Mistress Watson. Master Tireman."

She looked round, opening her mouth to return the courtesy, but he was already gone.

She returned to Thames Street to drop off the costumes and start work on the silver-laced gown. Usually she spent every performance backstage, helping the actors in and out of their costumes, but there were few changes in today's play and Master Naismith had said her time would be better spent on her other work. There was always plenty of it. Costumes formed a large proportion of the company's capital and they saw a lot of wear – and, not infrequently, tear – when the actors were touring.

Before settling down to work she slipped down the alley to the small barn behind the house where the touring wagon was kept. Her few mementoes of a former life were hidden in a small box in the hayloft, and she had not had a chance yet to check they were still safe.

To her surprise the barn doors were not locked. Master Nai-smith must have forgotten about it, she decided, being distracted by thoughts of the meeting with his investor. Nevertheless she entered warily, senses alert for any sign of an intruder.

The players' wagon stood where they had left it, taking up almost half the small building. A thin beam of sunlight picked out the gilded unicorn on the wagon's side: the badge of their patron the Duke of Suffolk. To the yeomen and townsfolk far from London, it was a wondrous sight, to be greeted with cheers and whistles; Coby had spent far too many hours trudg-ing along behind it – and helping to heave it out of yet another pothole – to find it the least bit marvellous.

As she headed towards the hayloft ladder, she caught sight of a movement behind the wagon.

"Show yourself," she cried out, trying to sound bolder than she felt, "or I shall call for aid."

She took a step backwards towards the barn door, and the lurker stepped out of the shadows. He was a young man, short but wiry of build, with heavy brows and a stubbled chin, as though he were normally clean-shaven but had decided to grow a beard.

"Ned Faulkner." Coby frowned. "What are you doing here?"

"Good to see you too, Hendricks."

"I hope you're not spying on our rehearsals," she said. "I know you work for the Admiral's Men."

"Just the odd copying job," Faulkner said. "A man's got to eat, you know."

"So you *are* spying."

"No!" He looked sheepish. "I came to see Gabriel. We used to meet here, sometimes."

Coby folded her arms. "He's not here. As you can see."

"But he returned to London with you?"

"Of course. He's at Newington Butts, probably on stage at this very moment."

Faulkner's eyes lit up. "I must go and see him."

"And lure him back to the Admiral's Men?" she said. "I do not think so. Besides, he told me he has forsworn your companionship. He does not wish to see you."

Quick as a snake Faulkner closed the space between them, grasping Coby by the upper arms and pinning her against the barn wall.

"Why are you keeping me from him, whelp? Have you become Naismith's guard dog all of a sudden?" He studied her face. "You blush very prettily, you know. Perhaps that's it: you mean to keep me for yourself."

She stared back at him, defiant. "I have no taste for such sinfulness, sir."

"Oh no?" He pressed the length of his body against hers. His lips were almost touching hers and his breath smelt of cheap beer. Her heart began to pound; any moment now he would feel the solid shape of the padded leather bulge sewn into her breeches' front and come to entirely the wrong conclusion. She leaned in closer as if to kiss him, and bit down. Hard.

"Son of a pox-ridden whore!" He pushed her away, wiping his bloody mouth with his sleeve.

"Go. Now." She folded her arms, willing her body not to tremble. "Or Master Naismith will have you whipped all the way back to London Bridge."

Faulkner pushed past her, deliberately knocking her shoulder. "Perhaps you should keep this place locked up, if you want no intruders."

She closed the barn door behind him and sank into the straw, wrapping her arms around her knees. Why had she confronted Faulkner like that, instead of calling upon her master to eject him? Had she become so accustomed to behaving like a young man that she forgot the danger she was in? She forced herself to breathe slowly. It wouldn't do for the other apprentices to catch her blubbing like – well, like a girl.

Emotions mastered, she went back to the house to work on the costumes, her box of keepsakes quite forgotten.

CHAPTER IV

After the visit to Court, Mal took to wearing his rapier every day. He had missed the weight of it on his hip, the reassuring reminder of who and what he was. And if it earned him a few suspicious looks from men, it also drew admiring glances from women. The leftovers from Leland's advance were too precious to waste, though, so glances were all he got.

Leland clearly had no doubt Mal would report for duty. He had already sent a tailor round to the Faulkners' house to measure him for livery.

"It had better not be all crimson velvet and goldwork," Mal muttered as the tailor fussed around him with lengths of measuring paper and a mouthful of pins. "I shall look like a popinjay. And do not pad it overmuch. I must be able to move freely."

The tailor said nothing, only wrinkled his nose at the squalid surroundings. Ned was not the most fastidious of bedfellows, and Mistress Faulkner was too stiff with age to run about after her grown son. Reaching out with one foot Mal slid the chamber pot under the bed. The tailor muttered imprecations under his breath and left as soon as he could, saying that next time Mal would have to come to his workshop, for he would not set foot in the place again, no, not if the Queen herself commanded it.

A few days later, Mal was walking back towards London Bridge after a fitting when two figures stepped out of a doorway into his path. By their elaborately slashed sleeves, Venetian lace ruffs and pearl earrings, he took them to be courtiers, or perhaps the sons of wealthy merchants.

"Forgive me, gentlemen," Mal said with a slight bow.

They did not give way. The slighter built of the two, a youth of sixteen or so, raised a silver pomander to his nose; the scent of cloves and orris root wafted from it, competing with the stink of the river.

"What have we here?" the other drawled, looking Mal up and down. "A sewer rat bearing the weapons of a gentleman. From whom did you steal them, sirrah?"

"They're mine, given to me by my father."

"Really? Is that how you northerners acknowledge your bastards?"

Mal's jaw tightened and he drew his blade a hand's breadth from its scabbard in warning. Passers-by hurried away, their eyes averted.

"Go on," the man said with a mocking smile. "Show us why you deserve the Queen's favour, when so many of your betters have been passed over."

Was that what this was all about, jealousy that he had been chosen to guard the ambassador? What irony, that they so coveted something he would give up in a heartbeat.

He glanced from one to the other. Taking them both would be easy enough, but what good would it do? This could end in one of only two ways: his own death, or an arrest warrant for murder. He slammed the rapier back into its scabbard.

"A coward as well as a bastard," the pomander bearer said with a sniff.

Mal snatched the bauble from the youth's hand and threw it across the street. It flashed in the sunlight, bounced off a shop front with a high sharp note like a hand-bell and plopped into a slimy puddle. A scabby dog trotted over to investigate, but backed off whining when the overpowering scent hit its nostrils.

The older man caught Mal by the front of his doublet and slammed him against the nearest wall.

"Don't think Grey will protect you, cur," he growled, craning his neck to look Mal in the eye. "His standing at Court is not so high as he likes to think."

"And yours is, I suppose?"

"I am a close friend of Prince Arthur. One word to him, and—"

"And what? Think you he will go against his mother's wishes?"

The man flushed. His was an empty threat and they both knew it. If he had so much influence with the prince, why bother to seek Mal out and threaten him?

He released Mal with a sneer of contempt.

"I shall enjoy watching your fall from grace," he said. "If not I, then someone will bring you down. 'Pride goeth before destruction, and a high mind before the fall'."

He gestured to his companion, who was fishing his pomander out of the puddle.

"Leave it, Jos. A gentleman," he glared at Mal, "does not grovel in the muck."

Mal watched them leave. Was the pomander bearer Josceline Percy, one of Northumberland's tribe of younger siblings? If so, who was his companion? Mal had paid too little heed to Court gossip in the past, knowing that what reached the ears of the common folk was for the most part a confection of lies and exaggeration. Perhaps it was time to start listening. And where better to begin than with those on the very fringes of Court: actors.

• • • •

Coby saw no more of Faulkner in the next few days, for which she was heartily thankful. She had enough to do helping Master Naismith ensure there were no delays in the new theatre's construction. He entrusted her with a great many more errands than usual, and she had been back and forth across London Bridge so many times, her shoes were more holes than leather.

On Friday morning she was sent to Bankside with a message for the foreman in charge of the builders. The new theatre, which was to be named the Mirror, was being built on the western edge of Southwark, in a field next to Paris Gardens. Workmen swarmed over the ladders and scaffolding that covered its sides, putting the finishing touches to the lattices of split branches that filled the gaps between the main timbers. Soon the wattle panels would be plastered over and it would start to look like its rival the *Rose*, barely a hundred yards to the east.

She found the foreman deep in conversation with a man she had never seen before. He was of middling years, with lank mousy hair parted in the centre above a round, clean-shaven face. Plainly dressed in a dark brown worsted doublet and hose, there was not a bit of lace or other frippery about him except for a heavy gold neck chain from which hung a unicorn badge. Another servant of their patron, and an important one at that.

At last the foreman made his courtesies and returned to his work. Coby ran after him and delivered her message, but as she turned to leave she found herself being addressed by the stranger.

"You are Naismith's tiring man?"

"Yes, sir. Jacob Hendricks, sir."

"I am John Dunfell, His Grace's private secretary." He motioned her aside, out of earshot of the workmen. "It has come to my attention that this theatre–" he broke off and looked around at the building with a grimace of distaste "–will be required in the entertainments for the Ambassador of Vinland."

"Indeed, sir."

"Indeed. Well, we must not disappoint or embarrass His Grace. I have therefore been charged with overseeing the completion of the building."

Coby nodded, unsure why she was being told this information. Unless Master Naismith did not yet know?

"If you wish me to convey any message to my master–"

Dunfell held up his hand. "Master Naismith is already informed of my intent. It was you I wished to see."

"Me, sir?" Her voice cracked, and she hid her embarrassment with a cough.

"You are a bright, trustworthy lad," Dunfell said, placing an avuncular arm across her shoulders. "Naismith would surely not rely on you otherwise. A man of talent can go far, with the right patronage, howsoever humble his birth. Your father is a tailor, I am told."

"Yes, sir," she lied; in truth he was a locksmith, but how else to explain her skill with a needle? "But… he may be dead for all I know."

"An orphan? Well, that need be no obstacle. It is in my power," he leaned closer, "to offer you preferment in the duke's service."

"That would be very generous of you, sir."

"Of course you would have to prove your worth."

"Sir?"

"A small task only. And, I am sure, well within your power." When Coby did not reply, he went on. "There is a man whom you may know, one Maliverny Catlyn. He lives in Bankside, or thereabouts."

Catlyn. Where had she heard that name before? Oh, no. Not him.

"Ah, you do know him, then?" Dunfell said.

"By sight, sir, that is all."

"Then you are to acquaint yourself further with this gentleman, and report back to me what you find. His history, character..."

"You want me to spy on him, sir?"

Dunfell nodded approvingly. "I knew you were a sharp lad when I set eyes on you. And a discreet one too, I'll warrant."

"Of course, sir."

"As you may be aware," he said, lowering his voice, "His Grace takes a great interest in all the affairs of our allies the skraylings, the better to advise His Highness the Prince of Wales. It has come to His Grace's attention that the skraylings are by no means as united as we have been led to believe. There is dissension amongst their ranks –" he pursed his lips in disapproval "– even with regard to the ambassador being sent to England."

"That is indeed grievous news," Coby said.

"Indeed. Worse still, this fellow Catlyn, who has been appointed as the ambassador's bodyguard, may owe his position to the scheming of the ambassador's own enemies. Our very alliance with Vinland could be at stake."

Coby stared at Dunfell. "This – this is too great a task for me, sir, I cannot–"

"Nonsense. I ask but a small thing, do I not? A mere acquaintance, a few questions asked as of a new friend... Surely I do not need to tell your master of your disloyalty?"

Coby shook her head miserably.

"Very well," she said. "I will do what I can to make friends with this man."

Ned sat at a table by himself, nursing a pint of beer and keeping an eye on the door. His stomach growled. If Mal didn't turn up soon, he'd be having dinner by himself.

The low-ceiling taproom held the July heat like a brick oven, and the air was thick with tobacco smoke and laughter. A favourite of both of Southwark's principal companies of players, the Bull's Head was the natural resort of every hireling actor on the look-out for work, as well as those gentlemen whose pleasure it was to mingle with the more famous denizens of the city's underbelly.

Ned spotted Gabriel Parrish weaving through the crowd, his bright hair unmistakable in the shadowy taproom. No wonder he had earned the nickname "Angel" before ever he ventured onstage. Ned sighed, remembering how those forget-me-not blue eyes could darken with pleasure in an instant.

Just as it seemed Gabriel would pass by without a sign of recognition, he paused and looked straight at Ned. He did not smile, but at least he did not frown or sneer. Ned swallowed past the lump in his throat, and found himself getting to his feet almost against his will.

"Gabe." He never called Parrish by his nickname in public. It didn't seem right, somehow.

"Ned."

"I heard you were back in London."

"As you see."

"So I thought—"

"Naismith doesn't like me even talking to you." Gabriel glanced back the way he had come. "He thinks you would lure me back to the Admiral's Men."

"Does he have a reason to fear it?" Ned replied, hope rising in his breast.

"Not at all."

"Pity."

There was a moment's awkward silence.

"I suppose," Gabriel said, "you've not lacked for work since the playhouses reopened?"

Ned grinned. "You angling to find out what play Henslowe has chosen for this contest?"

Gabriel looked around then sat down at the table, motioning for Ned to do likewise.

Ned sighed. "To be blunt, I don't know. He's got me working from dawn to dusk, copying sides for at least half-a-dozen different plays, and none of his men have been told anything definite either."

Gabriel made to leave, but Ned reached out and caught his wrist. The contact sent a shiver of pleasure down his arm to the base of his spine.

"I do know something that might interest you, though," he said. "Something better than finding out what the Admiral's Men are up to."

The actor sat down again. "Go on."

This time it was Ned's turn to glance around the taproom. There was still no sign of Mal.

"I have a friend. You've probably seen him in here with me a few times. Tall dark fellow, a bit foreign-looking."

"Oh yes, I remember *him*," Gabriel purred. "I thought it very unfair of you, keeping him all to yourself."

"It's not like that." Ned flushed. "*He's* not like that."

"You could have fooled me, darling."

Ned resisted the temptation to explain further. It was none of Gabriel's business. And this was going to be worth it in the end. Oh, yes.

"Do you want my news or not?" he asked.

Gabriel pouted and fingered his love-lock.

"I'm listening," he said.

"Well…" Ned leaned forward and whispered in his ear.

"No! You, my dear, are a treasure." He seized the front of Ned's doublet and kissed him on the mouth. "Bring him to our table when he arrives, and I promise you I will be *very* grateful."

• • • •

"You told him what?"

Mal stared at his friend in despair. Why did he ever bother trying to keep secrets, with Ned around? Thank the Virgin Mary and all the saints Ned hadn't overheard the conversation with Grey. Had he?

"Everyone will know soon enough," Ned replied, frowning. "I don't know why you're making such a fuss."

Mal hesitated. He had come here hoping to strike up a conversation with Edward Alleyn, the leading actor of the Admiral's Men, but perhaps Parrish would do just as well. Anything to keep Ned quiet.

"Come on, then," he said with half-feigned irritation. "Best get this over with."

He followed Ned to a table near the fireplace. On one side sat Ned's former lover, along with a glum-faced fellow of about thirty whom Mal didn't recognise; opposite them were two actors he did know by sight, Henry Naismith and Rafe Eaton. Squeezed between this latter pair was the young tireman he'd seen at Goody Watson's.

All eyes were on Eaton, whose mellow baritone carried easily over the hubbub. Mal only caught the end of the tale he was spinning:

"… And then I say to him, 'By Heaven, sir, I would not marry her if she shat gold!'"

Everyone around the table laughed, apart from the boy, who smiled nervously and clutched his tankard closer. Ned took advantage of the pause in conversation to address the leader of the troupe.

"Master Naismith?"

The actor-manager looked up.

"What do you want, Faulkner? I thought I told you to stay away."

Parrish said, "Ned has brought someone to see you, sir."

"I'm not hiring."

"I'm not looking for work," Mal said. "I have... connections you may find interesting."

"Go on."

Mal leant closer. "The skrayling ambassador. I am to be his bodyguard."

Coby stared down into her tankard, hardly able to believe her luck. She had been wondering how on Earth she could contrive to meet this man again, and here he was.

"Well, you are welcome, sir," Master Naismith was saying. "Henry Naismith at your service. Leader of this humble band of players."

"Maliverny Catlyn." He bowed in courtly fashion. "I saw your Hieronimo in Cambridge a few years ago. Very moving."

"A pleasure to meet a man who appreciates the dramatic arts," Naismith said. "Is that why you were appointed to guard the ambassador?"

"I am not at liberty to say," Catlyn replied with a smile.

Rafe Eaton got to his feet.

"Any friend of Faulkner is a friend of yours, eh, Parrish? And any friend of Parrish is a friend of ours." He slapped Catlyn on the back. "Sit down, sir, sit down!"

To Parrish's evident disappointment, Catlyn did not take the proffered space on the settle but pulled up a stool and sat at the end of the table. Faulkner rested his elbows on the back of the settle, his left hand dangling inches from Parrish's head. The actor seemed oblivious to his presence, though Coby noticed how he leant back casually in his seat so that his hair brushed against Faulkner's fingers.

"Have you dined?" Master Naismith asked Catlyn.

"No, not yet."

"Please, be my guest," he said. He glanced at Faulkner and added, somewhat grudgingly, "Both of you."

Faulkner's eyes lit up, and he slid around the settle into the seat beside Parrish.

"We are only having the ordinary," Naismith told them. He turned to Coby. "Run and tell Joan we are now seven altogether, there's a good lad."

She squeezed past Rafe and Catlyn and went in search of the tavern cook. By the time she had returned from her errand, beers had been poured and Rafe Eaton was engaged in a lengthy account of their latest travels. She slipped onto the seat next to the actor so as not to disturb the performance. This put her opposite Faulkner, and on Catlyn's left.

She hadn't got a good look at him in the gloom of the pawnshop, nor had she any reason to take notice. Now she took in every detail, her costume-maker's eye matching dress to character. Good-quality but threadbare doublet and hose. An expensive-looking dagger, its wire-bound hilt worn smooth with use, at his right hip. A knotted ribbon of black silk adorning his left earlobe, where a richer man might wear a pearl droplet or other bauble. A well-born man down on his luck, then: ambitious, no doubt bribable… He certainly fitted Master Dunfell's description of the situation.

She glanced from Catlyn to Faulkner and back again. The two were friends but evidently not lovers; Catlyn appeared unmoved by the fact that Faulkner and Master Parrish were exchanging glances and whispers like a courting couple. That suggested one approach, though it was her stratagem of last resort. The risk of exposure was too great.

When Master Eaton paused to take a drink of beer, she seized the opportunity to enter the conversation.

"Do you come to hear plays often, sir?" she asked Catlyn.

"Not as much as I would like," he said, with a polite nod towards Master Naismith. "And I fear that when I am on duty in my new position, my thoughts will be engaged elsewhere."

"You think there's a threat to the ambassador?" It was a crude gambit, but what if she did not get another chance to speak to him?

"Quiet, lad!" Master Naismith turned to her, glowering. In a low voice he added, "Walsingham and Cecil's spies are everywhere."

Chastened, Coby lowered her gaze. Since Sir Francis Walsingham's unexpected recovery from a grave illness three years ago, the rivalry between the Queen's private secretary and his understudy had become intense. It was not wise to attract their attention with careless talk.

A serving-man arrived with supper. Coby poked her horn spoon into the mess of boiled vegetables and gristly grey lumps of something vaguely animal. Tavern food was good work for the jaws, if not the belly.

The conversation turned to a comparison of the two royal princes. Robert, the elder, resembled his father in looks and his mother in temperament, and everyone agreed he would make a great king, perhaps one even more famous than his grandsire Henry the Eighth. It was his younger brother Arthur, however, who was the people's favourite, taking after Henry in his love of jousting and spectacle.

"Shall the princes attend, if we perform at the new theatre?" Coby asked, drawn back into the conversation despite herself. The thought of being mere yards from the Prince of Wales set her stomach a-flutter with nerves.

"Surely you will be invited to play at one of the royal palaces?" Catlyn asked.

Master Naismith recounted Master Cutsnail's instructions, leaving out the matter of whether the theatre would be ready in time.

"Thank you for this intelligence, sir," Catlyn said. "It explains why Her Majesty requires an additional bodyguard for the ambassador."

"This contest is a sham," Dickon Rudd, the company's clown, muttered, pushing away his empty bowl.

They all looked at him.

"How so?" Catlyn asked.

"Do you really think the ambassador will risk offending the Queen by choosing any but her own son's company of players? Mark my words, the Prince's Men will win. I would put good money on it."

Parrish leant forward, a sly smile on his lips.

"You will be close to the ambassador," he said to Catlyn. "Could you not put in a good word for your friends?"

"Why should I care who wins?" he replied. "And what makes you think I have any influence over the skraylings? I cannot so much as speak their tongue."

Coby saw her chance, and seized it.

"I can."

Everyone stared at her.

"Well, I can. Only a little Tradetalk, I confess."

Catlyn looked at her thoughtfully. "Could you teach me?"

"I–" She turned to Master Naismith. She would have to play this carefully if she was not to arouse suspicion. "I have work to do, have I not, sir?"

"I am sure you could be spared one afternoon a week," he said after a moment's pause. Leaning around Rafe's back he added, "A wise man does not turn down an opportunity for advancement."

"I am in your debt, sir," Catlyn told Naismith. "If there is anything I can do for you – within the bounds of my duty to Her Majesty, of course."

"Of course."

Catlyn got to his feet.

"Now, if you will excuse me, gentlemen, I have business elsewhere."

Coby joined the chorus of farewells and watched him leave. An afternoon a week for, what, almost two months? Surely she could find something out in that time, enough to satisfy Master Dunfell.

CHAPTER V

On his return to the Faulkners' house, Mal was met in the hall by Ned's mother, Mistress Faulkner. In the gloom of the narrow windowless passage her lined features resembled a death mask, pale as wax.

"What is it? Are you unwell, ma'am?"

She shook her head.

"There's a man waiting for you," she whispered. "I had to let him in–"

"What? Where's Ned?"

She held up a finger to her lips.

"Gone to Henslowe's house to do some copying work. I'm not expecting him back until curfew."

"Hell's teeth! Who is this man?"

She shrugged. "Never seen 'im before. He said he was come to talk to you about this new job."

Dear God, not another disgruntled young cockscomb looking for a fight. It was bad enough being accosted in the street, without them following him home and frightening poor old women out of their wits.

"Go and visit one of your neighbours," he told her. "I'll get rid of him."

She bobbed her head gratefully and hurried out of the door. Mal waited until she was out of earshot, then opened the door to the Faulkners' parlour.

A solidly built man of about forty stood to one side of the window, leaning against the crumbling lath-and-plaster wall. From his mousy brown hair to his workaday brown boots, he was as ordinary a man as Mal had ever seen. He made no move as Mal entered the room, only watched him calmly as if he were the host and Mal the unwelcome visitor.

"Who are you?" Mal said, drawing his rapier.

The man's eyes flicked to the blade then he raised his hands, holding them away from his own weapons.

"You can call me Baines." His accent was that of the city: gravel grating on the underside of a Thames wherry.

"What do you want?"

Baines looked him up and down. "Leland told you about the job."

"The ambassador? Yes."

"And you accepted."

"Yes. Look, what is this all about? Leland told me to report next month–"

"Leland ain't the one giving orders. Not directly, anyhow."

"I know this commission comes from the Queen. And you don't look like an officer of the Crown."

Baines sighed. "Are you going to put that pig-sticker away so we can discuss this like gentlemen?"

"Why should I trust you?"

"Because," Baines sneered "if I wanted you dead, you'd already be spilling your guts in the rushes."

Mal sheathed his sword. He didn't doubt the man's words.

Baines moved towards the empty fireplace. Mal noted he kept to the edges of the room, as if to avoid being silhouetted against the window.

"You work for Walsingham," Mal said. This was starting to make sense, of a sort. The Queen's private secretary was said to run the largest network of intelligencers in Europe.

"Give the man a round of applause. Yes, Walsingham. Christ's balls, you college boys aren't half slow on the uptake."

"What does he want with me?"

"That's for him to say. Me, I prefer not to know." He probed the corner of his mouth with a finger and flicked something into the fireplace. "Walsingham's house, Seething Lane, five o'clock. Tell no one where you're going."

Baines left, closing the door behind him. Mal watched him through the window, realising as he did so that this was where Baines had stood to watch for his own approach. He shook his head. What was he getting himself into?

After dinner Coby ran some more errands for Master Naismith, collecting the tradesmen's bills for the latest building work on the new theatre and delivering a list of the company's intended performances to the Office of Revels in Clerkenwell. She didn't mind the running back and forth; whilst her feet were busy, her mind was free to think and plan. It was one thing to arrange to meet this Catlyn fellow, quite another to get information out of him. Annoying he might be, but he was unlikely to be a complete fool, otherwise he would not have been chosen for whatever wicked scheme the ambassador's enemies had planned. She would have to be discreet and tactful.

On returning to Thames Street she found Gabriel Parrish in the parlour drilling the apprentices in deportment and womanly manners. Though apprenticed to Master Naismith, the boys took much of their instruction from Parrish since he had the most recent experience of playing women's roles.

"No, no, no!" Parrish cuffed Oliver around the ear. "Bend at the knee, not the waist. You're not a Bankside whore. Show him, Philip."

The older apprentice dipped gracefully and picked up the handkerchief that lay in the middle of the floor. At almost sixteen, Philip Johnson was at the height of his career, an experienced actor of female roles hovering on the brink of manhood. This would probably be his last summer of glory, before his voice broke and his boyish charms faded.

Coby cleared her throat.

"What do you want, Jacob?" Parrish asked without looking round.

"I need Philip for a short while, sir, to do a fitting for tomorrow's performance."

"If you got it right the first time," Philip said, "I would not have to–"

"It's your own fault. You fidget."

"Enough. Ladies, please!" Parrish rolled his eyes. "Philip, go with Jacob. Oliver, on with your practice. We will get this right if it takes all day."

Oliver dropped the handkerchief on the floor, and Philip pointedly stepped on it as he strode across to the door Coby held open for him. The boys were encouraged to behave like ladies at all times, in order that they avoid picking up masculine mannerisms, but this only added girlish spitefulness to their rivalry.

In the attic where Coby did most of her sewing, Philip stripped to his underlinens and stood in the centre of the room with arms folded. He was still at the gangly stage, all knees and elbows but yet to gain a man's full height or broad shoulders. Coby studied him out of the corner of her eye, anxious to learn every detail of boyish demeanour, even if her best model was one skewed by an actor's upbringing.

"How women stand this all their lives, I know not," Philip said, thrusting his arms into the corset she held out. Coby laced it up the front with brisk movements; it was much like the one she wore under her own shirt, but cut lower, to enhance rather than conceal. Not that Philip had anything to enhance.

"You should eat more," she muttered. "Being so skinny makes you look too much like a boy."

"I eat every scrap on my plate. It's Master Naismith's fault, the miserable old skinflint. Anyway, you're one to talk."

She stuck her tongue out at him. "I'm not the one who needs to look rounded and womanly."

She held out the farthingale, and he stepped into it. Coby fastened it at the back then walked around him with her head on one side, peering at the hemline.

"Are you standing on tiptoe again?"

"No. See?" He lifted the front of his skirts to mid-calf and dropped them again.

"Then stop growing, will you?" She placed the end of her measure on the ground and squatted to count off the markings. "I'll have to sew another two inches of guard on all your gowns at this rate."

She crossed to the baskets filled with neatly folded fabric remnants, and began searching through them for a length of black taffeta to match the farthingale.

"Short is fashionable. To show off my pretty ankles." He poked one foot from below the skirt, toes pointed.

"And your yard-long feet," she replied. "No, the hems must touch the ground, or the illusion is spoilt."

Philip heaved a sigh and folded his arms again. She draped the green-and-gold shot taffeta skirt over the farthingale and again measured the deficit.

"Want to come to the bear-baiting when we're done?" Philip asked. "I'll lend you an angel to bet with."

"No, thank you. I have far too much work to do, thanks to your sprouting. And where do you get so much money, anyway?"

Philip smiled slyly. "De Vere sent me a pearl carcanet. Said I ought to wear something queenly for the contest."

"And you sold it?" She stared at him in dismay. The cheap fake pearls from the costume chest would not pass muster from the lords' gallery.

"Pawned it. I can get it back any time before the performance."

She thought of Catlyn, pawning his lute and running behind on his payments.

"And what if you can't?"

Philip shrugged. "There'll be others. I reckon Southampton would cover me in pearls if I let him touch my cock."

Coby felt herself blush. "You wouldn't..."

"Course not. Sam from the Admiral's Men reckons you can get more with promises than surrender." He frowned, staring at his own raised hand as if imagining it adorned with jewels. "Still, could be worth it..."

"You don't mean that. I–"

"What? You going to rat on me, Jakes?" Philip unfastened the skirts and let them fall to the floor.

"No."

"Perhaps I should start spying on you. I'm sure you have some tasty little secret you wouldn't want Master Naismith to find out."

He stepped towards her over the silken folds. Coby turned away for fear her expression would betray her, and rummaged in her sewing basket.

"You Dutch are as thick as thieves," Philip went on. "What is it you get up to on Sundays, anyway? Can't spend the whole day at church."

"Master Kuyper reads to us from the Bible after dinner," she replied.

"Whited tombs!" Philip attempted a deep hectoring tone, like a street corner preacher. "Full of dead men's bones, and all filthiness!"

"Don't you quote scripture at me, Philip Johnson. Or I might turn the page to Saint John. Starting with the whore of Babylon."

The blood drained from Philip's face, and she thought he was going to hit her. Instead he growled something under his breath, snatched up his clothing and marched out. It sounded very like *You'll regret that, Jakes*.

"You have all the wit of a cow pat, and are less use withal," she shouted after him, but her words were lost in the slamming of the door.

She gathered up the fallen garments, shook them out and hung them back up. She really shouldn't goad Philip, but one of these days she was going to wipe the smile off his simpering, beardless face.

The streets were becoming busy by five o'clock, as the citizens of London swarmed home for their supper. No doubt that was Walsingham's intent; one more man amongst the throng was unlikely to be noticed.

Seething Lane lay a stone's throw from the Tower, a narrow street of tall, well-kept houses built close together to make best use of the valuable land. Second to last on the right, Baines had said, with a door knocker in the shape of a lion's head. Mal scarcely had time to lift the heavy bronze ring before the door opened and he was ushered inside.

He found himself in a bright atrium with white-painted panelling and a black-and-white tiled floor. A wide oak staircase dominated the space, and arched doors led off into the house to either side. The man who let him in wore servant's garb, but his face bore the same guarded expression Mal had seen on Baines's face. Was there anyone working here who wasn't an intelligencer?

"This way, sir," the man said.

He opened a door Mal had not noticed before, concealed as it was in the panelling under the stairs. Mal half-expected to see a flight of steps running down to a dungeon. There were many rumours about what went on in the house in Seething Lane.

Instead he was taken along a short whitewashed passage to a spacious parlour overlooking a walled garden. A gaunt-featured man of about sixty, dressed in a black gown and skullcap, sat in a high-backed chair by the fireplace.

"Maliverny Catlyn, sir."

Walsingham raised a hand in acknowledgment. The servant bowed and withdrew.

"Come closer, Master Catlyn."

Mal approached the Queen's private secretary and stood to attention, eyes fixed on the plasterwork coat of arms above the fireplace. The design was very plain: a horizontal bar on a vertically striped field. Either an ancient blazon, or one chosen by a man with no taste for the fantasies of the modern age.

"You understand why I sent for you?" Walsingham asked. His voice was deep, and surprisingly steady for one in evident ill health.

"No, sir." He had a shrewd idea, but he was not about to admit it.

"Sit down, Master Catlyn." Walsingham gestured to the chair opposite.

"I prefer to stand, sir."

"And I prefer not to crane my neck. Sit."

Mal obeyed. Walsingham leant back in his own chair, and Mal caught himself on the brink of doing likewise. Allowing himself to relax in this man's presence would be a grave mistake. Perhaps literally.

"You were seen at Court on Tuesday, talking to Blaise Grey," Walsingham said.

"He and I were at Peterhouse together. Sir."

"Yes, well, we will come to that later. But as to the present…
You would do well to take more care in the company you keep."

"Sir?"

"When the son of one of the most powerful men in England
rebels against everything his father stands for, you can be sure
it comes to my notice. Blaise Grey attracts malcontents like
wasps to a wind-fallen apple. For you to seek him out… well,
you must see how that looks."

For once Mal did not have to feign contrition.

"I'm very sorry, sir, I did not think–"

"You young fellows never do. What precisely were you
up to?"

"I–" A half-truth was safer than a lie. "Sir James Leland did-
n't say how long this commission would last, and as I am sure
you know, sir, I have no other means of support."

"Hmm. Well, you would do well to seek a better patron
than Grey."

"Yes, sir."

Walsingham folded his long pale hands in his lap.

"What think you of the skraylings, Catlyn?" he asked, in the
idle tones of a gentleman indulging in scholarly debate.

Mal paused, wondering what answer the spymaster expected.

"I believe they are part of God's creation," he said at last, "for
the devil cannot create any living thing, only the semblance of
it. I also believe that, since the Bible is the word of God and of
His Son, and there is no mention of skraylings therein, the message of Christ is not meant for them."

"Then they are damned?"

"That is for God in His infinite grace to decide, not I."

"A very pretty answer," Walsingham said. "But I speak of
policy, not theology."

"May I be frank with you, sir?"

"I wish for nothing less."

"I think they play a dangerous game," Mal replied. "They rely on fear and awe as a protection, on rumours that they possess magicks far more fearsome than the toys and fancies they show us."

"Dangerous to themselves, or to us?"

"Since we are allies against Spain, both."

"Then you think Her Majesty wrong to continue this alliance?"

"Not at all, sir." Mal swallowed. Men had had their hands cut off – or worse – for criticising the Queen. "Far better for them to be our friends than the friends of our enemies."

"Just so. The Spanish would gladly invade England and put a Catholic on the throne if they could muster the forces to do so, the French are allied with our old enemies the Scots... If the skraylings were to abandon us and seek friends in other lands, we would be hard pressed to defend ourselves."

"You fear the French or Spanish have designs on the ambassador?"

"If they have not, they are fools."

"I am already pledged to defend the ambassador with my life, sir, or will be once I take up my duties," Mal said. "Is there aught else you expect of me?"

Walsingham looked thoughtful for a moment.

"I knew your father, you know, in Paris. We were both at the English embassy, during the massacre on Saint Bartholomew's Day. Perhaps he mentioned it?"

"No, he... He didn't like to talk about his work when he came home." Mal paused. "I remember, the summer before my fifth birthday, Mother bought guns for the servants and said there would be no more riding or playing cricket for a while. At the time I was just jealous that Charles was old enough to be given a gun and I was not. Afterwards, I found out she feared reprisals against Catholics."

"You are a Catholic?" The spymaster's voice remained level, but a dangerous glint appeared in his eye.

"My mother was. I do as my queen commands, in all things."

"As should we all." He tapped the arm of his chair absent-mindedly, then looked up, fixing Mal with his dark gaze. "Do you know why you were chosen for this commission?"

"Sir James Leland told me it was the Queen's own command."

"A convenient fiction. Your name was presented to me by the head of the skrayling merchant-venturers, on behalf of the ambassador himself."

"What? How–?"

"How did the name of an obscure country gentleman of no fortune come to the attention of the most important skraylings this side of the Atlantic? Why did they choose you, when there are so many worthier men at Court? I was hoping you could solve that conundrum for me."

"I– I have no idea, sir." It was truth, of a sort. If the skraylings knew anything about the Catlyns, surely they would have chosen someone – anyone – else. "There must have been a misunderstanding."

Walsingham smiled thinly. "Our dealings have been beset with misunderstandings, as I recall."

The letter he had received at college. The one with a discreet "W" seal.

"That letter was from you, sir?"

Walsingham nodded, and Mal silently cursed his former naivety.

"I thought it was a prank by one of the older students." Or worse, a trap to flush out Catholic sympathisers. "I could not believe the Queen's private secretary had any use for me. And besides, there were my studies to consider."

"The masters at Cambridge know better than to punish those in my employ for lack of attendance at lectures," Walsingham said. "Arrangements could have been made. We did it for Marlowe, after all."

"Kit Marlowe? But he's–" Playwright Christopher Marlowe had been killed at an eating-house in Deptford, back in May; a quarrel over the reckoning, or so rumour had it.

"Dead? Yes. A pity. Brilliant fellow, one of the finest poets of our age." Walsingham sighed. "A shame he kept such ill company."

His words finally sank in.

"Marlowe was a spy," Mal said.

"He served his queen and country." Walsingham laced his long pale fingers together. "The offer stands, Master Catlyn. Except that it is no longer an offer."

"I see."

"Do you?" The spymaster leant forward in his chair. "Our alliance with the skraylings is of paramount importance. If our enemies make any approach, friendly or otherwise, I need to know of it."

"Surely, sir, you have men far more skilled than I in such matters."

"Of course I do. Unfortunately, none will have such intimate access to the ambassador and his party as you."

Mal groped around for a counter-argument, but could think of nothing. Damn Leland! Bad enough to be working with skraylings; now he was expected to get close to them?

"I want to know with whom they speak," Walsingham continued, "whether any letters are sent or received, and if possible I would like those letters intercepted and copied. Baines will train you in the art of seal-cutting."

"Yes, sir."

"Also, you will not come here again unless instructed by Baines, do you understand?"

"Of course, sir. A spy is of little use if it is known he is work-ing for you."

"Exactly."

"Then was it not unwise to invite me here at all?"

Walsingham smiled. "A calculated risk. I wanted to speak to you in person. And you *have* been appointed by the Crown, so what is more natural than that Her Majesty's secretary should wish an interview?"

Mal wordlessly indicated his agreement.

"One more thing," Walsingham said.

"Sir?"

"If you do find out why the skraylings asked for you, I want to be the first to know."

"Of course, sir." Over my dead body.

Walsingham went over to his desk and opened a drawer.

"I understand you negotiated a retainer from Leland."

"Yes, sir. Two shillings a day."

"Hmm." He held out a small purse. "For your expenses in car-rying out your… additional duties. I am informed you do not share your brother's vices, so that should be more than adequate."

Mal decided it would be impolitic to count the money in front of the spymaster. "Thank you, sir."

Walsingham rang a small bell which stood on the desk, and Mal was shown out by the manservant. In the street, curiosity got the better of him and he took out the purse. Silver crowns and half-crowns met his gaze, not a fortune but more than enough to cover his daily needs for the next few weeks. Did Walsingham know about Sandy? By "brother" Mal assumed he had meant Charles, whose gambling habits had been the stuff of gossip since Mal was a child. Still, perhaps he should not visit Bethlem for a while, just in case.

He shoved the purse back in his pocket with a grunt of an-noyance. Every time he thought his life could not possibly get any worse, Fate shat in his chamber pot again. Well, at least now he had some beer money to help him forget about it for another night. Except then Ned would want to know where the money came from. Christ's blessed mother! He stamped off down the street, cursing in every language he could remember, ignoring the stares and muttered comments from passers-by.

CHAPTER VI

The house in Culver Alley sagged between its neighbours like a drunk on his way home. Window shutters hung askew on their hinges, or were nailed shut. The decorative plaster work over the door had turned leprous with neglect, and the door itself was pitted and scarred, as if someone had tried to batter it down on more than one occasion.

Mal knocked. After a few moments footsteps approached the door, then after a short pause came the sound of bolts being drawn back. The door opened, though whoever had done so remained hidden behind it.

"Come in." The voice sounded like that of Baines.

Mal stepped inside and the door closed behind him.

Baines led him through to a dining parlour at the back of the house, looking out over a gloomy courtyard surrounded by other equally decrepit tenements. A straggly sycamore pushed its way through the mossy cobbles, and a cloud of metallic-green dung-flies buzzed around the midden. Mistress Faulkner's neatly tended vegetable garden was a vision of Paradise in comparison.

The room was dominated by a heavy oak table covered in the impedimenta of letter-writing: paper, ink bottles, quills cut and uncut, pen knives, a pounce shaker, sticks of sealing wax and a stub of candle burning in a pewter candlestick.

"Your first job," Baines said. "Make a pile of sealed letters to practise on later, when the wax is set hard."

He handed Mal a sheaf of papers, most with writing on them, and a small seal of the sort used by private persons.

"We'll practise with these first," the intelligencer said. "Later you'll learn to cut the larger seals of state and diplomatic papers. Now get on with it; I have other things to do."

Mal skimmed through the papers, but could make neither head nor tail of their contents. Some bore line after line of nonsense words, others had columns of pairs of letters as if meant as arithmetical exercises, though there were no totals at the columns' bases. Most, however, were in English – either everyday correspondence on a variety of subjects, or decidedly bad poetry. Mal chuckled to himself at the thought of Baines penning sonnets, then put the pages aside and set about his assigned task.

When Baines returned, he produced a sheaf of letters readysealed and taught Mal the various ways of softening sealing wax just enough so it would not snap when handled. He also gave him a small knife, not very sharp but flat and of such thinness that when heated in a candle flame it could be slipped under a seal without disturbing it.

"Watch you keep that hidden," Baines said. "We don't want the ambassador knowing what you're up to, do we now?"

Mal resisted the urge to point out he was not a fool. The intelligencer had already made up his mind, that was obvious.

After a couple of hours of painstaking practice Baines called a halt.

"What next?" Mal asked.

"When you've mastered the skill of cutting a seal and replacing it – without bloody breaking it in two – we'll move on to invisible writings and the use of ciphers."

"Is that what these are?" Mal said, pointing out the sheets of numbers and nonsense words.

"Aye, and the rest. Practice pieces, like your seals."

Mal scanned one of the letters. The phrasing was a little odd in places, but he could see no hidden meaning. He looked at Baines in puzzlement.

"That's work for another day," the intelligencer said, holding up a hand. "Enough."

He tidied their work away into a cupboard and locked it.

"Come back the day after tomorrow. If I'm not here, go straight home. I'll find you."

Mal caught himself on the verge of asking Baines where he was going. No, that would not be a good idea. Baines would not tell him, and in any case it was probably best he did not know.

"All the costumes?"

"All," Naismith said.

Coby sat down next to him on the gallery bench and watched the workmen fitting the balustrades and other finely turned woodwork, but her mind was elsewhere.

"But surely we do not need everything made new," she said at last. "There are some small parts–"

"All must be of one piece, or the harmony of the thing is spoiled." He stood up and leant over the railing. "You! Carpenter fellow in the mustard jerkin. That third baluster along is upside down." He sat down again. "A pox on Dunfell! He should be here by now to keep an eye on this lot."

Coby ran through her mental inventory of the costumes.

"We have those Roman breastplates," she said, "the boiled leather ones painted to look like steel."

"Lord Suffolk's antiquarians have determined that the Ancient Greeks wore bronze," the actor-manager said. "Besides, those breastplates have seen better days. I think they're older than I am."

Coby ignored the attempt at a joke.

"The soldiers will be standing at the back for most of the scene," she said. "No one will notice."

"What about the people sitting in the lords' galleries? They will have a close view of the back of the stage."

"All right, not the breastplates. And the helmets *do* need new plumes. But there must be something…"

Naismith sighed and turned to look at her.

"What's the matter with you, lad? Our patron has offered to restock our wardrobe with the finest costumes money can buy, and all you can do is protest. I thought you would be grateful not to have all that work to do."

"I am," Coby said, trying not to let her resentment show. "So, if I do not need to make any costumes, what about other things? There are sides to be copied, a plot sheet to be written out, properties to be bought–"

"All taken care of," Naismith said, putting a hand on her shoulder. "Master Dunfell is managing everything."

"Everything?"

"Oh yes. He has been most thorough."

So this was Dunfell's idea of helping her, by taking all responsibility out of her hands. No doubt if she confronted him about it, he would say he was making time for her to pursue the task he had set her. She wished he had chosen someone else to bestow his favour upon.

It was but a short walk from Ned's house to the new theatre at the far end of Bankside. The theatre field was empty of workmen for the moment, but the piles of sand, clay and straw spoke of recent – or imminent – industry. Sounds of hammering came from the theatre itself. The main doors stood open, so Mal wandered inside.

"Hello?" he shouted, looking around. "Master Naismith?"

"Who is that?" a voice called out from the galleries.

"It is I, Maliverny Catlyn," he replied, stepping out of the shadowy entrance tunnel. "I come by appointment, to speak with your tireman."

After a few moments he heard footsteps on the gallery stairs, then the young tireman appeared.

"You still wish for lessons in Tradetalk?" the boy asked.

"That's why I'm here."

"We had best go outside. We shall not be able to hear ourselves think in there. And in any case, Master Naismith doesn't like anyone from outside the company spying on our progress."

"Indeed not." Spying on actors? What would anyone want to do that for?

As if guessing his thoughts, the boy added, "The Admiral's Men would give a good deal of money to know our plans for the contest."

So that was what Ned had been up to, that night in the Bull's Head. Mal smiled to himself. Perhaps he should not have judged his friend so harshly.

"You have the advantage of me, lad," Mal said to his companion as they walked across the field.

"Sir?"

"You know my name, but I do not know yours."

"Jacob Hendricks, sir."

"Dutch?"

The boy nodded.

"Anxious to get over there and fight?" Mal asked.

Hendricks shook his head.

Mal gave up that line of conversation. If the boy was going to be so taciturn, learning a language from him promised to be hard going. He looked around.

"This is a poor spot to sit and talk. Look, there is shade, down there by the millstream."

He pointed to a knot of alders on the edge of the pleasure gardens.

Hendricks bit his lip. "I am not so sure."

"Come now, we cannot stand around in the sun like labourers. And it seems we cannot sit in the shade of yon theatre either, lest I am suspected of eavesdropping."

"Very well," the boy said. "It is just… Master Parrish said I should stay away from such lewd places. He–" Hendricks blushed like a girl. "He says I am too pretty for my own good."

"What, you think I would ravish you?" Mal laughed. "Jesu, you're a child, for Heaven's sake!"

"I'm not a child, I'm seventeen."

"Aye, well, tell me again when your voice breaks and I might believe you."

They crossed the little wooden bridge into Paris Gardens and sat down in the shade of the alders. Mal studied the boy's profile for a moment. Furrowed brow, a nose red and peeling from the sun, a bottom lip curled downwards in, what, frustration? Or misery? No sign of violence, but then not all bruises show. He wondered if that was why the boy hugged his ribs so protectively.

"I suppose tempers are running short," Mal said. "What with the contest and all."

"Something like that." The boy picked up an alder cone and threw it into the stream.

Mal made a sympathetic noise. It was none of his business, and he did not press the matter further.

"So, where shall we begin?" Hendricks said with forced cheerfulness.

"How should I know?" Mal said, sitting alert with forearms propped on his knees. "You're the teacher."

The boy glanced at him, ready with another retort, then seemed to change his mind. He smiled nervously.

"Well, the first thing you need to know," he said, staring off into the distance, "is that Tradetalk uses English words, more or less, but not in the way an Englishman would do. The skraylings refuse to make certain letters, to whit, m, b and p–"

"Why?"

"It is said they find them effeminate, like a lisp. The upshot is, they must find new words for many common English things, such as mother, brother and the like."

"And man and woman?"

The boy blushed again.

"Yes."

"So, how do you say 'man' or 'woman'?"

"Man is 'fellah'. Woman is 'she-fellah'."

"Like she-wolf?"

"Yes, I suppose so. But you address a man as 'sir', whatever his rank, and a woman as 'lady'. Not that you will need to address a woman in Tradetalk."

"Is it true there are no womenfolk here?" Mal asked.

Hendricks shrugged. "I have not seen any, nor no children neither. Perhaps they keep their women hidden, like the Turks are said to do."

Mal repeated the Tradetalk words a few times. It all seemed simple enough, if a little barbaric to the ear.

"Even the Turks are not so secretive," he said. "But then the skraylings seem fond of secrets."

"And stories," Hendricks said. "That's why they come to the theatres so much, even those who cannot understand the speeches."

"Your patron is a friend of the skraylings," Mal said. "And I hear yon theatre is being built with skrayling silver. That is a bold venture."

"You sound as if you do not approve, sir," the boy said, eyeing him suspiciously.

"On the contrary," Mal replied, cursing his clumsy approach to the issue. "I am all for seizing any advantage in a fight. Now, where were we?"

By the end of the afternoon, Mal had a grasp of simple greetings and a few phrases that might be useful in the marketplace. From time to time he was even able to forget why he was learning all this and simply enjoy a pleasant afternoon in the company of a new friend.

"I am indebted to you and your master," he said, getting to his feet and brushing dead leaves from his clothing. "If there is anything else I can do..."

Hendricks stared at the glittering millstream for a long moment.

"Teach me to fight."

So, it was the other boys giving him grief, not the master.

"I doubt I can help you," Mal said, not unkindly. "You will not come up against many apprentices armed with rapiers."

The boy looked up, his expression unreadable. "Anything you can teach me... about being a man."

Mal smiled. "Now that you really must learn for yourself. But–" Something about the boy's air of desperation reminded him of himself at the same age. "Part of my training was in unarmed combat and dagger-play. Perhaps that would be of some use?"

Hendricks' eyes lit up and he nodded.

"Though I warn you," Mal added, "if you ever come up against a man with a knife, your best stratagem is to run."

"Run, sir?"

"Like all the demons of Hell are after you."

Coby sat by the stream for a long time after Master Catlyn had gone. What was the point in going back to the theatre, if there was no work for her to do? And then there was this business of fighting lessons. She could not imagine what had possessed her to ask him. She didn't even like the man. No, that was not true. She had been determined not to like him after the way he had behaved at Goody Watson's, but he had changed his tune since then, indeed had been all politeness this afternoon. Not at first, perhaps, but then after they sat down together, he had suddenly changed. Was it something she said? Did he… oh Lord, did he suspect?

And what if he does? a voice in the back of her mind asked. She had assumed he shared Faulkner's tastes, but what if she were wrong? She felt herself grow hot all over, and not from the sun. What if he tries to seduce me? She leant over the stream, trying to make out her reflection in the rippling surface. Stupid. Why would he be interested in a plain, skinny creature like me, when London teems with women far better supplied with feminine charms?

She threw a twig in the stream and watched it float away. No, he did not know, she was certain of it. He would not have agreed to teach her to fight if he knew her to be a girl. The thought should have been comforting, but somehow it was not. She sighed. Anyone would think she wanted to be found out, like the guilty man in the proverb, running from shadows, afraid of everyone and everything.

Well, that was not her. She had nothing to feel bad about, the rest of the world was to blame for forcing her into these desperate straits. Getting to her feet she marched back to the theatre. She would find something useful to do if it killed her.

Walking back along Bankside towards Deadman's Place, Mal wondered when he had stopped trying to get out of Leland's commission and started looking forward to it and, more to the point, why. The lessons with Baines and Hendricks provided new challenges, it was true, but was that all? Perhaps a part of him was just sick of running away. Very well, so be it.

After crossing London Bridge he walked eastwards along Thames Street, emerging on the lower slopes of Tower Hill. In daylight the fortress looked far less ominous than it had by night. The crenellations of the walls and towers had begun to crumble with age, and moss and weeds had taken hold in every crack. The former Great Hall stood open to the sky, its roof timbers bare as the ribs of dead men. Only the Lieutenant's House, whitewashed and in good repair, gave any indication the Tower remained in active use. Mal hoped the ambassador's accommodation was in a better state than the rest of the fortress, otherwise the skraylings might be sorely offended.

No sooner had he thought of the skraylings than his eye was drawn towards the stockade on the far side of the river. Within it could be seen many domed tents of some heavy fabric woven in the same patterns of interlocking triangles as the skraylings' tunics. A column of bluish smoke rose from somewhere near the centre. He set off down the hill at a lope, determined to cross the river before he could change his mind.

"Westward ho! Eastward ho!"

The familiar cries of the wherrymen echoed across the water.

"What's the nearest stair to the skrayling camp?" Mal shouted to one of them.

"That'll be Horseydown. Tuppence, an it please you, sir."

Mal fished two pennies out of his pocket and stepped aboard the little boat. It felt good to have money to spare again.

A few minutes later he disembarked at Horseydown Stairs, a hundred yards downriver from the stockade. Unlike elsewhere on the Thames, there were no wherries waiting to take passengers, only a small boat with a prow carved in the likeness of a seabird's head, moored to the jetty and unoccupied. He assumed it belonged to one of the skrayling merchant vessels that stood at anchor along the Southwark docks. He gave the wherryman an extra halfpenny for his inconvenience, and set off towards the stockade.

The skrayling encampment stood on a narrow strip of ground, bordered on the north, south and west by the Thames and its tributary streams. Only a small wooden bridge connected it to Southwark at the western end. A pleasant enough situation, had it not been for the tanneries and forges upwind. If the intent was to isolate the skraylings whilst keeping them in plain sight, Mal could not think of a better location. It also made it impossible to approach the place unnoticed.

For a moment he considered skirting around the common land south of the encampment – but then why bother to come at all, if he did not improve upon the glimpse he had gained from Tower Hill? He took a couple of deep breaths, like a man steadying his nerves before charging into battle, then took the faint path that ran directly towards the skrayling stockade.

Not satisfied with the protection of river and streams, the builders had added a narrow moat connected to the Thames. On the south side, it was crossed by a wooden drawbridge where a double gate pierced the timber palisade. The gates were open, and skraylings armed with quarterstaves stood at either side of the entrance. The scent of tobacco drifted out across the common, along with unfamiliar cooking smells. He thought of all the strange peoples he had seen on his travels, but none were as strange as these creatures dwelling in his own country.

He paused at the landward end of the drawbridge. Should he announce himself? Seek an introduction to the chief skrayling? He still knew too little Tradetalk to be useful and besides, why would they believe him? He wore no livery, carried no badge to prove his position.

The distant murmur of skrayling voices stilled, and the notes of a woodwind instrument rose in its place. Soft, like a flute,

but tuned to an alien key, even stranger than the music of the
Turks. And yet the melody was hauntingly familiar, as if...
That was it. A lullaby his mother used to sing, in the house by
the sea. No. He had never heard it before, did not know it –
how could he? Derbyshire was about as far from the sea as
anywhere in England. Mal shook his head in confusion. Was
he being bewitched? He made the sign of the cross, and the
strange feeling faded.

He was uncomfortably aware of the two guards watching
him out of the corner of his eye. He swallowed and walked
away, heading westwards towards Southwark. His footsteps
echoed on the timber planking of the bridge as he crossed the
stream, and he had to force himself not to break into a run.

CHAPTER VII

Ned stripped the barbs from a crow quill and cut the tip into a nib. Only one more copy and he was done. Legal papers were not the most interesting of jobs, but at least he could do the work at home and keep an eye on his mother. And with Mal's new connections to draw on, he might even aspire to a post in one of the new scriveneries attached to the Inns of Court.

He had just sanded the last page when footsteps sounded on the stairs and Mal appeared in the doorway.

"Can I borrow a pen and a bit of paper?" Mal asked.

"What do you want it for?"

"A letter."

"Who are you going to write to? You don't have any friends except me." It was cruel, but Mal was at his most handsome when he was vexed.

"I have friends. Blaise Grey, for one."

"Grey's not your friend," Ned replied. "If he was, he'd have helped you by now. Trust me, powerful men don't help underlings like us unless there's something in it for them."

Mal glowered, but said nothing.

"I don't think you're writing a letter at all," Ned went on. "I think you're writing a sonnet to that pretty apprentice-boy of Naismith's, the one you've been spending all summer with."

"I am not."

"After all I've done for you…" Ned sighed melodramatically. "Putting you up here, sharing my bed with you–"

"And I'm grateful, truly. But *I* have a letter to write and *you* should be at Henslowe's."

Ned shrugged. "It's only eleven."

"That was twelve the clocks struck. Or can't you count either?"

"Christ's hairy arse!" Ned snatched up his satchel and waved at the desk. "Help yourself. I'm off!"

He ran down the stairs without a backward glance, through the kitchen and out into the garden, where his mother was hoeing the cabbages.

"I'll be back for supper," he called over his shoulder as he vaulted the gate.

The mastiffs in the bear-baiting kennels nearby bayed in response to his shout but soon they were well behind him, their clamour lost amongst the cries from the Clink prison. Desperate inmates stretched their arms through barred windows as Ned passed.

"Spare a penny for an old soldier down on his luck, sir," one prisoner rasped through his few remaining teeth.

Ned threw him a pitying glance before turning towards the house opposite the prison. Henslowe was generous in lending money to his employees, but visitors to his house could not avoid the grim reminder of what would happen if they abused that generosity.

Ned knocked on the theatre manager's door and was admitted by a serving girl. He didn't know her name; maids came and went with the turn of the seasons, and they all looked much alike to him. She showed him into Henslowe's study, a gloomy wood-panelled chamber on the first floor overlooking the street.

Henslowe's book chest stood open and empty, its contents
piled on the desk and floor. The theatre manager was sifting
through a pile of manuscripts bound with string. His greying
hair was unkempt and he wore a loose gown over his underlinens and slippers on his feet, as though he had not thought
to dress since rising.

"I don't suppose you have Marlowe's final masterpiece hidden about your person, do you, Faulkner?" he asked, without
looking up.

"Umm, no, sir."

Henslowe waved a hand at the piles of paper all around him.

"A fortune invested in the theatre business, and what do I
have to show for it? A chest full of feeble scribblings, and not
one of them fit to put on for the ambassador."

Ned doubted his words; most of the city's playwrights had
sold their work to Henslowe in recent years. All except Will
Shakespeare, who wrote exclusively for the Prince's Men.

"Does it have to be something new?" Ned asked, remembering what Mal had told him. "The ambassador's never been
to London before, and surely he cannot have heard any of our
plays put on in the New World unless they be transcribed into
Vinlandic."

Henslowe put down the pile of manuscripts and stared at him.

"You know, you may be onto something."

"And he won't understand a word of it anyway," Ned said,
warming to his subject, "so you could just put on something
that looks good."

"Looks good… Yes, yes. Pageantry, spectacle, that colour of
beast." Henslowe clapped him on the shoulder. "Good thinking, Faulkner. I knew there was a reason I liked you."

Mal finished his writing, sanded and folded it, and put it into
his pocket. It was not a letter, nor indeed a sonnet, damned be

Ned's lewd imaginings. Though even a sonnet would be easier to explain than the nonsense text he now carried: Baines' latest assignment, a letter transposed into cipher from memory. It was hard enough keeping his intelligence training hidden from Ned, without having cipher keys in his possession. He would present his work to the intelligencer later. Right now he had other things to do.

He was barely halfway along Bankside when he spotted Hendricks running towards him. The boy's straw-pale hair was dark with sweat, yet his doublet remained buttoned up. Mal had commented on it during their first wrestling lesson, but Hendricks had insisted he was more comfortable fully dressed. What kind of injuries must he be hiding, that he could not strip to shirt and hose? And yet the boy had not cried out when Mal threw him to the floor. Perhaps he was reading too much into the situation. Or perhaps the hurt was on the inside.

Hendricks' look of worried concentration was replaced by a broad grin when he caught sight of Mal. He shouted a greeting and stumbled to a halt, wiping the sweat from his sunburnt brow.

"I thought – I would not catch you," he panted as Mal approached.

"Is something amiss? Can I help?"

Hendricks shook his head, casting droplets of sweat about him. "Master Naismith is in the most dreadful temper, that is all."

"He has not changed his mind about allowing you to teach me?" Mal asked. "I would not have you disobey your master."

"Naught like that," Hendricks replied with a rueful smile. "It is the builders. They say it will take at least another two weeks to finish the carpentry, but we are due to perform at the end of the month and the stage is still not painted. Master Naismith blames Master Dunfell, Master Dunfell blames Master Naismith…"

Mal laughed. "Then we are well out of it. So, where shall we go?"

For a moment he thought of suggesting the Faulkners' house, but that would only add fuel to the fire if Ned found out.

"An it please you, sir, it is time you practised your Tradetalk with others."

"Others?"

"Skraylings."

Billingsgate was one part of London Coby knew well. The greater proportion of its Dutch inhabitants lived there, close to the wharfs where their ships put in. All foreign vessels coming into London were obliged to dock there for their cargoes to be measured and taxed, including those of the skraylings, and a market had sprung up nearby to offer the latest wares from both New World and Old.

To her surprise, Master Catlyn exchanged greetings with some of the Dutch stallholders in their own language. His accent was Flemish like her own, rather than the Zeelandic of the Amsterdam merchants, but he had no problem making himself understood.

"Not many Englishmen speak my tongue," she said, looking at him with renewed curiosity.

"I sailed to the Low Countries when I was nineteen," he said. "Living under siege, you learn what you need to survive."

"You were in a siege? What was it like?"

"Boring. Hungry. You don't want to know."

Well, that closed that line of questioning. She racked her brains for another topic of conversation.

"Did you never want to sail to the New World?"

"Not I." He laughed. "Crossing the Channel was bad enough. My home county is landlocked, and as far from the sea as any in England."

"Where is that?"

"Derbyshire. The Peakland. You would find it very hilly, coming from…" He paused. "Where do you come from?"

"Berchem, near Antwerp."

He nodded. "I think we marched through there."

"You did? Yes, I remember the banners…"

She broke off, remembering also her father's stern admonition to stay well away from the English soldiers. Drunks and blasphemers, he called them. Despoilers of women. She was only eleven years old at the time and had not understood what he meant. Half a decade in London had been… an education.

She steered the conversation, and their path, back to her purpose in coming here. Quickening her pace she led Master Catlyn through the market, past stalls piled high with fragrant Italian leather, baskets of almonds and garlic, and wheels of cheese studded with cloves. When she realised he was no longer at her side, she feared he had changed his mind about trying his skills out, but he had only stopped a few yards behind her to buy strings from a lute-maker.

The Vinlanders' stalls were set apart from the other strangers, marked out by their brown-and-white striped awnings. Strings of dried peppers and puffed corn festooned many, though rather for decoration than purchase. Neither were much to the taste of Europeans.

"You should talk to some of the skraylings," she said. "Perhaps buy something."

"I have little to spend, and no one to buy for," he replied.

"Then perhaps you could haggle badly and lose."

They passed a stall selling ribbons dyed in vivid iris shades, brighter than anything made in England. The colours brought to mind the lights that hung outside the skrayling guild house after dark.

"Why only blue, yellow and purple?" Master Catlyn asked,

as if guessing her thoughts. "Surely red and green would be just as simple to make, and more popular."

"You know how some men cannot tell red from green? So it is with skraylings. Red is dull in their eyes, so they do not use it."

"Really? You didn't mention it before."

"I'm sorry, sir. Names for colours are so little used in Tradetalk, I didn't think of it."

They paused at another stall. This one held boxes of straw in which nestled earthenware and porcelain, much of it glazed a bright turquoise highlighted with yellow or white. The items themselves ranged from dishes and plates to grotesque figures with leering mouths and bulging eyes.

The stall holder, a short skrayling with blue beads threaded in his mane, bowed to Master Catlyn and held out a small pottery figure of an animal, somewhat like a long-necked sheep. Its feet had been replaced with wheels, and a striped blanket was painted on its back.

"Toy, give little one."

Master Catlyn turned pale, and Coby thought he was going to puke.

"Are you all right?" she murmured.

"It is naught," he replied, rubbing his eyes with one hand. "Someone walked over my grave, that's all." He turned back to the skrayling. "No little one. No she-fellah of I."

So, he was not married. She had suspected as much, but the knowledge still pleased her. That in itself was worrying. She already risked too much by letting him touch her in their fighting lessons. Yet she felt at ease in his presence now, as she had never done with the actors. And if his kindness towards her was only that of an elder brother, it was for the best. Wasn't it?

They moved on to another stall, where a slim androgynous figure with bronze skin and sleek black hair was roasting brick-coloured tubers over a brazier.

"That is not a skrayling female?" Master Catlyn asked in an undertone.

"No," Coby whispered back. "It is a man from the New World. See, he has dark eyes, and his features are as human as yours or mine."

"What about his ears?"

The man's earlobes were as big as apricots, stretched out of their natural shape by roundels of ivory.

"It's not so very different from your earring, is it?" she said, then added, "He probably speaks Tradetalk, so he'd be as good a test of your skill as a skrayling."

Master Catlyn cleared his throat and pointed to the brazier.

"An they, sir."

The man speared a sweet potato with a fork and wrapped it in a scrap of coarse cloth, grinning at them with tobacco-stained teeth.

"An denna, thank ye," he replied, holding out a scarred hand.

As Master Catlyn fumbled in his pocket for a penny, a scrap of paper fluttered to the ground. Coby picked it up. It was a letter, and not sealed. This was her chance. Hardly daring to breathe, she turned her back on the stall and unfolded the paper.

My dearest Jane–

Her throat tightened. No, it might only be a letter to a sister. She read on.

–I do most heartily wish you well, and assure you I have not forgotten my promise to visit on the 22nd of next month. In the meantime I will send 13oz of sugared almonds for you and your 3 sisters–

"What have you there?" Master Catlyn asked.

She hastily folded the strange letter and turned back to him.

"You dropped this, sir," she replied, holding it out.

He snatched the paper from her hand.

"Did you read it?"

She dropped her gaze to the ground, unable to lie to his face.

"Did you read it?"

"Yes, sir," she whispered. She wished she had never agreed to spy on him.

"And what did you make of it?"

"Only th-that you have a sweetheart, sir. And she likes sugared almonds."

"Nothing more?"

"No, sir. I didn't read any more."

He put the letter back in his pocket, his expression thoughtful. She supposed she would have to report this to Dunfell. There was something odd going on, since sugared almonds were an expensive gift, an unlikely choice for a man who claimed to have no money.

"I think I have had enough of markets," Master Catlyn said, taking his purchase from the stall holder. "And your master will be expecting you home for supper."

"Yes, sir."

"Sunday afternoon again, at five o'clock?"

She stared up at him, hardly daring to believe, but there was no teasing look on his face. She had expected him to end their lessons together, after what she had just done. But why should he suspect her? She was just some boy to him, not a girl who might rival the mysterious Jane for his affections. She chided herself for thinking there could ever be anything but friendship between them.

"Sunday," she said. "At five."

On Saturday morning she accompanied Master Naismith on another business matter. He would not say where, but instructed her to wear her best suit. Another visit to Master Cutsnail? She hoped not – there was no good news for the merchant.

However, they turned north out of Thames Street, and a short walk up the hill brought them to the yard surrounding

St Paul's Cathedral, where the chapmen had their stalls hung about with ballad sheets and stacked with books of all sizes. Here one could buy a family Bible or a volume of love sonnets, sundry classics in the original Latin and Greek or English versions of works by Machiavelli and Castiglione. There were even a few printed editions of plays; were they perhaps going to visit one of the printers who had their workshops in the streets around Paul's Yard?

Master Naismith turned left through Ludgate, however, taking them outside the city walls. In Fleet Street, Coby's eyes were drawn towards the dark bulk of Bridewell Prison on the bank of the Thames. She shuddered. If she were ever found out to be a girl in men's clothing, she could be whipped through the streets and condemned to that horrible place, to be locked up with all the other "disorderly women" of the city.

They walked on and Fleet Street became the Strand, the main road between the city of London and Westminster. On the riverward side stood many fine houses belonging to the greatest lords in the land: Arundel, Bedford, Somerset... and Suffolk, she realised with growing excitement. Their patron had built himself a grand new mansion at Charing Cross, to be close to Whitehall Palace in Westminster. She exchanged glances with Master Naismith, and he smiled.

"You have guessed our destination," he said. "We are to meet Thomas Lodge, the playwright engaged by our patron to compose a play perfectly suited to the Ambassador of Vinland." He smiled again and added, "Master Lodge has been to the New World."

The New World! It was one thing to meet skraylings who had journeyed so far, but an Englishman who had ventured across the Atlantic and returned safe was a rare marvel indeed. She wondered if he was as handsome as Master Catlyn.

They reached the western end of the Strand, where the

ancient marble monument to Queen Eleanor dominated the
confluence of three roads: the Strand, King Street and Cock-
spur Street. On the southern side nearest the river stood
Suffolk House, its pale stone walls and many glazed windows
rivalling the nearby Palace of Whitehall. They entered through
a gatehouse into a large cobbled courtyard where servants hurried back and forth on the duke's business. On either side
stood the apartments of the gentlemen retainers; the great hall,
a single-storeyed building even taller than the wings, took up
the entire south side of the courtyard.

"His Grace lives beyond the hall, in fine apartments beside
the river," Master Naismith said. "I doubt we shall be invited
into such rarefied company."

A man of about forty, wearing the duke's blue-and-white livery and a harassed expression, greeted Master Naismith as one
well known to him, and they were shown through a door in
the west wing and up a spiral stair to one of the apartments.
Two men were waiting for them in the small but comfortable
parlour. Coby immediately and with a sinking feeling recognised
Master Dunfell; the other she assumed to be Master Lodge.

"Naismith, good to see you!" Lodge grasped Master Naismith's arm and shook it heartily.

Coby hung back in the shadows, eyeing the playwright with
disappointment. She had expected a dashing adventurer with
a taste for poetry, like Sir Walter Raleigh or Sir Philip Sidney,
not this short scrubby-bearded fellow with a feverish glint to
his gooseberry-green eyes.

"So, what do you have for us?" Master Naismith asked, once
the pleasantries were over.

Lodge gestured for them to approach the table, which was
covered in a chaotic layer of papers scrawled in a barely leg-
ible hand. She did not envy the scrivener who had to make
a fair copy.

"My best play yet," he said. "I have entitled it *The Queen of Faerieland*."

"Based on Spenser, is it?"

"Better than that." Lodge fairly quivered with excitement, like a child bursting to tell a great secret.

"What Master Lodge is trying to say," Dunfell put in, "is that he has borrowed from his recent travels, not from another poet. This is a skrayling story put into English."

"Devil take you!" Lodge turned scarlet. "You have ruined the ending, you pinch-souled capon. Go back to your accounts, and leave the recounting of tales to poets!"

Dunfell stepped back a little from the table, but did not leave the room. His fixed expression suggested he was used to the playwright's temper.

Lodge turned back to Master Naismith.

"It is a story I heard in Antilia, an ancient legend of three brothers of the Pescamocarti and their love for the Queen of the Forest. I have transposed it to the city of Athens..."

Whilst the playwright and the actor-manager bent over the manuscript, Master Dunfell motioned Coby to one side.

"Have you made any progress in the matter we spoke of?" he asked in a low voice.

"I- I found a letter," she said, "though it was only to his sweetheart."

"What did it say?"

"It was addressed to a lady named Jane, who has three sisters, and said he would be visiting her on the twenty-second of September."

"After the competition? Well, no matter. Go on."

"That is all, sir. I did not have time to read more."

"You do not have it."

"No, sir, I–" She could not tell Dunfell she had been caught red-handed.

"More than a month, and this is all you have found out? I must say I am disappointed. Very disappointed indeed." He wrinkled his pointed nose, as if she were a smear of dog shit on his shoe. "After all I have done for you and your master, I expected greater efforts to follow my instructions."

Coby hung her head and tried to look contrite.

"Needless to say," he went on, "I shall not be recommending you for a place in the duke's household. You may consider my own patronage of your career at an end."

She inclined her head submissively, though she was secretly relieved. The last thing she wanted was to work for such an odious man. She would rather take her chances amongst the actors, even at the risk of exposure.

"This is very good, Lodge," Master Naismith said, scanning a page. "Here, Dunfell, is this not most excellently written?"

Seeing Lodge bristle in anticipation of another argument, Coby put in, "Begging your pardon, Master Lodge, but why did you set it in Athens instead of the New World?"

"It is not your place to question your betters' judgement," Dunfell snapped.

Lodge looked taken aback at this unexpected ally, though Coby guessed it was only anger at herself that made Dunfell side with the playwright.

"No, let the boy speak," said Master Naismith. "'Tis a fair point."

Master Lodge launched into a long explanation full of words and allusions Coby did not understand. When he eventually paused for breath, Naismith put in: "Our scholarly colleague's point is, have you ever heard of these Peascod folk?"

"No, sir," Coby replied.

"And how much do you think the average playgoers know of them?"

"Not much, sir."

"Your first answer was nearer the mark. No, there is no drama in telling a tale of lands so far away that no one knows their names. No resonance with the audience, see? Instead, Master Lodge has taken the tale and reshaped it into something even the penny stinkards can make sense of. That's how you get bums on seats, lad."

Lodge gathered up his mess of papers into what Coby hoped was the correct order, and she stuffed them into her satchel. A skrayling play in a skrayling-sponsored theatre – let the Admiral's Men top that!

CHAPTER VIII

After church on Sunday morning Mal visited Bethlem Hospital again. To his relief his brother was improving, in both body and spirit. Either Mistress Cooke was being true to her word and giving him more care now Mal was a regular visitor, or... No, he could not let himself dare to think it. Sandy had had lucid spells before, but they never lasted.

The weather had turned cooler again, and they stayed indoors all morning. Mal had bought a book in Paul's Yard which he thought Sandy might like. Something to dispel evil humours, and bring his thoughts to greater order and harmony.

"*The Whetstone of Wit*'," Sandy read out, "'which is the second part of Arithmetic: containing the extraction of roots; the cossike practice, with the rule of equation; and the works of surd numbers'." He looked up at Mal. "It's just abridged Euclid, you know."

"You've read it."

He tried to keep the disappointment out of his voice, but Sandy knew him too well.

"I've read everything here a hundred times." He gestured to the small pile of volumes by his bed. "Something twice- or thrice-read will seem fresh in comparison."

Sandy settled down to read the mathematics treatise whilst
Mal took out his lute. It took some time to tune, being so sen-
sitive to the changes in the weather. The room was oppressively
warm now, and he wondered if he should suggest they go outside, but it was looking like rain again. August was always a
race to get the harvest in before the heavens opened.

He started as Sandy clapped his book shut with a loud thump.

"No," Sandy whispered, turning pale.

"What is it?"

Mal went to the door and pressed his ear against the rough
wood. A burst of laughter came from downstairs. Not the hysterical shrieks and giggles of the inmates, but a colder, more
mocking sound. Visitors.

He looked around. Mistress Cooke had locked the door as
usual, but what if she opened it from the outside? Surely she
would not do that with Mal in here, but if one of the gentlemen flashed a little gold in her direction, she might think it
worth the risk.

"Help me move the bed against the door," he told Sandy,
keeping his voice low but firm.

Sandy clutched the book to his chest, his face rigid with fear.
Mal sighed and leant his weight against the door, ready to resist entry bodily if need be. He was not about to attract
attention to their cell by setting off one of Sandy's fits.

Mal remained at his vigil for what felt like hours, listening
to Mistress Cooke and her husband's sycophancies and the
cruel laughter of the visitors, and watching Sandy twitch every
time footsteps came near their door. Eventually the ward fell
silent and Mal returned to his brother's side. This was not going
to be easy.

"Sandy?" He sat down on the bed. "I have to go soon and…
I don't know when I can return. I have to earn money to pay
for our keep."

Sandy said nothing, only stared into the distance.

"If I can't come," Mal went on, "I'll send Ned to see you, all right? You remember Ned?"

"Ned. Short for Edmund. Yes."

"Good. He'll keep you company well enough. I'll have him bring his deck of cards."

"He cheats."

"That he does." Mal forced a smile, and kissed his brother on both cheeks. "It won't be much longer, I promise."

Coby sat down on the grass by the front doors of the theatre, feeling conspicuous. In nearby Paris Gardens, revellers laughed, and a man was singing "The Pangs of Love" to the playing of a lute. A few passers-by gave her curious looks, but probably thought her just a young swain waiting for his sweetheart. If only…

Shortly after five o'clock the gate opened and Master Catlyn entered the theatre field. Coby leapt to her feet and tried not to look too pleased to see him. She led him round to the back of the theatre and unlocked the door. The theatre was of course empty on the Lord's Day, which was why it made such a private practice-space. As they passed through the tiring house and out onto the stage, Master Catlyn handed her one of the two cudgels they used for their practice. They were sturdy lengths of maple, three feet long and an inch and a half thick, shod with iron. Ostensibly for walking, they were a favourite weapon of apprentices, who would often gather to fight on one of the fields outside the city walls, much to the indignation of their elders.

After a few warm-ups and drills they sparred for a while. Master Catlyn's fighting technique was not at all like the moves the players used on stage; instead it involved a surprising amount of grappling and body contact, and she had been

thrown to the boards on several occasions. It was at once ter-
rifying and exhilarating, feeling his arms about her or his
weight pinning her down. Every night she prayed for forgive-
ness for her unchaste thoughts, and every day she thought of
little except her next meeting with him.

She did not only think and daydream, however. Every spare
minute she could get alone, she had been practising moves,
sometimes even using her tailor's dummy as a pell. It seemed
to be paying off. Master Catlyn did not swear at her quite as
often as on previous occasions, and she got a couple of solid
blows past his guard towards the end. As he was a good six
inches taller than her, with a grown man's strength, she was
pleased with herself for managing even that much.

"All right, time for something new," Master Catlyn said,
tossing aside his weapon. It rolled across the stage to fetch up
against one of the pillars.

"Sir?"

"I want to show you how to disarm a man. Come at me as
before."

She advanced towards him, cudgel gripped in both hands. As
she let go with her left hand and raised her weapon to strike,
he caught her right arm with both hands and twisted it behind
her back. The cudgel slipped from her grasp.

"Ach, God's teeth!" Master Catlyn let her go, muttering
under his breath.

"Are you all right, sir?" Coby asked, stretching her aching
arm and flexing her fingers.

"Dropped the damned thing on my foot," he replied. "I
swear to God, I would rather fight a man armed with steel
than one of these bloody things."

He kicked the cudgel across the stage. Sensing this would be
a good time to take a breather, Coby produced two bottles of
beer she had hidden in a shady corner of the yard before leav-

ing the theatre last night. Master Catlyn took one with a muttered apology for his foul language on the Lord's Day.

"Is something the matter, sir? You seem in an ill humour today."

"It's nothing." He uncorked his beer and took a swig.

Coby nodded sympathetically. One thing she had observed
about men was that they rarely unburdened their hearts. It
was a habit she tried to emulate, though in present circumstances it was so frustrating. There was more to her feelings
for him than mere girlish fancy, she was sure: she truly liked
Master Catlyn. Well, except when he swore at her. But at least
it was proof her disguise still held. She felt certain a gentleman
like him would not blaspheme so in front of a woman.

They sat on the edge of the stage in the late afternoon sun,
their legs dangling over, like two small boys fishing from a jetty.
It reminded her of her childhood, of long hot summer days
spent tagging along behind her brother Kees and his friends as
they explored the woods and pools around their home town.
She felt tears starting to prick her eyes and scrubbed hastily at
them with her sleeve.

"Worn out already?"

"I was just thinking of my family. I haven't seen them since…"

"Since the fall of Antwerp?"

She nodded. "Mother wanted to move north, to Amsterdam
where we have cousins, but Father insisted we would never
be safe with the Spanish in control of the Netherlands, so we
took a boat across the Narrow Sea. There was a storm – I don't
know if they are alive or dead. I asked everywhere I could
when I got to England, but…"

"Both my parents are dead," Master Catlyn said in a quiet
voice. "My mother died when I was small, and my father a few
years ago. My brothers…"

"Tell me about your sweetheart," she said on impulse. It was
like picking at a scab; she knew it was stupid, but there was

a grim satisfaction in reopening the wound. "Are you to be betrothed?"

He smiled. "There is no such woman, at least not of my acquaintance."

"Then what–"

"One of Ned's fancies, a foolish game he plays with Parrish. I needed a scrap of paper for a laundry list, and there it was."

"Oh."

"I have no means to support a wife," he went on, "and little hope of it hereafter."

He fell silent, and Coby risked a sidelong glance. He was staring at the ground, seemingly unaware of her gaze. His black hair curled like a lamb's in the humidity, though he had barely raised a sweat despite their exertions. Long dark lashes shaded his brooding eyes. She had only to lean over a little and she might kiss him–

He grunted and finished his beer. "Come, let us not speak of such melancholy matters. Your lesson is not over yet."

"I– I think it is. In fact, I think I shall not have time to see you again before you start your work for the ambassador."

It was not what she had planned to say, but she knew it was the right thing to do. If she did not see him, if they did not talk, there could be nothing to betray – and no temptation either. She scrambled to her feet and walked away, not trusting herself to be able to look him in the eye.

The sound of his footsteps approaching caused her to freeze, one hand on the nearby pillar for support. Her heart was pounding.

"If you need my help kicking some little bastard's arse…"

He sounded so deadly serious, she could not help but smile.

"It is a generous offer, sir."

As they headed towards the door, Master Catlyn handed her the cudgels.

"Here, you might as well keep these. They are of no more use to me."

She hugged them to her chest as she showed him out, wishing she could hug him instead.

"Farewell, then," he said, holding out his hand. "Good luck in the contest."

"Thank you." She tucked the cudgels under one arm and shook his hand, trembling a little at his touch. "For everything."

She lingered in the doorway, watching him until he disappeared around the curve of the theatre wall, then closed the door and leant back up on it. Her disguise had always been her armour; right now it felt more like a cage.

Mal ate alone in the attic that night. Ned had taken to spending more and more time with Parrish, which was all to the good since it meant he was seldom around to notice Mal's absences. It made for dull mealtimes, though. He dipped his hunk of bread in the thin pottage, wondering what kind of grand dishes the ambassador would be served. Not stewed cabbage and onions, that was for certain.

As for his other companion of recent weeks... it was probably for the best. He had noticed the way the boy looked at him, ever since that first day in Paris Gardens. At first he had thought it simple admiration, such as he himself had felt for the heroes of his youth – Edmund Campion, Sir Francis Drake, Sir Philip Sidney – but there was a girlish shyness to Hendricks' glances, and more blushes than even a fair Flemish complexion and summer heat could account for. At least it was not the simpering of the young ganymedes who frequented the Bull's Head. He could not have stood that.

Putting aside the empty bowl he took out his next assignment from Baines, but his eyes would not focus on the grid of letters. Damn Walsingham, for trapping him in this conspiracy. How long was it going to take, anyway? A chill ran over his skin despite the closeness of the evening air. Leland had not said when the ambassador was due to leave. What if he stayed in England indefinitely?

On the other hand, twenty-four shillings a week would be enough to get proper care for his brother, away from that dreadful place. Mistress Faulkner might know a reliable woman who would look after Sandy, especially if he continued to improve. And it would be most fitting for the skraylings to pay for what they had done.

With a smile he kicked off his boots and lay back on the bed. Some good was going to come of this after all.

The dream began as it always did, in darkness and cold. Mal was riding through trees, the wet leaves brushing his face. Around him, others were riding too, the only sounds the steady tread of hooves and the snorting of horses reined in. No jingle of harness – it had been muffled before they left – and no conversation. Mal looked around for his brothers. Sandy was a few yards away, separated from him by a couple of other riders; Charles was indistinguishable from the other masked men in the dark.

On they rode in silence, uphill and down and up again until the trees gave way to bracken and scattered birch, and finally to heather and gorse and clumps of rough grass. The constellation of Orion burned high in the northern sky. It was a week after the twins' sixteenth birthday, and only a few days until they were due to go up to Cambridge.

In a hollow by the side of the road, a camp fire flickered. The riders broke into a canter, then a gallop. He could see them to either side of him, hooded figures all alike, now carrying flaming torches. Across the moors they galloped in near-silence, as smoothly as on a beach, never stumbling or slowing down. The distant glow drew nearer. Three wagons, drawn into a U-shape, with a fire between them. The silhouettes of men moved against the flame, running in panic. There was a faint crack of musket fire, then they were there, riding around the camp so none could escape. Crossbow quarrels thudded into earth, wood, flesh. Screams rent the air.

A few of the men dismounted, swords drawn. The rest assembled at the open end of the U, watching and waiting. All that could be heard was the moaning of the wind. Then there was a scuffle in one of the wagons, and two riders appeared, dragging a third figure between them. Firelight danced across a tattooed face, turning it into a demonic mask. With quiet methodical movements, the riders tied the skrayling to the wheel of one of the wagons.

Mal glanced at Sandy, who had managed to evade his escort and rein his mount in next to his brother's gelding. Sandy's eyes were wide and white-rimmed behind the slits of the mask. He did not have to speak for Mal to know exactly what he was thinking. Mal shook his head. Even if they could somehow out-ride these men, they would never find their way home in the dark.

One of the men pulled something out of his doublet. He grabbed the skrayling's jaw and wrenched it open. Mal tried to look away, but something nudged him in the ribs. A pistol.

"Art craven, little brother?"

Mal's breath caught in his throat as the skrayling screamed. There was a roar from the riders. The one in the black hood took something in his left hand and threw it to the nearest rider, then bent back to his work. Another scream. Mal was glad he couldn't see from here, but he could hear well enough to imagine it. Then everyone was dismounting, and the men closed in on the skrayling. Mal turned away, trying to shut out the animal sounds.

Someone grabbed Sandy and pulled him off his mount.

"Come on, lad, it'll be thy turn soon."

The voice was answered with coarse laughter.

"Leave him alone!" Mal shouted at them.

Sandy began to make a strange whimpering sound in the back of his throat.

"No, no, please–" Sandy screamed. *"Sula, aneimaca! Eicorro niwehi mallä! De! De! Amayi!"*

The riders drew back, crossing themselves.

"The beast has unleashed a demon amongst us," one of them cried, drawing his dagger as he pushed his way into the knot of men surrounding the skrayling. The creature's screams ended in a gurgling moan. Sandy collapsed to the ground and curled into a ball, still whimpering.

Mal slid down from his horse. He knew he was the only one who had understood any of the strange words his brother had babbled. It was the secret language they used to speak together as boys, until their father caught them and whipped them black and blue. Something about "people coming", Sandy had said. Was he trying to warn the riders, or their victim?

Mal tried to get around the gelding to where his brother lay, but someone caught him by the arm.

"What about this 'un?" his captor asked the leader.

"Blood him."

"Aye, ye mun blood at least one," said someone else. "He's not one of us until he's blooded!"

He tried to turn and run away, but his path was blocked by the broad expanse of an oak trunk. He looked around and down and discovered he was tied to the tree, belly against the rough bark, naked but for the low boots skraylings wore. No, oh no...

"Amayiiii!"

Suddenly he was surrounded by three or four of the humans, towering over him in their slit-eyed hoods like carrion birds. Cold hands clawed at him, colder steel tore his flesh, burning like brands… White-hot pain exploded at the base of his spine, then his spirit fled into the howling darkness–

Mal awoke with a cry, his heart hammering in his chest. He felt himself all over. No wounds, no broken bones, nothing but the familiar scars of battle, long healed. He let out a shaky breath and looked around, half-expecting to see Sandy at his side, cheeks smeared in dried blood.

The cold half-light of an overcast dawn seeped through the shutters. In the distance a mastiff howled. Southwark. Ned's house. Home. He kicked off the sweat-soaked sheets. Where was Ned when he needed him? He wrapped his arms about his knees and bowed his head.

"Sancte Michael Archangele, deduc me per tenebras. Ferro tuo viam illumina…"

CHAPTER IX

"You off, then?" Ned asked, eyeing the gaping knapsack.

Mal grunted in affirmation and began rummaging in the chest at the end of the bed. His belongings were pitifully few: a spare doublet and hose and a few changes of underlinens, a pair of riding gloves, a brown velvet cap going bald in places, and a threadbare winter cloak, the lute, a dog-eared fencing manual in the original Italian, and what he thought of as his soldiering kit. The canvas pouch contained a small whetstone, a tinderbox, a corked bottle of neatsfoot oil, a bundle of greasy rags and a bobbin of thick silk thread with a curved leather-needle stuck in it.

He unrolled the cloak and retrieved the fist-sized pouch hidden there.

"Will you look after this for me?"

He tossed the pouch to Ned, who loosened the strings and looked inside.

"A rosary?" Ned raised an eyebrow.

"It was my mother's. I suppose it would have been safer to get rid of it but…" Mal shrugged. "Anyway, I don't want to be found with it in my possession. Not at the Tower."

"Very wise." Ned slipped the pouch into his pocket. "Don't

worry, I'll stow it somewhere it won't be found."

Mal stuffed the cloak into the knapsack, drew the strings tight and slung it on his shoulder.

"Farewell, then."

"Aye." Ned leant on the bedpost. "I'll miss you."

"No you won't." Mal reached out and snagged Ned's nose between curled fingers, giving it a shake. "You'll be able to have Parrish over whenever you wish."

Ned batted his hand away with a sheepish look. The next thing Mal knew they were embracing, pounding one another's backs in sudden bittersweet urgency.

"Take care," Ned murmured huskily, kissing him on both cheeks. "Don't do anything stupid."

"You know me."

"Exactly."

Ned released him, and Mal picked up the lute. After a last look around the room, he unlatched the attic door and left.

Twenty minutes later he walked up to the gates of the Tower to report for duty. At least this time he was entering through the landward gate, and of his own accord. Two guardsmen in scarlet livery blocked the entrance with crossed partisans. He handed the nearest guard the letter of appointment Leland had given him back in June. The man perused it, his lips moving silently. I suppose, Mal thought, I should be grateful he doesn't need to follow his finger.

"All seems in order," the guard said at last.

"Thank you." Mal took the letter back and headed through the gatehouse.

"So you're the new Keeper of the Royal Menagerie," the guard said as Mal passed him.

"What?"

"Don't worry, you'll soon get used to the smell. When the

wind's in the south..." The guard waved his hand in front of his face and wrinkled his nose.

"Do you know," Mal said, "I could do with a knowledgeable fellow like yourself on guard duty outside the ambassador's quarters. I think I'll ask the lieutenant to assign you to my command."

The guard's bloodshot eyes bulged. "No, sir, thank you, sir. I don't know nothing about skraylings, honest."

"That's a pity. Well, I'm sure you are best off here, then." Mal set off again. "Good day to you, gentlemen."

He crossed the causeway that spanned the moat, through a second, larger gatehouse and finally into the castle's outer ward. The narrow cobbled lane seemed to close in around him, and he hurried through the archway into the pleasanter surroundings of the inner ward.

As he approached the lieutenant's lodgings, Leland himself appeared at the main entrance. His golden hair and beard glowed in the sun, their curls merging into the bullion-work on his moss-green doublet.

"Catlyn!" The lieutenant beamed, as if Mal were an old friend. "Not run off to France, then, eh?"

Mal winced at the reminder of his elder brother's misdemeanours, but forced a smile and bowed.

"I'll have Captain Monkton show you around the place later," Leland said, "but for now I'll take you up to your quarters and you can get settled in." He strode off without waiting for an answer, leaving Mal to follow in his wake.

Monkton? Wasn't that the name of the man who had arrested him and thrown him in the Salt Tower for the night? Either Leland had a malicious sense of humour, which from what little Mal knew of him did not seem in character, or he had simply forgotten the circumstances of Mal's first visit.

The lieutenant led him back out into the outer ward, to the

water stairs where Mal had disembarked all those weeks ago. Above it stood the timbered upper levels of St Thomas's Tower, now stripped of their severed heads. Leland turned right and climbed the short flight of steps to the tower entrance.

He opened the door and ushered Mal inside. They passed through a tiny vestibule into a pleasantly domestic dining room with painted plaster walls and a large stone fireplace. A long table dominated the room, draped with a ruby and cream patterned carpet that overflowed the benches standing either side. A throne-like chair, age-blackened and carved in an antique style, stood at its head. Two doors led off the dining room, one into an empty stone-walled chamber in the corner tower, the other into the rest of the apartments, which were further divided in two by a thin lath-and-plaster partition.

Mal explored the large divided chamber beyond the dining room. A bed with embroidered hangings stood in the far half; in the other, which was set out as a parlour, a short flight of steps led up to a heavy oak door.

"Is this where I will sleep?" Mal asked, gesturing to the bed.

"That is for Master Lodge," Leland replied. "We are fortunate to have found an Englishman fluent in the skrayling tongue. You will sleep here."

He led Mal up the stairs into the chamber beyond. Like the rest of the apartments it had recently been painted, and fresh rushes covered the floor. A large bed with crimson damask curtains dominated the space. Realisation dawned.

"This is the ambassador's bedchamber."

"Of course. How else are you to guard him day and night?"

"I–" Mal shivered. If he had known he would be living cheek by tattooed jowl–

"Well, I'll leave you to it. Monkton will be along shortly."

After Leland left, Mal went back down to the small parlour to wait for the captain. He glanced at the door to the ambassador's room. Don't be ridiculous, he told himself. You're no longer a small boy scared of the ghosts in the attic. He marched up the stairs and wrenched the door open.

Really, it was not so very different from his parents' chamber in Rushdale Hall. In addition to the canopied bed, there were chests for linens, a washstand with basin and ewer, and a close stool containing a Delftware chamber pot. The walls were hung with thick tapestries, though on a blazing August day they were scarcely needed. Another large iron-studded door in the far left corner appeared to lead to the walkway to the next tower. Mal tried the handle, but it was locked.

He was about to leave the room when he saw one of the tapestries stir. Drawing his rapier slowly and silently he padded towards it. The tapestry remained motionless. He prodded it with the point of the rapier. Nothing. He stepped to one end of the hanging and raised the edge with his blade.

There was no one there, only a small door. It was locked, but peering through the keyhole he could make out a tiny chamber beyond with a carved wooden screen and coloured glass in the windows. A chapel? If so, it had been locked to prevent desecration. He let the tapestry fall and sheathed his blade.

It may have been a false alarm but it reminded him that, skrayling or not, the safety of the person sleeping in this room would be his responsibility. Lurking assassins were only one threat; Baines had told him of men being poisoned by all manner of cunning means. He put his old riding gloves on and ran his hands over the furniture, looking for concealed needles or protruding nails. Whilst examining the beds he even sniffed the sheets, in case they had been suffused with poison. The linen was musty from long storage, with a faint perfume of entombed lavender, but he could smell nothing amiss.

Satisfied he had done everything necessary to fulfil his duties, he returned to the dining room to wait for Captain Monkton.

Monkton's tour began at the old royal apartments south of the White Tower. The Great Hall had been hastily refurbished for the ambassador's visit, with a new timber roof and tiled floor, but the windows were still empty of glass.

"Why go to all this work, when the Queen has palaces aplenty?" Mal asked.

"The Prince of Wales ordered it done," Monkton replied. "All great royal ceremonies begin at the Tower. The Queen stayed here the night before her coronation."

As will the prince, when he succeeds to the throne? Perhaps he already looks ahead to his mother's death.

After a brief examination of the hall Monkton showed Mal up onto the walkway of the inner curtain wall and through each of its towers. There were no prisoners here at the moment nor, Monkton told him, had there been any since the Prince Consort's death. The whole country seemed to have settled into a sombre peace, untroubled by rebellion or religious strife.

"The calm before the storm, no doubt," Monkton said. "When the Queen dies, Robert will come down hard on Catholics. He is his father's son."

Last on their itinerary was Beauchamp Tower, where Mal was shown the bed in which Robert Dudley had died, and the elaborate carving made by his elder brother John many years previously, when he was imprisoned here during Queen Mary's reign.

"Did you meet the Prince Consort?" Mal asked.

Monkton grunted. "I was not here in his day."

He unlocked another door and they went down a narrow stair, emerging on the Tower Green near the lieutenant's lodgings.

There they were shown through the antechamber into a small dining parlour. Leland was pacing up and down before the fire, a sheet of paper in his hand. A stocky man in his mid-thirties with sunburnt features and bright, almost manic eyes sat watching him, his lips moving silently.

Leland greeted the two men somewhat distractedly, and continued with his pacing, muttering something unintelligible. Monkton appeared to be accustomed to the lieutenant's eccentric behaviour; he went straight over to the table, where a silver flagon steamed, giving off a scent of cinnamon and apples.

"Splendid idea," Leland said. "This damnable language turns a man's throat to dust."

Monkton poured a little of the hot, spiced wine into silver goblets and handed them to Leland, Mal and the stranger.

"Your health, sirs," Mal said.

"The Queen," Leland replied.

"Of course. The Queen."

Mal took a cautious sip. It was the last of the old vintage, its sourness tempered with sugar and spices.

"You have met Thomas Lodge?" Leland asked, gesturing to his other guest.

"No, sir," Mal replied. He sketched a polite bow, unsure of the other man's status. The stranger was fashionably dressed, but his garments lacked the jewels and intricate embroidery that only the very rich could afford.

"Lodge is newly returned from a voyage to the New World," Leland said, "and will be our translator for the ambassador and his party."

So this was the man with whom he would be working for the next few weeks. He would have to keep an eye on him, in case someone tried to use him as a go-between to get to the ambassador.

"You are a sailor?" he asked.

Lodge flushed a deeper shade of red. "I am a poet. You may have heard of *A Looking Glass for London and England*…?"

Mal racked his memory. Yes, Ned had once mentioned copying some sides of that play for the Admiral's Men.

"I have not heard it played," he said, "but I am told it is very entertaining, especially the casting of Jonah out of the belly of the whale."

Lodge sniffed in disdain. "There is a great deal more to it than spectacle."

Leland stepped into the awkward silence.

"The voyage must have given you many ideas for new plays," the lieutenant said.

"Indeed it did," Lodge replied, looking pleased with himself. "I have sold one already – but I say too much." He put down his wine.

"*The Queen of Faerieland*," Mal said. Now he knew where he had heard the name before.

Lodge narrowed his eyes. "Are you a spy?"

"Me? No!" Mal laughed nervously. "Merely an acquaintance of Suffolk's Men. I've been taking lessons in Tradetalk from their young tireman."

Lodge raised an eyebrow. "Really? What did you make of it?"

"It was surprisingly simple to learn."

"Simpler than this, then," Leland said, handing Mal the piece of paper he'd been studying.

The sheet of paper bore three short sentences written in clear round-hand.

Kaal-an rrish, senlirren. Kaalt tokuur London-an iin tuuraq. Iin kaal-an lish hendet tutheeq.

"His Grace the Duke of York insists the visitors are greeted in their own tongue," Leland said with a pained expression. "Wanted me to do the whole damned speech in it, but the Queen's ministers argued him out of it, thank the Lord."

"It certainly looks very odd," Mal replied.

"That's what I told Lodge here, though he swears he has it aright."

"I spent nigh on a year in Vinland," Lodge said, his pale eyes glinting. "I promise you, Sir James, this is their tongue, faithfully transcribed to the best of my skill."

"It had better be, sirrah, else Her Majesty will have you swinging from a gibbet faster than you can say 'Hey nonny nonny'."

Lodge muttered something under his breath, but did not press the point. Leland took back the sheet of paper, folded it up and slipped it into a pocket. Gesturing to his guests to sit down, he took his own place at the head of the table. The servants brought in dinner, and whilst they ate Leland regaled his guests with stories of the Tower's long history and its more colourful inhabitants, whilst Monkton tried unsuccessfully not to look bored.

"Do you smoke?" the playwright asked, holding out a leather tobacco pouch whilst tamping down his own pipe with a yellow-nailed thumb.

"Thank you, no," Mal said.

"Quite right too," Leland said. "Damned filthy foreign habit."

Lodge shrugged. He went over to the fire and lit his pipe with a bit of kindling.

"Of course it wouldn't do to say that in front of the ambassador," Leland added. "Help yourself to more wine, Catlyn."

"Perhaps Master Lodge could tell us more about his adventures in the New World," Mal said. Better put the man at ease, if he was going to get anything useful out of him.

"Absolutely," Leland put in. "Do enlighten us, Lodge. Did you see any of their women? What are they like?"

Mal leant in closer, curious to know if Lodge had better information on the topic than young Hendricks.

"I regret to say I cannot confirm their existence, except in legend," Lodge replied. He paused to suck on his pipe. "Though I sailed all along the coast of Vinland and round the Isles of Antilia, I was unable to gain admittance to the Seven Cities. The race dwelling therein is quite different from the skraylings who visit our shores, and they are not welcoming to strangers."

"They are hostile?" Monkton asked.

"No," Lodge said. "Merely aloof. Almost monastic, one might say."

"But no women, eh?" Leland said.

"That was the peculiar thing," Lodge replied. "My skrayling guides referred to the city-dwellers as *iiseth*, which in other contexts translates as 'women', but from the little I saw of them, I can only assume it was a misunderstanding. The citizens were squat burly folk with bluish skin and short raven-black hair. They wore no face paint but in other respects were unmistakably skraylings."

"Perhaps the word was intended as an insult," Mal suggested.

"No," Lodge said, "my guides were very respectful towards them."

"No accounting for foreigners, eh?" Leland said.

"Well, if you gentlemen will excuse me, I'm for bed," Lodge said. He tapped out his pipe on the hearth, refilled his goblet and carried it off with him.

When the playwright had gone, Leland went over the arrangements for the visit at length: who would be attending the arrival ceremony, which noblemen were out of favour and especially to be watched, and the duties expected of Mal.

"Day and night, mind," Leland said in conclusion. "I want no assassins creeping up on our guests whilst they are my responsibility."

"Will the skraylings not bring their own bodyguards?" Mal asked.

"Undoubtedly," said Leland. "But what do they know of Christians? Can they even tell an Englishman from a Spaniard?"

"Even if they could," Monkton said, "I hardly think our enemies would be so clumsy as to send one of their own openly."

"Perhaps not." Leland drained his glass, and looked at Mal, his eyes narrowing. "But there are plenty of Papist sympathisers here in London. A man who could claim to have broken up our alliance with the skraylings would find rich rewards in Spain. Or France."

Mal nodded. "Sark."

"Quite. The French haven't forgiven us for handing the island over to the skraylings."

"I will be most vigilant," Mal assured him. "No villain will get within five yards of His Excellency, I swear."

As Ned walked home from the Bull's Head, the sun was sinking between the houses at the far end of Bankside in a blaze of gold. Perhaps that was why he didn't see the man standing in his path until it was too late.

"'Scuse me." He tried to step around the fellow, who was built like the piers of London Bridge, the ones they called "starlings". The man clamped an enormous hand on Ned's shoulder.

"We want a word with you, sirrah," a voice hissed in his ear.

Ned tried to turn, and found himself being pushed into an alley by two men. Alleys he was used to, but two men at once was more than he cared to handle.

"Look, gentlemen, I'm happy to have all the words you want, but is this the place for it?"

Starling slammed him against the wall. "Shut yer gob!"

First they want a word, then they want me to shut up, Ned thought. I wish they'd make up their minds.

At last he got a look at the second man, or at least as good a look as could be managed in the shadows. He was about

Ned's own height, a slight, weasel-faced man wearing a fustian doublet that had seen better days. Ned felt sure he had seen the fellow before, but then there were plenty like him in Southwark.

"You a friend of that whoreson Maliverny Catlyn?" Weasel Face asked.

"What?"

"You 'eard him." Starling took Ned's left bicep in his huge fist, and squeezed.

"Ow, yes, yes I know him. But not all that well—" He clenched his teeth against the pain as the big man squeezed again.

"You sure about that?"

"Yes," Ned gasped.

Starling squeezed, his iron-hard nails biting into the muscle, until Ned was sure his fingers must meet in the middle. He felt tears welling in the corners of his eyes, but he refused to make a sound. He'd had worse than this from some of his customers.

"That's enough," Weasel Face said. "We're not getting anywhere."

The iron grip loosened and Ned sagged against the wall, nursing his bruised bicep.

"Nah," he went on, "there's a much easier way to get what we want."

Ned looked up. There was something in the man's voice that made his flesh creep.

"Got your attention, have I? So, you're going to tell me everything you know about Catlyn."

"And if I don't?"

"Well, now, let's see." The man took a knife from his belt and began paring his nails. Ned watched him, waiting for the threat to come. Sweat trickled down the back of his shirt. The knife didn't look particularly sharp, but depending on what they had in mind, it might not need to be. He weighed up his options. The big man wasn't holding him. How far could he get before they grabbed him again? Probably not far enough.

The knife slammed into a timber beside his ear.

"Don't think of running," Weasel Face said. "Won't do you no good anyway."

"Why not?"

"Because when you hear what I have to say, you'll be glad we're here with you and not somewhere else."

Ned stared at him.

"What's the phrase?" His captor leered. "Oh yes. 'We know where you live.'"

"You wouldn't," Ned growled.

"Ah, but we would, you see. And you'd better believe it." He sheathed the knife. "So, are you going to tell us what we want to know, or are me and my friend going to pay a visit to your dear, sweet, silver-haired old mother?"

The dream began in darkness, but this time it was different. One moment he was riding through the woods, surrounded by masked men, next thing he knew he was on foot and alone. The trees thinned and he found himself on open moorland. Short wiry grass rippled underfoot, though there was no wind. The sky above was a dull nacreous grey; not storm clouds, he realised with a shock, but a sky without moon or stars, as if all the lights of heaven had been smeared like paint across a black canvas.

The moor was studded with great limestone boulders, some taller than himself. *Things* lurked behind each one; he couldn't see them but he knew they were watching him. He wanted to turn and run but he knew they would pursue him. He looked beyond the boulders, wondering if he could slip past the waiting creatures. In the distance, warm lights burned here and there – farmsteads perhaps? No, too many. A town, a city even. The lights seemed to multiply before his eyes; a few winked out, but were replaced by more. He watched for what felt like an eternity, and eventually the lights began to disappear. He sensed the creatures' disappointment. They had been hoping he would try to cross the moor.

Then from the edge of sight came a new light, searing blue-white that flooded his vision. He flung up his arms and squinted, desperate to see if this new arrival were friend or foe, but his eyes would not obey. He had to keep his eyes open or the others, the cruel ones, would be upon him in an instant–

Mal jerked awake. A valet was setting down a plate of bread and a tankard on a small table.

"Did you say something, sir? Anything I can get you?"

"No." His mouth was sour and sticky with sleep. "Wait. I need a clean shirt–"

"We have your new livery laid out ready, sir," the man replied.

"Livery? Oh, of course."

The valet snapped his fingers, and two body-servants stepped forward, linen towels draped over their arms. "Perhaps a shave, sir, before you break your fast?"

Mal gratefully accepted. The last thing he wanted was to turn up to the ceremony with bloody scrapes on his face. He got out of bed and took a chair by the hearth, leaning his head against its back and listening to the crackle of the kindling as the fire caught. Rain rattled against the many-paned windows. Autumn was coming early this year.

"Stayed at the Tower before, sir?" One of the body-servants brushed rose-scented lather onto Mal's cheeks whilst the other stropped a razor.

"Uhnnee unce," Mal replied, keeping his mouth shut against the soap.

"Grand place, sir. At least for those of us on the right side of the locked door, eh?" The servant gently turned Mal's head to one side and began scraping the dark stubble from around his beard.

The new livery turned out to be a surprisingly good fit, and less gaudy than Mal had feared; no crimson velvet or gold braid to be seen. True, the short trunk hose were a little old-fashioned and showed rather more of his leg than he was accustomed to, but the black silk doublet was cunningly tailored to allow ease of movement, as he found out when he drew his rapier and tried a few feints and lunges. The servants retreated in alarm, not even bothering to take the dirty towels with them. Mal continued his exercises, losing himself in the familiar moves almost to the point of forgetting where he was, and why.

His concentration was broken by a fanfare from the direction of the river. The ambassador! With a curse Mal sheathed his sword and ran down the tower stairs, praying he could find his way through the maze of buildings in time.

CHAPTER X

At the main gatehouse he was greeted by a red-faced Leland.

"Catlyn, where the hell have you been?"

"My humble apologies, Sir James, I–"

"Never mind that. The barge is almost across the river. Come on!" He directed Mal through a side door and across a narrow drawbridge to the wharf.

The rain had eased off, but a fine mizzle drifted in from the west. Mal recalled from the briefing that the visitors would be disembarking at the Queen's Stairs, with the opening ceremony being held on the wharf-side, as was traditional. Awnings had been set up between the river and the moat, some in royal red, white and green, others striped blue and white. Courtiers clustered beneath the dripping canvas, complaining about the unseasonable weather that threatened to ruin their plumed bonnets. Several of them glared or muttered as Mal was escorted to the foremost canopy, by the edge of the Thames.

At the front of the royal pavilion the princes sat side by side, resplendent in matching black velvet and cloth-of-gold. Robert's three children – ten year-old Princess Elizabeth, her younger sister Isabella and little Prince Edward – sat on cushions nearby under the watchful eye of their nurse.

"Why isn't Mama here?" the little boy asked in a loud voice.

The ladies in the crowd laughed at this, but the nurse quickly hushed him. Princess Juliana had gone into her fourth confinement, and whilst she had birthed three healthy children so far, no one was taking further success for granted.

The Prince of Wales, dark-complexioned and dour as his father, was gazing out over the Thames, a faraway look in his grey eyes. Mal made his obeisance in the fashionable French style as he neared the thrones, bowing so low his forehead nearly touched the ground. Prince Arthur gave him an appraising look, but Robert seemed scarcely to notice him. Mal bowed again for good measure, and took his place near the rear of the royal pavilion.

Trumpets blared. Mal craned his neck to see over the black velvet caps of the noble lords who crowded the royal pavilion. Dozens of small barges and wherries rowed back and forth at a discreet distance from the wharf, crammed to the gunwales with eager spectators. Beyond them, a ceremonial barge decked out in blue and gold was gliding across the murky water, oars dipping to the beat of a pair of deep-voiced drums.

Though English in design, the vessel was manned entirely by skraylings. Most were tall by skrayling standards and broad-shouldered, clad in geometric-patterned tunics of dark blue and white. In the centre stood two older skraylings in merchants' robes and a dark-haired figure wearing vivid blue. More than that he could not make out at this distance.

"Historic day, eh, Catlyn?"

Mal turned to see Leland beaming at him. Lodge hovered at his elbow, clutching a sheaf of papers.

"Oh?" Mal said.

"First time their ambassador has set foot in England."

"Didn't he set foot in Southwark before boarding the barge?" The words slipped out before Mal could stop himself.

Leland flushed.

"A trivial detail. This is the landing history will recall."

Of course. This is what will get put in the chronicles, not some unceremonious disembarking observed only by dock-hands and wharf-rats. He fidgeted with his lace-trimmed cuffs, wishing his first introduction to a skrayling didn't have to take place in such a public manner.

"The Master of the Queen's Music has outdone himself again," Leland said. He waved towards another awning, where a trio of flautists were doing their best to murder a rondeau.

"Is that meant to be skrayling music?" Mal asked. It sounded little like the playing he had heard at the stockade.

"It has a wondrous melancholy air, has it not?"

The music was soon drowned out by the approach of the royal barge. As it came closer, the rhythm of the drums quick-ened into something almost dance-like. Mal was surprised to see that two of the skraylings were in the bows of the barge, leaping back and forth between the two drums and striking them with their bare hands. Two others in the aft clashed cym-bals in a complicated counterpoint. The rest of the crew pounded on the deck with elaborately carved and ribbon-be-decked staves.

The barge bumped against the jetty, and the crowd drew back. The drummers concluded their performance with a final flourish and the skrayling guards, as Mal supposed them to be, disembarked, rapping their staves on the stones as they went and chanting in their own tongue.

The skrayling guards arranged themselves in two lines, their teeth bared in an unmistakable warning, and between them walked the guests of honour. The elders had the typical white-streaked manes of their kind, and their faces were covered in swirling tattoos of a subtly different design to those of the guards. The leading figure, who must surely be the ambassador, wore long robes similar to those of English scholars, made of lapis blue brocade and fastened with a broad sash of white and gold. He was also a good deal younger than his companions, perhaps no older than Mal himself, though with a serene air that belied his age. He wore his black hair cropped short, and his face, though mottled pink and grey in a symmetrical pattern, had no tattoos at all. Without the patterns obscuring his features he looked, if anything, less human: the high-bridged, flattened nose and thin bluish lips were more reminiscent of a beast's muzzle, the pupils of his eyes more obviously oval than round. An Antilian? He certainly resembled Lodge's description of the city-dwellers.

Leland stepped forward and cleared his throat.

"Carlan rich, sen leeren. Calt toe-cure London an een tourak. Een carlan lish endeth toothache."

The ambassador raised his eyebrows at this unexpected attempt to greet him in his own language, but said nothing. He waited until Leland had finished speaking, then bowed in the English fashion as gracefully as any courtier.

"*Kaal-an rrish, Ingilandeth,*" he said in a clear voice that carried to the back of the crowd, then added in English with only a slight sing-song accent, "We thank you for your kind welcome."

A gasp ran around the assembled company. If a beast in the royal menagerie had spoken, they could hardly have been more astonished.

"W-well, indeed, we are most honoured," Leland murmured. "I... Your Excellency, may I introduce you to His Highness the Prince of Wales and his noble guests?"

Leland waved Thomas Lodge away, and ushered the skraylings towards the royal party. Out of the corner of his eye Mal saw the playwright turn scarlet with impotent rage at being robbed of his moment of glory.

"Your Excellency," Leland said, "this is Robert, Prince of

Wales, Duke of Cornwall and heir to the throne of England. Your Highness, this is…"

"I am Outspeaker Kiiren of Shajiilrekhurrnasheth," he said, "and this is eldest of our clan, Judge Sekaarhjarret, and Chief Merchant Hretjarr."

He gestured to the elders, who bowed awkwardly.

"We are honoured to meet you, Lord Outspeaker," Robert drawled, "and your elders also. I trust your voyage was not too unpleasant?"

The introductions droned on, each of the notables in the royal pavilion being presented in strict order of precedence. The visitors bowed to each one, the elders' faces inscrutable behind their masks of tattoos. The ambassador on the other hand seemed to take an interest in everyone and everything. Mal wondered if he was some kind of prince amongst his people, to be entrusted with such an important role so young.

Master Naismith had hired a boat to attend the ambassador's arrival, at a ridiculous price as far as Coby was concerned. She had been surprised by her master's extravagance until she discovered that Mistress Naismith and the other wives had insisted on being taken along as well, to see the Court in all its splendour. Thus it was that Tuesday morning found a dozen people squeezed into a boat meant for half as many.

"You should have hired a larger vessel, Henry," Mistress Naismith said for the hundredth time, as they bobbed amongst the other spectators. "By my troth, if we are not all drowned it will be a miracle."

Coby scanned the crowd of nobles and gentlemen gathered on the wharf, but could not see Master Catlyn. She hoped nothing was amiss.

"There's my lord Suffolk," Naismith shouted over the noise of the crowd.

They all waved their hats in the direction of the man in the great pavilion. Coby had seen their patron at the playhouse on several occasions, but he usually sat in the lords' box above and behind the stage, where he could be seen by the audience as clearly as the play itself. A tall man of middle years with grey in his sandy beard, he wore a well-cut suit of garnet-red silk, elegant but restrained. A younger man, taller still and fairer of hair but with an obvious family likeness, stood at his elbow. Was this the prodigal son Master Catlyn had told her about, now standing there in unity with his father? The skrayling ambassador seemed to be spreading peace by his very arrival in England.

For a moment she thought Suffolk would not deign to notice them, but then he smiled and inclined his head in acknowledgment. Naismith bowed low, causing the boat to rock and the ladies to shriek.

They watched as the ambassador and his companions were introduced to the royal party and courtiers. As usual, Coby paid little heed to the individuals; she was too busy storing away the details of their appearance in her memory. Her eye was caught by a middle-aged man whose heavily padded doublet and trunk hose only served to emphasise his spindly calves, whilst his purple-dyed beard clashed with his florid complexion. Such a look would be perfect for the role of the self-serving Lord Villuppo in *The Spanish Tragedy*.

"Isn't that Catlyn?" Parrish asked, leaning over her shoulder and pointing.

A slender man dressed in sombre black livery and bearing a long silver-hilted rapier was being introduced to the skraylings. As he swept the black velvet cap from his head and made a formal bow, her breath caught in her throat. He was even more handsome in uniform than in his threadbare doublet and slops. She chided herself for such foolish thoughts; they were worlds apart now and likely to stay that way.

"He is a very picture of manly grace, is he not?" Parrish murmured in her ear.

"I had not noticed," she replied coolly, praying her treacherous complexion would not give her away.

"You dissemble very ill, my dear. I know you spent a great deal of time with him this summer, dallying in Paris Gardens." Parrish placed an arm around her shoulders. "And after I was so careful to warn you."

"Nothing untoward took place between myself and Master Catlyn, I can assure you, sir."

"If you say so."

"I do say so. On my honour."

She glanced around. Luckily the other actors and their wives were too absorbed in the spectacle on the riverbank to pay any attention to their little exchange.

"Now, now, no need to be so stiff about it," he said. "Anyone would think you had a maidenhead to defend."

Again he came too close to the truth. Perhaps the best way to get him off the scent was to let him think the worst. She gave an exaggerated sigh.

"You are right, sir. I do love him, and I am ashamed of my unnatural desires." She gazed into his pale blue eyes. "Please, you will not tell anyone?"

Parrish's teasing expression gave way to a smug grin.

"I knew it!" He gave her shoulder a squeeze. "Never fear, your secret is safe with me."

Coby turned back to the ceremony with a genuine sigh of relief. Her plan had worked for now, but she did not like to think what the consequences might be. She only hoped the actor would think twice about crossing swords – literal or figurative – with Master Catlyn.

"Your Excellency," said Leland, "this is Maliverny Catlyn, who has been appointed as your bodyguard whilst you sojourn in our city."

Mal swept the velvet cap from his head and bowed low, determined to hide his nervousness at all costs. When he raised his head again, the ambassador was staring at him. He knew, Mal was certain of it. He knew about that night nine years ago and was about to denounce him in front of the entire Court. He quelled the instinct to bolt as he had done at the Catherine Wheel. Perhaps he was mistaken and this was his guilt speaking.

Long moments passed, and still the skrayling held his gaze with inhuman amber eyes. A murmur, faint as a summer breeze, passed over the crowd.

Leland coughed. "Your Excellency?"

"Forgive my poor manners, *Catlyn-tuur*," Kiiren said. "Your service honours us."

Mal inclined his head and forced a smile.

"It is my honour to serve you, sir," he said with another bow.

Ambassador Kiiren smiled back, showing neat, even teeth. No fangs? A memory of iron pincers, and a bloody trophy held aloft, flashed before Mal's eyes. Sweet Mother of God, surely not?

The heralds blew a fanfare, and the princes rose from their seats.

"If you would come this way, Your Excellency," Leland said, guiding the skrayling party into the procession that was beginning to form.

Kiiren beckoned to his guards, who formed up before and behind him. Then he gestured to his new bodyguard to join them. Mal took up a position amongst the rearguard, heart still pounding from the confrontation with the ambassador, conscious of both the stares of the courtiers and the closeness of so many skraylings. This was something he was just going to have to get used to, he told himself.

The Prince of Wales led the company in solemn procession along the wharf to the main entrance of the castle complex.

As they passed the Lion Tower the beasts roared, causing the skraylings to halt and look around them in alarm.

"No fear," Mal told the skrayling guards, hoping they knew Tradetalk. "No fear. All good."

They looked doubtful, but after a brief discussion in their own tongue they moved on, much to Mal's relief.

The procession continued across the moat, through the outer ward and under the Garden Tower, and thence to the innermost ward and the newly refurbished Great Hall. Yeoman warders in bright ceremonial uniforms flanked the doors, which stood wide open.

Inside, long tables had been set out covered in snowy linen and laden with baskets of bread and flagons of wine. The ambassador was invited to sit at the high table on Prince Robert's right hand; Mal took up his station behind Kiiren's chair, a not very subtle reminder to all present that the Crown took threats to this alliance most seriously. The elders were seated at the near end of the lower table and the skrayling guards lined up against the side wall, as close to their masters as was courteous.

Whilst the rest of the Court filed in, Mal stared up at the painted beams, trying to ignore the rumblings of his stomach. The flautists appeared on the makeshift minstrels' gallery and took up their positions. Trumpets sounded again, and a troupe of serving-men began carrying in an endless stream of silver and gold platters.

Mal tried not to stare and drool. Even his Cambridge college's Christmas Feast had not had so many courses and subtleties. There were pies in the shape of skrayling ships, with sails of crisp-fried bacon; open tarts filled with candied sweet potatoes and other exotic vegetables from the New World; and wines of every colour and type that Leland's cellars could supply. The latter were being consumed in larger quantities than even the most profligate courtiers were accustomed to; some of the dishes had been spiced with the fierce pepper favoured by the skraylings, and many a lord's face flushed and streamed with sweat as a result. The noise in the hall was deafening, quite drowning out the flautists in the gallery – which was no bad thing, to Mal's mind. One could take a compliment too far.

"You speak English very well," the Prince of Wales said.

"Thank you, Highness," Kiiren replied. "I learn from English travellers to our land. John Cabot and his men."

The prince paused, cup halfway to his lips. Some of the other guests glanced at one another.

"Cabot's second expedition disappeared nearly a hundred years ago," Prince Robert said quietly.

The skrayling inclined his head in agreement and smiled. The prince covered his confusion with a feigned cough, and dropped the conversation. After a discreet pause the other guests began murmuring together over this extraordinary revelation. From the little Mal could overhear, most dismissed it as a misunderstanding. The foreigners might parrot English speech, but only a fool would expect them to make sense.

The Duke of Suffolk cleared his throat.

"If the effort of speaking our tongue grows wearisome, Your Excellency, you are welcome to use the services of my man Lodge. He speaks Vinlandic very well, I am told."

"Thank you for your kind offer, my lord, but I am *senlirren*. Outspeaker. It is my duty to speak for my people; I have trained my whole life for this."

Suffolk's face was a mask of politeness. He could hardly press Lodge's services upon the ambassador further, but the snub clearly rankled. Mal wondered what the duke felt he had to prove. He was already a member of the Privy Council and a confidant of both the Queen and her elder son. On the other hand he was not a young man, and perhaps he feared a fall from grace once Prince Robert succeeded to the throne.

After yet another showpiece dish – a roast peacock in gilded pastry, with its tail feathers arranged as if in life – had been brought in and presented to the bemused ambassador, Leland got to his feet, and the trumpets blared.

"Pray silence for His Royal Highness the Prince of Wales!"

A hush fell over the company, then everyone stood up in a deafening scraping of wood on tiles.

"Once again, I welcome our guests to this our fair city," Robert said, when the noise had died down, "and to the seat of my ancestors of blessed memory. May this be only the first of many visits, which will confirm and seal the alliance between our two peoples for all time."

He continued in this vein at some length. Mal scanned the company, wondering how many of the courtiers shared their prince's sentiments. Some had profited immensely from the new goods and ideas brought to England by the skraylings, but many felt threatened by the skraylings' mysterious devices, and even more by their dogged refusal to convert to Christianity. The erstwhile interpreter, Thomas Lodge, watched the ambassador from his place at one of the lower tables, his complexion flushed with wine and ill-concealed jealousy.

"... and in token of that friendship and fellow-feeling," Prince Robert was saying, "I hereby announce that there will be a contest between the city's three finest companies of players, to be judged by Your Excellency, if you would do us the honour."

Mal glanced from one patron to another. Prince Arthur's regal calm was spoilt by the twinkle of boyish delight in his blue eyes, the Lord High Admiral sat back in his chair with a confident smile on his face, and even Suffolk's grim visage softened a little at the compliment to his retainers.

"This sharing of tradition is most pleasing to us, Your Highness," Ambassador Kiiren said, and bowed low.

The prince inclined his head in acknowledgment and took his seat. At this signal, servants began clearing away the dishes, and the courtiers took advantage of the bustle to gossip about the contestants' relative merits.

When the servants were done, Leland stood up and cleared his throat.

"It is my great honour, sir, to be your host for your visit. You are no doubt weary after your long journey; allow me to escort you to your quarters."

Mal sent up a silent prayer that the skraylings would baulk at being housed in a dismal fortress, but the saints were not on his side today.

"Thank you, Sir Leland," Kiiren said. "We are greatly honoured by your hospitality. As we say in my homeland, 'Friendship is forged in cooking-fire'."

"Ah, yes, indeed," Leland replied. "Very… profound, sir. Catlyn, will you lead the way?"

Mal escorted the ambassador's party up the steps to the now-familiar apartments. Two of the ambassador's attendants followed him through the door, carrying a large trunk made of dark polished wood. They set it in the middle of the room, then left again. Another trunk followed, and another, then four more skraylings appeared carrying armfuls of some kind of matting. This latter was laid before the hearths in both rooms, after the rushes had been swept aside. From one of the trunks the skraylings brought forth several small translucent bowls which they placed on the hearths and tables in both rooms and filled with clear liquid that soon began to glow like the lamps of the stockade.

So that was their magic. An alchemical secret – and a bargaining chip to be kept back for future negotiations? England's enemies would certainly love to get their hands on anything

that made the creation and control of fire – and therefore guns
– easier and more efficient.

At last the attendants seemed to be satisfied the rooms were
comfortable, and all but two of them retreated to the dining
room. Mal breathed out, a deep breath he had been unaware
of holding. Kiiren looked around, an expression of puzzlement
plain upon his face. Mal cleared his throat. They are just people, he told himself, in a strange land far from home.

"How can I help you, Your Excellency?" he asked. As an af-
terthought, he made an obeisance in the skrayling fashion, as
he had seen the elders do, inclining his head back and to his
right rather than bending forward. It felt like he was inviting
a blow. He straightened up hurriedly, discomfited by the experience. As a gesture of submission, it was far more effective
than any bow.

"Perhaps you can tell me where I sleep?" Kiiren said.

Mal led him to the bedchamber, trying to shake off the feeling of vulnerability his action had aroused. He held the
curtains of the bedstead aside whilst the ambassador peered at
the interior, head cocked on one side. Was the young skrayling
really so ignorant of English customs, Mal wondered, or was
he waiting to see Mal make a fool of himself?

"It's a bed," Mal said. "You sleep on it."

"But it is so high," Kiiren said at last. "How do you not fall
off in sleep?"

"You… just don't," Mal replied in some confusion, gesturing
at the wide expanse of mattress. It made the bed he shared
with Ned look like a child's cot.

"It is not our custom to sleep this way."

"I will speak to Sir James," Mal said. "Perhaps the mattress
could be moved to the floor, though I'm afraid Your Excellency
may find it very draughty."

"What is this word, 'draf-tee'? It was not taught to me."

Along with a great many others, no doubt. Perhaps he should offer to help the ambassador expand his vocabulary in new and interesting directions… He dismissed the thought with an inward smile. Leland would not thank him for teaching the Ambassador of Vinland to curse like a Billingsgate fishwife.

"It means wind coming in through a crack in the wall, or under a door," he said instead.

The ambassador nodded. "And you will sleep in next room, in other bed?"

Mal recalled that it would be empty now Lodge was no longer needed. Tempting, but…

"No, sir. The lieutenant instructed me to sleep in here, the better to protect you."

He reached under the bedstead.

"See, there's a servant's bed here," he said, pulling out the wheeled truckle bed. "Cunning, eh?"

The ambassador seemed impressed by this piece of human ingenuity, and ran the truckle bed in and out of its hiding place several times.

"I will sleep here," he announced, pulling the bed out and kneeling on it. "You have high bed."

"Ah, no, Your Excellency, that is most generous but I cannot, it would be unfitting–"

"I insist."

So, they did teach him the important words.

"The truckle bed won't be very comfortable," he said as a last resort.

"Nor will high bed, if I cannot sleep for fear of falling."

Mal gave up the argument. How he was going to explain this to Leland, he had no idea.

CHAPTER XI

Coby was getting ready for bed when a hammering on the front door made her start. The noise was followed by muffled shouting that sounded like threats. She ran down the stairs two at a time and found Master Naismith by the front door, looking worried.

"Open up, Nocksmith!" the voice came again. "I know you're in there!"

"Is that Master Lodge?" she asked her employer.

She glanced around the hall, hoping to see a walking stick or cudgel to hand. It was high time she made use of Master Catlyn's lessons.

"Aye," Naismith said. "Cup-shot as a rat in a malthouse, by the sounds of him."

"Shouldn't he be at the Tower, aiding the skrayling ambassador?"

Lodge banged on the door again.

"Oi, open up, I say! Or shall I tell th'whole parish how you were cuckolded by—"

Master Naismith unbolted the door and pulled Lodge inside. The playwright tripped on the threshold and made a grab at Coby, who dodged back so that he sprawled on the floor at her feet.

"What is all this, Lodge?"

The playwright stared up at him.

"S'all your fault," he moaned. "I wish to God I'd never heard of Suffolk or his Men."

"What happened?" Coby asked. "We saw you at the Tower this morning–"

"Did you? Did you see it all?"

"Well, not everything. We could not get close."

"Passed over, I was." Lodge mumbled something incomprehensible that sounded more like Vinlandic than English. "Like, like a spare prick at a wedding. Three years, it took me, three puking years…"

He demonstrated by rolling onto his side and throwing up on the floor.

"Tell Betsy to get a bucket of water, lad," Master Naismith told her. "And a mop."

A few minutes later, Coby returned with the unhappy maid-servant in tow. Lodge was still moaning incoherently.

"Help me get him to his feet," Master Naismith said.

Coby took hold of one grimy sleeve and together they hauled him up. The playwright stank of brandywine, sweat and vomit. He stared from one to the other with unfocused eyes, then pulled himself free.

"Give it back," he said, gazing wildly around him. "I know you have it here." Seeing the open door of the dining room, he staggered away from them. "Where do you keep 'em, eh? Locked up safe as virgins in a nunnery, I'll be bound."

"What are you talking about?" Master Naismith called after him.

Lodge spun around and nearly fell over again.

"My play." He began to weep. "My beautiful, magnificent play."

His knees crumpled and he sank to the floor, head in hands.

Coby exchanged glances with her master, who shrugged. She crouched by Lodge.

"What about your play?"

"He shan't have it," Lodge muttered. "Wasted. All that work…"

"Who shan't have it?"

Lodge looked up, a cunning glint in his pale green eyes. "Suffolk. Snubbing me before the Prince of Wales. If he thinks he can profit from my hard-won scholola – schoraly – learning, he can think again."

"Then you are not in the skrayling ambassador's service?"

"He will have none of me."

"Surely your services as a speaker of Vinlandic–"

"His Eske – Excellency speaks the Queen's English. I am… superfluous." Lodge hid his face in his arms again.

Coby got to her feet. All those lessons in Tradetalk she gave Master Catlyn, and the ambassador turns out to speak English? She began to laugh.

"S'not funny!" Lodge scrambled to his feet. "How would you like it, eh? Eh?"

He tried to grab the front of her doublet, but she caught hold of his wrist, ducked under his arm and threw him to the floor. Master Catlyn would have been proud, she thought, staring down at the limp body of the playwright. Then she realised he was not moving.

"Sweet Jesu," she whispered, stepping back with her hand over her mouth. "I think I killed him."

Betsy gave a shriek, dropped her mop and ran into the kitchen.

"Nonsense," said Master Naismith. "He is passed out, nothing more."

He was right. Lodge's chest was moving up and down steadily. A moment later the unconscious man began to snore.

"What are we going to do with him?" she asked. "We can't turn him out into the street in this state."

"We'll haul him out to the barn. He can sleep off the drink there, without troubling the rest of the household." He took hold of Lodge's shoulders. "Come, let us get him away so Betsy can finish cleaning up."

Fortunately the street was almost empty, this close to curfew. Between the two of them they managed to manhandle the playwright's dead weight out of the front door and down the alley to the barn. They dumped Lodge on a pile of hay by the opposite wall where he lay, slack-jawed and snoring, as if in his own bed. Master Naismith wiped his forehead with his shirt-sleeve, then ushered her out of the barn and closed the door.

"Aren't you going to lock him in, sir?" Coby asked as he turned back towards the house.

"What, and have him cause more damage when he wakes? No, let him crawl home unremarked, like the misbegotten worm he is. If Lodge is out of favour, I want as little to do with him as possible."

"Should we then look for another play?"

"I fear it is too late. All we can do is carry on as planned, and hope His Grace's wrath is spent ere we come before him again."

Ned woke from uneasy dreams, though he could not for the life of him remember what he had been dreaming about. Something to do with… No, it was gone. He opened his eyes to total darkness. Gradually his sight adjusted, and he could make out faint shapes, black against grey. His heart skipped a beat. For a moment he thought he saw Mal standing at the end of the bed, pointing at him accusingly, but it was only Gabe's doublet hanging lopsided on a peg. A phantom wrought by a guilty conscience, that was all.

He rolled over and snuggled up to Gabriel, kissing his lover's back and neck and wishing he would wake up and distract him from this dark humour. They lay uncovered, the night being too hot for bedclothes, and in the pre-dawn light Ned could just make out the pale shapes of limbs side by side, darkly hairy against marble white. He moved against Gabriel, hunger woken now. The younger man stirred, rolled over, hands and mouth seeking Ned blindly. Ned turned his back and Gabriel took him, slow and sleep-drunk at first, then more urgently, their bodies turned slick with sweat. Gabriel nipped the back of his neck with sharp teeth, like a tomcat with his queen, and Ned yowled in ecstasy. Someone next door knocked on the wall in protest, but Gabriel only laughed, wild and defiant.

When they were both spent, Ned lay back with a heavy sigh.

"Why so melancholy?" Gabriel asked, brushing a stray lock from Ned's brow with damp fingertips.

"Just wondering what I did to deserve such bliss."

"Nothing good, I hope."

Ned turned to him with a start.

Gabriel frowned. "Something wrong, love?"

"No. I–" He shook his head. "Thought I heard something moving around."

"Probably just a rat. Go to sleep."

Ned shut his eyes, but sleep would not come. He had told his assailants as little as he dared about Mal, things that surely didn't matter. What if it wasn't enough? What if they came back here, threatened his mother, threatened... Oh God, what if they were watching him, knew about Gabe? The thought of those bastards hurting his darling boy...

They would have to stop seeing one another. Gabriel would not understand, might never forgive him, but Ned could not forgive himself if anything happened to him. It could wait until morning, though. For now, he could enjoy a last few hours' bliss. Taking Gabriel's unresisting hand in his own and pressing it to his lips, he settled down to watch his lover sleep.

• • • •

Mal did not bother to undress that night, though he unstrapped his rapier and laid it on the counterpane within easy
reach. He lay awake for a long time, listening to the castle's
night noises and the faint sound of the ambassador's breathing.
From time to time he got up and went to the window, but saw
only the blue and gold glimmer of lights reflected in the river.
He looked back at their counterparts arrayed about the bedchamber, and the motionless shape of the sleeping skrayling.
Day and night, Leland had said. Well, he would do his best.

Some time before dawn the skrayling lamps faded and went
out. The next thing Mal knew, the room was filled with early
morning sunlight and the skrayling attendants were bustling in
and out with jugs of water and armfuls of linens. He looked
around for Kiiren and found him kneeling by the fireplace with
his back to Mal, stark naked, washing his face in an ornate basin.

"I– I'll return when you're dressed," Mal muttered, and hurried down the stairs to the lower chamber, suppressing the
urge to vomit.

He had seen mercifully little of the Huntsmen's bloody victim, but now he knew what drove them to such fear and
loathing. The ambassador's spine ended in a stubby hairless
tail, about the size of Mal's thumb, which twitched obscenely
like a rabbit's scut. Making the sign of the cross Mal retreated
into the bedchamber that had been set aside for Lodge. Tonight
he was damned well going to sleep in here, and to Hell with
Leland's instructions.

He could not hide forever, unfortunately. Steeling himself,
he walked through into the dining room, where breakfast had
been laid out. A dozen of the skrayling guards were lined up
behind the benches awaiting their master. Mal took a stool at
the far end. His appetite had fled, but he snatched up a tankard
of small ale from the breakfast table, wishing it was something
stronger as he downed it in one.

Kiiren arrived a few minutes later, dressed once again in his blue robe.

"Good morrow, Catlyn-*tuur*," the young skrayling said.

Mal got to his feet and bowed, though more to cover his own discomfort than out of courtesy. The ambassador took his place at the head of the table and a servant helped him to slices of bread and cold beef. Mal couldn't help but watch the skraylings closely, expecting some new and dreadful revelation of bestiality, but as at the banquet the ambassador conducted himself with a prim courtesy that would not have shamed a prioress. Even the skrayling guards ate in a civilised manner, though they slouched on the benches in a way no English lord would have tolerated from underlings. The ambassador, on the other hand, sat bolt upright on the hard wooden chair. Mal hid a smile. Having a tail really was a pain in the arse.

When breakfast was over the ambassador retired to the parlour, and Mal felt obliged to follow. He scarcely had time to wonder what to do or say next when one of the castle servants entered the room, carrying a velvet cushion to which was pinned a large gold pendant.

"A gift for His Excellency," the servant said to Mal.

"Bring it here," Kiiren told him.

The servant looked taken aback at being addressed by a skrayling, but complied. "From my lord the Earl of Northumberland," he said, kneeling before Kiiren.

The centre of the pendant was an oval of blue fluorspar the size of a hen's egg, with faint veins like ripples in water; around it were set seed pearls and tiny beads of jet in a pattern reminiscent of skrayling designs.

"Allow me, sir," Mal said.

He took the pendant and examined it. Henry Percy was famous for his knowledge of alchemy, an interest which had helped earn him the nickname "the wizard earl". The back of the pendant was smooth, however, with no sign of poisoned needles or hidden mechanisms. He handed it to Kiiren.

"I thank your master for most kind gift," the ambassador said, bowing low.

"A splendid offering," Mal said, after the servant had gone. "No one who sees it can doubt the giver, either."

"How so?"

"Blue and gold are the Percy colours, and the central gem may have been mined in Northumberland; my own home county produces a similar mineral. And these lozenges," he pointed out the design of the setting, "are found on their family's coat of arms."

"Coat of arms?"

"A shield bearing symbols of great antiquity, which is passed down from father to son. Each family has its own design."

"Our people are not so very different, then," Kiiren said.

"How so?"

The skrayling ran a grey-nailed thumb under the necklace around his own throat. It consisted of cylindrical ivory beads carved into elaborate patterns similar to the ones on their clothing, interspersed with round beads of gleaming grey-black metal. Mal had noticed all the skraylings wore them, though he had assumed they were merely a fashion.

"This is marked with signs telling name of my father and his clan. Father gives to mother, and then mother to child, as proof of kinship."

"Proof? Do fathers not acknowledge their children amongst your people?"

"We are not like you. We do not take mate for always. There is mating, and then we part."

Mal laughed. "A lot of men would prefer your way."

The pendant turned out to be only the first of an endless

flow of gifts, sent by courtiers eager to show off their loyalty to the Queen by favouring her guest. Scented gloves, jewelled daggers, falcons, books of poems: all had to be checked for signs of poison or other treachery. The gifts were then arranged on a cabinet, apart from the falcons, which were taken to the Royal Menagerie for safekeeping.

Examining the gifts for poison was one thing; looking for secret messages was going to be more difficult. Mal needed privacy and time, neither of which was likely to be in generous supply for a while. So far no letters had been sent to or by the ambassador, at least not openly, and Mal's initial examinations of the gifts had revealed no hidden notes or suspiciously blank pages that could hold invisible writing. If anyone was trying to communicate privily with the ambassador, they were using more subtle means.

He had just handed over the latest gift, a pair of German pistols inlaid with ivory panels depicting the death of Actaeon, when he realised the ambassador was addressing him.

He inclined his head. "Sir?"

"Please, have this gift from us."

He gestured to a skrayling servant, who held out a small box of pale wood about the size of a child's palm. Mal took it, quite forgetting to bow. As he opened the box, he let out a low whistle. Nestling in folds of velvet was a black baroque pearl as big as his fingernail, attached to a hoop of the same dark metal as the beads on the skraylings' necklaces.

"I…" Mal closed the box. "This is too rich a gift, Your Excellency."

"It is fashion of your people, is it not?"

"Yes, sir."

"Then wear it, in honour of our visit."

Mal inclined his head in submission. Drawing his dagger he cut the silk ribbon threaded through his earlobe and replaced it with the pearl earring. The unfamiliar weight and movement would be a distraction for a while, but he supposed he had better get used to it. Much like the skraylings themselves.

"It's… beautiful."

Coby stood in the yard of the new theatre, gazing up at the painted canopy over the stage. On a background of deepest blue, figures representing the moon and planets paraded around a gilded sun, and the canopy itself was supported by thick pillars painted with such artifice, she would have sworn they were made of marble.

"Worth the wait, eh, sir?" Master Naismith said, beaming at Master Cutsnail. "Come, let's around to the tiring house and you can see it from within."

Coby followed them back out into the field and round the outside of the theatre to the back door. Master Naismith produced a large iron key and unlocked it, then ushered his business partner inside.

"This is where the players dress for their parts," Coby translated for Master Naismith.

The tiring room took up almost the entire ground floor behind the stage. Benches ranged down both sides, with pegs above them awaiting costumes. Already the room held a faint hint of the dusty, magical smell Coby always associated with the backstage of a theatre, though here it was masked by the resinous scent of new wood.

"What is this?" Cutsnail asked, going over to the staircase in the centre of the room.

"The under-stage, sir. Please, come this way."

Master Naismith stayed above whilst Coby and the skrayling went down to the cramped area under the stage, backs bent and heads scraping on the underside of the boards. Fresh sawdust drifted down on them at every footfall from above.

"Here we store all the engines needed for our play," Coby said, trying not to sneeze.

She pointed out the miniature wooden castle on its wheeled base, the pair of wave engines, and the cannon. The wave engines were her favourite, a pair of complicated contraptions of blue and green canvas sheets attached to cables, wheels and gears, long enough between them to span the entire stage and each powered by a crank handle at the off-stage end.

She ran a hand over the surface of a wave, making the canvas ripple like the real thing. "I wish I could show you how they work, but you will have to wait until the play is performed."

"And this is the new trapdoor?" Cutsnail gestured to the complex mechanism of timber, iron and wood in the centre of the under-stage.

"Yes, sir," Coby said, biting her lip and watching his reaction.

Cutsnail inspected the pulleys and gears, rubbing the engine grease between two fingers and sniffing it with professional interest. Coby unlatched the trap, then released the counterweight so that the bottom section rose smoothly upwards to become flush with the stage.

"There is another in the stage canopy," she added, "to lower gods and the like from the heavens. I can take you up to see it if you wish."

"Gods? I thought you Christians had only one god."

"Yes, but some of our plays are about ancient times, before Christ came to save us. In those days people believed in many different gods."

"Ah, I think I understand. But thank you, I have seen enough."

She showed Cutsnail back up to the tiring room and thence upstairs to the office. To her annoyance Dunfell had turned up, and was fussing over some paperwork with Master Naismith. The duke's secretary fell silent when he saw Master Cutsnail, however, his expression turning to one of guarded politeness. It was a strange reaction from a man in the duke's service, who must see more than his fair share of skraylings.

Cutsnail appeared not to notice anything amiss, but it was impossible to know if that was through genuine ignorance of humans or simply lack of visible reaction. The foreigners' faces were hard to read at the best of times, their expressions concealed or distorted as they were by the tattooed lines.

"Thank your master for showing me the new theatre," he told Coby. "Now I must be about my other business."

"Certainly, sir."

She showed him out of the back door, lingering a while to enjoy the sunshine. It was oddly quiet without the constant hammering and cursing of the workmen. For a moment she was taken back to Sunday afternoons with Master Catlyn, sneaking into the empty building to spar and talk. She closed her eyes, lost in blissful memory.

"Naismith! Is Naismith there?"

She blinked against the light as Master Eaton came running round the curve of the theatre wall.

"In the office," she said as he pushed past her. "Why, what is it?"

She ran after him, heart in her mouth. Judging by the look on the actor's face, something was very wrong.

"Rafe?" Naismith put down his ledger.

"It's – Hugh Catchpenny," Eaton panted. "He's dead."

Coby stared at Master Eaton, aghast.

"What?" Naismith looked almost as shocked as she felt.

"Killed in a brawl last night. Skull smashed in, so they're saying."

"Dear God in Heaven."

Dunfell stepped forward. "Who is this Catchpenny?"

Coby bit back a snide remark. Six weeks with the company, and he still could not remember the names of the men on stage.

"A hireling, a player of small parts only," Naismith replied distractedly. "Still, he must be replaced."

"Certainly he must," said Dunfell, "and with someone less quarrelsome, by Heaven. My lord Suffolk–"

"With all due respect, *sir*," Master Eaton said, advancing on him slowly, "this is too little a matter for the notice of a great man like Suffolk. Is it not?"

Dunfell retreated, his round visage as pale as the moon.

"Ah, um, yes. Yes, I suppose so."

"Well, there's nothing for it," Master Naismith said. "We shall have to hire a replacement."

CHAPTER XII

At eleven o'clock a yeoman warder announced that the ambassador's barge was ready. Baron Howard of Effingham, the Lord High Admiral, had offered to show the ambassador around the royal dockyards at Deptford. Effingham also happened to be the patron of one of the competing theatre companies. Mal wondered how many palms the admiral had greased in order to get this early introduction to the judge of the competition.

The two skrayling elders, Scarheart and Greatyard, had also been invited, and they sat with the ambassador under a canopy in the centre of the barge, shaded from the heat of the sun. Even at this early hour it was beginning to get uncomfortably hot. Mal soon began to wish some other colour than black had been chosen for his livery, or even that he could join the skraylings in the shade. Instead he stood behind the ambassador, hand on rapier hilt, though in situations like this his role was more ceremonial than practical. If anyone chose to take a shot at the ambassador from the riverbank or a passing boat, there was little Mal could do short of throwing himself in front of the arrow or bullet. And he was not about to throw away his life for a skrayling, no matter how important.

"Catlyn-*tuur*?"

"Sir?"

"Please, talk with us. Sekaarhjarret-*tuur* wish to know more about you."

Mal sat down on a cushion opposite the skraylings, arranging his rapier behind him. Perhaps this was an opportunity to find out why they had asked for him in the first place.

"What would you like to know, sir?" he asked warily.

"You are from place called Peak, north of here?" Kiiren asked.

"Peakland, in Derbyshire." His heart sank. So that was it. No sense in trying to conceal things, then. "Rushdale Hall," he added.

Kiiren conveyed the information to the elders, who nodded and smiled at Mal. He smiled back, confused. If the skraylings knew about him and Charles, why were they so pleased? Foreigners! They made no sense.

"May I ask when you are born?" Kiiren said.

Mal frowned. "In the ninth year of Queen Elizabeth's reign, the year of Our Lord fifteen hundred and sixty-seven."

"Twenty-six years ago."

"Yes."

Kiiren leant forward. "What count of days? What time?"

"The first day of November," Mal replied. "I know not the hour. Why, do you desire to cast my horoscope, sir?"

"I do not know this word. What is... *horror scope*?"

Mal spent the rest of the journey to Deptford explaining what he knew of astrology; anything to keep the skraylings from enquiring further about his own history. Fortunately they seemed well acquainted with the movement of the stars, though they called the constellations by different names. Kiiren seemed keen on teaching him the names of everything, and he did his best to oblige, though the skrayling tongue was harder to pronounce than any language he had come across in his studies. He was relieved when the massed white sails of the shipyard came into view, and he could rest his dry throat a while.

Ned woke late to find Gabriel gone and a note on the pillow. *Gone home to fetch clean linens,* it said. *Meet me at the Bull for dinner?* Dammit, how was he to break the bad news to Gabriel there? Still, he had to get it over with. He whiled away the rest of the morning practising his card shuffling and dealing, then slipped the pack in his pocket and headed out.

The Bull's Head was abuzz with gossip, something about a fight outside the Castle on the Hoop. He found Gabriel with the rest of Suffolk's Men at their usual table in a nook near the fireplace, and slid onto the settle next to him. Gabriel reached for his hand and squeezed it. His face was drawn and pale, and his free hand gripped his tankard like a vice.

"Something wrong?" Ned murmured.

"One of our hirelings is dead," Gabriel replied. "Killed in a fight."

"Anyone I know?"

Gabriel shrugged. "Hugh Catchpenny."

"Thin, pockmarked fellow? Works for whatshisface, next door to the Lewes Inn?"

"That's the one."

"Huh." Ned beckoned to a passing pot-boy. "Another ale, if you will." He glanced at Gabriel. "No, make that two."

Naismith was going over the parts with Eaton and Hendricks, trying to work out if they could double up and manage without the lost actor.

"I don't see how it can be done, sir," Hendricks said at last. "The costume changes for some of the smaller roles are tight enough as it is. There will be mistakes made if we try for more."

"We could give Catchpenny's part to Fletcher," Rafe added, "and hire someone to take his place. There would be few lines and cues to learn, it's mostly walk-on parts."

The actor-manager got to his feet. "Gentlemen!"

The taproom fell silent.

"As you know, there has been a terrible tragedy this day, the loss of our good friend Hugh Catchpenny. Now, melancholy as this business is, some good may come out of it for someone. Suffolk's Men are left a player short, and as you know, we are set to perform before the Ambassador of Vinland next week."

There was a murmur of interest from some of the assembly.

"Yes, I am hiring." He held up his hands. "Only the one part, and that small. Two shillings on the day of performance itself, and an angel if we win."

"What's the play?" someone shouted.

"A new one, by Thomas Lodge, never before played on any stage."

Eaton and Rudd cleared a space amongst the tables, and arranged some stools for themselves and Naismith.

"Not going to join them?" Ned asked Gabriel.

"It's not my place," he replied. "I am the lowliest of Suffolk's Men, barely more than a hireling."

"Early days yet," Ned told him. "You'll be up there with Eaton one day, mark my words."

Gabriel smiled, like the sun breaking through clouds. Ned swallowed. God in Heaven, I can't do this.

"Now, gentlemen," Naismith said, turning to his companions, "let us see what the tide brings in."

The first to approach was a pallid, gangly youth in clothes that had once been apprentice blue but were now faded to colourlessness, where they had not worn to holes. He mumbled a name.

"Say on, lad," Naismith told him.

The young actor coughed, then recited:

"Stay, Roman brethren! Gracious... conqueror,
Victorious Titus rue, the tears I shed.
A mother's tears in passion for her son.
And – if thy sons were ever dear to... thee,
O think my son to, be as dear to me!"

"Thank you." Naismith looked around. "Next, please!"

Next up was a short shiny-faced fellow who looked more like a pastry-cook than an actor; indeed the stink of rancid butter preceding him was as good as an advertisement.

"Next!"

Ned turned back to Gabriel. "Where are all the decent players? Usually you can't spit in here without hitting a Tamburlaine or a King Henry."

"All hired by Henslowe or Burbage, or else on tour for the summer. With our three companies tied to London by this contest, there's rich pickings to be had elsewhere."

Hendricks nodded. "We'd only got as far as Sheffield before we were called back by my lord Suffolk, but Master Naismith would have pressed on to York if he could."

When Gabriel got up to go to the jakes, Ned leant across the table. The news of the murder had given him an idea.

"Hey, Hendricks," he whispered. "Do me a favour, will you?"

The boy drained his tankard and frowned at Ned. "Why should I?"

"Because if you don't, Suffolk's Men will lose this contest."

"Is that a threat?"

"No!" He looked around at the other actors, but they were busy watching the auditions, "I'm just worried about Gabe. I don't think he should be left alone right now, not after this attack on Catchpenny."

"You think someone's out to ruin us by murdering our players?"

"Probably not. But better safe than sorry, right? And Gabe's the only one who lives alone." *The only one who matters, anyway.*

"Can't he stay with you?"

"No," Ned said hurriedly. "Mam's got a cough, and I don't want him to catch it and lose his voice. No, he's better staying at Naismith's."

"Tell him that yourself."

"He won't listen to me. Thinks I fuss over him too much already. That's why I need you."

"All right," Hendricks said at last. "What am I to say?"

"I don't know. Use your wits. Flatter him. Tell him your apprentice lads are crying themselves to sleep with fright over this contest and need a ministering angel."

Hendricks eyed him suspiciously.

"I still reckon you're up to something."

"What do you want me to say? That I'm in love with the man, and can't sleep at night for fear of anything happening to him? There, I've said it." He looked over his shoulder. "Ssh, here he comes."

The Lord High Admiral was a stern, hawk-nosed man in his late fifties, with a sunburnt complexion and an energy that belied his years. He showed the ambassador and the elders around the shipyard, pointing out the differences in design between English and Vinlandic ships, of which he seemed to have a great deal of knowledge. Mal followed behind, with half an ear on the conversation. He had been on a ship scarcely a handful of times, and then only to cross one sea or another on his way to war.

Whilst Effingham pointed out one of the cranes used to lift the masts into position, Mal scanned the dockyard for any sign of potential trouble. There were tools here aplenty that could be used to kill a man, in addition to the weapons proper to naval warfare: cannons with their various forms of ammunition, arquebuses and calivers for the marines, and boarding axes.

"And this," Effingham was saying, "is the pride of our fleet, *Ark Royal.*"

The elders nodded as Kiiren translated, gazing up at the snowy sails of the galleon. Effingham gestured for the skraylings to precede him up the gangplank.

"With your permission, my lord–" Mal put in.

The admiral grunted, then motioned for him to proceed. Mal edged up the gangplank; the galleon was rolling in the water even though it was well anchored, and the plank pitched and wobbled alarmingly. At last he reached the comparative safety of the ship and scanned the decks and rigging. A couple of the sailors stared at him, an interloper on their territory, but none of them looked ready to murder an ambassador in cold blood. He waved down to Kiiren, and the skraylings followed him up the gangplank.

They were shown all over the vessel, from poop deck to beakhead. When Effingham enquired if they wished to go below decks to examine the guns, the ambassador shook his head, but gestured to the elders to proceed. The admiral and the two skraylings disappeared through the hatch. After a few moments Effingham's voice rumbled from below as he went from gun to gun, giving the range and poundage of each, as proud as a man showing off his sons.

"Very wise, Your Excellency," Mal said to the ambassador, lowering his voice to avoid being heard by the sailors all around them. "The stench of the bilges is enough to put any man off his dinner. And the admiral keeps a fine table, I am–"

"Be gone, ye foul demon!"

Mal pushed the ambassador aside as a sailor swung past on

the end of a rope, axe blade whistling through the space where they had stood. The man hung for a moment in the air over the river, and Mal drew his rapier. The sailor's eyes widened in horror as his momentum brought him swinging back over the ship, straight towards the blade. Mal leant into the stroke, a shudder running up his arm as the rapier punched through the man's belly.

The sailor let go of his rope and sagged to a halt, staring up at Mal with bloodshot eyes. Mal pulled the blade free and stepped back, edging round between the ambassador and his attacker. The man lurched forward, clutching his blood-soaked shirt, and Mal managed a slash to his legs before he got in too close for rapier work. Mal drew his dagger with his left hand and, as the sailor raised his axe, plunged it into the soft flesh of his opponent's armpit. Blood spewed from the severed artery and the man dropped his weapon with a cry, collapsing to his knees at Mal's feet.

"What in Heaven's name is going on?" Effingham barked, emerging from the hold.

"An assassin," Mal replied, holding the rapier point at the wounded man's throat.

"Captain!" The admiral looked around. "Who is this man?"

The captain, drawn sword in hand, crossed the deck. Mal suddenly realised no one had moved to help him, not even the captain. Had it happened so fast, or were they all in this together? In the sudden silence he was conscious of the warm, sticky blood coating his dagger hand and dripping onto the deck.

"Edwards?" The captain seized the sailor by his hair and wrenched his head back.

Edwards' eyes rolled up into their sockets, and he sagged, a dead weight in his captain's grasp. The captain grunted and let him go, and the dying sailor slumped to the deck.

Mal turned to Kiiren. A spatter of red dots marred the ambassador's robe at knee height.

"Are you hurt, Your Excellency?"

Kiiren shook his head slowly, never taking his eyes off his assailant.

"He almost kill me," he said in a low voice.

The skrayling elders hurried forwards, muttering in their own tongue as they stepped around the spreading pool of blood on the deck. The ambassador seemed to be assuring them he was unhurt, but the elders closed in around him as if to protect him from further attack. Mal wished that he had asked the ambassador to bring his escort aboard the ship. In future he would be more cautious.

He wiped both blades on the sleeve of his doublet – it was soaked in blood already, a little more would make no difference – and sheathed them.

"I think His Excellency has seen enough," he told the admiral.

"Indeed," Effingham replied. He turned to the captain. "See to this mess, Fosdyke. I want every man aboard questioned. Someone will hang for this."

"Aye-aye, sir."

The captain snapped a salute, his expression that of a man determined to find a scapegoat lest his own neck feel the hempen collar.

Mal wiped his hand absentmindedly on his hose. Only the first day of the visit, and already he had drawn steel in the ambassador's defence, aye, and bloodied it too. How many more zealots and desperadoes would try their luck? And how long before he failed to stop them? With a last glance round at the crew of the *Ark Royal* he escorted the skraylings down the gangplank to the blessed safety of the dockside.

There was only one problem with Faulkner's plan, Coby realised.

Where was Master Parrish going to sleep? Philip and Oliver shared a bed in the room opposite Master Naismith's, and Coby and the maidservant Betsy had the two servants' rooms on the top floor. Master Parrish would have to have a pallet on the floor in the boys' room. Either that or Coby would surrender her own bed and sleep in the costume store.

Faulkner got to his feet.

"So, mayhap I'll see you later, Gabe," he said with forced casualness. "Got a lot of work to do, though."

Parrish made an affirmative noise, still with half an ear on the debate over hirelings. Faulkner gave her a wink over Parrish's shoulder and left.

"Master Parrish," Coby said. "Sir?"

"Hmm?"

"I need your help. It's about Pip."

"Oh?"

"He's…" Perhaps the truth would be best, even if it cost her dear. "He's running wild, sir. Master Naismith has been so busy with the new theatre and the contest, he hasn't been keeping an eye on the apprentices like he should. I think… I think Philip is taking costly gifts from admirers and spending the money on… on…"

"On what?"

"Gambling, sir. And whores."

Parrish frowned, suddenly attentive. "How long has this been going on?"

"I don't know, sir. Since we came back to London, at least."

"Why did you not say anything sooner?"

"I wanted to, sir, but I was scared. I know I shouldn't be, he's more than a year younger than me, but he's always been jealous that I get to come to the tavern with you and the other adults whilst he has to stay at home with Oliver, and–"

"Very well, I'll speak to Master Naismith–"

"No!" She caught his sleeve. "If you do that, he'll know it was me."

"What would you like me to do?"

She swallowed, caught his cool blue gaze with her own.

"Come and stay at Master Naismith's for a few days. Tell him you're worried about this attack preying on the boys' thoughts, giving them nightmares, and want to keep them company for a while."

Parrish smiled. "You have this all thought out, haven't you?"

"It has been on my mind for a while, yes."

She looked away, praying he would agree. Faulkner was right. If anything happened to Parrish or, worse still, Philip, their chances of winning the contest would be scuppered.

"All right," he said at last. "Ned will not be happy about this, but I dare say he'll live."

He put an arm around her shoulders and gave her a brotherly hug. For once she did not shy away. She was beginning to realise she had misjudged this man. He had never been interested in her, not in that way.

"Thank you, sir," she whispered.

The temptation to pour out her heart to someone had never been greater. No, she must not succumb. The company was already under threat, without adding new kindling to the flames.

At Trinity House Mal was shown into a side-chamber and clean clothes were brought to replace his ruined livery. Mal changed hurriedly, reluctant to let the ambassador out of his sight for a moment. He emerged into the dining hall a few minutes later to find the admiral and his guests sitting at table, along with a number of naval officers. The hapless Captain Fosdyke was not amongst them.

"... most regrettable," Effingham was saying. "Can't question a dead man, though."

"The ambassador's assailant is dead?" Mal asked, taking a seat at the far end of the table, where he could see the skraylings clearly. He noticed the elders had placed themselves either side of Kiiren, and wondered how many English noblemen would defend their ambassador so readily.

"Bled to death," Effingham replied, picking up a gobbet of meat and gesturing with it. "You know how to wield that fancy sword, sir, I'll give you that."

Mal inclined his head at the backhanded compliment.

"Do you think the fellow was a Spanish spy, sir?" a young officer asked the admiral, his eyes gleaming with patriotic fervour.

"Unless Fosdyke finds a purse of doubloons in his hammock, how will we know?" The speaker was an older man, weather-beaten like the admiral but less richly attired.

"Not all men betray their country for pay," the young officer replied. "Damned Papists will do anything to harm the Queen's cause."

"Enough of such talk, gentlemen," Effingham said, gesturing to the skraylings. "Don't want to bore our guests with our petty squabbles, eh?"

Conversation turned to more friendly matters for a while: the ambassador's voyage from the New World, expeditions of trade and exploration on both sides. What it must be like, Mal thought as he sipped his wine, to sail for weeks without sight of land, and no certainty of reaching the other side? Like marching into battle, he supposed, only against a foe more implacable than any army, and with no means of retreat.

"I wish more of my men would learn to swim," the young officer said, echoing Mal's thoughts, "but they prefer to put their trust in God."

Kiiren translated this for his companions.

"We have seen this in your people," the ambassador said, "but never understood."

"Damned foolish nonsense, if you ask me," Effingham muttered. "Here, have a slice of quince tart."

"Thank you, no. We are much sated."

"Ate too much of the roast goose, eh?" The admiral beckoned to the servants, who cleared the dishes away. "Now, about this play–"

Kiiren held up a hand. "I am sorry, Effingham-*tuur*, but I cannot talk about contest."

"I was just going to ask–"

Kiiren stood up. "Please, you must excuse me."

He bowed low, and walked out of the room. After a moment's hesitation the skrayling elders did likewise.

"Damned foreigners!" Effingham slammed his glass down on the table, slopping wine over the tablecloth. "I was only going to ask how many of these contests that young fellow has judged. None at all, I'll warrant. I've seen cabin boys with more hair on their upper lips."

Mal refrained from pointing out that the skraylings did not appear to grow facial hair at any age.

"I am told they take their traditions and rules very seriously, my lord," he said. "If you will forgive me–"

He sketched a bow and all but ran from the room, his footsteps echoing round the high ceiling.

Kiiren was pacing a terrace overlooking the river, deep in conversation with the elders. Mal took up his station by a clipped box tree, where he could see most of the gardens at a single glance.

Shaded by the house behind him, the terrace was cool despite the afternoon sun. Balustraded steps ran down to a parterre divided into elaborate geometric shapes by low box hedges, and taller hedges either side framed the view of the river. Mal's attention was not on the formal beauty of the gardens, however, nor on the spectacle of so many ships sailing back and forth on the glittering waters. He scanned the shadowed arbours for lurking threats, calculated lines of sight and angles of attack. After the morning's events, he was taking no chances.

The gardens were disappointingly empty, however. A lone gardener was snipping the deadheads from the roses and tying in the climbing stems, and in the distance he could hear the shouts of a lieutenant of marines drilling his new recruits, but otherwise it was all very peaceful. He was just beginning to wonder if he should ask the ambassador if he wished to return to London yet, when he spotted a figure slipping from bush to bush. Not another so soon?

There was no point calling out; no one apart from the gardener was within easy range, and the intruder would easily get away. Mal stepped back into the shadows of a column and watched.

The man paused in a gap in the hedge, waiting for the gardener to turn his back. He was a short, dark-haired fellow, dressed in dull green and russet as if to go unnoticed in his current surroundings. He wore no cloak that would hide a pistol, and did not appear to be armed with more than a dagger. No immediate danger, then, unless he got a good deal closer to the ambassador.

The gardener picked up his trug and turned towards the next group of rose bushes. For a moment Mal was afraid the intruder would leap out and stab him, but the gardener walked away unharmed. The intruder looked straight at Mal and beckoned.

Mal hesitated. He was not about to walk up to another assassin and let himself be murdered. On the other hand, this could be some kind of contact from Walsingham. He strolled down the steps to the garden, as if going to admire the sundial. Glancing back, he reassured himself that the ambassador was still busy with the elders. He stepped aside into a rose bower and drew his rapier, then walked towards the waiting man.

"What do you want?"

The stranger said nothing, only took out a sealed letter, dropped it on the gravel path and walked away. Mal glanced around, but the gardener had his back to him. Crouching, he retrieved the folded paper. The seal was a plain one, a simple cross within a circle. On the other side were two initials: M C.

He slipped the letter into his pocket and sheathed his blade, then hurried back to the terrace. His only thought was to get the ambassador safely back to the Tower so he could read the letter at his leisure.

CHAPTER XIII

After a quiet supper in the dining room of St Thomas's Tower, the ambassador and the two elders settled down to a game of Five Beans. Greatyard produced a bag of counters and a roll of leather on which was painted the X-shaped board, and the skraylings began haggling good-naturedly over the items to be provided for the bets. The ambassador chose six gifts from the cabinet, much to the annoyance of the elders, who seemed to be disputing their value. Mal excused himself as early as possible, and retreated to the privacy of the small bedchamber.

Taking the letter from his pocket he cracked the seal.

Esteemed sir, it has come to our attention that one true to the Old Faith has, by the Grace of God, been granted access to His Excellency the Ambassador of Vinland. It is the fondest wish of His Holiness that the foreigners be brought to knowledge of Christ for the salvation of their souls, and it is certain that any man who could claim to have converted the ambassador himself would gain eternal salvation. He would also earn the undying gratitude of His Most Catholic Majesty King Felipe, to his undoubted benefit and worship. I pray to Our Lady that this message reaches one whose heart is true, and wish him all success in this endeavour.

Mal crumpled the letter in his fist. Goddam Spanish, using faith as an excuse for conquest. He looked around the bed-chamber. Even to possess such a letter was enough to condemn a man. It mattered not that there was no signature, nor any re-cipient named; the initials on the outside were as good as a noose around his neck. Were they genuinely trying to recruit him, or was this a more subtle ploy, aimed at removing him from his position by exposing him as a Catholic? No matter. He would not give them the satisfaction of either.

He ventured into the ambassador's bedchamber, where one of the lamps rested on the hearth. He dipped the letter into the glowing liquid, but it failed to burst into flames. When he lifted it out, it dripped pale light back into the lamp but was other-wise unharmed. With a sigh he retrieved his tinderbox and placed the damp letter on the hearth, arranging a small heap of wood-shavings and other dry scraps in the centre.

After a few strikes of flint and steel the tinder caught fire. Flame gulped at the dry stuff and spread to the paper, turning it to wisps of black ash that floated about the room in the draught from the fireplace. Only the corner dampened by the skraylings' lightwater remained, the ink smeared into illegibility. He picked it up, wadded it and stuffed it in his pocket. One more thing that Walsingham would never hear from his own lips. Perhaps he should make a list, as Cecil was reputedly so fond of doing.

Item: one treasonous letter from the Spanish.
Item: one initiation into an illegal secret society.
Item: one murder of a skrayling, witness to.

Brushing the soot from his hands, he turned to leave. Should he do as he had vowed and sleep in the side-chamber tonight? Perhaps not. It would only cause more trouble and besides, the skraylings were not so monstrous, in truth. He had seen far more noisome creatures begging on street corners, and they were God's children also.

He suddenly realised he had not had the old nightmare last night, despite the close presence of the ambassador. On the contrary, he had slept better than he had since learning about this job. Perhaps it was relief that the waiting was over. Or perhaps it was just the calm before the storm.

The next day, Coby rose at dawn. Master Naismith might have delegated most of her work to Master Dunfell, but that did not mean she could not keep an eye on the secretary herself. What did he know about the theatre? Sooner or later he would slip up, and then what? Naismith and his men would get the blame, of that she was sure.

First order of the day was to head over to Bankside so she could be at the theatre before anyone else arrived. The actors were usually late to rise, but Dunfell no doubt scorned such idleness. Fortunately Master Naismith had given her a spare key to the back door of the theatre before Dunfell took over, and she had neglected to return it.

Shoes in hand, she crept in stockinged feet down the stairs, hopping over the creaky tread halfway down. On the first floor, snoring came from Master Naismith's bedchamber; the room opposite, where Master Parrish was sleeping with the two apprentices, was silent. At the bottom of the second flight of stairs she paused to put on her shoes. The sound of a brush scraping on hearthstones came from the kitchen, which meant their maidservant was already awake and at work. Coby's stomach grumbled. Perhaps she had better eat breakfast first. With Master Parrish to watch over them, there was much less chance that Philip or Oliver would come downstairs early with the same idea, and no one else was likely to be up at this hour, not even Mistress Naismith.

She wandered into the kitchen, trying to look nonchalant, and took a heel of yesterday's bread from the pantry.

"Morning, Jacob," Betsy murmured, brushing her hands on her apron.

"Uh, morning," Coby replied in her best Philip-surly voice, and sat down at the table.

"You're up early."

"Uh, yeah. Get us some ale, will you?"

The girl bobbed a curtsey, and returned with a tankard and a smile.

"Going to the fair today?" Betsy asked, sliding onto the bench opposite and pushing the tankard towards her.

Coby looked up, noting the girl's intent expression and the mock-coy way she rested her chin on her hand. She cursed under her breath. Sometimes her disguise was far too convincing.

"No." Coby stuffed some bread in her mouth and washed it back with a mouthful of small ale.

"What about tomorrow?"

"I doubt it."

"Sunday?"

"Certainly not. I shall be at church on Sunday, as you should be."

Betsy pouted. "Never mind. Master Philip will take me. If I ask him."

"Philip's going to the fair?"

This was more interesting. They were supposed to be rehearsing for the next three days, thanks to Master Dunfell, who was convinced everyone would forget their lines by next week. She would have to remember to warn Master Parrish to keep an extra-sharp eye on the apprentices.

"Oh yes. He promised me a half-angel to spend all to myself." Betsy sighed. "What colour ribbons should I buy for my hair, do you think?"

"Green," Coby replied without thinking. Betsy's copper hair looked good with green.

"How do you know so much about what women should wear?" Betsy asked, her eyes narrow with curiosity.

"It's my job to," Coby said quickly. "I make up the costumes for the stage, remember?"

The girl's mouth formed an "oh", then a look of guile crossed her features and she looked sidelong at Coby through lowered lashes.

"I wish you would take me, Jacob," she murmured. "You're much nicer than Philip."

Coby was saved by the sound of movement upstairs.

"Got to go," she said, draining the tankard and stuffing the rest of the bread in her pocket. "Tell Master Naismith I've gone to the new theatre, would you?"

After breaking his fast Mal was summoned to the lieutenant's lodgings. He was shown into the same dining parlour where he had met Lodge a few days ago, now bright with morning sunlight. Leland was still at breakfast, leafing through a pile of papers with one hand whilst the other held a spoon that dripped congealing porridge onto the tabletop. Mal stood to attention, hands clasped behind his back, and waited.

"I hear you saved the ambassador's life yesterday," Leland said eventually, frowning at a document he had just picked up.

"Well, yes I suppose—"

"Effingham says you killed the man."

"I didn't intend to, sir," Mal said. "But—"

"No?" Leland put the porridge spoon down and looked up at Mal. "Just mortally wounded him by accident, eh?"

"No, sir. But he would not back off, and I feared for my own life as well as that of the ambassador."

"Hmm. Well don't let it happen again."

"The attempted assassination, or my killing the assassin?"

"Either."

Leland picked up the spoon again and waved him away, spattering the paperwork with porridge. Mal bowed and left, wondering if he had just been praised or reprimanded.

The morning was fine and cool, with a flawless blue sky promising a scorching hot day to come. Even the turbid waters of the Thames were bright with sunlight. As Coby walked across London Bridge the city came to life: bleary-eyed shopkeepers unbolted their shutters and began setting out their wares, and the great gates at the southern end of the bridge swung open, letting in the first street-vendors with their baskets of eggs and pails of milk.

When she arrived at the field where the theatre stood, she was surprised to find the gate open. Fresh hoof-prints marked the damp earth at the entrance to the field, and by the gatepost were the imprints of booted feet – going in through the gate, but not leaving. She froze, scanning the field beyond.

There was no one to be seen, but on the other hand there were places enough for concealment. The wooded gardens nearby were thick with new growth at this time of year and of course there was the bulk of the theatre building itself, casting a long shadow on the dewy grass. A flicker of movement caught her eye. Something white, pinned to the front door of the theatre and fluttering in the early morning breeze. Paper?

She looked at the ground again. The boot marks went one way only, but the hoof prints faced in both directions, and the outgoing ones lay uppermost. Someone had dismounted to unlatch the gate, but had ridden out again without closing it. Why be in such a hurry, unless one was up to mischief? Heart in mouth, she ran up to the theatre doors.

A sheet of paper had been nailed to the door by its top edge; it was slightly askew and one nail was bent, as if the job were hastily done. On it, written in a neat hand, were four verses of doggerel, signed "Jonah". Coby's breakfast turned to lead in her stomach. Just such a pseudonymous notice had been posted on the Guildhall door only a few months ago, intended to stir up violence against skraylings, Jews and other aliens in the city. The aldermen of London had offered a reward of one hundred crowns for information on the perpetrator, whilst the Privy Council had issued a blanket arrest warrant for all possible suspects, their lodgings to be searched for evidence and their persons to be tortured if they would not talk.

Thankful she had discovered the libel before it could be made public, she tore it down and took it in both hands, ready to rip it into pieces. No, Master Naismith needed to see this. If the theatre company had enemies, he ought to know about it, lest the villains try again.

Around mid-morning a servant arrived from Trinity House with Mal's livery, which had been rinsed of blood and dried. Mal gave the servant his borrowed garments and sixpence for his trouble then returned to the bedchamber to get changed. Unfortunately the delicate silk and silver embroidery on the breast was ruined by the scrubbing. A clicking noise caused him to turn. Kiiren stood in the doorway, looking him up and down and frowning.

"You need new clothes," the skrayling said.

"Probably, Your Excellency, but…"

"But?"

Mal hesitated. Perhaps it was better to be honest. "This livery must have cost a great deal. Even if Sir James docks my entire pay for this commission, it might not be enough."

"I will give Sir Leland money," Kiiren replied. "It is small price for saving of my life."

"Thank you, sir, that is most generous."

Mal put aside the livery and donned his own clothes once more. His best doublet and hose were of plain English wool, nothing like as fine as the royal livery, but good enough for a dinner at the Guildhall followed by trade negotiations, which was all the "entertainment" planned for today. After yesterday's excitement, it would be a relief to guard the ambassador in surroundings that did not bristle with deadly weapons. Still, he would have to remain watchful and alert. There must be a few merchants whose trade had not benefited from the alliance with the skraylings.

Though he was getting used to the skraylings' presence, he longed for the company of his own kind. He wondered if it was against ambassadorial protocol for him to invite Ned over one evening, or perhaps young Hendricks. No, not the boy. The ambassador had made it plain he could not discuss the contest, so asking one of Suffolk's Men to sup with them would not be wise. And even Ned had theatre connections, through Parrish and Henslowe. Dammit, the sooner Sunday came around the better. He would go and see Sandy after church, and perhaps have a drink with Ned before returning to the Tower. Leland had assured him he would be allowed time off duty on the Lord's Day; though the skraylings might not care to hear the word of God, they respected Christian custom at least that far.

He returned to the dining room, where the ambassador was greeting yet another well-wisher, a foreigner by his clothing.

"I am Monsieur D'Arrignan, aide to His Excellency the Ambassador of France," the man said in heavily accented English. "The ambassador regrets he cannot visit you himself, but he has been much distracted by bad news from Paris. A Catholic assassin tried to kill His Most Christian Majesty since only a few days."

"I do not understand," Kiiren said. "Is not your king of same faith as his people?"

"Since one month only, and not all believe he is sincere."

The ambassador shook his head. "It is very sad thing, that some men are so blind from own hatred they cannot see good in others."

Mal glanced at the ambassador, wondering if this statement was aimed closer to home. Had the ambassador understood the remarks at the admiral's dinner after all? He must surely have been briefed on the political situation in England, even if his people could not understand the details.

D'Arrignan presented Kiiren with an inlaid wooden box containing a gilded spoon and fork. Mal had seen table forks used in Italy, though Englishmen considered them unnecessary and effeminate. After a cursory examination he took the box and handed it to a servant, with instructions to wash the implements thoroughly in case the ambassador wished to use them at dinner.

As he was leaving, D'Arrignan addressed Mal in French.

"My master wishes me to convey his regrets that your family has suffered so much in recent years. Your late mother was truly an ornament of the French court, and she is sadly missed."

"Thank your master for his kind words, sir."

"He also wishes me to say that your mother's family's legal affairs are very… complicated. It is possible that mistakes were made in assigning the dowry, and that her sons may yet be entitled to certain modest estates currently in the possession of our sovereign, Henri."

More bribes, eh? At least the French had the delicacy to couch it in terms that almost sounded reasonable and just. Treason was still treason, however.

"Please tell your master I appreciate his concern for my family. Should any such matter be presented to an English court of law, I would be most happy to accept the outcome."

The diplomat smiled thinly at the rebuff.

"As you wish, monsieur."

Mal was relieved when D'Arrignan left. First the Spanish, now the French; who else was lining up to bribe, threaten or cajole him into betraying his commission?

Master Naismith cancelled the day's rehearsals and called a meeting of the principal actors at his house in Thames Street.

"'Tis a Papist plot to put us out of business!" Rafe Eaton's bellow made the door tremble on its hinges.

Eaton was pacing back and forth, shaking his fist at the ceiling and slopping beer on the floor from the tankard in his other hand. Coby slipped into the dining parlour, trying to stay unnoticed. She sat down at the table not far from Master Parrish, who was staring at nothing, his chin resting on interlaced hands.

"Give it a rest," Master Rudd said, his weary tones so unlike his onstage persona. "It's only words, after all."

"Only words?" Eaton hauled the clown from his seat by the back of his doublet. "Will you still be saying it is only words when you are dragged off to Bridewell to be tortured, like poor Tom Kyd?"

"Gentlemen, please!"

Naismith separated the two men, and Rudd resumed his place at the table.

"He's right," Parrish said quietly. "Kit Marlowe was arrested just because some libeller used the name of one of his plays as a pseudonym. Then they found an old essay of Marlowe's in Kyd's lodgings and arrested him for nothing more than that. Do any of us dare to come under such scrutiny?"

The actors pondered these unhappy events in silence. Though Marlowe had been released from prison almost immediately, he was killed in a brawl only a few days later. To many within the theatre, this seemed too convenient a happenstance.

"It is God's judgement," Rudd said, peering into his tankard as if seeing revelation there. "We have blasphemed and he is punishing us."

Eaton paused in his pacing. "What are you blathering about now, buffoon?"

"This aping of the skraylings," said the clown. "Until they came along we had only pageants and mystery plays, honouring the Lord and telling His scriptures."

"Nonsense," said Naismith. "My grandsire told me there were worldly plays when he was a boy, ere any skrayling ship was seen in these waters."

"But you can't deny the playhouses were not built until after our nations became allies, or that King Henry banned women from playing, just to curry favour with the skraylings."

"No," Naismith conceded. "But God did not do this dreadful deed; it is the act of men. Or a man, at any rate." He peered around the shadowy room, as if expecting the miscreant to leap out and declare himself.

"Who is this Jonah, do you think?" Coby asked.

"Whoever he is, he writes very poor verse," Eaton said. "If 'twere not for the foul libel therein, no one would pay it any mind."

"Might there not be something in the writing?" Parrish said. "All poets have their own style, and we here must know every scribbler in Southwark. Perhaps we might make a guess?"

"You read it out, lad," Master Naismith said, passing the notice to Coby. "I will not dignify it with an actor's oratory."

Coby cleared her throat, and began to read.

"When Christian men should be at prayer
The trumpet sounds and every player

Gathers to hail their great naysayer,
The smith who forges blasphemy.
Alas! 'Tis plain for all to see
A tarnished glass this Mirror be."

Her voice shook, and she eyed Master Naismith anxiously. His features were dark with controlled anger, but he gestured for her to continue.

"Chains of silver bind their souls.
Their capering doth fan the coals
Of Satan's fires and turn the whole
Of virtue into venery."

"The refrain is the same as before," she added.

"So we perform for money," Dickon Rudd said. "And if my japes bestir a woman to lust, what of it?"

Coby put her hand over her mouth to cover a nervous snigger. The thought of anyone lusting after Master Rudd was, well, laughable.

"Peace!" Master Naismith glared at the clown. "Have some respect for those more cruelly defamed. Go on, boy."

Coby glanced at Master Parrish and swallowed. This next verse was perhaps the most venomous of all.

"Unnatural actors, aping graces,
Flaunt their shorn and painted faces
Like the New World's savage races—
Whoring boys in sodomy."

Parrish's face betrayed no emotion as she read, only a slight tightening of the clasped hands hinting at the turmoil beneath. The city authorities usually turned a blind eye to their citizens' sexual misdemeanours, unless it involved children. And now Parrish was staying under the same roof, sleeping in the same chamber as the apprentices. The accusations in the poem would be hard to ignore.

Eager to have the business over, Coby read the final verse.

> *"Set apart from God's creation*
> *And Christ's message of salvation,*
> *How should any Christian nation*
> *Hold with such vile heresy?"*

"There," Eaton said. "What did I tell you? Does not the Pope himself rail against the skraylings' rejection of the Gospels?"

"And you are the good Protestant, I suppose," Rudd replied. "Who was it cried God's vengeance? And who is least slandered in this doggerel?"

Eaton turned pale. "You think I wrote that?"

"Can you prove you did not?"

"Enough!" Master Naismith moved between them, holding up his hands. "No one here is the perpetrator of this foul deed, of that I am certain."

"Then who?" Eaton asked, looking round at them all. "There is nothing in the style to suggest any playwright of my acquaintance. 'Tis more like a street ballad."

"This is futile," Rudd said. "We should take the matter to the Privy Council. Such infamous deeds should be rooted out."

"No," Parrish said in a low voice. "I beg you, do not."

"Angel is right," said Master Naismith. "Mark the mentions of a glass, and the name Jonah. This quarrel may be aimed at Master Lodge, but we are all tainted by association."

"Then what are we to do?" Eaton asked.

"Do? We do nothing," Master Naismith replied. "Coby here has already thwarted the villain's evil intent by finding the notice before anyone else could read it. The failure of his scheme is justice enough."

"He may try it again," Parrish said. "He must have a copy of the verse – what is to stop him from posting it anew?"

"We must set a guard on the theatre," Coby said.

They all looked at her.

"Splendid idea," Master Naismith said. "And since you were so diligent in rising at sparrow-fart to catch this fellow, who better to do it?"

Coby's heart sank. This was not what she had planned at all. On the other hand she was in no position to argue, since she had no other work to speak of.

"Very well," she said. "I will pack up my belongings and install myself at the theatre until the performance."

CHAPTER XIV

As she passed the boys' bedchamber on her way up to her own room, Coby realised she had not seen either Philip or Oliver all morning. Had they used the confusion to slip away to the fair, as Betsy had told her? After gathering her belongings together, she went back downstairs, and found Master Parrish doing the same in the boys' room.

"You're not leaving, are you, sir?"

She recalled Faulkner's warning, and the desperate look in his eyes.

"How can I sleep in here," Parrish replied, "after what has been said today?"

He snatched up his razor and wash-ball from the night stand and stuffed them into a side pocket of his knapsack.

"You can have my room," Coby said. "I shan't need it for a few days, and there's a bolt on the inside so you won't be disturbed in the night."

Parrish managed a tight smile. "Thank you. I wasn't easy about going home tonight. I would not have it thought I was turned out, or had any reason to feel guilty."

"There is one thing, sir." She told him about her conversation with Betsy. Well, all the relevant parts anyway.

"Gone to Bartholomew Fair, you reckon?"

Coby nodded.

"Then I think we need to fetch him back," Parrish said. "By force of arms, if need be."

Coby produced the two cudgels from her bundle.

"Will these do?" She handed one to Parrish and he hefted it thoughtfully before tucking it into his belt.

"You know how to use it?" he asked her.

"A little."

"Good. I hope it won't come to it, but the fair's a pretty rough place."

Bartholomew Fair was one of the great events of the London year. Ostensibly limited to the three days of Bartholomew's Eve, the saint's day itself and the day after, in practice the fairgoers often lingered for a week or more afterwards, much to the inconvenience of the traders of Smithfield, whose ground the fair occupied. Craftsmen and entertainers of all kinds flocked from miles around, creating a miniature city of booths and tents whose alleys were even more noisome and crowded than those of the rest of the capital.

What hit Coby first was the smell, a thick smoky mix of roast hog, beer, sweaty bodies and of course the mud of Smithfield, permeated by generations'-worth of cow dung and urine. After that came the noise: the clamour of voices, beating of drums, the occasional blare of a trumpet.

"What d'you lack, sir?" A pedlar flourished a sample of his wares at her. "A plume for your bonnet, a ribbon for your hair!"

She thought of Betsy, stuck at home whilst Philip ran off to enjoy himself, and was almost tempted to buy a ribbon for the girl. No, that would be a big mistake. Bringing home fairings was the opening sally of many a courtship, and Betsy was already too interested in her for comfort.

They walked up and down the aisles of the fair for what felt like half the day, to no avail. The place swarmed with youths of Philip's height and build, and they were led on several wild goose chases when one or other of them spotted a lad who looked overmuch like him.

"If only he had red hair, or flaxen like mine," Coby sighed, when they paused to get their bearings.

"Then we would mistake him for half the whores of Cheapside," Parrish replied with a laugh. "Come on, let's go back. We could search all day and never find him here."

"We don't have to," Coby said.

She pointed to a skinny boy who was sitting on a barrel picking at a scab on his hand. His nose was red and his eyes swollen as if from weeping. Oliver.

Parrish motioned for her to go around behind the boy. She did so, and tapped him on the shoulder. He looked round, gaped, leapt up – and ran straight into Parrish.

"Going somewhere, Noll?"

Parrish pushed the boy backwards, and Coby caught him by the arms from behind. Parrish drew the cudgel from his belt and pressed its steel-shod tip under the boy's jaw. A few passers-by, the women at least, gave Oliver pitying glances, but most acted as if they saw nothing.

"Where's Philip?" Parrish pressed the tip of the cudgel into the soft flesh under the boy's jaw.

"Dunno, sir–"

The cudgel flashed down and caught the boy on the shin. He yelped and started blubbing again, shivering in Coby's grasp. She frowned at Parrish, but he took no notice.

"Where is Philip?"

"Th-th-the Saracen's Head, sir."

"And you weren't tempted to join him?"

Oliver mumbled something, too quietly to make out.

"What was that?" Parrish asked.

"They... they wouldn't let us in at first, then Pip gave 'em an angel. I said to him, lend me one, but..." He sniffled noisily. "He s-said I had to earn it first."

"Did he now?"

Oliver nodded, lips pressed together to stop them trembling.

"Get off home," Parrish said, more gently.

Coby released him, but before he could take a step the cudgel came up again, not in a blow but a gentle touch under the jaw that nonetheless froze him to the spot.

"Next time, don't sit around waiting for some bawd to come along and cozen you out of your last sixpence. Now get you gone."

They watched him slouch away, wiping his nose on his sleeve.

"Was that necessary, sir?"

Parrish shrugged. "Boys needs discipline. If Naismith won't do it..."

He led the way through the crowds to the edge of Smithfield. Beyond the fairground the streets of London stretched in all directions, spilling out of the city walls northwards towards Clerkenwell. They passed the hospital of St Bartholomew towards Aldersgate. Every other building here seemed to be an alehouse or tavern. Craning her neck, Coby soon spotted a carved and painted sign showing the severed head of a swarthy beturbanned warrior, complete with dripping scarlet blood.

Like most taverns of its kind the Saracen's Head doubled as a brothel, the girls circulating amongst the customers until deals were struck and more comfortable accommodation sought. Parrish marched straight through the taproom, Coby trailing in his wake, and up the stairs. The upper floor was divided with lengths of sacking into narrow cubicles with just enough floor space for a mattress. Parrish peered into one after another, ignoring the complaints of the customers so disturbed. Coby stared at the floor, trying to shut out the chorus of grunts and moans. If Master Kuyper ever found out she had been in this place, she would be on psalm-reading duty from now until Christmas.

Parrish gave a cry of triumph. Coby looked away just in time as he seized a curtain and pulled it aside.

"Get your rat's pizzle out of there, Johnson!"

The whore shrieked, and there was a brief scuffle. By the time Coby looked back, the woman was clutching her unlaced bodice to her doughy breasts, and Philip had got to his feet and was tucking himself back into his breeches. When he saw Coby waiting behind Master Parrish, his defiant expression twisted into a sneer of contempt.

"Might have known it was you, Jakes. Always got to lick the pretty boys' arses, haven't you?"

Coby's grip on her cudgel tightened, but Parrish held up his hand.

"I was the one noticed you were gone," Parrish said. "And if you will plot to run off to the fair, perhaps you shouldn't boast to the servants about it."

"That little bitch–"

Parrish snapped the length of maple at the back of the youth's legs, and Philip collapsed to his knees, cursing.

"I see one bruise on that girl," Parrish said softly, lifting Philip's chin with the tip of the cudgel, "one tear in her eyes, and I'll make sure you get to play women's roles for the rest of your miserable life."

"You cut my balls off and I'll shove 'em down your throat. Sir."

"That's not what I meant," Parrish replied. "I meant that your next performance will be your last."

The blood drained from Philip's face. At a twitch of the cudgel, he scrambled to his feet and all but fell down the stairs in his haste to get away.

"You didn't really mean that, did you, sir?" Coby asked in a

low voice, as they followed Philip out of the brothel. "About...
you know?"

He paused on the threshold and winked at her. "What use
is there in being a player, if you cannot adopt a role at need?"

By the end of the afternoon, Mal had learnt more about customs duties on *aniig*, the grading of tobacco and the keeping
properties of dried potatoes than he ever wanted to know. The
ambassador did not seem interested in the discussions either,
but protocol demanded that he be included and so he had to
offer an opinion when asked. He proved surprisingly knowledgeable on every topic, and quoted Vinlandic traditions from
memory when the English merchants disputed their skrayling
colleagues' claims. Mal wondered if the skraylings had univer-
sities or similar places of learning, and what was taught there.
Did they learn merchantry and magic, the way English students studied theology or law?

The coach came to collect the ambassador at five o'clock,
and they returned to the Tower for a quiet supper alone. Afterwards, at Kiiren's insistence, Mal played his lute for a while.
At first he felt uncomfortable being watched so intently, but
after a while he forgot the skrayling was there. He thought instead of Sandy, away on the northern outskirts of the city,
alone. The thought was almost enough to make him wish he
had accepted the French ambassador's offer. An estate in
Provence, where he and Sandy could live together in peace
and comfort; was that not worth a little treason?

The curfew bell had scarcely finished tolling eight when
there was a knock at the door of the ambassador's quarters.
Two cloaked and hooded but recognisably female figures, accompanied by a similarly clad man, entered the outer room.
Mal leapt to his feet and put a hand to his rapier hilt.

"Hold!"

The newcomer lowered his hood, and Mal sank to one knee.

"Your Highness," he murmured. That explained why the guards had admitted the visitors despite the lateness of the hour.

"Enough, you may stand," Prince Arthur said. "I am not here on state business."

Mal got to his feet but kept his eyes lowered. The two women had not removed their hoods or spoken.

"Your Excellency!" The young prince strode across the room to greet the startled ambassador. "It was so good to meet you on Wednesday. How are you enjoying London?"

"It is very... different to what I expect, Your Highness," Kiiren replied, bowing.

"Splendid. Travel broadens the mind, or so my tutors always said." He looked around the dining room. "I see they've done the old place up. Don't think anyone's stayed here overnight since Grandfather's day."

He strolled around the room and paused to admire one of the skrayling lamps. His hair looked even redder in this light than it had at noon, and Mal wondered if the prince really resembled King Henry as closely as everyone said. He was certainly the image of his mother in masculine form.

"I suppose you are wondering what brings me here so late?" Prince Arthur said, turning his attention back to the ambassador.

"Your Highness is welcome to visit at any time."

"Yes, I am, aren't I? Privilege of being a prince. Well, I have a gift for you. Two, in fact. Only for the night, I'm afraid. This is England, not the Turkish Empire."

"I do not understand," Kiiren said, his brow furrowing at the prince's seemingly random train of thought.

"Forgive me, I do rattle on," Prince Arthur said, and clicked his fingers. "Ladies!"

The two women shed their velvet cloaks in midnight pools about their feet. They were younger than Mal expected, barely eighteen, and decidedly pretty. Their hair was almost as black as his own, and their lips had been stained crimson with kermes. Underneath the cloaks they wore shifts of the finest milk-white silk, so transparent Mal could clearly make out the dark circles of nipples and darker triangles below. The blood stirred in his veins, and he dropped his gaze once more. Lord, must you so torture a starving man with the sight of a feast meant for others?

"I trust these are to your taste, Your Excellency," he heard the prince say.

"You are most generous, sir," Kiiren replied, staring at the girls.

"Well, I won't keep you from your pleasures. My men will return at dawn to take the ladies home. Good night, Your Excellency."

Prince Arthur bowed curtly and swept out without another word.

"Ladies," Mal said with a bow of his own, "I suppose I have no excuse to search you for concealed weapons, not in those garments."

The girls exchanged glances and giggled. He turned to Kiiren. The young skrayling looked about as comfortable as a virgin on his first visit to a brothel. Mal supposed it was up to him to take charge of the situation.

"This way, please, ladies," he said, shepherding the girls towards the ambassador's bedchamber.

When Kiiren did not follow, Mal went back to the dining room.

"Sir?"

"I am… uncertain of what this means, this gift of women."

"Well, I suppose His Highness thought it unmeet for an ambassador to haunt the stews of Southwark."

"Stew?"

"Brothel. House of pleasure. Place of resort."

The young skrayling continued to look puzzled. Mal sighed.

"A place to buy a woman's favours, to bed her as you please."

Kiiren sat down by the hearth and looked up at Mal. His eyes reflected the lamplight like a cat's.

"It does not seem right to me," Kiiren said, "this buying and selling of flesh. Women are honoured amongst our people."

"And amongst some, at least, of ours," Mal replied.

"I cannot accept this gift."

"It is unwise to offend a prince, sir."

The young skrayling looked wretched but did not answer.

"Is it...?" Mal hesitated, unsure he wanted to pursue the topic further, but was not any intelligence valuable? "You are not like other skraylings."

"No, I am not." Kiiren stared down at the ground.

"I reckoned as much from the first."

"I have been set apart from birth, raised to the role I now play."

"You said as much at the banquet," Mal replied. "You were taught English by our sailors."

"There is more to it than that."

"How so?"

Kiiren sighed. "Amongst my people, as yours, women do not act upon stage. Men take their parts, or rather *senlirren* do."

"Sen... leeren?"

"Man who has been... changed as boy, to make him able to speak like woman."

"Oh?" He thought back to his brief glimpse of Kiiren naked. He had not been able to see much from behind, admittedly, nor was he sure what to expect a skrayling eunuch to look like.

"You need not be sad for me," Kiiren said. "It was long time ago, and I chose it freely. And we have herbs to take away pain, and heal mouth so it is as if–"

"Mouth?" Mal stared at him.

"Why, yes." Kiiren bared his even, yellowish teeth. "Our women have no long-teeth, so I must have mine taken out."

Mal's blood ran cold at the image: bloody trophies being ripped from a skrayling's mouth. Had Charles and the others known the symbolism of what they did?

"You are upset, Catlyn-*tuur*," Kiiren said. "I am sorry for talking of painful business. You must think we are barbarians."

"Not at all," Mal replied, trying to shake off the memory. "We do the same – or worse – to our own children, for much the same purpose. At least, the Italians do. It is not practised in England."

He recalled Lodge's account of the "women" of Antilia.

"Is this commonly practised in the Seven Cities?" he asked.

Kiiren looked at him curiously. "I am from Vinland, not Antilia."

"Then those were women Lodge saw, when he approached the city. Short hair, no tattoos…?"

"Of course. All our women live in safety of cities." He smiled. "Humans are thought most strange by my people, to live together. Your men seem so – what is word? – effeminate, to us."

"Begging your pardon, sir, but I'm not the one dressed like a woman."

He fell silent, fearing he had said too much and Kiiren would take offence, but after a moment the ambassador returned his smile.

"So," Mal said, "*senlirren* or not, sir, do you wish to lie with the whores tonight?"

The familiar scents of the theatre enveloped Coby and she stood for several minutes, back to the door, letting her eyes adjust to the gloom. All around her the huge wooden building creaked like a ship under sail as it cooled. Coby told herself firmly there was no one else here and nothing to be afraid of.

After a moment's thought she fetched some cushions from the box-office, and arranged them on the floor of the lowest gallery between the front bench and the low wooden partition that kept the groundlings out. Sleep did not come easily, however. She kept thinking back to Betsy's words. Philip was determined to go to the fair and, lo and behold, the rehearsals were cancelled. What was more, the most sorely defamed of the players was the man who had been set to watch over Philip. And who but the players knew where he had slept last night?

No, that couldn't be right. How had Philip managed to sneak out of the house and back under Master Parrish's nose? And then there were the prints of hooves and booted feet. It had to be coincidence. Unless... Philip had money. Quite a lot of money. Enough to bribe someone to post a libel? Perhaps. But then who wrote it? She sighed. Philip might recite his lines with surprising delicacy of feeling for such a villainous ill-headed lout, but he could barely write a letter to his mother, never mind a poem.

She would find an excuse to go back to Thames Street during tomorrow's rehearsals and search the boys' room. At least that way she could eliminate one suspect. She was only glad this watch duty would keep her well out of the apprentices' way for a while. After what had happened at the fair today, she knew the reprisals would not be long in coming.

Mal paused at the foot of the steps. How to politely decline a gift from a prince? He supposed the girls would have to stay the night; he could hardly send them home now. And what if they were not common whores, but the daughters of ambitious noblemen hoping to win the ambassador's favour? It was scarcely good Christian behaviour, but it had been done before; indeed, it was said that the princes' own grandmother, Queen Anne, had been thus put into King Henry's path to snare him.

Nor could he tell these girls the truth. God knows who they might report back to, and Walsingham and the Queen would not thank him for revealing that the Ambassador of Vinland was some kind of eunuch. The skraylings received little enough respect in some quarters; he would not let Kiiren become a laughing stock. He realised with a shock he had become rather fond of the young skrayling during their short acquaintance. There was something familiar about him that Mal could not put his finger on. He felt like they had met before, long ago, impossible as that was.

He took a deep breath and entered the bedchamber. For a moment he thought the girls had somehow slipped past him, or out through the door to the Wakefield Tower. Then he saw them. They had shed their thin garments and were sitting in bed as naked as the day they were born. He swallowed, feeling his own skin burn in response.

"Ladies," he began. "I am afraid His Excellency is indisposed. Our English food does not agree with him and he has a dreadful bellyache and other… illnesses that I could not in all courtesy mention in female company."

The girls sighed with evident relief, though the prettier of the two mustered a pout of disappointment. Mal had a sudden inspiration. Waste not, want not…

"He has therefore asked me to fulfil his duties on his behalf, so as not to insult the prince's generosity."

After a moment's puzzlement the girls' eyes widened with delight. As they scrambled, giggling, across the counterpane he approached the bed, then stood in a haze of blissful anticipation whilst they attacked the buttons and laces holding his clothing together.

CHAPTER XV

Coby woke at first light, and immediately went to check the outside of each of the theatre's doors. Nothing. She went back inside and waited for a good couple of hours, listening to the cows lowing in the fields nearby and the sparrows quarrelling in the hedgerows. The folk of Bankside would not stir for a good while yet. When no hammering came to disturb her watch, she tidied away the cushions, hung up the keys on a hook by the back door, and prepared for another working day.

The actors arrived promptly for their rehearsal at nine o'-clock, the principals looking as though they had slept far worse than Coby. After a few minutes she realised Master Parrish was not amongst them.

"Hiding his face in shame," Eaton muttered. "Naismith's got one of the hirelings to take his part for the nonce."

In the wake of the libellous notice, Suffolk's Men were more nervous than usual. Philip, who had been given the lead role as the eponymous Queen of Faerieland, kept forgetting his lines, and Coby had to be drafted in as prompt after Master Eaton had a blazing row with the company's book-holder. She was not at all happy with the arrangement, but since Master

Dunfell had taken over most of the backstage work, she had no excuse that she was needed elsewhere.

She took some small comfort in the fact that Dunfell did not seem to be happy with his new duties either. Unaccustomed to the ups and downs of theatre life, he treated every little set-back as a catastrophe.

"I must say I am very disappointed by Parrish's abandonment of his role," he said to Master Naismith during a break in rehearsals.

"I am sure he has not abandoned it," the actor-manager replied in his most conciliatory tones. "Our Angel lives for the stage, does he not, Coby?"

"Aye, sir." She did not add that there were other stages in London, less plagued by troublemakers. The last thing they needed right now was for Master Parrish to leave them for a rival company.

"If Parrish does not return tomorrow, I shall have to inform my lord Suffolk," Dunfell said.

"There will be no need for that, Master Dunfell, I assure you," Naismith said. "I will impress upon him the importance of his role." He gestured towards the stage. "But apart from that small interruption, everything goes very well. Very well indeed."

"Well?" Dunfell sniffed. "I would not say so. Scarcely a single speech rendered without stumbling. My lord wishes – nay, demands – they be word-perfect."

"Oh, they will be, sir," Coby said. "Once they are in front of an audience, they lose themselves in the playing and the words flow like water."

"They had better do. His Grace is most anxious that your company be ready in time, and trusts he will not have cause to regret his patronage."

"I will speak to Master Parrish," she told her wan-faced master. "I might be able to talk some sense into him."

It was the perfect excuse to go back to Thames Street whilst Philip was busy here at the theatre. Handing the playbook to a glowering Dunfell, she left before Naismith could stop her.

Ned laid down his pen and flexed his cramped hand a few times. He glanced over the contract, checking he had included all the standard clauses the lawyer had requested, then put it aside. A moment later he heard his mother's slow, uneven tread on the floor below.

"Some gentlemen to see you, son," she called up. "Masters Kemp and Armitage."

Ned frowned. He didn't have any legal contacts of that name. Must be someone new to the Inns of Court. "Show them up, Mam."

He scooped the papers back into their satchel, made sure the ink on the contract was dry, and put it away with the rest. Getting to his feet, he brushed himself down and prepared to greet his guests. When the door opened, the words of welcome shrivelled on his tongue and it was all he could do to remain calm. Standing behind his mother were two all-too-familiar figures.

"Master Faulkner, how good of you to see us." Weasel Face stepped into the attic room, smiling benignly. He was dressed in lawyer's robes and carried a leather document wallet, all very respectable-looking. "My name is Samuel Kemp, and this is my client, Tom Armitage."

Ned waited until his mother had left the room before speaking.

"What are you doing here? I tell you what you want to know, and you stay away from my house. That's the deal."

"Deal's changed," Kemp replied. "We need you to do a little job for us."

"What sort of job? If it's paperwork you want, fine, but anything else–"

Kemp glanced meaningfully at the door. "You're not in a position to argue, Faulkner."

"All right." Ned sagged onto the stool. "What do you want me to do?"

"You told us Catlyn has a twin brother, locked up in Bedlam." Kemp began pacing back and forth with his hands behind his back, for all the world like a lawyer in a courtroom.

"Yes, that's right."

"You met him?"

"Once or twice."

"Is he dangerous?"

"Sandy? No. He wanders in his wits a lot of the time, and some days he doesn't say a word, but dangerous..." He shook his head.

"Would he recognise you if you visited him without Catlyn?"

"I don't know. Possibly."

"You say his wits wander. Is he slow? Can he learn?"

"Why do you need to know?" Ned asked. "What's going on?"

"Master Kemp is asking the questions," Armitage growled, looming over him.

"So, can he learn?" Kemp asked.

Ned sighed. "When he's in his right mind, he is sharper than any man I know. Reads Latin and Greek, and is learned beyond my wit to tell of."

Kemp seemed pleased with this information, though for the life of him Ned couldn't work out why.

"How often does Catlyn visit him?" Kemp asked.

"I don't know. Most Sundays, when he's in London."

"What about during the week?"

"Not that I know of. If he's working, he's rarely free to visit, and if he's not, then he usually hasn't got enough money to bribe the porter."

"Perfect," Kemp said to Armitage with an unpleasant smile. "We do it Monday, it'll be days before anyone notices."

"Do what Monday?" Ned asked.

"All in good time, Master Faulkner, all in good time." Kemp patted him on the shoulder. "We'll see you outside Bishopsgate at ten o'clock on Monday morning. In the meantime, I do indeed have a bit of paperwork for you."

"Oh?"

"Catlyn lived here for a while, right?"

"Yes."

"So, perhaps he left something, some letter or the like, with his signature on it."

"No, nothing." He had expected something like this when Kemp first latched on to him, and had destroyed what few papers Mal had left behind.

"Pity," said Kemp. "Just make it look good, then."

He handed Ned a sheet of paper and a large, official-looking seal. The document was a draft copy of a power of attorney; the name at the top read "Maliverny Catlyn Esq., of Rushdale in the county of Derbyshire".

"I think you know what to do with those," Kemp said softly. "See you Monday."

The front door of the Naismiths' house was locked, so Coby went round to the back. A clattering and reedy singing from the scullery told her Betsy was busy with the laundry. Perfect. Mistress Naismith was probably at the market or visiting friends, so she had the house to herself.

She let herself in and walked through the kitchen and upstairs to the apprentices" room. The spartan bedchamber held a plain bedstead, a washstand and a clothes chest cracked and stained with age. She rummaged in the chest amongst the tangle of clean and dirty linens, but found only the usual scant possessions of a boy: a comb with several teeth missing, a cup-and-ball, a set of skittles. There was nothing under the mattress either, apart from dust and an odd sock. What Philip did not know, however, was that this room had been hers, briefly, after Master Naismith had first brought her to London. If he had explored it thoroughly since then, he would have found her old hiding place.

She moved the washstand to one side and levered up the short piece of floorboard with her knife. Reaching down into the dusty depths her fingers brushed against something smooth and cold. A leather pouch. She took it out and tipped the contents into her lap.

The gold and jewels blazed like beacons in the gloom. A handful of angels and half-angels, mixed with gold chains, finger rings and the rope of pearls Philip had boasted of pawning. Had he taken the hint and redeemed them? Still, by themselves these treasures were useless to her. Everyone knew that boy players received gifts from their admirers, and the canny ones like Gabriel Parrish saved them up for the day when their admirers sought newer, younger idols.

She reached inside the hiding-place again, but found nothing. Either Philip was cleverer than she thought, or he was not behind this wicked scheme. She put the pouch back and returned the room to the way she had found it. She was just about to leave when she heard noises coming from upstairs. Not the room above, which was Betsy's. That only left her own room and the costume store. Heart in mouth, she padded up the stairs.

As she neared the top she heard someone cry out, a man's voice. In her own room. She crept up the last few steps and turned right onto the landing. The only sound from the room up ahead was a fast rhythmic creaking. She tiptoed to the door and pressed her ear to the worn planks.

The cry came again and this time there were words, in a voice she recognised. Ned Faulkner.

"Oh God… Oh God… I die, I di– Aaaahhh!"

Blood rushed to her cheeks and her heart stilled its clamour. Ned Faulkner. Gabriel Parrish. They were fornicating like the sinners of Sodom, in her own bed no less, and blaspheming as they did so. She leant back against the wall and drew a deep breath, then another. Reaching out to her left she pounded on the door with the side of her fist.

"Master Parrish?"

There was a scuffling noise from within, and muttered curses. Coby recited the Lord's Prayer under her breath, then knocked again.

"Master Parrish!"

Silence. Try once more.

She had just got to the part about forgiving trespasses, when the door opened a crack. Parrish stepped out onto the landing clad in shirt and hose, his feet bare. His pale hair was disordered and limp with sweat, and his features were as flushed as her own, though not, she feared, with shame.

"Hendricks? What are you doing here?"

"What are *you* doing here?" she countered. "We have rehearsals today."

Parrish made a derisive noise.

"Please, sir?" She tried a different tack. "Philip is still forgetting his lines, and now he reckons his voice might be breaking."

"And how am I to help with that?" He lowered his voice. "I want nothing to do with this play. Not any more."

Coby sighed. This was all she needed.

"How could you?" she muttered, jerking her head towards the door. "In my bed."

He shrugged. "Ned was… persistent, and we could hardly use the boys' room, or anywhere else for that matter. You did take pains to point out that this door has a bolt on it."

She pushed past him, unwilling to acknowledge he was right. If Betsy had found… evidence in Philip's bed, it would go ill for Parrish.

The air was heavy with the smell of violets and fresh sweat. Memories of another man's scent, the warmth of his breath on her neck as they grappled in combat, rose unbidden. How was that any different from this? the voice of temptation asked. It just is, she replied.

She shook off the troublesome thoughts and forced herself to return to the matter at hand. Parrish was making a show of straightening the bedding, but since Faulkner was still sprawled across half of it with only a corner of the sheet to hide his modesty, there seemed little point.

"Hullo, Hendricks," Faulkner said, grinning. "What brings you here?"

"Master Parrish is supposed to be at rehearsals," she replied.

"So you're Naismith's retriever now, as well as his mastiff?" He exchanged knowing glances with Parrish. "Methinks he would make a better spaniel, eh, Gabe?"

"Oh, he's that already." Parrish gave her a wink.

"Alas, my horn is winded," Faulkner sighed. "The hunt is over, and the quarry brought to its fall."

Coby ignored him. "Sir, we really do need you at the theatre. Everyone's so upset–"

Parrish's eyes flicked towards his lover, and Coby realised he hadn't told Faulkner about the poem yet.

"They're always like this before a new play," he said, a little too loudly. "They can live without me for one afternoon."

"As long as it is only one."

"Why should it not be?" Faulkner levered himself out of bed and slithered naked over to Parrish, slipping his arms around the other man's waist. "Or is there something you're not telling me, love?"

Coby looked away, her cheeks burning. The shamelessness of the man knew no bounds.

"It's nothing," Parrish said. "Just the usual squabbling over who gets the best parts."

"I know which parts I like best," Faulkner purred.

"Stop it, Ned, you're embarrassing yourself as well as Hendricks."

Faulkner flounced back to bed and wrapped himself in a sheet, muttering.

"Don't mind him," Parrish told Coby. "He's been in a queer humour all morning."

She made no comment. As far as she could see, Faulkner was his usual self: lewd, discourteous and nasty.

"So, how are the rehearsals going?" Parrish asked her, leaning on the bedpost. "Is Pip's voice really breaking?"

"I don't think so. It's just nerves, or a summer chill."

"Naismith should get him some physic from the skrayling apothecary in that case."

"They would be happier if you were there, sir. And not just the boys. The company feels incomplete without you."

Parrish bit his lip. He looked somewhat mollified, but she decided this was not the time to take chances.

"You are the very pinnacle of the actor's art, in both male and female roles," she went on, "and thus invaluable to Suffolk's Men."

"Invaluable, eh?" Parrish fingered his lovelock and looked about the room.

"Absolutely."

"All right. Tell Naismith I'll turn up if he pays me the same as Rafe."

"I–" She could hardly say no, but if she agreed, Master Naismith would be furious. For one thing, actors were normally fined for failing to turn up, not rewarded when they deigned to appear. She supposed she could offer to pay the difference out of her own meagre wages. After all, it would only be for a few days. Once the competition was over, Parrish could run off to Vinland for all she cared.

"Ten shillings a week, or naught," Parrish said. "It's his choice."

"Very well," she said. "I'll tell him."

Gabriel shut the door behind Hendricks and sat down on the edge of the bed, staring down at his clasped hands. He sat there for so long, silent and unmoving, Ned began to fear that this was it; he had gone too far this time, offended Gabriel as well as that uptight little Puritan Hendricks, and now he was to be cast off. He slid out of bed and began dressing. Better to leave now of his own accord than be thrown out.

He got as far as buttoning his doublet before Gabriel spoke.

"You trust me, don't you, Ned?"

He paused. This was not how he'd expected it to begin. When he didn't answer, Gabriel looked up, an expression of such despair on his face that Ned went to him and knelt at his feet.

"Of course I do." He took Gabriel's hands in his own.

"I– I know I've done some wicked, sinful things in my life," Gabriel said. "But I never forced myself on anyone, nor forced them–"

"What's this all about, love?" He moved to sit on the bed, and put his arm around Gabriel's waist.

Gabriel proceeded to tell him about the previous day's discovery, though his account was so garbled Ned could scarcely make head or tail of it.

"A libel?" he said at last. "About Suffolk's Men?"

The actor nodded, biting his lip. "Such terrible things it said…"

"Come on, it can't be that bad."

In a small voice Gabriel recited the verse pertaining to himself.

"Lies and conjecture," Ned said, trying to convince himself as much as his lover. "Like you say, you never forced anyone to do anything they didn't want to, did you?"

"No, of course not. But…"

He glanced up at Ned. No words were needed; they both knew to what depths a man could sink, if his very survival was on the line.

"But that was long ago, surely?" Ned replied. "And the rest is but idle gossip, and scarcely a secret."

"It's one thing for tongues to wag," Gabriel said, "no one expects otherwise. But when it is written down, published for all to see, and in a point-by-point list of such slanders–"

"I thought you said it was a poem?"

"Poetry?" Gabriel grimaced. "I would not grace it with such a title. Rank doggerel of the feeblest kind."

"So that's it. You are ashamed to be insulted in bad verse. Now if Marlowe–"

The slap came out of nowhere, leaving Ned's cheek stinging. Suddenly they were both on their feet, eye to eye.

"Leave Kit out of this, you puny upstart scratcher of other men's words!" Gabriel's eyes filled with tears. "You're not fit to speak his name."

Ned said nothing. He knew Marlowe had had many lovers, but had never been able to get Gabriel to admit how he felt about the playwright. Until now.

"I'm sorry, Gabe," he said quietly.

He slipped his arms around his lover's waist and pulled him close. As angels went, Gabriel was a pretty sorry specimen at the moment, dark circles under his eyes and hair unkempt. Ned lifted a hand to smooth those golden locks, but Gabriel shrugged him off.

"Three months," the actor said, pacing the narrow room. "Three months since those bastards murdered him."

"I know."

"Atheist, my arse. They killed him to shut him up. Didn't want him confessing to debauching half the Court. He had nothing to do with that libel, and they knew it."

"You think it's happening again?" Ned asked. "The sedition, the arrests, the…?"

He fell silent, sick to his stomach at the images running through his head: Gabriel tormented, broken… dead.

Gabriel snorted. "Who needs torture when you have a willing informant?"

"What do you mean?"

The actor sank down onto the bed again, hands clasped before him.

"If the Privy Council find out, they will question everyone here. Including Philip."

"So?"

"What if he lies? What if he tells them I… that I…"

"He wouldn't."

"You don't know him." Gabriel shook his head. "I thought I was doing the right thing, hauling him out of that stew and knocking some sense into him, but you should have seen the look in his eyes. He'd denounce me in a heartbeat, and probably accuse young Hendricks of being complicit in the crime."

"You're serious, aren't you?"

Gabriel nodded.

"How will anyone find out?" Ned asked. "Would Philip go to the city fathers himself?"

"We haven't told the boys why the rehearsal was cancelled, and Naismith burned the cursed thing when we were done with it. I think we are safe for now, unless the villain posts a copy somewhere else. In any case, perhaps we are not his only target. These things seldom appear alone, but spring up in clumps like toadstools on a cowpat."

Ned closed his eyes, trying to shut out the knowledge that Gabriel was right. Someone was targeting the skraylings and anyone connected with them, and Ned would bet his life it was the innocents who would suffer. The villains doing the dirty work, and their masters pulling the strings, would get off scot-free as usual.

He should tell Gabriel about Kemp, warn him of the real dangers facing him – No. Let him calm down a little before plying him with more bad news. He would be safe enough here for a couple of hours.

"I have to go," he said, clapping Gabriel on the shoulder. "And I'm not sure when I'll be able to come back."

"What is it? Where are you going?"

"There's something I have to do, and it's best you know nothing about it."

The actor caught hold of him by both arms.

"Can't it wait a while?" Gabriel gazed down at him with red-rimmed eyes. "Please, Ned."

He sighed. "All right. A few more hours can't hurt. I'll stay here until supper, on one condition."

"Anything." Gabriel smiled, his face lighting up with a hint of his old wickedness.

"Tomorrow you go to rehearsals," Ned told him, trying to sound masterful. "The show must go on, remember?"

"I promise," Gabriel murmured, and pulled him down onto the bed.

CHAPTER XVI

Mal woke just before dawn to find the girls preparing to leave. He tried to persuade them to stay a little while longer, but they shook their heads and continued dressing. They had not spoken a word since they arrived.

When they had gone Mal rose and dressed, too alert now to sleep longer. The truckle bed was empty, and for a horrible moment he feared this had all been a clever ruse to distract him and abduct the ambassador. He wrenched open the door and leapt down the stairs into the parlour. Running into the side-chamber he pulled the bed-curtains aside – and found Kiiren curled up in the centre of the bed like a cat, fast asleep.

With a smile Mal let the curtain fall. This was the perfect opportunity to re-examine some of the gifts for signs of secret correspondence. He picked out three books from the cabinet and carried them through into the bedchamber. The lamps had all gone dark and he had no idea how to relight them, so he found a candle and lit it with his own tinderbox.

Without a key there was little hope of even recognising one of the more subtle ciphers, so he contented himself with skimming the pages for passages containing numbers, incongruous phrases or illustrations containing odd symbols. Nothing jumped out at him, and in the end he returned the books to the cabinet, frustrated. If someone was communicating directly with the ambassador, they were using means beyond his skill to uncover.

Eventually servants arrived with hot water and breakfast, and Mal vacated the bedchamber so the ambassador could wash and dress in private. Snatching up a hunk of bread, he wandered out into the ward. The rising sun was already warm, but leaden clouds massed on the horizon. He climbed to the wall-walk and leant on the parapet, watching Southwark stir to wakefulness.

The sound of approaching footsteps woke him from his reverie, and he looked round.

"Shirking your duties already, Catlyn?" Monkton said. "I should report this to Leland."

"Can't a man break his fast in peace?" Mal threw the heel of bread into the river below. With a shrill cry a seagull folded its wings and plunged after it, followed by several of its fellows. "Where's the ambassador going today, anyway?"

"Bedlam."

"Bedlam?" Mal tried to keep the panic out of his voice. "Why?" Monkton shrugged. "Why not?"

"Where is Leland?" Mal pushed past him, heading down the steps towards the inner ward and the lieutenant's lodgings.

"He's gone to inspect the fort at Tilbury," Monkton called after him. "Won't be back until after noon."

Mal skidded to a halt, turned, and ran back along the outer ward. If Kiiren went to the hospital, he might see Sandy, and surely even a skrayling could not miss the resemblance. His other brother's gambling debts were shameful enough, but insanity in the family... There had to be a way to stop this.

The ambassador's coach was stopped outside St Thomas's Tower, with the mounted skrayling guard lined up behind it, and Kiiren was already climbing in. Mal ran up to the driver.

"There's been a change of itinerary." A plan was starting to form in his mind. Yes, that would do it. "Rumours of plague at the hospital. It's not safe for our guests."

The coachman made the sign of the cross. "Wild horses wouldn't drag me there, sir, not if there's plague about. Where to, then?"

"Bartholomew Fair," Mal said, climbing up beside him. "Where else?"

Today being the day after St Bartholomew's, the fair was still in full swing. By the time the coach reached Newgate Market, near the western end of Cheapside, the traffic was so thick they could make no headway at all.

"Best walk from here, good sirs," the coachman yelled down. Kiiren leaned out of the coach window and shouted some instructions to the skrayling guards. Eight of them dismounted, leaving the remaining four to look after the horses. The guards gathered around the coach door and then moved outwards to form a clear space in which the ambassador could safely disembark. The skrayling party was now causing an even bigger obstruction as fairgoers stopped to watch this latest diversion.

After a moment's hesitation Mal jumped down from the driver's seat. He pushed his way through the crowds, scanning every face for any hint of malice towards the skraylings or, worse still, guarded neutrality. He saw nothing to arouse his suspicions, only open curiosity and the natural impatience of people whose holiday was not starting as quickly as they wished. Even so, he remained on alert. After Wednesday's attack he was taking no chances.

At last the guard was formed up in a U-shape around Kiiren, with Mal at the front to close the square, and they moved off. He felt uncomfortably conspicuous, the object of so many stares that, in truth, probably slid straight past him to the peculiar party trailing in his wake. He led the skraylings through Newgate, the massive gatehouse in the city walls that also served as a prison, and up Giltspur Street towards the fair. The traffic was at its worst here, though no one seemed to want to get too close to a group of fearsome skrayling warriors, so they were able to move comparatively swiftly into Smithfield itself.

The permanent buildings of London gave way to a temporary town of stalls and alleys, punctuated by larger spaces where entertainers tumbled, played instruments or performed tricks – or sometimes attempted all three at once. On a low wooden stage a fire-eater, stripped to the waist and with a belly even bigger than Sideways Jack's, was flourishing a blazing torch. A drum rolled, and the fire-eater thrust the torch into his mouth. His eyes bulged, his scarlet face dripped with sweat, then he removed the extinguished torch from his mouth with a grand gesture and bowed thrice. His audience whooped and cheered. The fire-eater's assistant, a lad as skinny as his master was gross, carried round his drum, which doubled as a collecting bowl. A rain of small coins beat a second drum-roll on its surface.

"It is custom to give money for shows?" Kiiren asked Mal when the noise had died down enough to speak.

"It is how these men earn their living, sir."

Kiiren nodded thoughtfully, then produced a purse from his belt and took out a shilling. Mal dropped the coin onto the drum, reflecting that the sum was nicely calculated to be generous but not ostentatious. The fire-eater's assistant thanked him profusely and bowed towards the ambassador's party, hand on heart.

The skraylings moved on, eager to see all the sights.

"What are they?" Kiiren asked, leaning close to Mal to be heard over the crowd. "They are shape of people, but what is purpose?"

Mal saw he was looking at a stall heaped with Bartholomew Babies, the gingerbread dolls decorated with dried fruit and gold leaf which were bought by the thousand to take home to children and grandchildren. He explained they were for playing with, and for eating.

"Your children eat images of people?" He shook his head. "It is… most strange to us."

"It's traditional," Mal said. He had never thought about it before, but he supposed it might seem odd to a stranger.

Out of loyalty to his own culture rather than any particular desire for gingerbread, he purchased one of the dolls, a fashionably dressed lady about eight inches high, in a gilded ruff and saffron-painted gown with currants dotted over her skirts.

"For your little one, good master?" the stall-holder asked.

"Erm, no," Mal said, though it occurred to him as he handed over his pennies that Sandy would like it.

The man peered around Mal at the skraylings. "If you're looking for their quarter," he said, "it's over that way, at the Cow Lane end."

"Thank you." He ought to have known the skraylings would be here in force, being ever ready with goods and trinkets to sell. He smiled to himself. This plan of his was turning out better and better.

He turned back to the ambassador's party.

"I'm told your people have a number of stalls here; perhaps Your Excellency would like to visit them?"

Kiiren nodded. "It is my thought also. Please, lead on."

Mal headed westwards, hoping the gingerbread-seller had not been wrong. The day was warm and humid after the recent rains – too warm to be traipsing round a crowded fair. He eased a finger under the collar of his doublet and wondered if he dare unbutton it. Leland wasn't here to see him after all, and the skraylings doubtless knew little of English etiquette.

Fortunately, either the directions had been correct or luck was on Mal's side again. The rough rectangular booths of the regular stallholders gave way to circular tents with domed roofs, their sides decorated with the same geometric patterns as the skrayling guards' tunics. Everywhere Mal looked there were tattooed faces, silver-streaked manes and bared fangs. He swallowed hard. Daniel in the lion's den, he told himself. Stay calm. He wondered if this was how the skraylings felt whenever they walked the streets of Southwark.

The crowds thinned out a little as the ambassador's party entered the skrayling quarter. The narrow lanes of the fair were still crowded, but people did not push or jostle as much, and their demeanour was more sober and reserved. Those here on serious business had no wish to offend the foreigners, and those who came to gawp were content to keep their distance.

The skrayling merchants were selling their most popular wares at the fair: tobacco, carved beads and exotic herbal mixtures guaranteed to cure any ill. Here and there a charcoal brazier topped with a heavy clay pot shimmered in the summer heat, giving off an enticing scent. A sudden rattle of explosions from one had Mal reaching for his rapier, until the vendor lifted the lid with a flourish to reveal a pile of fluffy white grains. He offered a dish of them to Mal, who picked up a grain and cautiously put it in his mouth, expecting this new delicacy to be hot and perhaps spicy. It turned out to be chewy and rather bland, not nearly as flavoursome as the scent it gave off when cooking. He politely declined the rest.

He continued to scan the crowd for signs of trouble, though what he expected to see, he was not certain. The skraylings' facial tattoos exaggerated some expressions and concealed others, making their intent difficult to read. Perhaps that was why he felt more at ease with the ambassador than he had expected. Perhaps old wounds were healing at last.

Lost in these thoughts, he suddenly realised Kiiren was addressing him.

"Catlyn-*tuur*, our esteemed Master of Lines wants know if you like have tattoo."

"Ah, well, I don't know..." Mal glanced around. All the skraylings were staring at him, their patterned faces intent.

"It is token of belonging, done to all men of our people," Kiiren added. "Is... traditional."

"In that case, I can hardly refuse." He hesitated. "I don't have to have it on my face, do I, sir?"

Kiiren shook his head and smiled. "That is clan-marking, not for your people."

The "Master of Lines" turned out to be a stocky skrayling with ink-stained fingers and hair more silver than black. Tattoos spread across his cheeks like ripples on water. He looked Mal up and down, his amber eyes expressionless, then took down a booklet which was hanging from the roof-pole and handed it to Mal.

"Do you choose," he growled, and sat down on a stool. He took up a pestle and mortar and began grinding some pigment.

The booklet was a single long strip of paper, folded this way and that like a bellows, and on it were painted dozens of designs for tattoos. None of them were much like the ones on the faces of the skrayling guards: these were simpler, mostly roundels containing stylised animal heads, leaves or flowers. He wondered if they were genuine skrayling designs or just made up to suit English tastes.

Kiiren peered around his shoulder, and shook his head. He said something in Vinlandic to the tattooist, who handed over a sheet of paper and a charcoal pencil. The young skrayling sketched a design: a knot of thorns surrounded by five-petalled flowers.

"You like this?" He looked expectantly at Mal.

"Well, yes, sir." He could not say no, not without offending the most important skrayling in England. "Very well, have him do it now before I change my mind."

"Where you like he?" the tattooist asked.

"Here.' Mal patted his left arm, just below the shoulder. No sense in damaging his sword-arm.

"Do you neked," the skrayling instructed, and gestured to a low stool just inside the tent.

Mal hesitated. He was starting to get the hang of Tradetalk, even without more lessons from young Hendricks, but this wasn't the time for a misunderstanding. He turned to Kiiren. "Did he really say what I thought he said?"

"He ask you bare your arm," Kiiren said. "What did you think he say?"

"It doesn't matter, sir," Mal muttered. The young skrayling might feign innocence, but there was a twinkle in his eye that said he understood more than he liked to let on.

Mal took off his doublet and shirt and sat patiently whilst the tattooist copied Kiiren's design onto his bicep with a brush and ink. Then the old skrayling took up another bowl of pigment, and a needle. He grasped Mal's elbow with a rough grey-nailed hand.

"Tell me about the design, if you would, sir," Mal said to Kiiren, partly because he was curious but mostly because he wanted a distraction from the fact that he was now at the mercy of a skrayling armed with a sharp instrument.

"It is ancient Vinlandic symbol, tree of our homeland. There is English tree, much like it, with thorns and small berries."

Mal thought for a moment. Blackthorn was too bushy to be considered a tree. "Hawthorn? The leaves are shaped like a hand, and the berries are –" he was about to say "red", but remembered what Hendricks had told him "– about so big." He measured the small size of the haws with thumb and forefinger.

"Yes. Hawthorn."

"May I ask why you chose it?" He winced as the needle punctured his skin.

Kiiren looked down at him, his expression inscrutable. "It is for remembering."

Mal looked away. The last thing he wanted to do was remember. For a brief moment he was tempted to pull away and refuse the tattoo, but the old skrayling had hold of him too tightly and besides, Leland would probably have Mal dismissed if he offended the ambassador. He forced himself to breathe slowly and deeply. It occurred to him that he was not exactly in a position to do his job right now, and he wondered what he would do if another assassin struck. It seemed unlikely, here in the heart of their own community, but stranger things had happened. Was not Caesar murdered by his best friend, on the steps of the Roman Senate?

Preoccupied by these thoughts and by planning possible strategies, he hardly noticed the rest of the tattooing process. The next thing he was aware of, it was all over and the Master of Lines was bandaging his arm with a piece of snowy linen. Through Kiiren the old skrayling instructed him to keep it covered until morning and to keep it clean, though his expression suggested he had a low opinion of English cleanliness. He also gave Mal a pot of evil-smelling grey salve, to be used twice a day. Mal put his clothes back on, wincing as his sleeve rubbed against the bandage. "How much do I owe him?"

"For you, is gift," Kiiren replied.

"Thank you," Mal said, wondering if this put him in the skraylings' debt, and if so, what would be expected of him in return. Unlike the earring, he could not give this gift back.

He looked up at the sky. The sun was high overhead, silvering the leading edge of an enormous grey cloud that had blown in from the west.

"We should be getting back to the Tower, sir," he said. "Sir James will be expecting you for dinner."

"You took him where?"

Leland was scarlet with rage, pacing up and down in front of the fireplace like a lion in the menagerie. The parlour, now emptied of dinner guests, suddenly felt cramped to Mal, as though the panelled walls were closing in.

"Bartholomew Fair, sir," Mal said.

"Bartholomew Fair. Were you *trying* to get him killed?"

"No, sir, of course not."

"Yet you took the Ambassador of Vinland to the most crowded, filthy place in London, to be jostled by pickpockets and drunkards, gawped at by bawds and, and–" Leland broke off, almost apoplectic with fury. He took a deep breath. "Why did you not take them to Bethlem as had been arranged?"

"I thought it an unfit diversion for a gentleman, even a skrayling one," Mal said truthfully.

"You thought? You are not paid to think." Leland stopped in front of him. "You are paid to keep your eyes open and your sword at the ready."

"Yes, sir."

"What the Queen will say when she hears of this, I dread to think," Leland muttered.

"The Queen, sir?"

The lieutenant caught him a backhanded blow across the face. "Speak when you are spoken to, sirrah!"

Mal kept his eyes on the floor. He could feel his lip swelling already. He heard the door open and booted footsteps approach.

"Ah, captain," Leland said. "Take this man out to the barracks and have him flogged for insubordination."

Mal's head jerked up, but he bit back a retort when he saw

the malicious look on Monkton's face. No sense in goading the man further. He turned to Leland.

"Permission to speak, sir."

Leland inclined his head.

"Sir, am I to be dismissed?"

"If it were in my power, you would be out of this place faster than shit off a shovel." Leland grimaced. "Fortunately for you, the ambassador has the final say in the matter."

Mal was marched across the green to the barracks. Leland had increased the garrison for the duration of the ambassador's visit, and there were around four dozen off-duty militiamen sitting around smoking and playing dice after dinner.

"Right, lads," Monkton barked. "Look sharp! I have here for you a lesson in what happens to men who fail to follow orders."

He held out his hand for Mal's sword, then gestured to him to remove his doublet. Mal complied, trying to ignore the soldiers' catcalls. Monkton led him over to the wall, where a pair of manacles was fastened at head height. Evidently this was a regular punishment.

"Shirt off as well," Monkton said. "We don't want you dying of a festering cut."

Mal stripped off his shirt, revealing the bandage on his left arm.

"Been in the wars already, have we?" Monkton said with a sneer.

Mal faced the wall and raised his arms, and the manacles were closed around his wrists. He sank his forehead on his hands, bracing himself for the first blow. Monkton exchanged banter with the soldiers, stretching out the moment of anticipation until Mal was almost ready to scream at him to get on with it, for God's sake. Then there was a whistle and snap of leather and sudden sickening pain that drove the breath from his lungs. Again and again the lash fell, until the soldiers' jeers blurred into the sound of blood roaring in his ears.

After a while he was aware of Monkton unlocking the shackles, and surmised his punishment was over. Someone pressed a tankard of ale into his hands. He gulped it down, hoping to dull the pain, and the soldiers laughed. When he had drained the tankard, Monkton thrust Mal's bundled-up garments and his sword into his hands and escorted him back to the tower. Mal stumbled along, his guts a cold knot of shame. He should have let the ambassador go to Bethlem; nothing he might have seen there could have been worse than this humiliation.

Ned trudged along Thames Street in the pouring rain. He wanted to run back to Gabriel and forget all about yesterday's visit from Kemp, but his laggardly conscience had pricked at him all day. With the courage of several pints of beer inside him and Gabriel urging him to get it over with, it had seemed such an easy thing to do. Now, as he neared the Tower, his courage began to desert him.

He emerged into Petty Wales and stared at the massive fortress, grey and forbidding under the lowering rain clouds. In there, men were imprisoned, tortured and executed, or simply left to die. Why, he asked himself for the umpteenth time, had he ever thought this was a good idea?

It was the right thing to do, that was why. Mal would have done this long ago, if their situations had been reversed. He only hoped his friend could protect him, though he knew he did not deserve such consideration.

With feet like lead he followed the path round to the left, through the Bulwark Gate and up to the crenellated gatehouse at the near end of the L-shaped causeway that spanned the moat. Two guards in the familiar livery of scarlet cloaks and dark blue jackets stood in the inadequate shelter of the passage under the gatehouse. Torches in iron cressets hissed as the wind drove veils of rain through the archway. In the flickering light, the entrance to the fortress put Ned in mind of the gates of Hell.

One of the guards stepped to the edge of the passageway, squinting through the rain dripping off the brim of his helmet. He levelled his partisan at Ned and looked him up and down.

"What do you want?"

Ned drew himself up to his full height, aware he must look like a drowned rat, with his hair plastered to his skull and his shoes leaking rainwater.

"I'm here to see the Ambassador of Vinland's bodyguard. M-Maliverny Catlyn."

"Catlyn, you say?"

Ned nodded, looking from one to the other.

"What do you want with him, anyway?" the second guard asked, peering at him suspiciously. "Here, aren't you that little runt we ran into last time we had trouble with Catlyn?"

"Who, me? No, that wasn't me," Ned lied. "Must have been someone else. So, can I see my friend?"

"Wait there."

The guards flipped a coin, and the one who had first pointed his partisan at Ned lost. He set off across the causeway, grumbling at his ill luck.

"Can I at least come in out of the rain?" Ned asked the remaining man.

The guard shrugged and stepped back a couple of yards to let him under the archway. Ned was already as wet as he was going to get, but at least he would be out of the wind. He stared at the worn stonework and tried not to shiver too obviously.

As they waited in silence, Ned ran the previous conversation back through his mind. What was it the other guard had said? Last time we had trouble with Catlyn… He blanched. If Mal was in trouble again, he had to get out of here. He began to back away.

"Oi, where are you going?" the guard shouted.

He blocked Ned's escape with his polearm and glared at him in what Ned assumed was meant to be a menacing manner. It might have worked better if the man had not possessed a nose like an over-ripe strawberry and the flaccid build of a habitual drunk.

"Having second thoughts, are we? Makes me wonder what's so important you come all the way here in the pouring rain."

Ned slumped against the wall in defeat. He just wanted this to be over with.

After what felt like an age, the other guard reappeared, crossing the causeway at a brisk walk. Mal was not with him. Ned resigned himself to having to go further into the fortress. This plan was getting worse by the minute.

The guards conferred in low tones, and the red-nosed man laughed.

"It's more than whips he'll get where he's gone, poor sod," he said to his companion, just loud enough for Ned to hear. "I bet you a pint to a bucket of piss he'll not be able to sit down till Michaelmas."

"What's going on?" Ned asked, dread curdling in his stomach.

"You're too late," the other guard told him. "He ain't here."

"What do you mean, not here?"

"He's gone. Skraylings up and left this afternoon, and took Catlyn with them."

"Left? Where did they go?" He had sudden visions of Mal being shipped off to Sark, or even the New World.

"How should I know? Now clear off, before the curfew bell rings and we have to arrest you."

Ned turned and set off for home. There was nothing for it; he would have to go along with Kemp's plan, and God have mercy on his soul.

CHAPTER XVII

Coby stood on the balcony, watching the rain pour down into the theatre yard. The actors had finally gone home to their suppers after spending the entire day in rehearsal. They seldom had the luxury of such lengthy preparation, but with the contest only days away, Master Naismith was doing everything in his power to ensure they were as ready as their patron desired. The actors seemed to have forgotten the business with the poem already, and even Master Parrish was back with the company as if nothing had happened. Master Naismith was not so complacent, however, and had bade Coby stand watch again, even though it was the Lord's Day tomorrow.

Well, tonight she was not going to sleep in the open gallery and get rained on, that was for certain. Not when there was a snug box-office to sleep in, and no one around to gainsay her. Why carry the cushions down to the gallery, when she could make her bed right here?

She went inside, shrugged out of her doublet and shoes then, after a moment's indecision, pulled up her shirt and began unlacing her corset. Though she had grown accustomed to wearing the constricting garment, it still itched on warm, humid nights like this, and she was glad to put it aside for a while. After all, it wasn't as if anyone was here to see her. Comfortable at last, she tucked her shirt back into her hose, stretched out on the cushions and closed her eyes.

Their departure from the Tower was heralded by a low rumble of thunder, and moments later the heavens opened. The little gull-headed boat that ferried them across the river offered no cover from the weather, and Mal found himself wishing for one of the royal barges with its canopied seats. The guards seemed untroubled by it, however, and bent their backs to the oars without complaint.

By the time they reached the south bank of the Thames he was soaked to the skin and shivering in delayed reaction to the flogging. One of the guards pounded on the gates with his staff until they opened, and the ambassador's party splashed across the little drawbridge. Walkways made of wooden planks raised a few inches above the ground criss-crossed the encampment, bridging runnels that guided the rainwater back into the moat. Apart from themselves and the gate guards, the camp could have been deserted, all its inhabitants having apparently retreated to the shelter of their tents.

Mal assumed he and Kiiren were being led straight to the enormous pavilion that rose in the centre of the encampment like a mother hen over her brood of chicks. Instead the guards turned aside at the last moment and escorted them to an otherwise unremarkable-looking tent. In size it was not unlike the ordinary soldiers' campaign tents he was accustomed to, about a dozen feet across and slightly higher than a tall man, though it was round instead of square. Next to the tent stood a large shrub of a kind Mal had never seen before, with enormous drooping oval leaves that were just beginning to turn yellow. Somewhere nearby a slow, mournful melody was being picked out on a stringed instrument. He felt like he had crossed the seas to the New World and entered the skraylings' own country.

One of the guards pointed at Mal's feet. "No shoe," he said.

When Mal had removed his boots, the guard held up the tent flap and gestured for them to go inside. Mal made the sign of the cross and whispered a prayer, then ducked through the entrance in his stockinged feet.

The tent was lit with the same lightwater lamps that the skraylings had used at the Tower. Panels of azure-blue silk hung from the sides of the tent, catching the lamplight on their glossy weave. Each panel had a different design on it, though what they were intended to represent, Mal could not make out. On one side of the tent stood a low table and some kind of enclosed brazier which gave out a welcome heat.

The tent smelt strongly of tobacco smoke, mingled with the dry musk of skrayling and another scent Mal could not place. He was uncomfortably aware of the fact he was dripping rainwater onto the expensive Turkish rugs that covered the floor. Kiiren began stripping off his wet clothes and was soon down to singlet and breeches.

"Please to take off your shirt and sit."

Mal peeled off the wet, blood-stained garment he had hastily donned before their departure from the Tower, wincing as the fabric parted company with the weals on his back.

"I am sorry you could not be tended more soon," Kiiren said, taking a bundle of linens from a skrayling who had appeared at the tent flap.

"It's nothing," Mal muttered. He was just glad to be out of that place.

The light shifted as Kiiren knelt down behind him and raised a lamp to examine his wounds. The skrayling's hissing intake of breath sent waves of shame through him. Mal had witnessed plenty of men flogged during his time in the army, but he guessed Kiiren had never seen anything like it before. He longed to make some jest, break the tension, but the words stuck in his throat.

Something ice cold touched Mal's back and it was all he could do not to cry out.

"What is that?" he gasped. A sharp woody scent began to fill the tent.

"*Ashaarr.*"

Mal wondered if that was the name of the stuff in the bottle, or if Kiiren were trying to hush him. He braced himself as he heard the slosh of liquid again. But where the stuff had first touched his shoulder the pain was already fading, to be replaced by a pleasant warmth. He breathed shallowly, trying not to flinch away every time Kiiren dabbed the searing fluid on another cut. Eventually all his wounds were salved, and Kiiren corked the bottle and put it aside.

"We must cover these," Kiiren said. "You English are so dirty."

He began winding a smooth bandage around Mal's torso.

"Are you angry with me, sir?" Mal asked, trying to take his mind off Kiiren's closeness. The skrayling's breath was hot on his raw back.

Kiiren sighed. "Not with you. With – Leland, and *Ingilandeth*. Unkindness to one of our clan is unkindness to all."

"But–" Mal twisted round. "I am not of your clan."

"You are one of us." Kiiren reached out and traced the line of Mal's cheek, his eyes never leaving Mal's own. "You are touched by Erishen, I can feel it."

Mal willed himself not to pull away. "Is this... *Erishen* your god?"

"He is light of my soul," Kiiren whispered.

Mal swallowed.

"Whatever you think, sir," he said, as politely as he could, "you are wrong."

Kiiren lowered his hand. "I fear so." He picked up a heap of folded cream wool and held it out towards Mal. "Please to put this on."

Mal took the robe gratefully and, turning his back on the skrayling, stripped off his wet hose and stockings. The garment was very like the one the ambassador wore in the evenings, after he changed out of his ceremonial robes. Mal felt a little self-conscious wearing it, but at least it was dry and warm.

The tent flap opened again. One of the skrayling guards who had accompanied them back from the Tower crouched there, his eyes lowered in respect. He spoke briefly to Kiiren, who beckoned to Mal.

"Come, it is time."

He handed Mal a pair of sheepskin moccasins, then ducked through the tent flap.

"Time for what?" Mal asked, hopping after him with one moccasin on.

Four of the guards waited outside, this time with a canopy to hold off the rain, and Mal and Kiiren were escorted to the central pavilion. Inside, it was packed with skrayling men of all ages, from youths of perhaps fourteen or so to silver-haired elders. The central area was empty; around its periphery, tall wooden standards stood at intervals, hung with three or four of the coloured lamps, whose light turned the skraylings' tattooed features into tiger masks of black and silver.

"Wait here, Catlyn-*tuur*," Kiiren said as they reached the inner edge of the ring of skraylings.

"What's going on?" Mal asked.

"Elders of clans wish to know what happen today, and why we are here," Kiiren whispered.

The young ambassador walked into the centre of the open space, and the crowd fell silent. He began his account of events, pointing northwards at intervals. Mal caught the occasional name here and there, mainly "Leland". Judge Scarheart, Chief Merchant Greatyard and the other elders seated in the front row of the crowd asked many questions. Kiiren's account went on for a lot longer than seemed necessary to describe such a simple incident.

At first Mal could not make head nor tail of what was going on, then he realised it was not so different from the debates at university. If one ignored the words and watched the expressions and gestures, it was possible to make out the general intent, if not the detail.

Kiiren appeared to be on the defensive, as if he were trying to justify his decision to leave, but without a sound argument to back it up. Mal began to think he had been wrong about Kiiren's status; throughout the debate, participants referred back to the judge, as if seeking his expert opinion on a point of contention.

Eventually Kiiren came over to where Mal was sitting and held out his hand, gesturing for him to rise. Mal followed him into the centre of the circle, wondering what this was all about. Suddenly the ambassador seized the shoulder of his robe and pulled it down. Mal glanced at him in alarm.

"Do you neked," Kiiren murmured in Tradetalk, smiling.

Mal let the robe fall to the ground, so that he was wearing nothing but his linen drawers. Kiiren untied the knots holding the bandages in place. As the strips of linen fell around Mal's feet, those of the crowd sitting behind Mal gasped. The ambassador put a hand on Mal's shoulder and turned him gently so all could see.

"Was that necessary?" Mal muttered to Kiiren, clutching the robe to his chest, as they returned to the front row of the crowd and sat down.

Kiiren smiled apologetically. "Our people must see what is done, so they understand why we leave."

Judge Scarheart now took the floor. This time Mal did not even try to follow the discussion. He sat, eyes downcast, whilst Kiiren rewound his bandages, trying to ignore all the stares the two of them were attracting. He felt totally out of his depth, alone amongst a people whose customs made no sense to him. Men who took on the role of women; an ambassador who was at once revered by his people and yet as humble as Our Lord... He caught himself at this blasphemous thought. He must not allow himself to be led into heresy and damnation by a skrayling, no matter how charming.

The skraylings fell silent, then one by one they began to remove their necklaces, placing them on the ground at their feet. Mal glanced at Kiiren, but the young ambassador was too intent on his own part in this apparent ceremony. Once the crowd was still again, Judge Scarheart began chanting, low and soft. Others took up the song and soon the tent reverberated with their joined voices, rising and falling like waves on the shore. Memory stirred, and a terrible loneliness swept over him. Without thinking he reached up and removed the earring, placed it in his lap...

He was there, under the strange starless sky, but he could no longer see the moor with its distant lights. A wall of mist surrounded him, not quite close enough to touch. Shapes swirled within it, and he thought he heard voices, but when he turned to locate the speaker he found only an echoing silence, like the memory of words just spoken.

He ought to be afraid, the creatures were still out there, he was sure of it, but somehow he knew the mist protected him. Together we are strong, the mist voices seemed to say.

"Who are you?" he shouted, but no sound reached his ears.

A brighter patch of mist weaved back and forth in front of him, as if examining him. He was reminded of the blinding light from before, only this time it was veiled, a pearly glow like the moon behind clouds. The light retreated, and he plunged into the mist after it. The light flared around him, engulfing him, drowning him in shining water like the skraylings' lamps. He cried out – and woke with a start in the musty dimness of the little tent.

Kiiren was kneeling by the brazier, watching him intently.

"Wha' happened?" Mal mumbled, sitting up and rubbing his face. He felt as if he'd woken from a long fever.

"You took this off," Kiiren said, handing him the earring. "That was not wise." The force of the reprimand was rather spoilt by the gleam of delight in his eyes.

Mal fastened the heavy pendant in place. "I don't understand."

"You will," Kiiren said. "Now, you must sleep."

He placed a hand on Mal's shoulder as if to urge him to lie down. Mal's breath hissed between his teeth as his raw back protested at the touch.

"Please forgive," Kiiren said, inclining his head to the side in obeisance. "I did not think – I mean no hurt."

"It's nothing." Once again he was taken aback by the young skrayling's peculiar mix of friendliness and humility.

When Kiiren had gone he stripped off the robe and lay face down on the pallet, covering his lower half with a blanket for modesty's sake. There were no pillows, so he pulled a cushion over and rested his head on it. He closed his eyes. His mind still buzzed with the memory of the dream. If it had been a dream. Though it must be well past midnight, he did not feel the least bit sleepy. Not sleepy at all…

Coby was woken by sounds from the tiring room below. Footsteps? She groped for the cudgel, her heart pounding. Surely she had locked and barred the doors before coming to bed; at least, she thought she had. No, she was certain of it. How then had someone got in?

The footsteps sounded on the stairs now. She pulled the cloak over her head, hoping not to be noticed in the shadows. If a thief were after something, it was better she spied on him and reported to Master Naismith later. She lay there, hardly daring to breathe. Yellow light, as of a candle or lantern, outlined the door at the far end of the office. The footsteps halted, and the door opened to reveal the face of a devil.

She clapped a hand to her mouth to stifle a scream. The devil advanced into the room, holding the lantern so that its hideous blood-red face was lit from below like the fires of Hell. Its eyes glinted, and the hooked nose cast enormous shadows on the walls and ceiling. Coby moved her hand very slowly to the little wooden cross that hung on a cord around her neck.

The devil went from one chest to the next, unlocking each and examining the contents. At last he found what he wanted. Coby's heart skipped a beat. It was the chest containing the actors' sides. Master Naismith did not trust the hired men with even a fraction of his new play, and insisted that all copies were returned to the chest after each rehearsal. Pieced together, they could be made into a complete manuscript.

"Lodge," she muttered under her breath and got to her feet. The playwright was probably drunk again.

"Who's there?" the man growled.

He set his lantern down on the nearest chest, reached under his cloak and brought out a snaplock pistol. Never take on a man armed with a blade, Master Catlyn had told her. Or a gun, she added mentally. On the other hand, unless she fancied jumping over the balcony, there was nowhere to run from this particular devil.

After a moment she let the cudgel fall. The noise was loud as a pistol shot in the empty theatre, and in the long silence that followed, Coby realised no one would hear them and come to her aid. The intruder apparently came to the same conclusion.

"Make one more move and I shoot." He cocked the pistol with his free hand, then thumbed the flash pan open.

She froze, her heart pounding in her chest. If this was Lodge, he had grown a pair since Coby last saw him. Come to think of it, this man was too tall to be Lodge, and his mask could not quite hide the bald patch gleaming above a circle of mousy brown hair.

"Who are you, and what are you doing here?" she asked.

"That's none of your business, Hendricks."

So, he *was* an acquaintance, just not the one she had supposed. An actor, perhaps, or one of the workmen? His voice was familiar but, distorted as it was by the mask, she could not immediately identify him.

"Open the chest," the intruder said, stepping back slightly and gesturing with the pistol.

She crossed the room slowly, not wanting to come within arm's reach of the man. Most of all she had to keep from getting between him and the lantern, lest the transparency of her shirt betray her. Reaching the chest, she crouched and raised the lid. Neat stacks of pages lay where she had left them earlier that day, bound into sets with string. The handwritten lines seemed to blur before her gaze.

"Now, take out all the sides for *The Queen of Faerieland*."

She had been afraid the masked man intended to burn the contents of the chest, and perhaps the entire theatre, but if he were interested only in the new play, that suggested his motivation was monetary. The question was, what would he do with her once she had done everything he asked?

"If you are going to take these away with you," Coby said, trying to keep her voice steady, "it would be easier if I rolled them up into a document case."

She stood slowly and gestured towards the desk behind them, where there was indeed a cylindrical leather case. As she had hoped, the masked man turned without thinking, and she snatched up a nearby stool and hit him across the back of the head. He went sprawling across the floor, dropping the pistol. Coby stood over him, trembling with relief, but he did not move. She prodded him with the toe of her shoe. Out cold – or dead. Right now she was not sure she cared which.

There was no rope in the box-office, but a foray to the attic produced some offcuts from the fitting of the trapdoor and hoist mechanism. She bound the intruder hand and foot, and only then did she dare roll him over and remove the mask.

It was John Wheeler, the new hireling. Planning to sell them out to the Admiral's Men, no doubt. Well he could await Master Naismith's wrath. Grunting with effort she dragged the unconscious man over to a supporting timber and secured him with a further length of rope. She examined the back of his head, but his skull seemed unbroken and there was only a little bruising where she had hit him. He also had a lump on his forehead where he had hit the floor. At least he was not dead, though this knocking men out was getting to be a bad habit.

She got dressed, feeling vastly safer in the reassuring embrace of canvas and lacings, and settled down with a flagon of small ale to watch over her captive. Much as she wanted to run back to Thames Street and alert Master Naismith, there was nothing for it but to wait here. The wherrymen went home at curfew, and the city gates wouldn't open again until dawn.

The thought came to her that if the villain was the man hired to replace Catchpenny, he might have killed Catchpenny to gain a place in their company. She shivered despite the heat. If she had known she was taking on a murderer, she might have been more cautious, and that in itself could have got her killed. She picked up Wheeler's pistol and examined the intricate mechanism. She didn't know much about guns, but surely a pistol needed to be primed with powder and loaded with shot? This one looked as clean as the day it was made. An empty threat, then; Wheeler had not had any murderous intent this time. That was a relief of sorts. But she had acted on impulse, risking her life for what? A few sheets of paper, and those a mere copy of the original that Master Naismith kept safe at his home. The actor-manager might praise her bravery in capturing their would-be thief, but she did not think Master Catlyn would agree. She sighed, and put the pistol down on the desk.

After about an hour Wheeler regained consciousness and began to struggle against his bonds.

"Wha–? Where am I?" he slurred.

"You don't remember?"

Wheeler shook his head, and winced.

"You're at the Mirror," she told him. "I caught you breaking into the box-office and trying to steal the sides for the new play."

"I – There were rehearsals."

"Yes, all day. Everyone went home for supper this evening."

"I don't remember," he groaned.

"You don't remember going home?"

"No. Where am I?"

Coby sighed. Perhaps she had hit him too hard after all, and knocked his wits awry.

"At the Mirror. Why were you stealing our manuscript?"

He looked up at her with unfocused eyes.

"You're that Dutch boy who works for Naismith. What are you doing in my house, and why am I tied up?"

"You are at the theatre," Coby said through gritted teeth.

"Am I?" He looked around, puzzled. "What am I doing here?"

"That's what we'd all like to know," she sighed.

It was useless; she would not get any sense out of the man tonight. Picking up an armful of cushions she went out onto the balcony and closed the doors behind her. The rain had cleared the sky, and stars twinkled in the cloudless black. She lay down, pulled the cloak over her head to muffle the sound of her captive's shouts for help, and prayed for dawn.

CHAPTER XVIII

Mal woke slowly, stiff with cold. The brazier had gone out in the night, and his back was no longer numb from the skrayling salve. He rolled onto his side. Needles of sunlight pierced the seams of the tent, threading the gloomy space with lines of sparkling dust. The blue silk panels on the tent walls glowed softly.

He rubbed his eyes. Kiiren sat behind the brazier, watching him with those catlike amber eyes. Had he been sitting there all night?

"Good morrow, Catlyn-*tuur*," Kiiren said. "You sleep well?"

"Tolerably," Mal replied, grimacing. He shifted into an upright position. "I have to go to church today. I could be fined if I don't."

"Of course you go," the skrayling replied. "You must spend time with your people."

Mal needed no further prompting; he thanked Kiiren and left for Southwark as soon as his own clothes were returned. His shirt was in a sorry state, so he gladly accepted Kiiren's offer of a plain linen tunic in its place. It felt a little odd, wearing it under his doublet, but hopefully no one would notice.

He attended service at his parish church of St Mary Overie,

hoping to see Ned there, but oddly there was no sign of his friend amongst the congregation. He thought to ask Mistress Faulkner, but she was with a gentleman friend whom Mal had never seen before. Well, good for her; a poor widow deserved companionship in her old age.

After the service he went straight to Bethlem Hospital. Sandy was in much better health than he had been two months ago, though still rather thin and unkempt. As the weather was so hot today, indeed too humid to be cooped up indoors, the non-violent patients had been allowed out into the courtyard, to see the sky and feel the sun on their faces. Sandy, however, remained in his cell.

"I would like the keys to my brother's shackles," Mal told Mistress Cooke.

"Oh, I can't do that, sir. Master Cooke says the bad cases ain't to be let out, no matter what."

"I will take responsibility for my brother."

The matron shook her head, her chins wobbling. "I'm sorry, sir."

"I would reward you for your pains," Mal said, taking out his purse. "Let us say, an extra week's fees?"

The woman's eyes lit up at the gleam of silver.

"Just for an hour, mind," she said, tucking the coins into her soft, freckled bosom. It would be a bold thief who dipped for that.

Mal took Sandy out into the courtyard and sat him on the bench under a great linden tree. His lute was left behind at the Tower, alas, but a few pence procured the loan of a draughts board from the warder.

When Mal returned to the bench, Sandy had something cupped in his hands and was examining it closely.

"What have you there?" Mal asked, sitting down next to his twin.

Sandy held up his hands. Perched on one palm was an enormous hawkmoth with dusky pink-and-black wings. The moth's feathery antennae quivered.

"Very fine. Perhaps you should let it be about its business, though. Whatever that might be."

He set out the board and pieces and let Sandy make the first move.

"They are treating you well?" Mal asked. He prodded a counter forwards.

Sandy shrugged. A lock of dark hair fell over his face, and he pushed it back absentmindedly – a painfully familiar gesture.

"I'm sorry I didn't visit last week," Mal said. "I have a new job, and there was much to do in preparation."

"You didn't come yesterday either," Sandy said, hopping his piece across several squares.

Mal stared at him. "You know about that?"

"I heard the girl telling someone, out in the hall. He sounded angry."

"Probably one of Leland's men." Mal did not voice his real concern, that it could have been another assassin. Had his plan inadvertently thwarted a second attack? "I'm sorry about that. I was supposed to come here with some other people, but I thought they would rather go to the fair instead."

Sandy nodded. "I would rather go to the fair than come here."

"I did bring you something," Mal said. He produced the Bartholomew Baby, retrieved from his knapsack after the hasty retreat from the Tower. It had broken in half and some of the gilt had rubbed off, but Sandy's face lit up when he saw it. Taking it from Mal he glanced around the courtyard, broke off a piece of the lady's gown and stowed the rest of the gingerbread doll inside his shirt.

Mal rubbed his left arm. The tattoo was healing well, thanks to the skrayling's salve, but the morning was already hot and sweat was trickling down inside his tunic sleeve, making the still-tender skin sting like nettle rash.

"Fleas?" Sandy asked, taking a bite of gingerbread.

Mal laughed and shook his head. He took off his doublet, rolled up the tunic sleeve and pulled the bandage away to display the tattoo. "What do you think, Sandy? Sandy!"

His brother had given a strangled cry and turned as stiff as the gingerbread doll, arms and legs rigid and trembling. His eyes rolled back in their sockets and he began to toss his head from side to side, moaning.

"Help! Someone help us!" Mal shouted, taking hold of Sandy's head and trying to get the piece of gingerbread out of his brother's mouth before he choked on it.

One of the warders came running. "Gawd help us, the lad's possessed!" he wailed.

"Don't be an ass." Mal glared at him. "It's just a fever brought on by the sun's heat."

He didn't believe it himself, but it seemed to reassure the warder, at least for the moment.

"Let us get him inside," Mal told him. "Cool shade and a drink will soon bring him to rights."

The warder fetched a stretcher and they carried Sandy, still twitching and moaning, back to the gatehouse and his own bed. Some of the other inmates watched them go, moaning in sympathy. Back indoors the air was humid and pungent, promising little respite for any fever victim, but at least the cell was out of public view.

"Bring wine – the good stuff, mind, none of that vinegary swill," Mal said, pressing a shilling into the warder's sweaty palm. "Now, if you please."

Sandy had stopped moaning but was now muttering to himself in the secret language of their childhood.

ANNE LYLE   245

"Sandy? Sandy, are you all right?" Mal whispered, crouching on the edge of the bed.

His brother opened his eyes and sat up. His pupils were enormous, great pools of darkness that seemed to draw Mal in…

"*Itë omiro*?" Sandy asked. Who are you?

"It's me, Mal. Remember?"

Sandy screamed. Mal threw his arms around him, trying to quiet him before he set off the whole ward. Sandy writhed in his embrace but despite having a madman's desperate strength he was too frail from his long confinement to break free. Mal held him tight until he stopped struggling, then reluctantly snapped the gyves around Sandy's wrists and ankles before he could gain his second wind. Sandy's pupils shrank in an instant, like a door slamming shut, and he slumped back on the bed. Mal stroked the sweat-damp hair from his brother's brow, blinking back tears, then sank to his knees beside the bed and prayed to St Giles, patron of madmen, cripples and those with the falling sickness.

The warder eventually returned with a cup of sweet hippocras, made the sign of the cross at the sight of Sandy, and fled. Mal coaxed a few drops of the wine between his brother's lips.

Sandy gazed up at him with wide eyes. "Mal? What happened?"

"A brief fit, nothing more," Mal said. "We should not have sat out in the sun so long."

Sandy closed his eyes again, and soon his breathing began to slow and his features relaxed in sleep. Mal stayed with him whilst the sun traced its slow path across the floor, alternately pacing the cell with soft tread and kneeling in prayer for his brother's soul.

At last the bells of nearby St Botolph's tolled five, and Mal remembered he had promised to return to the skrayling compound by six. He knocked on the cell door to be let out. The thought of leaving Sandy in this condition and being unable to visit him for a whole week tore at his heart, but what could he do? They would both have to endure the separation as best they could.

When Mal returned to the compound he was shown back to the small tent. Kiiren was seated cross-legged on a large woollen cushion next to the brazier, where a lidded metal jug stood heating. The jug's spout emitted a thin wisp of steam. That smell again: bitter and woody yet strangely pleasant.

"Please, sit," Kiiren said in a low voice.

He took the pot off the fire and whisked the contents, sending up a cloud of steam. Mal breathed it in, and felt his spirits lift a little.

"What happens now?" Mal asked. "This… is not a good start to your stay in London."

"We go back to Tower, perhaps tomorrow."

Tomorrow, the day after, a week from now; Mal didn't care any more. He just wanted to see Sandy again.

"Next Sunday," he said firmly, "I must have time for my own affairs."

"Of course. We honour your customs." Kiiren looked thoughtful. "Day of sun. So many of you humans revere sun in different ways, yes?"

"We do not revere the sun as the pagans of old did," Mal replied, trying to shake off his melancholy. A discussion of history would perhaps take his mind off his troubles. "But we kept their names for the days of the week. You know about the gods of the Greeks and Romans?"

"I speak of humans that live near my homeland."

"I have heard rumours," Mal said. He leant forward, hoping to learn something of use to Walsingham. "Beyond Antilia, a mighty empire rich in gold."

"Always it is gold with humans." Kiiren gave a hissing laugh. "Gold, tears of sun… And yet you Christians still not agree if sun travel round earth, or earth round sun."

They sat in silence for a while, listening to the hiss of steam and the distant strains of Vinlandic music.

"Last night…" Mal began cautiously. "Last night you said it was unwise to take my earring out, but that I would come to understand."

"It was not safe for you to join us." Kiiren lowered his voice. "The others may have set spies amongst the clan. And even if they have not, the elders must not know about you. Not yet. As soon as you came amongst us, I hurried to conceal you. I am sorry if I hurt you, but it was needful to be swift."

Mal felt none the wiser after this "explanation", but he let it pass. Kiiren had just admitted there were factions amongst the skraylings and that they spied on one another, just like the nations of Christendom. That fact alone was a useful titbit to take back to Walsingham. The strange vision of the mists, on the other hand, was not something to reveal to the spymaster, at least not yet. The skraylings had powerful magics, that was clear, but he needed to know more.

Recalling the vision brought another memory to mind: his conversation with Kiiren before the meeting. *Light of my soul*, the ambassador had said. Perhaps it meant something different to skraylings.

"This is something to do with Erishen," Mal whispered.

Kiiren produced a wooden box from which he took two small cups carved from lapis lazuli. Mal stared at them. The skraylings valued the deep blue stone more highly than gold, and these cups comprised enough to buy a fleet's worth of skrayling cargo. Kiiren whisked the contents of the pot again, then poured the foamy brown liquid into the cups.

He passed one to Mal. "What believe your people is happen to them after they die?"

Mal hesitated, wondering what to make of this sudden change of topic. He took a sip of his drink.

"What is this?" he asked, trying not to pull a face.

"We call it *shakholaat*," Kiiren replied. "It is good for weariness, of body and spirit."

Mal took a longer drink. The hot, bitter liquid was definitely an acquired taste. His mouth began to tingle slightly. The stuff must be spiced with the hot pepper the skraylings loved so much.

"Their souls pass on," he said, returning to the question Kiiren had posed, "to whatever destination God deems fit: Heaven, Purgatory, or Hell."

"I hear much talk of Heaven and Hell," Kiiren said, "but what is this... Purgatory?"

"It is a place – some say a great mountain on the other side of the world – where the souls of those who did not turn away from God in life, but who are yet too sinful to enter straight into Heaven, are purged of their sins so they might be fit to enter therein."

Kiiren smiled and nodded politely, but said nothing.

"You do not have similar beliefs?" Mal asked.

"Beliefs, no. There are things we know as fact." He put his cup down, and leant towards Mal, hands clasped in his lap. "We have no stories of afterlife, as you call it, no Heaven or Hell, no Purgatory. When man dies, his spirit is gone. Like candle flame." He made a gesture, touching his fingertips together with his hand pointing upwards, then spreading them suddenly, like a flame dispersing into smoke. "But there are those amongst us whose spirits are strong, and they can be born again and again. If they find mortal shell."

"Pythagoras believed as much, though Christians call it heresy," Mal said, trying to frame his argument in terms that would not offend. "My people are... not tolerant of other faiths."

"And yet there is disagreeing between Christians, is there not? Some follow Great Father in city beyond Inner Sea, and some defy him."

Mal guessed he was referring to the Pope.

"That is true. For fifteen hundred years we were one Christendom; but in the last few generations, everything has changed."

"This does not please you."

Mal couldn't help but glance around the tent, fearful they were somehow being overheard – and not by skraylings. Foolishness. If there was anywhere in London they could speak freely about religious matters without some informant overhearing, it was here.

"My mother was of the Old Faith," he said. "She taught us – she taught *me* to follow the old ways, but it had to be in secret. The Pope – the Great Father of whom you spoke – declared Queen Elizabeth a heretic and urged his followers to kill her. As a loyal Englishman I cannot of course condone this, but anyone of the Old Faith is suspect. I have no choice but to obey the edicts of the Established Church."

"And if Church say we are demons?"

Mal drew a deep breath. "If I may be honest with you, sir, a month ago I would have said they were right."

"And now?"

"Now I am not so sure. You do not seem like demons to me. Of course the theologians would say this is merely a clever deceit of yours, that in hiding your true nature you prove your demoniacal power... but in truth I could never follow such subtle logic. I have not the wits for it."

Kiiren smiled. "I am glad you not think us demons. We are friends, yes?"

Mal nodded cautiously. He could not help but like the young skrayling, even if half the time Kiiren's conversation made no sense. Perhaps in time he could tease out more of the skraylings' secrets, but only if he retained the trust of his one ally amongst them.

He raised his cup in salute.

"Friends, yes."

As soon as the city gates were open, Coby ran back to Thames Street and told Master Naismith about the intruder. Then she went to St Augustine's church as was her custom, and afterwards ate dinner with the Kuypers, one of the Dutch families of her acquaintance. As Master Kuyper was wont to remind her, the Lord's Day was for contemplation, not worldly matters. It was a relief to forget about the theatre for a while and enjoy the simple company of friends.

She knew she could not long avoid the events of last night, however, and late afternoon found her returning to Thames Street on reluctant feet. Though she was glad to have prevented the theft, she felt guilty about injuring Wheeler; men did not always recover from such hurts.

Master Naismith called her into his study as soon as she got back. He was sitting by the fire, reading by the light of a single candle. The shadows carved deep lines in the old man's features, and for a moment Coby recalled the lamplit visage of the masked intruder.

Naismith looked up.

"I wanted to thank you again, lad, for catching that viper in our bosom," he said. "We are well rid of the cur."

"What has been done with him, sir?"

"He has been handed over to the sergeant of the watch and thrown in the Compter to await trial. Perhaps," he added with a humourless smile, "they should have put him in the Clink, where his erstwhile master could watch over him."

"Wheeler was working for Henslowe?"

"He admitted as much, when pressed."

"Then he has regained his wits," she said with relief.

"Such of them as he ever possessed. He still claims to have no memory of yesterday afternoon or evening, but he did recall Henslowe offering to pay five pounds to anyone who could obtain the manuscript."

"Five pounds?" That was barely half what Lodge had been paid for the play.

"It's a lot of money to a poor player like Wheeler," he said. "Enough to tempt even an honest man to crime."

"But why steal the sides now? We have had the play for almost three weeks, and the contest begins a few days hence – surely it is too late for the Admiral's Men to profit by it now?"

Naismith shrugged. "Perhaps it was done principally to cause mischief, with Henslowe's reward only a side bet. Better to do that as near the performance as possible, no?"

"But why would he want to harm us? It makes no sense for a man to bite the hand that feeds him."

"Who knows why anyone of these dissident fellows chooses to do a thing? There are Puritans enough who will pay their penny entrance fee to the latest play, just to have something new to rail against."

He got to his feet and put the book back on its shelf. It was not the Bible, as would be most fitting for the Lord's Day, but *A Mirror for Magistrates*, an old book of poems examining the lives – and falls – of England's great men, including kings and dukes. Coby wondered if Master Naismith had been seeking the libeller's inspiration in its pages.

"You think Wheeler wrote the poem as well?"

"Probably. Half these actors are would-be playwrights, are they not?"

"But you did not ask him?"

"I thought it best not to mention it. The fewer people who know, the better. Besides, it is too much of a coincidence for us to be the target of two enemies at once. No, trust me, the villain is caught and our troubles are over."

Coby nodded, wishing she could be as certain.

"P-perhaps I should continue as nightwatchman anyway, sir," she said.

"No need for that now, lad," Master Naismith replied, patting her on the shoulder. "You shall have the reward of your own bed after this."

She smiled, grateful at the reprieve. Though she was still not convinced their troubles were over, she was not keen to spend another night in the empty theatre.

"What about Master Parrish?" she asked.

"If he wants to stay, he can sleep in the storeroom," Naismith replied. "Or the barn. Don't trouble your head about him, lad."

A final niggling thought prompted her to ask: "How did Wheeler get in, sir? The doors were all still locked and bolted on the inside as I had left them, and I doubt he would have blocked his own escape thus."

"Wheeler confessed to me that he hid in the under-stage and did not leave with the others after the rehearsal. There was no need for him to break in."

Coby stared at him. "He was there all along?"

She shivered. What if he had come up whilst she was taking off her corset? That had been a foolish risk to take, to assume she was alone. Had Wheeler known she was upstairs? Perhaps not. As a hireling, he was not privy to the company's secrets: the regular actors had been warned to say nothing about the poem to anyone, and the whole purpose of Coby's watch had been to catch the miscreant in another attempt, not to scare him away. Wheeler must have assumed the theatre was empty that night and everyone gone home to their beds like good Christians.

"Do not blame yourself," Master Naismith said. "I should have kept a sharper eye on the hirelings and made certain they all left at the end of the day. I will not be so blind a shepherd in future."

Coby thanked him and made her way up to her attic room. Tonight she would sleep fully clothed, whatever the weather.

She knelt by her narrow bed and said her prayers: for her family, wherever they might be, for her Dutch friends, and Master Naismith and his family. And for Master Catlyn, standing between the ambassador and who knew how many wicked assassins. There would be no heroic swordplay, she feared; traitors preferred the subtlety of poison, or a close-wielded knife. Even Caesar could not escape such a fate... She shook the thought away. Worrying would not make Master Catlyn any safer. Her only concern for the next few days was to ensure that Suffolk's Men were dressed and on stage when their cues came, so they could do their best to win this contest.

CHAPTER XIX

Ned arrived outside Bethlem Hospital just as St Botolph's was tolling ten. He felt as if the forged document tucked inside his doublet were glowing like a beacon, pointing him out as a counterfeit and a betrayer of his friend. He knew that, regardless of Mal's absence, he should go and confess to his involvement in this plot, but he was afraid Kemp would find out and get to his mother in his absence. Besides, the Lieutenant of the Tower would probably have him tortured, just to make sure he wasn't holding anything back.

He was starting to think the risk of torment might be worth it if it meant getting out of this mess, when a coach drew up outside the hospital and Kemp and Armitage got out. Kemp was dressed as a lawyer again. Ned recalled the two men standing in the doorway right behind his mother, and his nerve deserted him.

"Right then," Kemp said. "Let's see the paperwork. Yes, very good. This'll do nicely."

"I've done my bit," Ned said. "Now let me go home."

"I haven't finished with you yet, Faulkner, not by half. You just come along with us, and keep your mouth shut until I say the word."

Kemp walked up to the gates of the hospital and knocked. A hatch slid open and the porter peered out. Before the man could say a word, Kemp held up a gold angel. The porter's eyes lit up, and within moments they were inside.

"We are here on behalf of my client, one Maliverny Catlyn," Kemp said in crisp tones befitting his assumed profession, "to oversee the discharge of his brother from this place." He waved the writ under the porter's nose.

The porter frowned. "Why ain't he here then? He told me he was in London until Christmas."

"Master Catlyn is a man of substance now," Kemp said, pressing the gold coin into the man's grimy palm. "If he chooses to send his servants on this errand, what business is that of yours?"

"None at all, sirs, none at all." The porter pocketed the bribe. "Master Alexander is in the west gatehouse, wonderful well cared for, as you will see."

Mistress Cooke was equally surprised to see them, and exclaimed woefully at the news they were taking Sandy away. An angelic visitation soon calmed her nerves, however, and they were let into the cell.

Sandy was crouched in the corner of his bed, eyeing them warily. A book lay open on the blanket nearby.

"He's a bloody sorry specimen," Armitage said, after the wardress had gone.

"He'll clean up," Kemp replied. He gestured to Ned to proceed with the plan.

"Hello, Sandy." Ned stepped a little closer to the bed. "Remember me? Mal's friend?"

"Ned Faulkner," Sandy replied. "Yes."

"Your brother has sent us to take you out of here."

"I know."

Ned paused, dumbfounded. "You do?"

"It's all part of the plan," Sandy said calmly.

"Here, what's he talking about?" Armitage said. "You been telling tales, Faulkner?"

"Not I," Ned said quickly. "Look, I told you he was–"

"Enough!" Kemp held up his hands. "If he thinks this is his plan, all to the good. Now let's go."

He unlocked the heavy iron shackles, then produced a pair of much lighter restraints from his lawyer's document wallet and snapped them around Sandy's wrists. The young man winced, though the blued steel bands seemed loose enough.

"What are those for?" Ned asked.

"Don't want him causing no trouble, do we?" Armitage growled.

Ned refrained from commenting that, without a chain between them, the handcuffs would be of little use. There was something odd going on here, something he couldn't quite put his finger on.

Sandy gathered up the pile of books on the table. "I can't leave these," he muttered. "Mal would be angry with me."

"All right, we'll take the books," Kemp said. "Armitage, you can carry them."

"Me?"

A look from Kemp cowed the big man. Ned wondered what hold Kemp had over him. Something even worse than he had over himself, probably.

Sandy hugged the books to his chest.

"It's all right," Ned told him. "You'll have them back as soon as we get to…" He broke off, realising he had no idea where Kemp was taking the young man.

"To your brother's lodgings," Kemp put in. "Now, come along with me and Ned."

Ned took off his cloak and draped it around Sandy's shoulders.

"Here," he said, "it's starting to rain."

They escorted Sandy out of the ward and across the courtyard. The porter waved them through the gates, bowing obsequiously. "Thank you, sirs. My kind regards to your master."

Ned helped Sandy into the coach, and they set off southwards down Bishopsgate Street. He wondered if the coach would be searched on entry into the city. Even if it were, what would be found amiss? Sandy was cooperating fully with his abductors, indeed seemed in control of the situation. Which was odd in itself. On the other hand Mal's brother was, after all, insane. Who knew what was going on inside his head?

In the event, the gate guards' inspection of the coach was curtailed by another of Kemp's seemingly endless supply of angels, and they passed through into the city without further obstacle. Whoever was behind this did not lack for money, Ned reflected. A pity nothing but threats came his own way.

From Bishopsgate the coach headed south-west down Threadneedle Street. Just before St Pancras they took a sharp turn left towards the river, and after a few more minutes the coach stopped.

"Out," Kemp told Ned.

"Why? Where are we?" Ned looked out of the window. On the far side of the river he could see the familiar Bankside skyline, dominated by the bear-baiting and bull-baiting arenas to the east and the theatres to the west.

"Three Cranes Stairs. Here's the wherry fare." Kemp handed him a meagre two pennies.

"What about Sandy? Where are you taking him?"

"That's none of your business. Is it, Catlyn?"

Sandy said nothing. He had been staring out of the coach window since they entered the city, taking in all the sights and sounds.

"This is an end to my part, isn't it?" Ned asked in a low voice. "You don't need me any more."

"That remains to be seen," Kemp said.

"What do you mean?"

"This isn't over yet, Faulkner. You think we sprang the idiot boy out of Bedlam for the pleasure of his company? There's bigger matters afoot, my friend. And don't even think about betraying us. You're in this up to your neck, and it's more than your neck that'll get stretched if you fail us."

"An audience with the Queen?" Mal asked.

That explained why servants had been sent at dawn to fetch his replacement livery from the tailor. Kiiren inclined his head in acknowledgment. He was dressed once more in his blue silk robes and looked every inch the foreign ambassador.

"I fear I have caused great offence," he said. "It is my duty to put things right between our people."

Just inside the gates of the compound the skrayling honour guard were waiting, mounted on matched bay geldings. Kiiren was escorted to a pretty grey mare and helped to mount; Mal could only assume the chestnut with the white blaze was for his own use.

Outside the compound they were joined by more guards, this time men in scarlet-and-gold royal livery, with banner-bearers in the vanguard. To show the ambassador the way to Nonsuch, Mal wondered, or to protect the skrayling party from unwanted attention? Few of the foreigners ventured outside London nowadays. There had been too many… disappearances.

The journey to Nonsuch Palace took most of the morning at the gentle pace set by the mare. At each village and hamlet, people flocked to watch the cavalcade pass, waving their hats as the royal banners appeared and then falling silent when they saw the ambassador. A few made the sign of the cross discreetly whilst others cried out "God save the Queen!" or "Christ bless you, Your Honour!" Even this close to London, many had probably never seen a skrayling before.

As they rode, Kiiren was full of questions about the English countryside: its crops, the manner of their cultivation and the cycle of the year. Mal explained that the main harvest – wheat, barley, peas and beans – was now over, leaving only the autumn fruits and roots to be gathered before the frosts.

"Your people do not grow many kinds of vegetables," Kiiren observed.

"Not in the fields," Mal replied. "In gardens."

He thought of the Faulkners' back garden, with its rows of onions and cabbages and herbs. It seemed a world away from the circles he now moved in.

If it had not been for dread at the thought of facing his queen, Mal would have enjoyed the journey a good deal. A strong breeze tempered the heat of the sun and blew away all memory of the stink of London. As the riders passed each farm, flocks of swallows weaved through the air above them, filling their bellies with the last flush of summer midges before they departed who knew where.

At last they neared the fabled palace built by King Henry the Eighth and now inhabited by his widowed daughter Elizabeth. At first nothing could be seen through the trees apart from an unremarkable crenellated gatehouse. As they approached, however, the scale of the building became apparent. Massive octagonal towers rose at each corner of the palace, topped with gilded onion domes flying the royal standard. Thousands of lozenge-shaped panes of glass glinted in the midday sun.

"It is called Nonsuch because it has no equal in Christendom," Mal said, noting with amusement Kiiren's awed expression. "Perhaps not in the world, unless Your Excellency knows better?"

Kiiren shook his head. "Your Queen lives in this great place all alone?"

"Not alone. There are many servants here, to attend to her every whim. I am told her sons visit as often as their duties allow."

"And her daughters?"

"There are no daughters, Your Excellency."

"That is sad indeed. Every woman needs daughters, for sons must leave her."

"Because only women live in your cities?" Mal asked.

"Yes."

"Then where do the men go?"

"They journey from place to place and trade, as we do here in England. Amongst our own people, and between human peoples also. This is how it has been since long before time."

"But your people do not live with humans."

"No. They have their ways, we have ours. We learn from them, they learn from us. Now we learn from you English, and perhaps you learn from us also?"

"I am sure there is a lot you could teach us," Mal said. "Like how to make those lamps without fire?"

Kiiren smiled. "That I cannot tell you. Only our women know secrets of making such things. Men trade, or make show of music and storytelling and games of skill and strength, one company against another."

"Like the theatre contest in London?"

"Yes, except…" Kiiren glanced at him sidelong. "In my lands, purpose of contest is for choosing of mates."

Mal was prevented from further enquiry into skrayling customs by their arrival at the gatehouse of the palace. The royal escort led them through a large outer courtyard to an inner one, less spacious but far grander. Rows of dazzling white stucco panels adorned all four sides of the quadrangle, depicting heroes of classical myth and English legend: Hercules, Perseus, Brutus and of course King Arthur, the prince's namesake.

"You must tell me some of their stories," Kiiren said eagerly, gazing around in wonder.

"Perhaps after the contest, sir," Mal said. "I would not want to spoil any surprises the players might have in store for Your Excellency."

The skraylings dismounted, and the ambassador and his bodyguard were escorted alone through the echoing corridors of the palace, across expanses of black-and-white marble floor and up a noble stair into one of the octagonal towers. Mal felt very small and wretched amongst all this magnificence, which was no doubt its purpose. He wondered for the thousandth time how much the Queen had heard about Saturday's incident, and what she made of it. He only prayed he might come out of this with his head and other limbs intact.

They were shown into an antechamber, and after a short wait the ambassador was announced. Tall doors decorated with bronze bas-reliefs swung open and Mal followed Kiiren into the chamber beyond.

If he had not already been perspiring from a long ride in the sun and the anxiety of meeting his monarch, Mal would have broken out into a sweat the moment he stepped through the doors. Though the palace's many windows caught and held the midday heat, fires blazed in both great hearths of the audience chamber. A thick layer of rushes covered the marble floor, sprinkled with drifts of yellow bedstraw flowers. No courtiers thronged here to wait upon their monarch, only a handful of servants, silent and watchful.

On a dais at the far end of the audience chamber stood twin thrones, The left was empty save for a narrow coronet ringed with ruby crosses and clusters of pearls; on the right sat Elizabeth. The sixty year-old Queen was her own death mask, a thick layer of white ceruse rendering her features immobile. She wore a gown of plain black damask with cuffs of tarnished

silver thread and a cartwheel ruff that framed her face in what
had perhaps once been a flattering manner. A wig of tight red-
gold curls made an incongruous splash of colour above her
sombre attire; a double rope of enormous pearls was her only
adornment.

Mal walked towards the dais behind the ambassador, gaze
lowered. His booted feet bruised the tiny yellow petals, releasing their honeyed perfume. As Kiiren bowed in a courtly
manner, Mal sank to one knee and remained there, eyes on
the floor. A mouse stared at him from the shadow of the dais,
jet-bead eyes glinting in the firelight, then it scuttled away.

"Ambassador." The Queen's voice was still sharp, accustomed to absolute obedience; only a faint quaver betrayed
her age.

"Majesty."

"How did you like the fair?"

So much for the pleasantries. Mal wondered how quickly
news had reached her. Probably the same night, which meant
the Queen had been waiting a day and a half to hear this story
at first hand.

"It was most entertaining, Your Majesty," Kiiren replied.
"Seeing our people together, as one – it remind me of home."

"Ah, your home. We have heard much from our advisers
about the wide lands of the New World, its richness, and our
great good fortune in attracting your friendship. And now we
are honoured by an ambassador. Tell me, Your Excellency,
which prince do you represent?"

"Prince, Majesty?"

"There is some leader amongst your people, a chief or po-
tentate or king?"

She gestured regally, taking in the portraits of her ancestors
lining the walls.

"There are many leaders, Majesty," Kiiren said, "and many

peoples. I speak only for Shajiilrekhurrnashet, as most numerous of all clans of Vinland to visit your shores."

"The other clans and nations do not wish to send their own ambassadors?"

"Perhaps in time they shall. I do not know their minds."

The Queen laughed sharply. "Would that I had so little care for the plans of my enemies."

"The other clans are not our enemies, Your Majesty," Kiiren replied.

"Then you are indeed fortunate, Your Excellency." She peered more closely at him. "You are not like the others. Are there as many different races amongst the people of the New World as of the Old?"

Kiiren shrugged. "There are *hurraqeth*, who are my people, and many nations of your kind, though they are darker of skin and black of hair. No others."

"Hmm." The Queen turned her attention to Mal. "I understand it was your idea to divert the ambassador to Bartholomew Fair, Master Catlyn."

Mal risked a glance upwards, into heavy-lidded bronze eyes as watchful as a hawk's.

"Yes, Your Majesty."

"To what end?"

"Sir James is not so well acquainted with the ambassador as I am, Your Majesty. I knew His Excellency would not think well of us if he saw the way we treat those sick in mind."

"You refer to Bethlem Hospital."

"Yes, Your Majesty."

"You think Sir James did wrong in this matter?"

"In arranging a visit to Bethlem?"

"In punishing you for disobeying orders."

"No, ma'am. I would have done the same in his place." Had done the same, on campaign. It was the only way to maintain discipline amongst the lower ranks. He was only glad he had never had to order a man's death.

"You consider yourself as skilled a diplomat as your father?"

Mal blinked at this change of direction. The Queen was as unpredictable a questioner as Walsingham.

"No, Your Majesty."

"Very wise. A diplomat who caused this kind of... upset would not hold his post for long."

"I am of course yours to command, Your Majesty. I will resign my commission forthwith, if that is your desire."

"Hmm."

"Majesty." Kiiren bowed again. "Please forgive my loyal companion; it is my fault alone. I should have more respect for customs of my hosts."

The Queen leant forward slightly, her eyes moving from one to the other of her visitors.

"It seems you have made a powerful ally, Master Catlyn."

"Yes, ma'am."

"Since no hurt has been done, we are willing to overlook this incident – if the ambassador is agreeable."

"Of course, Majesty," Kiiren said in grateful tones.

"It would be a great comfort to our enemies to learn that our two nations were at odds. We will not give them that satisfaction."

"Your Majesty is very wise."

"Now, leave us. We are wearied by all this talk."

The Queen rang a small bell that hung at her side, and a hidden door in the panelling opened. A lady-in-waiting hurried into the audience chamber, bearing a tray of refreshments. Her eyes widened at the sight of the skrayling.

They made their exit, stepping carefully backwards across the crackling rushes until they were out of the royal presence. Mal heaved a great sigh of relief as the doors closed.

"Your people are very fortunate to have so great a queen," Kiiren said, smiling.

"Yes, we are," Mal replied. "England shall not see her like again."

He did not add that his people would not think themselves truly fortunate until they had a king once more.

Ned went straight home after crossing the river. He wanted to stay on Bankside and see if he could make out which way the coach headed next, but he saw Kemp watching him like a hawk as he disembarked and thought better of it. The less he knew, the better. But even that might be too much.

His feet led him towards the Mirror at first, unconsciously seeking the comfort of Gabriel's presence, but as he reached Gravel Lane he changed his mind. He would not be at all welcome if the actors were rehearsing, and if they were not, there was no point in going. Perhaps he should try Gabriel's lodgings, or Naismith's house? Then again, Hendricks had made it pretty clear he was not welcome there either. And whilst Armitage and Kemp were busy enough for the present, there was no telling what they would do when they returned to London. Either Ned had finally outworn his usefulness, or they had some new villainy in store for him. Well, he would not oblige them either way.

There was only one thing for it: he had to get his mother away from here. They had cousins down in Sussex; they could hide out there and Kemp would never find them. How they would shift for themselves in the country, he had no idea, but it had to be better than this. With the thought of perhaps never seeing either Mal or Gabriel again gnawing at his guts, he made his way through the back garden and into the kitchen.

His mother was bent over the fire, stirring an iron pot hanging on a hook. A savoury aroma rose with the steam, making Ned's stomach growl.

"Sit down," his mother said. "I got a nice ham-hock from the butcher's this morning, and there's soup–"

"Mam, we should leave. Now."

He took down the shopping basket from its peg and began filling it with supplies: bread, cheese, a jar of newly pickled onions, and several bottles of beer. After a moment's thought he added a carving knife and a small roasting-spit.

"Leave?" Mistress Faulkner put the lid back on the pot with a clank and sat down at the table. "What are you talking about, our Ned?"

He looked around the kitchen distractedly. What else did they need?

"We have to leave Southwark, Mam."

She cocked her head on one side.

"Have you been getting into trouble again, my lad?"

"It wasn't my fault." He put the basket down with a sigh.

"It never is."

She patted the bench beside her, and he sat down reluctantly.

"If your father was alive," his mother said, "you wouldn't have to scrape around for a living with them actors. I always knew they'd lead you amiss one day… Well, no use crying over spilt milk, eh?"

"I suppose you're right, Mam."

He leant his head against hers, and she put her arm around his shoulder. Her fingers were cold through the thin linen of his shirt, and her breath sounded even more wheezy than usual. How could he ask his mother to go tramping the high roads like a beggar at her age?

"O' course I'm right." She ruffled his greasy hair. "Now, get yourself some supper and stop worrying."

CHAPTER XX

After the audience with the Queen they rode straight back to the skrayling encampment and Kiiren excused himself, saying he must report to the elders. A servant brought a plate of spiced rice scattered with strips of fried meat and chunks of vegetables, and a jug of *aniig*. Mal picked at the food, pondering the day's events. The fragile alliance between England and Vinland hung in the balance, and he had been the one to disturb the scales by switching his allegiance between the two. Who was this Erishen, that the mere possibility of his existence could rule the fate of nations?

Kiiren returned after about an hour, looking grave.

"Clan leaders say we must go on with visit and do nothing more to offend Queen Elizabeth," he told Mal. "I am to tell you to obey Leland in all things."

So sudden a capitulation? The clan leaders must have been very persuasive. Perhaps they feared the loss of profits if the Queen cancelled her extravagant celebrations.

"And you?" Mal asked him.

"It is not my place to gainsay our leaders. I am… vessel for words, nothing more."

Mal was not convinced by Kiiren's explanation. Something

was going on, some matter of skrayling politics he could not begin to grasp. He had assumed the ambassador had been sent by some greater authority back in Vinland, and the merchants here in England were no more important than the guild masters of London in determining their nation's policy abroad. Now he was not so sure. Perhaps he should not be surprised that the merchants were the ultimate authority amongst the skraylings. But where did that leave Kiiren, and why were they so deferential to him one moment then overruled him the next?

Returning to Horseydown Stairs, they boarded the little gull-headed boat and were rowed to the Tower by six of the skrayling guards. It seemed they were expected, for the water gate had been raised and they quickly passed into the little pool underneath St Thomas's Tower. Mal could not help but recall his first, ignominious arrival here, only two months ago. Then he was a nobody, a landless, penniless gentleman with few prospects; now he was an employee of Her Majesty Queen Elizabeth and companion to one of England's most powerful allies. The thought gave him a warm glow of satisfaction. For the first time since he had learnt of Charles' flight and their family's ruin, he allowed himself to hope that better times were ahead.

At the top of the steps, Leland was waiting with a group of gentleman warders in scarlet livery.

"Welcome back, Your Excellency," Leland said, smiling broadly at Kiiren, though the smile did not quite reach his eyes.

"Thank you, Leland-*tuur*," Kiiren replied. "Judge Sekaarh-jarret wish to say he hope we put this *tuqanishet*, this... misunderstanding, behind us, and go forward in friendship."

"Yes, of course. Her Majesty is most anxious our people remain allies."

I bet she is, Mal thought. If we turn the skraylings away, the French will be in the New World like a shot.

"I've had fires lit in your rooms," the lieutenant went on. "Can't have been pleasant, camping out in that downpour. Mind you, could be worse. I remember when I was a youngster, campaigning in Ireland..."

Leland escorted the ambassador to his lodgings, rattling away about his military career. He had not for a second acknowledged Mal's presence.

Leland eventually left them in peace, and servants brought a light supper of cold meats, cheese, oatcakes and hot spiced wine. Whilst the skraylings gathered around the dining table Mal lingered in the bedchamber, eager to be alone for a while. The fact that he had spent the best part of two days surrounded by hundreds of skraylings was only just beginning to sink in. Not long ago that would have been the stuff of his worst nightmares. Now... He was surprised at how calmly he had taken it.

For want of anything better to do, he rummaged in his saddlebags for his soldiering kit. The river-crossing in the rain had not done his sword belt and scabbard any good, and he had been too distracted by the sudden turn of events to attend to them. He uncorked the bottle and upended it against a wadded rag, then set about rubbing oil into the dark leather, following the grain in gentle strokes.

If Kiiren had not been at the council meeting, things would have been different, of that he was certain. There was something reassuringly familiar about the ambassador, something on the edge of memory, like the music he had heard on that first reconnoitre outside the stockade. Was Kiiren indeed a great deal older than he looked, as his words at the banquet suggested? Had Mal met him, perhaps as a child, and forgotten about it? There had been visitors to Rushdale Hall, sometimes important ones, but he was certain no skraylings had been amongst them. He wondered, not for the first time, if his father had been a Huntsman and introduced Charles into their company, the way Charles had done with him and Sandy. He hoped not.

The rain returned in a violent downpour that rattled the windowpanes and turned the sky black. After a few minutes it slackened off and the setting sun gleamed briefly on the waters of the Thames.

Lost in his task, Mal barely noticed the passage of time until the curfew bell tolled its warning. He looked up, and found Kiiren watching him from the doorway. The skrayling's expression was, as far as he could judge, a mixture of anticipation and anxiety.

"Can I help you, sir?" Mal asked. As an experiment, he added, "Kiiren-*tuur*?"

"Yes, yes!" The skrayling's mottled face relaxed into a smile. "Please to come this way."

"Of course, sir."

Mal put away the cleaning materials and wiped his hands on a towel. The greasy animal scent of the oil hung in the air, a comforting reminder of his normal routine. From the dining room came the sound of Tradetalk: skraylings and humans talking together? The tower door creaked, and footsteps rasped on the steps outside.

"What's going on?" Mal asked.

"There is something I need to ask of you, Catlyn-*tuur*. Something important."

"Very well." He followed Kiiren through into the empty dining room. The table had been cleared of the remains of supper and the fire banked for the night. A row of the little lightwater lamps glowed in the hearth, throwing eerie shadows against the plaster walls.

"Where are your guards, sir?" Mal asked, suddenly wary.

Kiiren smiled. "They go to play dice with captain's men."

"Monkton invited them?"

That seemed highly unlikely. The captain had not openly expressed an opinion of the visitors, but if the attitude of his men was anything to go by, he did not discourage prejudice against the skraylings either.

"I ask him to ask them," Kiiren said. "English and Vinlanders should not be apart so much. Bad for friendship."

"I suppose so," Mal muttered. Kiiren was being hopelessly optimistic. Most likely the experiment would end in broken heads and another retreat to the camp. Why Leland was allowing such a foolish venture so soon after the last incident, he could not fathom.

"If we cannot trust our friends, what is purpose to come here?"

Mal had no answer to that. Either Kiiren was far too naive for the role assigned to him, or – no, there was no "or". He shook his head in despair.

Kiiren paused, looking nervous once more.

"I wish to share ceremony with you this night," he said, his voice loud in the empty room. "If it be your will."

"Will it be… like the meeting?"

"Somewhat like. But we two only." He smiled shyly. "No one to spy on us here."

Mal swallowed. More magic. But he had to find out the secret of the skraylings' power, for his own satisfaction as well as the safety of the realm.

"Very well, I accept."

Kiiren produced an armful of cream wool that had lain folded on one of the benches.

"It is also our custom," Kiiren began, "to wash body and wear robe–"

"No more robes, I beg you!" Mal backed away, hands raised. "I will do this as I am, or not at all."

Kiiren wrinkled his nose, but did not press Mal further. He crossed the dining room and opened a small door in the corner.

The western tower chamber was the twin of the chapel at the other end of the ambassador's apartments, a small circular space with whitewashed stone walls, though the floor was of plain terracotta tiles and the windows unglazed. The window openings had been blocked with rush matting and covered with patterned silk, and carpets laid on the floor, so it looked more like the interior of a skrayling tent than a castle tower. Lamps hung from four iron stands positioned at what Mal guessed were the four cardinal points, and a low brazier stood in the centre of the room.

"Please to sit," Kiiren said. "Take off shirt and uncover tattoo."

Mal removed his doublet and shirt and threw them aside. It was almost a relief to strip off in the humid confines of the little chamber, and with his torso swathed in bandages he scarcely felt undressed. Sitting down cross-legged on the matting, he unwound the dressing over his tattoo. The skin around the inking was still red and tender, but with no sign of festering.

Kiiren unfastened his necklace, and gestured for Mal to remove his earring. He did so, and stared down at the pendant.

"Is there magic in this?" he asked the skrayling, examining the pearl.

"Power is in touch of metal." Kiiren held up his necklace, rolling the beads between his fingers. "In English I think it is called 'lodestone'. Powerful protection against evil spirits."

Mal remembered the nightmare presences lurking amongst the rocks, and shuddered. He knew without being told that these were the creatures the lodestone protected him from.

"If it is such a powerful protection, why put it aside?"

"Because it is anchor also, to hold spirit in body. Tonight we must be free."

Kiiren sat down opposite, then opened a small wooden box and threw a pinch of fine powder onto the coals. Mal sneezed repeatedly as a cloud of pungent smoke filled the small room, and wiped his streaming eyes with the back of his hand.

"Please to breathe slowly," Kiiren murmured. "Empty thoughts."

Mal drew a deep breath. The smoke smelt somewhat like tobacco but with an acrid edge. His throat burned and his toes and fingertips tingled, as if he had taken a draught of raw brandy. Kiiren's features blurred, and the lamps within his line of sight dissolved into a rainbow aura.

"Again," Kiiren said, his voice barely audible. "All is quiet. All is forgetting. All is remembering."

Mal breathed in again. He should be afraid, a small detached part of his mind observed, but he felt more content than he had done in months, perhaps years. The feeling combined the bliss of lying spent in a woman's arms with the heightened awareness of combat. He breathed out and closed his eyes, allowing his other senses to fill that awareness.

Linen and wool against his skin, a faint draught from the window. Kiiren's musky scent, the clinging odour of neatsfoot oil, a faint trace of wine and spices drifting in under the door, the stink of the river outside. The crackle of the charcoal brazier, the sentries on the wall walk, and an owl setting out on its evening hunt. His own heartbeat pounding in his ears, becoming one with the voice of the sea, the hiss and rattle of pebbles as each wave sighed its last upon the land.

He opened his eyes. The four walls of the tower room were gone; only the brazier remained, the shimmer of its coals echoing the molten gold of the sun, just rising above the ocean. Mal looked about him in panic.

"Where are we?"

Kiiren smiled and ran his fingers through the gravel. Mal stared down at the beach. Every pebble demanded his attention, begging to be touched, examined, chosen. He scooped up a double handful and let them go again, watching in fascination as they fell through his fingers. Tiny shards of stone clung to his damp skin: flecks of amber, grey and white.

"Come," Kiiren said, holding out a hand.

Now they were walking along the beach in the bright light of noon, the sea at their right hand, low wooded hills to the left. An ochre-sailed ship stood at anchor offshore.

"You remember this place," Kiiren said, grinning.

Mal realised with a start that the skrayling was now his own height, with the fangs and tattoos typical of his kind. And yet he was the same Kiiren, Mal knew it in his bones.

"This is a dream," he whispered.

"Of course." The skrayling held out his arms. "Remember."

"No."

Mal backed away, the pebbles crunching underfoot. Blood began to pour from the skrayling's open mouth. Mal turned to run, but the trunk of the tree blocked his path. No, not this. He could not let Kiiren see this…

Digging his fingernails into the bark he began to drag himself upwards, his lower body a dead weight, as if his legs were paralysed. The bark scraped the skin from his belly but he felt nothing, heard nothing, saw nothing but the stars overhead, impossibly distant. Only a little further. He grasped a branch and tried to haul himself up, but it snapped under his weight and he fell, twisting in the air, and landed on hands and knees on the hard stone floor.

"*Erishen*? *Amayi*, is it you?"

Mal's eyes snapped open. They were back in the tower room. Was he awake now? He sat back on his haunches, blinking away the last shreds of the nightmare. *Amayi?* Where had he heard that word before?

Kiiren leant across the brazier, his eyes reflecting the lamplight like a cat's.

"*Ë amayi, niníhami anosenno. Einotabe'ë mallä.*"

It sounded like – No. That could not be.

"*Mallä,*" Mal whispered. That was the word he and Sandy had used to mean "people, grown-ups". He had always assumed it was a play on his own name. Sandy had made it all up to entertain him. Hadn't he?

"*Lerr – lerrä'a ohilanno,*" Kiiren said, his voice trembling. You know my words.

"*Hä.*" Yes.

The skrayling gave a cry of joy. Crossing the small space between them he flung his arms around Mal, who gritted his teeth against the pain of his still-fresh wounds. Kiiren was babbling in the strange language, between hoarse sobs. All Mal could catch was "people" and something about "dead", and over and over that name, *Erishen*. He stroked the skrayling's spiky black hair awkwardly, his mind a whirl of confusion. What was going on here? Who was Erishen, and why did Sandy know the skraylings' tongue? More importantly, who was dead?

Mal pulled himself free of Kiiren's embrace and got unsteadily to his feet.

"*Erishen! Amayi!*"

Ignoring Kiiren's protests he staggered out of the tower and across the dining room. Too hot in here! He opened the outer door and drew in a deep breath of cool, moist evening air. He stepped out onto the landing, towards the stair that led down into the outer ward, but the stones buckled and twisted before his eyes. Clutching the balustrade he sank down onto the top step and pressed his cheek against the blissfully cold stone.

Sandy. Had Kiiren attempted some kind of scrying through him, and seen – but he had visited Sandy only yesterday, surely the fit had not been fatal? Mal jumped to his feet and stumbled down the stairs.

The more he moved about, the better his command of his limbs became. By the time he reached the main gates, he felt almost whole again. He hammered on the ancient timbers.

"Let me out!"

He had to get to Sandy, find out what was happening–

A door opened in the passageway under the tower, and a guard poked his head out.

"What do you want?"

"I– I need to leave."

"No one leaves the castle after curfew. Lieutenant's orders."

"But–"

"No one. Now clear off before I report you."

Mal turned around and headed back the way he had come. Before he had gone ten yards the heavens opened and rain began to fall. Seconds later, thunder rumbled in the distance.

Mal ran for the meagre shelter of the archway linking the ambassador's lodging to the Wakefield Tower. Beyond it was a garden, one of the many remnants of the Tower's former role as a royal palace. Rose bushes drooped in the downpour, water dripping from their leaves into the puddles that stretched across the gravel paths. White petals streaked with crimson fell to the ground under the onslaught and melted into slush. He stared at the squat rectangle of the Cradle Tower, where the welcoming glow of a fire gilded the windowpanes of a guard-room on the lower floor. Perhaps he could find a way out through the sally-port?

He skirted the garden and its betraying gravel, then went down a short flight of steps into the sunken pathway around the foot of the tower. Rainwater pooled on the worn paving and lapped around the toes of his boots. He edged towards the gateway, ducking down as he passed the window.

Sounds came from within: the idle conversation of bored men, the thump of a tankard on wood. He scouted all the way round, but the only exit was through the gate in the tower. Barred, of course, and most likely locked. Even if he got out, there was Bedlam itself to break into. And if Monkton caught him trying to escape… He shivered. The weals on his back were stinging again beneath their sodden bandages.

His mind was clearing now. What was he doing running around the castle half naked in the rain? Sandy was fine, he told himself. He had made a foolish assumption based on a few words of a language that just happened to resemble a childhood game, when his mind was fuddled with the drugged smoke. A misunderstanding, nothing more. Certainly not worth risking arrest – and another flogging – for.

No, it was his duty to find out what was going on. The skraylings believed in the reincarnation of souls and, unless he was very much mistaken, Kiiren believed him to be this Erishen reborn. But who or what was Erishen? A prophet, or perhaps a great hero of legend, like King Arthur? That would explain why he was picked out to guard their ambassador. He caught himself grinning like a fool, and had to remind himself this was just a heathen superstition, though perhaps one he could use to his advantage.

It was part of the intelligencer's stock-in-trade, the assumption of a false identity to gull his victims into revealing what they knew. Baines had drilled him on the essentials; now it was time to put his training into practice. With a last wistful glance at the sally-port, he made his way back to the ambassador's lodgings.

Kiiren was waiting by the window overlooking the outer ward, his whole body tense with anxiety. He must have been watching all this time – assuming he could see anything through the gloom. Mal rubbed a hand over his rain-damp face, unsure how to proceed. If Kiiren started telling everyone about this Erishen business, it could go ill for them both.

"You are cold, *Erishen-amayi*," Kiiren said, retrieving a towel from the bench by the fire. "Sit, dry yourself. Others return soon."

Mal sank onto the bench and began scrubbing his wet hair with the towel. To his surprise Kiiren knelt at his feet, gazing up at him. In the darkness his shadowed face looked almost human.

"I am sorry it had to be this way, *amayi*," Kiiren said. "I knew when first I saw you, something was wrong and you did not remember. I hoped that to see me again, to share our memories, would bring all back."

"Only pieces," Mal replied, realising with a shock that it was true. He did remember things he could not possibly know. Was Kiiren right after all?

"That is why I had to try *qoheetsakhan*." Kiiren glanced towards the tower room. "I am sorry if it frightened you to remember so much so quickly."

"I... I thought I understood your words, but already it is fading again."

Kiiren nodded. "It may take time, and perhaps more *qoheet-sakhan*."

Mal said nothing. He did not relish the thought of another dose of the skrayling drug, if it muddled his thoughts so.

"Please, *amayi*, tell no one of this night," Kiiren said in a low, urgent tone, glancing at the door. "It is too soon. If you – if *we* are found out..."

"I understand," Mal lied, hoping his relief did not show. Say as little as possible, Baines had told him; let the gull fill in the blanks and his own hopes and fears will betray him. Still, he could not help but wonder why Kiiren wanted to keep this a secret. Some incomprehensible matter of skrayling politics, perhaps, in which the ambassador did not care to show his hand too early.

Kiiren smiled and touched Mal's cheek, then leapt to his feet. The sound of skrayling voices, slurred with drink, drifted up from the outer ward.

"They return," Kiiren said.

He disappeared into the tower room and returned a moment later with Mal's shirt and doublet.

"Quick, into chamber."

He thrust the bundle of clothing into Mal's arms and all but pushed him towards the doorway into the bedchamber. Mal needed no further prompting. Within moments he had re-treated to the bed and closed the curtains. Belatedly he remembered he still had his wet, muddy boots on. He pulled them off and slipped them to the floor just as the front door banged open.

The guards' rowdy chatter faded into muttered apologies. Mal guessed that Kiiren had waited behind in the dining room, and was giving his men a good telling-off for coming back in such a drunken state. He smiled at the thought of the slight, soft-spoken ambassador facing down a dozen burly skrayling warriors. Like a raw young captain on his first command? his memory prompted. No, he and Kiiren were nothing alike.

With a sigh he lay down on the bed, ignoring his stinging back. So many questions buzzed around his head, but they all came down to one central point. Why was Kiiren being so se-cretive about this Erishen business? Mal thought back to the debate in the skrayling pavilion. Had Kiiren only suspected then what he now believed? It seemed to be the real reason he was so concerned about Mal's treatment, and yet he was hiding it from his own people. The young ambassador was up to something, and whether it boded well or ill for England, Mal could not tell.

With a soldier's sense of priorities, he forced himself to relax. Sleep now; tomorrow was time enough to worry about the dangers that lay ahead.

CHAPTER XXI

Ned woke with a start. The grimy light of dawn crept in through the shutters, promising another day of rain. He rolled over, seeking the warmth of a fellow living creature, but the bed was empty. He buried his face in the bolster – and almost missed the creak of footsteps on the stair.

"Mam?"

His mother often woke early, but she didn't usually venture up the stairs in the near-dark, and the lodgers gave the attic a wide berth. Heart pounding, Ned groped for his knife. His hand closed around the hilt just as the door swung open.

A tall, heavily built man filled the doorway. Ned couldn't make out the intruder's features in the dimness, but he didn't need light to know who it was. Armitage. So, his usefulness to Kemp had come to an end.

He edged out of bed, heedless of his own nakedness.

"How did you get in here?" he asked, hoping he sounded less terrified than he felt.

Armitage made no reply, only advanced into the room. He didn't appear to be armed, not that he needed weapons with fists like that. Ned crouched in a knife-fighter's stance, wondering what his chances were of slipping past his opponent.

Speed was his one advantage; speed, and knowledge of this house and its environs.

Armitage paused, his eyes flicking to the blade then back to Ned's face.

"Not so stupid, are you?" Ned muttered. "Kill me if you must, but I'll plant this knife in your guts before I die."

He dodged to one side, but in the narrow space it was child's play for Armitage to block his escape. He was going to have to rely on his wits. With a cry of rage Ned leapt onto the bed, giving himself the advantage of a couple of inches of height, though he had to crouch to avoid hitting his head on the canopy.

Armitage took hold of the two uprights at the foot of the bed and began to shake the whole bedstead from side to side. Ned shifted his weight, trying to keep his footing. The ancient, worm-riddled woodwork was beginning to shake apart under the assault. Clouds of dust fell from the canopy. Ned coughed and spluttered, barely able to see his opponent through streaming eyes. He felt rather than saw Armitage lunge, and rolled aside just in time, landing on the floor next to the bed with a thud and nearly dropping the knife. As he scrambled to his feet, an enormous fist caught him in the ribs with a sickening crunch.

Ned fell backwards, coughing, pain tearing into his side. Armitage grabbed an ankle and began to pull him out of the narrow space. Ned flailed his arms, trying to get a purchase on the wall and bed-frame, and his groping fingers touched cold stoneware: the chamber pot. He snatched it up and hurled the stinking contents into Armitage's face, followed by the pot itself. The big man brushed the missile aside, cursing. Free of Armitage's grasp, Ned launched himself upwards and buried the knife in his opponent's belly.

Armitage roared in pain and enveloped Ned in a piss-stinking bear hug that threatened to crush the life from his body.

Ned screamed as his cracked ribs exploded in fresh agony. The hilt of his knife was digging into his own belly now. With a last effort he leant against it, pushing it upwards into the man's chest towards the heart. As blackness took him, he heard Armitage give a strangled moan, and then he was falling...

He came to in a pool of blood and piss, half-buried under his attacker. He drew a cautious breath, and wished he hadn't. He felt like a dog after a bear-baiting, and not one of the winners either. He extricated himself from Armitage's final embrace and limped over to the wash stand. The water was cold but clean, and Ned spent a long time scrubbing at his skin with a damp flannel, trying not to think about what had just happened. He had killed a man. Not a good man, admittedly, but a man nonetheless. Ned knew his Ten Commandments, and whilst kidnapping was not on the list, murder certainly was. If he had ever doubted he was going to Hell for his sins, he could not do so now.

The house was silent; no sound came from the lodgers' rooms below, though they surely could not have slept through the fight. Ned thought back to some of his nights with Gabriel; no doubt the lodgers had long since learnt to ignore the noises from the attic. Clean at last, or as clean as he was ever likely to get, he pulled on his clothes with trembling hands. Where was his mother? She must have been woken by the noise, unless–

He crept down the stairs, sick to his stomach with dread, and made his way down to the ground floor and along the passage to the kitchen. A faint glow from the banked fire gave shape to the room and its meagre furnishings. Ned knelt at the hearth and lit a spill from the embers, then touched the flame to a candle stub and looked about him.

At first he could see nothing amiss.

"Mam?"

There was no reply. He went to his mother's bed and pulled aside the thin woollen hangings, but found only crumpled sheets and blankets. The back door creaked in the morning breeze, making him jump. Perhaps she was out in the garden.

Just as he reached the door, his foot caught against something. He looked down. A pale face stared up at him from the floor.

"Mam!"

He fell to his knees, patting her face and looking in vain for any sign of life. The old woman lay still, not a mark on her, only a slight frown of pain marring her features. Had the shock of Armitage's arrival at such an early hour caused her heart to fail? He took her hand. So cold. But her hands were always cold these days, that didn't mean anything, it didn't mean she was – He probed her wrist with his other hand, feeling for a pulse. Nothing. He pressed the back of her hand to his cheek, tears trickling down to pool where their flesh met.

"I'm sorry, Mam. I'm so sorry…"

After what felt like hours he rose, shaking with exhaustion. Now he really had to get out of here. There was a dead man upstairs, another man kidnapped… The parish priest would see his mother buried. Reluctantly he went back upstairs to gather his few belongings.

"Craven swine!" he screamed at the closed doors. "I should burn the house down with you lot in it."

Only the thought of his mother lying downstairs, and the innocent neighbours in the adjoining houses, prevented him from carrying out the threat.

With only a couple of days left before their performance in the competition, Suffolk's Men were spending every morning and afternoon rehearsing. The theatres had been closed all week in order to increase the public's anticipation of the great event. Nerves were stretched taut as bowstrings, and Coby was still needed as a prompt even though every man knew his lines backwards by now.

Master Parrish arrived late, and was even more distracted than usual. After yet another fluffed speech, he retreated to the back corner of the stage, where Coby was sitting on a stool with their one full copy of the script in her lap.

"May I speak with you privily?" he asked.

Coby glanced around. Several of the actors were in earshot, though they were engaged in the current scene and not paying her any attention.

"If it's something important, should you not tell Master Nai-smith?" she said.

Parrish hunkered down next to her.

"This isn't theatre business," he said quietly. "It's… personal."

She was tempted to remark that she had seen more than enough of his personal affairs.

"I have too much work to do today, sir," she replied, turning a page. "As well you know."

"A few minutes of your time, that is all…"

"Is it about…?" She jerked her head towards Philip, who was arguing with Oliver about a bit of stage business involving a fan.

Parrish shook his head.

"Very well," she said. "You can talk to me when we break for dinner."

"Thank you."

The rest of the morning went smoothly enough, and Coby soon found herself leaving the theatre with Master Parrish at her side. They walked along Bankside in silence, until Coby had to ask: "So, what is so important you must drag me away from my dinner?"

Parrish halted, and took hold of her shoulders.

"First, you must swear to tell no one what I am about to re-late; at least, not yet."

"I cannot swear to something when I know nothing about it, nor whether it is honourable to do so."

"And I cannot tell you unless you swear."

"Then we are at an impasse," Coby replied.

She pulled free of his grasp and carried on walking. He ran to overtake her, standing in her way like an ill-behaved child thwarting his mother.

"I thought you were in love with that fellow Catlyn," Parrish said. "Or do you not care if he lives or dies?"

She stared at him, heart in mouth.

"What are you talking about? Is Master Catlyn in danger?"

"Not yet. And you can help – but only if you swear to secrecy."

"I swear," she whispered.

"Then come with me. We should not speak of this in the street."

Coby went with Master Parrish to his lodgings, all thought of her day's work forgotten. Master Catlyn was in danger, and it was in her power to help...

Parrish lived above a draper's shop in Bermondsey Street, not far from the skraylings' guild house. Coby had been to the shop a few times, buying oddments of Holland and sarcenet for costume repairs, but had never ventured into the actor's home before. She followed him down a short alley to the shop yard, where a rickety wooden stair led up to a walkway that ran round the upper storey of the tenement.

"Is he here?" she asked.

"Catlyn?" Parrish shook his head. "Someone else."

He opened the door and ushered her inside. Coby's eyes widened in surprise. The single-room lodgings looked more like a cross between Master Cutsnail's office and a brothel than an impoverished actor's home. A motley collection of old tapestries, lengths of painted cloth, and threadbare velvet and damask cloaks covered the walls. The close-curtained bed was hung with rich fabrics too, dotted with embroidered animals in appliqué: harts, leopards and other heraldic beasts. Numerous chests stood about the room, some shut, some with lids wide open; one was piled high with hats of every colour and style.

"Gifts from admirers," the actor said, waving a hand in the general direction of the heaped treasures. "You can come out, love! He's here."

This last was not addressed to Coby. The bed-hangings twitched aside and Ned Faulkner emerged, looking even paler and grimmer of visage than Master Parrish.

"What's going on?" Coby asked, glancing from one man to the other.

"Sit down," Master Parrish said, dumping a heap of linens on the floor to reveal a plain three-legged stool.

Coby did as she was bidden, whilst Master Parrish sat on the bed next to Faulkner and placed a hand over one of his, gazing at his lover with a troubled expression.

"Ned has a story to tell."

Coby listened in horror to Faulkner's account of the men who had threatened him, and their plot against Master Catlyn and his brother.

"You betrayed him," she said. "He is your friend, and you betrayed him."

Her hand tightened into a fist, and she almost wished she had brought a cudgel. Master Catlyn would be avenged, one way or another.

Faulkner buried his head in his hands. "Tell him, Gabe."

"One of the villains broke into Ned's house before dawn today," Parrish said, "and tried to kill him. The fellow is dead – but so is Mistress Faulkner."

"No," she whispered. She looked at Faulkner with renewed pity and horror. "You killed a man?"

"It was kill or be killed."

"But – they will be looking for you," Coby said. "You must face charges."

Faulkner stared at the floor. Parrish put an arm around his shoulders and kissed the top of his head.

"A formality, love. No jury is going to convict a man of murder when he was simply protecting himself in his own home."

"You still must give yourself up. Otherwise they will assume you are guilty."

"I know," Faulkner muttered. He looked up. "That's why I need you."

"Why should I help you?"

"Don't do it for me; do it for him." He started to laugh, but broke off, grimacing. "I've seen the way you look at him," he said through gritted teeth.

Coby felt herself blush. Had she been that obvious?

"You want to be careful with that one, duckling," Parrish put in. "He might surprise you."

Hope warred with frustration in her heart. Best not to think about such things. It was impossible.

"Very well," she said. "What must I do?"

"You can get a message to Mal," Faulkner said. "I can't confess to my real business with Kemp and Armitage, not unless someone with connections can speak up for me."

"But why me? Cannot Master Parrish convey your message?"

Not that an excuse to see Master Catlyn was unwelcome. But there was something else going on here, something Faulkner was not telling her.

Faulkner sighed. "The skraylings took Mal from the Tower on Saturday night."

"What? Took him where?"

"I don't know. Perhaps all the way back to the New World…"

She gaped at him, caught between laughter and tears. "The New World?"

"Not that far, God willing," Parrish put in. "The Admiral's Men are due to play today, so the ambassador must surely be in London yet."

"But he might still be at the camp," Faulkner put in. "You speak their language, Hendricks. You have to go there and warn Mal. Those villains were up to something dreadful; they were too free with their money not to be working for someone very rich and powerful."

"And if he is not at the camp?"

"Then find him, wherever he is, and get a message to him. Lives depend on it, I'm certain."

By midday a persistent drizzle had set in, and the atmosphere in the ambassador's quarters was more dismal than ever.

"Will play go on in rain?" Kiiren said as they went down to the outer ward.

"As long as there's not a downpour," Mal replied. "I fear there's been too much preparation done for anything less to stop it."

"It rains very much in England," Kiiren said mournfully. "Perhaps that is why you think nothing of dirt everywhere."

They arrived at the theatre in good time, before the crush of people assembled at the gate had been let in, and were shown upstairs. Usually the most honoured guests sat on the stage itself, but Mal feared this was too close to both the actors and the audience for safety. Instead the ambassador's party were accommodated in a side gallery, separated from the paying audience by a sturdy oak door. A table had been set with cold meats and a silver flagon of wine, and cushioned chairs placed to get a perfect view.

"Sir Leland tells me this play is called *Locrine*," Kiiren said to Mal, "and is history of your people."

"I have not heard it played, but I understand it tells the story of the founding of London by the Trojans, many centuries ago," Mal replied.

"Trojans?"

"People of Troy."

"Ah, yes, I have heard tale of great horse. Is that in play?"

Mal shrugged. "I have not read much history, and never learnt Greek. I regret to say I neglected my studies a great deal."

It had been hard to concentrate on the niceties of Latin rhetoric when all he could think about was Sandy. His brother had not been able to join him in college, not after that dreadful night in the hills.

He realised Kiiren had asked him another question.

"Sorry, sir. What did you say?"

"You studied at… What is word?"

"University?"

"University, yes."

Mal nodded. "Cambridge."

They spoke of libraries and lectures, astronomy and music, but he steered the conversation away from his own sudden departure. If the ambassador did not already know his family history, Mal was not about to tell him now.

In the yard below, servants laid down straw to soak up the worst of the rain, carried piles of cushions to the lords' galleries, or ran back and forth on unknown errands. Three archways at the back of the stage led to the tiring house, and the occasional billow of a curtain or raised voice from within hinted at the frenzy of nervous preparation going on inside.

After about half an hour a small group of men entered the yard and made their way up to the gallery where the ambassador was seated. At the head of the group was the admiral himself, patron of this theatre company. Effingham greeted

Kiiren with the same blunt courtesy as on their first meeting, and asked after his health.

Also amongst the party was a thin, stooped figure whose richly coloured brocade doublet and hose contrasted grotesquely with his sallow, wasted features: Lord Brooke, former English ambassador to Venice. He was seldom at court owing to frequent bouts of illness, and Mal was surprised to see him here today. Perhaps he came to discuss diplomacy with Kiiren, under cover of the drama contest.

A rising hubbub from beyond the gates told of a gathering crowd. At last a shrill trumpet sounded in the street and the gates swung open. A multicoloured torrent of people surged through the opening: apprentices in blue, burghers in wine red or rusty brown, rakes in their slashed and embroidered doublets, and of course the whores in their tawdry gowns of scarlet and buttercup yellow. The groundlings jostled for places in the yard, the aldermen and their wives paid their extra pennies for admittance to the galleries and a cushion for their municipal rears. Serving-men stood at the doorways with bottles of beer and baskets piled with bags of hazelnuts. Mal was a little surprised they weren't selling the popped corn he had tried at the fair, though in truth it was more fit for throwing at bad actors than for eating.

Speaking of which… Prominent amongst the crowd were the skraylings in their striped and chevroned tunics; they were frequent theatregoers in any case, but today they had turned out in force, perhaps feeling safer for the presence of their ambassador. The foreigners occupied almost the entire top gallery, having been separated from the locals by a thoughtful doorman.

Soon the theatre was packed to bursting. Some of the crowd had noticed the guests of honour in their gallery and begun pointing them out to their neighbours. At that moment, however, their attention was diverted by a rumble of thunder from the gallery. A boy actor, dressed as a Greek goddess in robes of black, walked onto the stage.

"*In poenam sectatur et umbra*," the actor intoned.

"For punishment, even a shadow pursues," Lord Brooke added, for the ambassador's benefit.

A man dressed as a lion ran on, roaring, and paced to and fro across the front of the stage, clawing in the direction of the audience. Having seen the real lions in the royal menagerie, Mal found the actor's feeble roars singularly unimpressive.

A second actor, dressed in green and carrying a bow, slipped from the other stage door and hide himself behind a canvas bush, whilst the goddess continued her speech in English.

> *"A Mighty Lion, ruler of the woods,*
> *Of wondrous strength and great proportion,*
> *With hideous noise scaring the trembling trees,*
> *With yelling clamours shaking all the earth,*
> *Traverst the groves, and chased the wandering beasts.*
> *Long did he range amid the shady trees,*
> *And drave the silly beasts before his face,*
> *When suddenly from out a thorny bush–"*

The archer leapt out and drew his bow, nocked with an imaginary arrow.

> *"A dreadful Archer with his bow ybent,*
> *Wounded the Lion with a dismal shaft."*

The invisible arrow was loosed, and the lion clutched his chest and fell to the stage with a roar of agony.

> *"So he him stroke that it drew forth the blood,*
> *And filled his furious heart with fretting ire;*

But all in vain he threatened teeth and paws,
And sparkleth fire from forth his flaming eyes,
For the sharp shaft gave him a mortal wound.
So valiant Brute, the terror of the world,
Whose only looks did scare his enemies,
The Archer death brought to his latest end.
Oh what may long abide above this ground,
In state of bliss and healthful happiness."

The archer and lion stood and bowed, and all three actors left the stage.

"What was all that about?" Effingham grunted. "Damned foolish nonsense."

"It was an allegorical masque," Lord Brooke replied. "See, here comes the dying Brutus carried on a chair, and his Trojan courtiers."

Mal left the ambassador and his guests to enjoy the performance, and withdrew a discreet distance along the gallery, where he had a better view of the audience. Many of them were paying more attention to the ambassador than to the play, and their eyes flicked towards Mal from time to time. He returned their gaze levelly, and they soon looked away.

A disturbance in the crowd caught his eye, but it was only a woman fainting. Perhaps the lion had been too much for her, though it was more likely she was overcome by the press of bodies. In truth there was scarcely space for a would-be assassin to draw his pistol, never mind aim it. Mal retreated to the back of the gallery and considered the party gathered around Kiiren. The admiral could have been behind the attack onboard the *Ark Royal*, but surely that was too obvious even for him? The rest of the party were unknown to Mal. Once again he found himself wishing he had paid more attention to the goings-on at Court. Any one of

these men could be in the pay of France, Spain or the Holy
Roman Emperor. And he might never find out who until it
was too late.

CHAPTER XXII

Coby jogged along Bankside, her hair and clothing uncomfortably damp from the summer drizzle. She had been to the skraylings' camp, only to discover the ambassador had returned to the Tower after all. She took a wherry across the Thames to save time, but was told by the Tower guards that the ambassador had already left for the Rose by coach, in order to arrive before the crowds. For fear of missing them again she took the same route on foot, along Thames Street to London Bridge and thence to Bankside. By the time she arrived, however, the theatre doors had closed and people were being turned away.

"Please, you have to let me in," she said to the doorman. "I have an urgent message for the ambassador's bodyguard."

"Aye, and I'm the Queen of Sheba," the man replied.

"Here, aren't you with Suffolk's Men?" his companion asked. "Clear off. We don't need any of you lot getting anywhere near the judge of this contest."

"That worried, are you?" Coby replied, her impatience getting the better of her.

The man raised two fingers at her and jerked them upwards in the favourite English gesture of defiance.

Coby backed away. She didn't want to get into a fight, and there was no other way into the theatre but past these men. She would have to wait until the ambassador came out, even though it meant missing the afternoon's rehearsals. If this business was as important as Faulkner seemed to think, Master Naismith would have reason to thank her in the end.

She crossed the lane and sat down in the shelter of a large oak tree to begin her vigil.

The rain continued, thin but steady, adding to the ominous atmosphere of the play. Act Two began with more imitation thunder and lightning and another dumb-show narrated by the goddess Ate, in which Queen Andromeda was taken captive by a band of Ethiopians, to the dismay of her husband Perseus. "Divine will rules all" was the motto of this allegory.

This second prologue was followed by the invasion of England by Scythians and then a comic interlude in which the cobbler, Strumbo, was pressed into military service by a captain of Brutus' army. It reminded Mal uncomfortably of his own situation; indeed this whole play made him uneasy. Surely a story of invasion and war was not a happy choice for a diplomatic visit?

Judging by the expression on Kiiren's face, he was indeed somewhat perplexed by the play. He frequently turned to his guests with questions, and Lord Brooke was eager to be of service in showing off his broad knowledge of history and mythology, which was perhaps the reason Effingham had invited him. Mal wondered what had moved the admiral to patronise a theatre company in the first place, as he seemed to have little interest in the dramatic arts. Simple ambition perhaps? Queen Elizabeth had been very fond of plays before her husband's death drove her into seclusion.

After a particularly long explanation of the geography of

England and its relation to the homelands of the Trojans and Scythians, Lord Brooke fell to coughing, and a servant pressed a goblet of wine into his trembling hands.

"You should not have come out in this inclement weather, Brooke," Effingham said.

"It is a mild ague, nothing more," Lord Brooke wheezed. He took out a small bottle and tipped some of the contents into his wine.

Kiiren held out his hand, and the bemused Brooke passed him the bottle.

"Don't taste it, it could be poison!" Mal cried.

Everyone stared at him. Effingham sprang to his feet.

"Are you accusing my guest of trying to kill the ambassador?" The admiral's weather-beaten features were flushed with rage.

On stage, the actors fell silent, and everyone turned to stare at the lords' gallery.

"No, my lord." Mal fell to one knee and bowed his head, cursing inwardly.

"Please forgive our man Catlyn," Kiiren said, bowing low to the admiral and his party. "It is my error, being curious."

"Apology accepted, of course, Your Excellency."

Effingham sat down again, gesturing for the play to continue. Mal felt a touch on his shoulder, and looked up. Kiiren motioned for him to return to his position on guard.

"This medicine, Lord Brooke," the ambassador said, "you take it often?"

"Whenever the ague returns," Brooke said, and drank his wine down in one draught. "Bought it from an apothecary in Venice. Very learned folk, the Turks, for all their barbarity. Why, think you can do better?"

Effingham turned pale, and an awkward silence descended on the party.

"I commend your apothecary," Kiiren said. "We did not know trade in our herbs had spread so far, or their virtues had such renown."

Lord Brooke muttered something under his breath. Effingham burst into laughter.

"Hoist with your own petard, Brooke," he said, wiping a tear from the corner of his eye. "That'll teach you to try to best the skraylings at their own game!"

At that moment, thunder rumbled and the goddess Ate reappeared to narrate the prologue to Act Three. Mal took advantage of the distraction to retreat to his lookout post at the far end of the gallery. What had he been thinking? That Brooke would risk poisoning himself on the minuscule chance the ambassador would take an interest in his medicine? Leland had been right. He should think less and apply himself to the job he was hired to do.

After about an hour, the theatre door opened and several serving men left, complaining loudly about the crush within. Coby watched them from her vantage point across the lane.

"Run out of beer already?" the doorman asked them as they trooped away.

"Aye. And that skrayling brew as well."

"Better get plenty more, then," he shouted after them. "There's nigh on three thousand thirsty folk in there. The more you sell, the happier old Henslowe will be."

Coby leapt up. This was her chance. She strolled away down the lane, but as soon as she was out of sight of the theatre doors she backtracked towards a nearby inn which she knew belonged to Henslowe. Sure enough, the serving men were there, knocking back pints of ale to quench their own thirst before getting back to work.

"Master Henslowe told me you needed more help supplying

the theatre crowds," she said to the innkeeper. "He promised me sixpence."

"Don't I know you from somewhere?" The man squinted at her in suspicion.

"I'm a friend of Ned Faulkner, Henslowe's copyist."

The innkeeper laughed, showing several missing teeth.

"Good luck to you, then, lad," he said. "Faulkner's lackey or no, that'll be the hardest sixpence you earn all year."

When the men from the theatre had finished their break, Coby lined up with them outside the brewhouse door. Someone passed her a crate of beer, which she balanced on one shoulder. With a bit of luck, she could walk straight in past the doormen and they would never see her face.

Leaning against the pillar at the end of the gallery, Mal felt rather than heard a knock on the connecting door. He opened it a crack.

"Master Catlyn?"

"Hendricks!" he said, breaking into a smile at the sight of a familiar face. "What brings you here?"

The boy looked graver than usual, and he glanced warily around.

"There is something I must tell you, sir, in private."

"Then it must wait," Mal replied. "We cannot speak privily here. I am on duty."

"Please, sir, this is very urgent," Hendricks said in a low voice. "It's about your brother."

"Which one?"

"Sandy."

Mal's heart lurched. This was too much of a coincidence. After a brief glance towards the ambassador, he beckoned the boy inside. The audience were roaring with laughter at a comical fight between Strumbo and his wife; even the ambassador and his guests were paying too much attention to the antics on stage to notice a visitor.

"Is something wrong?" he asked Hendricks, leaning close to make himself heard. "Is he – Is he dead?"

"I– I don't know, sir. I don't think so."

"All right. Tell me everything–" He held up his hand and glanced pointedly at the ambassadorial party. "Tell me in your own tongue. Speak slowly, and use simple words I can understand."

The boy cleared his throat.

"I come from your friend, Ned," he said in Dutch. "Two wicked men found him, said they would hurt him if he did not tell them about you and your brother."

"Ned is hurt?"

"Only a little. But they used him to steal your brother away."

"Steal?" Mal asked. He knew the word well, though he had only heard it used in the context of looting.

"Yes, sir."

Mal made the sign of the cross. *Sweet Mother of God, Ned, what have you done?*

"When?"

"Yesterday morning."

Whilst we were far away at Nonsuch. Very convenient. But the implications of that line of reasoning did not bear thinking about…

The comic scene ended, and Kiiren looked round at last.

"What is happen? Who is this?"

Mal bowed low, and gestured to Hendricks to do likewise.

"Nothing of import, sir, merely a servant come to ask if we need more refreshments."

He took a shilling from his pocket and gave it to Hendricks.

"Here's for your trouble, lad," he said in a loud voice, then added in an undertone, "Wait for me outside the theatre."

"Thank you, sir," Hendricks replied brightly, though his eyes were filled with concern. Bowing again to the lords and gentlemen, he left the gallery.

Mal spent the rest of the play in an agony of frustration, scarcely able to stay still. The clamour of the crowd was no more than a murmur in his ears, the drama onstage hollow puppetry devoid of meaning. One thought alone raged back and forth in his mind like a wounded bear: the bastards who had done this would suffer, and soon.

Coby didn't sit and wait for the play to end. First she ran to the nearby Mirror and made her excuses to Master Naismith.

"I have a chance to meet the ambassador and find out what he thought of the Admiral's Men," she added, after her initial apologies.

"Not tonight," Master Naismith said. "By skrayling tradition, the judge of a drama contest must withdraw from company after the performance, to meditate upon what he has seen."

"But–" She racked her brains for another excuse. "Master Catlyn has need of me. If I can continue to be of service, I might get to speak to the ambassador tomorrow."

"Very well then. This shabby crew need to practise without their leading strings for a while. Get back to the Rose, but do not stay o'erlong."

She thanked him profusely and ran back to the other theatre. The Rose was situated in the old gardens of the brothel of the same name, which was also owned by Henslowe. Access to the theatre was via an archway piercing the brothel, there being no lanes or alleys interrupting the continuous row of stew-houses on this stretch of Bankside. She could hardly stand around on the street here, lest she be mistaken for either a prospective customer or a male varlet. Instead she took herself along the riverbank to Falcon Stairs, where she could at least feign to be waiting for someone.

As it was, she was propositioned at least thrice before the play ended and the audience began pouring out onto the street. Her disguise might not be a complete defence, but she dreaded to think how much worse it would have been, were she dressed as a girl. No wonder the city fathers forbade women to wear men's clothes; if her sisters knew how much freedom it might win them, none would willingly don skirts again.

Theatregoers swarmed out of the narrow archway like ants from a nest, covering Bankside in a mass of noisy, sweating humanity. Fearing to be lost in the crush, Coby crossed the street and walked back towards the Rose, flattening herself against the buildings as much as possible. Better to be mistaken for a whore than be trampled or cast into the river.

After what felt like an age, the flow of people eased from a torrent to a trickle, and she spotted a coach standing outside the Rose with four mounted skraylings as escort. More skraylings, armed with long staves, issued from the theatre exit, and behind them came the ambassador in his blue robe, with Master Catlyn towering above him.

The swordsman helped the ambassador into the coach, then looked around for Coby. Catching his eye, she hurried over.

"Get in the coach," he said in a low voice.

"Sir?"

"Just do it, will you?"

She did as she was told, cowed by his sudden grim demeanour. His anger was understandable, she told herself, and not directed at her. She knew well that feeling of panic at being separated from one's family.

The ambassador frowned at her as she got in, and looked questioningly at Mal.

"This servant accompanies us?" he asked.

"Forgive the subterfuge, Your Excellency," Master Catlyn said, climbing in after her. "It may be your custom to spend the evening in seclusion, sir, with no talk of the theatre –" Mal glanced meaningfully at Coby "– but I need to confer with my informants if I am to protect you."

The coachman flicked his whip and they rattled off. For a while it was all Coby could do to keep her seat. The little vehicle bounced over the cobbles like a pebble skimmed across a pond; if its purpose was to shake its passengers senseless, it was doing a good job. After a while she began to get the rhythm of the movement, however, and she was able to observe the ambassador more closely.

He was very different from the other skraylings she had seen in London, even allowing for the magnificent robes and lack of tattoos. Most skraylings were polite to the point of coldness; they kept their eyes averted and showed little emotion apart from rare flashes of anger. This one gazed about in open curiosity, and even smiled at her in sympathy when she nearly fell from her seat into the footwell of the coach.

"I am Outspeaker Kiiren," the skrayling said, inclining his head.

"Jacob Hendricks, of Su–" She caught herself, just in time. "Of Berchem, in the Low Countries."

She glanced at Master Catlyn, but he was staring out of the window, a muscle working in his jaw and his left hand clenched white-knuckled over the pommel of his rapier. Her elation at seeing him again was turning to lead in her stomach. She wanted to reassure him that she would do anything to help – but not here. Besides, what could she do that Master Catlyn could not manage himself, and ten times better at that?

For the rest of the journey she diverted Ambassador Kiiren with tales of her homeland. He was particularly interested in the dykes and dams, though she struggled to explain how

they worked; she had been too young when her family fled
to England.

"There is great city in New World with canals," Kiiren said,
"but this holding back of sea is unknown to us. I like to see it
one day."

"So would I," Coby replied. All this talk of her homeland
had brought back so many memories.

The coach rattled under the gatehouse of the Tower, and a
chill of fearful anticipation washed over her, knowing she
was now inside the dread fortress where so many good people had been imprisoned and executed. Some bad ones, too,
like wicked Queen Anne. No wonder the place was said to
be haunted.

They came to a shuddering halt outside a half-timbered
building in the outer ward. Coby shook her ringing head, half
falling out of the coach behind the ambassador and Master
Catlyn. She followed the party up a short dog-leg flight of steps
to the building's entrance, uncomfortably aware of the
skraylings' curious eyes upon her. She wondered if any of
them had seen her at the guild house with Master Naismith
and thus suspected her of spying for Suffolk's Men.

Ambassador Kiiren retired to his private apartments for the
evening, and the skrayling guards gathered in the dining
chamber to await supper. Master Catlyn showed her through
a door in the corner into a small octagonal room with walls of
bare whitewashed stone. The air was thick with dust motes
and smelt faintly of smoke. A charcoal brazier, cold and full of
ashes, was the only furnishing.

"Tell me everything you know," he said, closing the door behind him.

She stood in the middle of the room, arms clasped behind
her back, and began to relate the morning's events: Master
Parrish's insistence on speaking to her, the visit to his lodgings,

and Ned's account of the men who had pressed him into the service of an unknown master. When she came to the part about Mistress Faulkner's death, he placed his palms either side of one of the small windows and rested his forehead against the glass.

"And Ned has no idea where they took Sandy?" he asked, his voice cracking on his brother's name.

"None. I'm sorry, sir."

"Will he give himself up?"

She shrugged.

"He is not safe, either way." Master Catlyn pushed himself away from the window and came to stand before her. "There is something more I need you to do."

"Of course, sir." She gazed up into his dark eyes. Anything…

"You know where Seething Lane is, off the near end of Tower Street?"

"Yes, sir."

"Run to the house of Sir Francis Walsingham and tell his servants I need to speak to him immediately, here in the Tower."

Coby stared at him. If Master Catlyn was so intimate with the Queen's private secretary, that could only mean one thing. Her mind ran back over everything she had told him in the past few weeks. Had he been spying on Suffolk's Men all along? Was all this somehow connected to the attacks on the theatre?

He placed a hand on her shoulder. "Do not fear for your friends. I have no love for Walsingham or his methods."

"But you work for him."

"Yes."

"Can you not go to him yourself, sir? I am sure he will not listen to a mere errand boy."

"I must not leave here, not until something can be arranged."

"I don't understand."

"Someone has taken my brother captive. A man who looks exactly like me. And the ambassador trusts me with his life."

"Oh."

"Quite." He went back to the door. "Wait here for a moment."

He returned a few minutes later with a letter, unaddressed and sealed with a plain blob of wax.

"If my lord secretary is not at his house or will not see you, ask for a man named Baines. Do not say who the note is from; Walsingham is not the only one with informants everywhere."

She tucked the letter into her doublet and left, assuring him of her discretion. If there was one thing she knew, it was how to keep a secret.

CHAPTER XXIII

Coby delivered the letter as promised then set off for the theatre, her thoughts in turmoil. Master Catlyn an intelligencer? She smiled bitterly at the irony of being set to spy on him.

Dunfell's account of his master's suspicions came back to her. *This fellow Catlyn, who has been appointed as the ambassador's bodyguard, may owe his position to the scheming of the ambassador's own enemies.* Did that mean Walsingham was one of those enemies? Master Catlyn himself must surely be innocent; why else would they be using his brother against him? Unless it was a threat to ensure his cooperation, as they had done with Ned. That made more sense than trying to pass a madman off as the ambassador's bodyguard.

By the time she reached the theatre, Suffolk's Men were packing up for the day and heading for their suppers. To her surprise Master Parrish was there, though he was uncharacteristically silent amongst the laughing, chattering actors.

"Well, how did it go?" Master Naismith asked in a low rumble that was scarcely audible over the hubbub. He turned away for a moment and slapped Master Eaton on the back. "Good work today, Rafe. If that does not win us the contest, I shall eat my boots with gravy."

Eaton laughed. "It is many a year since we had so mean a supper. Do not wish those days back again, sir!"

The actor-manager turned back to Coby. "So?"

"Ah, um, it went well enough," Coby replied, trying to remember what she had said earlier. "Sir, did you really eat your boots, in the old days?"

"Aye, and count myself fortunate for even that. At least I did not set out barefoot." He laughed. "But enough of reminiscences. What did Catlyn want you for, anyway?"

"He, uh, wanted to learn how to play Five Beans with the ambassador's guards, since he has nothing to do this evening. He needed me to translate the skraylings' explanations of the rules."

She grinned, congratulating herself on her quick thinking.

"Did you warn him how seriously the skraylings take the game? I've heard of men sold into bondage after making an over-ambitious wager."

"Of course, sir. I did my best to discourage him from playing." She decided it was best to change the subject, before her tongue ran away with her. "Do you really think we can win, sir?"

"Think it? I know it," he replied loudly, then added in a lower tone, "though if you can put in a good word for us tomorrow with the ambassador, it can do no harm, eh?"

"No, sir."

"Lock up here, will you? We're off to the Bull's Head to find out how the Admiral's Men got on. Are you expected back at the Tower this evening?"

"I don't think so, sir."

"Well, then, join us for a drink. I've promised the lads a day off tomorrow, to rest their spinning heads before the performance on Thursday."

Whether he meant the spinning of a hangover or the exhaustion of a full day's rehearsals, Coby was not sure. Probably both.

"You too, of course," he added. "I need you fresh and ready to look after these miscreants on the big day."

"Of course, sir."

She glanced at Master Parrish. The actor looked pale and withdrawn, and in no better humour for carousing than herself. He gave her a wan smile in return.

"Would you help me tidy up, sir?" she asked him, with a meaningful look. "You know almost better than I where everything belongs."

He nodded acquiescence, and began picking up discarded garments, though he seemed unable to remember what to do with them after that. The other actors appeared not to notice, however; intent on their evening's enjoyment, they filed out into the rosy evening light. Soon the tiring room was empty but for the two of them.

Parrish went to the door and watched until everyone was out of earshot.

"Did you speak to Catlyn?" he asked, turning back to her.

"I told him everything Ned told us."

"And? Will he protect Ned?"

She had no answer for him. Master Catlyn had been very angry, and rightly so. No doubt he would do anything to get his brother back.

Master Parrish enveloped her in an embrace, catching her off-guard.

"Ned gave himself up this afternoon," he mumbled against her hair.

She patted his back awkwardly.

"You should go home," she said, pulling away.

He sighed and rubbed his hands over his face.

"Thank you for trying to help," he said at last. "Men like us must stick together, eh?"

"I was simply doing my Christian duty," she replied. "Now,

I really must lock up and meet Master Naismith at the Bull, or
he'll be wondering what kept me."

After Master Parrish had gone she locked the back door of
the theatre and crossed the field to Gravel Lane, but she did
not go to the tavern as promised. She was in no mood for the
actors' chatter this evening. Perhaps she ought to go back to
the Tower after all: Master Catlyn was not going anywhere
tonight, and she had not had a chance to tell him about the
attacks on the theatre. They might be nothing to do with the
plot against the ambassador, but what did she know of con-
spiracies? Older and wiser heads might see a connection where
she could not.

On the other hand, she was not sure how far she could trust
Master Catlyn. It pained her to think how naive she had been,
trusting a man she had known only a few weeks. What if Master Dunfell was right, and Catlyn was in collusion with
Walsingham and the shadowy enemies of the ambassador?
Was it too late to apologise to the duke's secretary and fulfil
her abandoned mission? She sighed, letting her feet lead her
towards London Bridge. After that, she did not know which
way to go. East to the Tower, or west, to Suffolk House?

After what felt like an interminable wait but was probably less
than an hour, Mal heard Walsingham's slow footsteps on the
outer stair. He wished this had not been necessary, but if the ambassador's enemies wished to get to him by substituting one twin
for the other, they could do that much more easily if Mal left
the Tower.

"Master Secretary." He bowed low as Walsingham entered.

"Catlyn. I hope this is important."

"Rest assured, sir, I would not have asked you to come here
if there were any alternative."

Walsingham raised an eyebrow in disbelief, but allowed

himself to be shown to the seat at the head of the table. Mal paced back and forth, trying to get his thoughts in order.

"Well?" Walsingham said.

"I have reason to believe someone is plotting against the ambassador." There, it was said.

"Tell me something I do not know," the spymaster replied.

"You know who is behind this plot?"

"Of which plot do we speak?"

"Which plot?"

"Master Catlyn, my intelligencers bring me news of plots daily. Spare an old man's memory and tell me which one has you so concerned you must drag me from my supper."

Mal apologised, and told Walsingham everything Hendricks had told him, and as much of Sandy's history as he thought necessary.

"And it never occurred to you to tell me you had a twin brother?" Walsingham asked, when Mal's account was over.

"No, sir. He is – *was* locked up in Bedlam, and often so mazed in his wits that I cannot fathom how he could be of use to anyone."

"But he does have spells of lucidity."

"Yes, sir."

Walsingham nodded. "That might be enough to give a desperate man hope."

Mal hung his head. His own hopes had been raised – and dashed – so many times in the past nine years.

"Well, there is only one thing for it," Walsingham said at last. "The ambassador must have a new bodyguard."

"Sir?"

"If you are no longer guarding him, then they cannot use your brother as a false replacement. We will have to make the dismissal public, of course, to the damage of your reputation, but…"

"No." He had wanted release from this job, but not at such a price. "Sir, you cannot."

"Do you presume to tell me my business?"

"They will kill my brother the moment he ceases to have any usefulness."

"Alas, I fear you are correct."

"But–" Mal stared at the Queen's secretary. "He's my brother."

"We must all make sacrifices in the name of our Queen and country, Master Catlyn."

Mal shook his head, desperately trying to come up with a way out of this.

"Surely you want to know who is behind this?" he asked Walsingham.

"My agents will look into it, of course."

"And what will they find? One of the abductors is already dead, the second was no doubt using a false name, and the third…" Mal hesitated. Vengeance is mine, saith the Lord. No, he would not return betrayal in kind. That crime was on Ned's conscience alone. "I swear on my honour he knows nothing more than he has already told."

"What do you suggest?"

Mal took a deep breath. "A two-pronged attack. First, hold the hearing into the deaths of Mistress Faulkner and her killer as soon as possible, and have Ned Faulkner acquitted and released."

"You think to use him as bait?"

"This Kemp fellow wanted him dead. He may try it himself this time."

"And I thought you were merely asking a favour for a friend," Walsingham said, smiling thinly.

"The favour I ask," Mal said, "is that your agents catch Kemp *before* he kills Ned."

"I will instruct them to do their best."

Mal inclined his head in thanks. He was putting Ned in terrible danger, he knew, but it was better than allowing him to be tortured for information he did not have.

"Second, let me continue in my duties. I will find an opportunity to expose myself to the plotters, that they may be drawn out. The men who took my brother were mere pawns, I am certain. But we may capture a rook, or even a king, if we are patient."

"And if they succeed?"

"We must bring the ambassador into our plan. Each time I leave his presence and return, I must give some secret word or sign to prove who I am. If the sign be not given, his guards will arrest me, or rather, my brother."

"You hazard much," Walsingham said. "If these plotters lay their hands on you, they may kill you."

"They will most certainly kill my brother if I do not try this."

"Very well. I will leave it to you to inform the ambassador of his part in this, and to arrange your watchword."

Footsteps sounded on the stair outside, and the door to the apartments flew open.

"Sir Francis!" Leland strode into the room, beaming. "To what do we owe this honour?"

"You will forgive me if I do not rise," Walsingham said. "This damp weather gets into my bones."

Leland made a sympathetic noise.

"I came to pay my respects to the ambassador," Walsingham went on. "Alas, I fear I timed my visit very poorly. I had quite forgotten that His Excellency would be seeing no one tonight."

"Damned peculiar custom," Leland replied. "Still, we have to respect our guest's wishes, eh?" He turned to Mal. "Any trouble at the theatre today?"

"No, sir, not a thing," Mal said, taking his cue from Walsingham.

"Excellent, excellent." He bowed to the spymaster. "Would you join me for a cup of wine before you leave, Sir Francis? I would appreciate your opinion on some plans I am drawing up."

"Of course."

Walsingham gestured to Mal, who helped him out of the chair.

"Please pass on my greetings to His Excellency," he told Mal. "I will endeavour to return at a more auspicious time."

"I am sure you will be very welcome, sir," Mal replied.

After they had gone, Mal paced the dining chamber, deep in thought. Walsingham apparently did not trust Leland enough to reveal his knowledge of the plot against the ambassador; did that mean he suspected the lieutenant of being involved, or had the spymaster become over-cautious in his old age? Leland made no secret of his contempt for the skraylings, but on the other hand he seemed too blunt and straightforward a man to plot in secret. Either that, or he was a better actor than any at the theatre.

The door to the ambassador's bedchamber stared at him accusingly. He was just putting off the inevitable. Kiiren had to be told, and watchwords agreed on. He would keep Sandy's name and identity out of it, though. He was not ready to discuss his brother – or his past – with a skrayling, no matter how friendly. And there was still this Erishen business to get to the bottom of. No, he would play his cards close to his chest, and see what more he could find out. Sandy's life might depend on it.

Coby headed west from London Bridge, but not along the Strand. It occurred to her she could defer her decision, and be useful to both sides, by investigating the disappearance of Master Catlyn's brother. Ned Faulkner had said he didn't see which way the coach went after the wherry returned him to Bankside, but perhaps others had been more observant.

Reaching the head of Three Cranes Stairs, she looked around. The first crush of playgoers returning across the river had long dispersed, and a number of wherries bobbed idly in the current, awaiting new passengers. She thought of asking if any of them recalled seeing Sandy and his captors, but the wherrymen had a poor view of the lane from the river.

She turned into the Vintry, a triangular quay surrounded on its two landward sides by warehouses. The quay swarmed with sailors, dockhands and customs officials, as well as the whores and pickpockets who infested every crowd like lice on a beggar. The larger ships could not sail this far up the Thames, but lighters ferried wine and other luxuries to the warehouses around the Vintry. Though it was some distance from their camp, many of the skrayling merchants also rented storage here, away from the stink of Billingsgate and the coal market.

Coby ducked as a crane loaded with wine barrels swung overhead. As she turned away she collided with an ebony-skinned dockhand. The man grimaced through the sheen of sweat and grime coating his features and swore at her in a fluent mix of English and Arabic. She backed off, muttering an apology; the man was twice her size, with biceps as big as her head.

Heading away from the riverside she noticed a group of perhaps half a dozen skraylings at the doors of a warehouse. Their leader was arguing with a short, red-faced man, punctuating his Tradetalk with angry gestures towards a barge moored at the quayside.

"What's going on, mistress?" Coby asked a middle-aged woman in the fine woollen gown of a merchant's wife.

"My husband just inherited that warehouse from his cousin," the woman said, "and now the foreigners want to pay their rent to *his* widow, as if it belonged to her."

"They do seem to have a lot of respect for women," Coby replied.

Not that she knew a great deal about their customs, but if Lodge's play were anything to go by, skrayling queens were revered more than any Christian king.

"Perhaps I can help," she said. Getting on a good footing with these people might help her investigation.

Before the woman could protest, Coby stepped forward.

"Excuse me," she said to the red-faced man. "In the name of the Queen's peace, perhaps we could come to some agreement here?"

The man stared at her. "Who are you to butt in here, whelp?"

"I am a servant of the Duke of Suffolk, and have assisted in his transactions with Merchant Cutsnail."

"You? You are scarcely more than a boy. Be off with you, before I call the watch!"

The skrayling merchant held up his hand and addressed her in Tradetalk. "You know Qathsnijeel?"

"I have drunk *aniig* with him."

This appeared to satisfy the skrayling.

"These English think they can change our contract," he said, baring his teeth, "because of the death of one of their men, and now they try to double our rent."

"Double?" She looked at the warehouse owner. "Is that true?"

"Well, I–" The man mopped his face with a striped kerchief. "There are running costs. And taxes. My cousin didn't keep the roof in good repair, and the price of vermin control has tripled in the last year–"

She held up her hand.

"Are you happy, sirs, with the state of the warehouse?"

The skrayling stared at the ground. "It has not been as good as we would like."

"But you would pay more if it were better."

"Yes."

She turned back to the warehouse owner. "If you were to begin repairs before increasing the rent, that would be a show of good faith, would it not, sir?" He seemed about to protest, so she added, "They always pay on time, do they not?"

"Oh yes, my cousin did praise them for it."

"And you," she said to the skraylings, "will pay your rent to this man's wife?"

She gestured to the woman in the crowd, who turned pale as the skraylings bowed to her in unison.

"If she is the new mistress of this property, yes."

"Good," Coby replied, clapping her hands together. "My lord Suffolk will be most pleased with this happy outcome."

"I– I will send him a butt of my finest sack immediately," the warehouse owner said, shaking her hand.

"Thank you."

She wondered what on Earth the duke would make of this unexpected largesse. Given the size of his household, he would probably not even notice.

"There is one more thing," she added. "You have men patrolling this wharf night and day?"

"Of course."

"Then perhaps they may recall something that happened yesterday, around noon."

The warehouse owner beckoned to a tall, heavy-set man in a leather jerkin.

"Wat, you were on duty yester noon, were you not?"

"Aye, sir."

Coby cleared her throat, picking her words carefully. "Master Wat, did you see a coach arrive here yesterday, with four men in it? One got out and caught a wherry, and the rest drove away again."

"A coach, you say?" He scratched his head. "Plenty of coaches fetch up here in the early afternoon, bringing folk what want to cross the river." He nodded knowledgeably. "That's when the plays start."

"But not so many before noon, I dare say," Coby prompted.

"That's true enough. Aye, come to think on it, I did see one betimes. I remarked that the fellow who got out looked more like a servant, and an ill-kempt one at that."

That certainly sounded like Ned Faulkner. "Do you remember anything else? Which way did the coach go, afterwards?"

"Now that was the odd thing. They waited a long time, until the servant was well across the river and out of sight. I was going to go and ask their business, but just as I stepped out, three more men got out and boarded another wherry, and the coach left without them."

"Was one of them tall and thin, with black hair?"

"Aye," the watchman said. "I got a good look at his visage; he was staring about him like he'd never seen the river afore."

"Which way did the wherry go?"

"Why, upstream of course. I watched it for a good while, until it disappeared round the southward bend towards Westminster. Beyond that, I can't say."

"Thank you again, gentlemen." She bowed, trying not to show her elation. "My master will hear of your faithful service."

Heart pounding, she ran back to Thames Street to make her excuses to Mistress Naismith. The thought of that unfortunate young man being carried away by ruffians, and to who knew what fate, had made up her mind. Tonight she would return to the Tower, and hazard the consequences.

CHAPTER XXIV

The Borough Compter was attached to the courthouse in Long Southwark. It had once been part of the parish church of St Margaret, its jewel-coloured windows replaced with plain glass and its Biblical murals whitewashed over. The walls were not white any more, but stained brown with the sweat of guilty men.

Ned hunkered on his heels against the wall to which he had been shackled by one ankle, unwilling to sink into the vermin-infested straw that covered the floor. At least he was in one of the upper rooms, where prisoners who could pay the gaolers' fees were kept. Down below, in filth and gloom worthy of Hell, were the debtors and other wretches who had run out of money or had no one to support them. Ned patted the purse hanging round his neck under his shirt. Gabe had given him a few shillings, since he had fled the scene of his crime with almost nothing. All Ned had to do was avoid being robbed by the other prisoners within reach of his chains.

The cell had room for perhaps a dozen men, with heavy staples cemented into the walls at intervals of a few feet. If the gaolers chose to use short chains, they could easily keep the prisoners apart, but they seemed to find it more entertaining to allow them enough freedom to torment one another. Word soon got around that Ned had murdered a man twice his size, and thankfully so far no one had seen fit to challenge him to prove it.

He glanced from side to side. The man on his left was curled up in the filthy straw, shivering as if with a fever; Ned noticed that the prisoner beyond him gave the poor wretch as wide a berth as the chains would allow. Plague? Ned muttered an oath and turned his attention to the man on his right. A scrawny fellow with thinning mousy hair, he sported a large purple-and-yellow bruise on his forehead that did nothing to improve his homely looks.

"Don't I know you?" Ned asked him.

The man peered at him, but said nothing.

"I saw you in the Bull's Head, when Naismith was hiring," Ned went on. "You're an actor, right?"

"Now and again," the prisoner said with a shrug. "Beats real work."

"Ned Faulkner. Philip Henslowe's copyist, amongst other things."

"John Wheeler," the man grunted. He looked Ned up and down. "They say you killed a man."

"He broke into our house and–" He could not say it out loud, not in this place. "It was kill or be killed."

To Ned's surprise, Wheeler broke into laughter. "Then I should count myself lucky the fellow who did this was armed with naught worse than a three-legged stool."

He touched the bruise gingerly, and winced.

"Are you – were you playing in the contest?" Ned asked.

"Not any more. I had a small part with Suffolk's Men, but..." He moved his leg, rattling the chain that pinned him to the wall.

"They play for the ambassador tomorrow, I hear," Ned said.

"Without me. Not that I care."

"Oh?"

"My part is already played," Wheeler said with a smirk.

Ned stared at him. Was this the fellow who had been sowing discord amongst Suffolk's Men with libellous doggerel? He launched himself across the gap that separated them, and pinned the unsuspecting actor to the floor.

"I should beat you into a bloody pulp for what you've done," Ned growled, and punched Wheeler in the mouth, splitting his lip. "That was for Gabriel."

The rest of the prisoners whistled and stamped their feet at this new entertainment. Wheeler pulled his arms free, shielding his battered face with one and reaching for Ned's wrist with the other. His groping fingers connected with Ned's nose and clawed at the tender flesh within, sending spikes of agony through Ned's skull. Ned caught the man's hand and forced it back to the floor, arching his own back to increase the space between them.

The purse swung free of Ned's half-unfastened shirt and Wheeler made a grab for it with his free hand, twisting the cord tight. As Ned tried to pull away, Wheeler pushed upwards, flipping Ned over onto his back. He did not press his advantage, however, but got to his feet and staggered backwards. Ned scrambled up after him, testing the limits of his shackles. Nowhere near long enough, unless Wheeler was prepared to advance.

"Ready for another bout?" he growled, retreating a little in the hope that his opponent would follow.

"You're not worth swinging for, Faulkner." Wheeler spat blood into the straw.

"You've already earned your hempen collar, and more," Ned replied. "Spreading sedition is near enough to treason that they will gladly gut you like a herring for it."

Wheeler turned pale for a moment, then regained his composure.

"No one can prove anything. This," he touched his forehead, "this was a mistake, I grant you. But it's the boy's word against mine."

"So you've taken to beating up children, as well as spreading lies?" Ned sneered. "You're a worse coward than I took you for, John Wheeler."

"At least I walk out of here, tomorrow or the next day. Or the one after that. You they'll save for the Michaelmas Assizes."

Ned swallowed. A whole month? Surely Mal would get him out of here before then?

Wheeler swayed again, stumbled against the wall and slid down to a sitting position. His face was pale and clammy, as if he were about to vomit. Several of the prisoners jeered or threw filth at the actor. Ned turned away in disgust and returned to his own station.

When it became obvious neither of them could be provoked into further fighting, the other prisoners lost interest. All but one, who continued to watch them closely whilst feigning not to. A spy? It was common practice to put informants amongst prisoners, to gain their confidence and trick them into betraying themselves. Ned felt certain it was more than coincidence that had placed him right next to Wheeler. But was it Providence at work, or did a more sinister hand direct his fate?

Master Catlyn was delighted at Coby's report, though she protested it was little enough intelligence to go on. He pressed her to stay the night in the ambassador's quarters, offering her the use of the canopied bed in a side room. There was no door, only an open archway, but the curtains of the bed gave enough privacy for her to feel at ease, provided she did not undress completely.

Before they retired for the night they took supper in the

small parlour between the ambassador's bedchamber and the dining hall. She told Master Catlyn about the poem and Wheeler's attempted theft, and her theory that they were part of a stratagem to spoil the contest and perhaps even harm the ambassador.

"There is certainly a great deal of malice directed at the skraylings and anyone associated with them," Master Catlyn said when she had finished, "though whether from one source or several, I would not like to conjecture."

"Do you have *any* idea who it might be?"

"Unfortunately, yes." He sighed. "Have you heard of the Huntsmen?"

"Only rumours. I have heard there are scurrilous ballads about their activities, but Master Naismith will not have them sung in his presence. His fortune depends upon our company's alliance with the skraylings."

"Not all the ballads are invention," Master Catlyn said softly. "That I can vouch for myself."

She stared at him.

"It was a long time ago," he went on, "and I was but a callow boy, led astray by those who should know better. I disavowed their company as soon as I could."

She wanted to believe him. And surely he would not have taken the job as the ambassador's bodyguard if he were still a Huntsman, would he?

"And you think the Huntsmen are behind the attacks on our theatre, and the taking of your brother?"

"I don't know. The man whom you caught–"

"Wheeler."

"Yes. He, and any allies of his, are probably just sympathisers to the Huntsmen's cause. The real Huntsmen would not dare pursue their activities here in London, not with informants on every corner and the might of both princes ready to crush them on the slightest suspicion. But they surely have eyes and ears of their own, and friends at Court. Friends like Blaise Grey."

"The Duke of Suffolk's son? That cannot be. His father is our patron, and a friend of the skraylings."

"The duke may be, but his son is not. And Blaise has income enough to fund a conspiracy, despite the breach with his father. You said Ned told you these villains of his were well supplied with money?"

"Several gold angels at least. And that was just to bribe the warders at Bedlam."

Master Catlyn stood up and walked over to the window. Moonlight silvered his hair and caressed the pommel of the dagger on his right hip.

"I should be out there, looking for Sandy," he muttered, slamming the side of his fist against the stone wall.

"It is long after curfew, sir. You cannot behave in any strange manner that might betray your suspicion of their plans, otherwise…"

He turned abruptly to look at her.

"There is no Otherwise."

"No, sir."

The following morning Coby woke early, startled by the croaking of ravens on the battlements above her window. She washed her face in a basin of tepid water and pulled on her doublet before anyone else stirred.

Master Catlyn finally appeared, dishevelled and grey from lack of sleep, as breakfast was being set out in the parlour.

"You said that Naismith gave you the day off today," he said, taking his place at table.

"Yes, sir."

He poured himself a flagon of small ale, but waved away

the platters of bread and cold meats. The servants bowed and retreated.

"Then you must go to the hearing at the Compter," he told her, "and report back here."

Coby put down her hunk of bread. "Are you not going?"

"I think it wise for me to stay away from Ned as long as possible. I already risk much by using you as my go-between; Kemp mustn't suspect that I know about Sandy's disappearance."

She nodded. *Otherwise Sandy is dead,* she added silently. *And there can be no Otherwise.*

"Of course, sir. I... I was going to go anyway. Master Parrish is giving evidence, and Master Naismith will be most wroth if he is too distraught to act tomorrow."

"Then you must do your utmost to help your friends." He stood and bowed curtly. "Now, if you will excuse me, I have much to do."

As he left, she thought she heard him mutter *Though what, I do not know.* She sighed, picked up her woollen cap and headed for the door.

The hearing had been set for eleven o'clock, so she went round to Master Parrish's lodgings first. The actor looked even worse than Master Catlyn, white as new curds and with an uncharacteristic golden haze of stubble around his jawline.

"Will they hang him?" Parrish asked for the hundredth time, as they walked along St Olave's Street towards the Compter.

"I am sure they will not. Master Catlyn has friends in very high places."

"But Ned betrayed him."

"And is forgiven." A small lie, but she had sworn not to reveal Master Catlyn's plan to anyone.

All too soon they arrived at the tall arched doors of the courthouse. The church buildings had been divided up, concealing most of their high vaulted ceilings, but many details of their former purpose remained: narrow Gothic windows, finely carved stone doorways and blank-faced niches that had once held the statues of saints. The nave had been converted into a panelled courtroom, and the magistrate's bench stood where the priest had formerly distributed the Host to the faithful. A fitting end to the corrupt idolatry that had been swept away by the Reformation, Coby had been taught, though she was too young to remember how things had been. To her, the name *Catholic* had always signified soldiers and enemies; it had nothing to do with ordinary pious folk.

Sixteen men in their Sunday best occupied the front bench: sixteen citizens of the borough where the crime took place, as required by law, to form a jury of Ned's peers. A thin couple in threadbare homespun sat close together near the back of the courtroom, looking duly terrified by the grand surroundings, and a little way along the bench sat the Faulkners' parish priest, black-garbed as a crow and about as genial. Peering over the heads of the jurors, Coby realised with a shock that what she had taken for an ancient marble tomb was a bier on which lay two corpses, each draped in a linen sheet. There was no sign of Ned.

Feeling somewhat queasy, she allowed Master Parrish to show her to a seat halfway down the room. She sank down onto the bench and stared at her chipped fingernails, praying for the hearing to be over soon. Eventually the magistrate appeared, flanked by not one but two coroners, in robes of black lined with scarlet. The officer of the court rapped his polearm on the tiled floor, and everyone stood.

"Pray silence," the magistrate intoned, "for Their Worships William Danby, Coroner of the Queen's Household, and John Derrick, Coroner for the County of Surrey."

The jury and witnesses sat down again, and the legal proceedings began.

"Let it be recorded," the magistrate went on, "that in the presence of the aforesaid coroners, on the twenty-eighth day of August in the thirty-fifth year of the reign of Elizabeth, by the grace of God, Queen of England, France and Ireland, et cetera, et cetera, and upon view of the bodies of Mistress Margaret Faulkner, widow of the parish of St Mary Overie, and of a man calling himself Thomas Armitage, both lying cruelly slain, upon the oath of–"

He paused and gestured to the jurors to stand. The sixteen men took their oaths on the Bible, whilst the clerk of the court scratched down their names and stations.

"Bring forth the accused."

The rattle of chains echoed around the stone walls of the former church as Ned was escorted to the stand, fettered and manacled and stripped of all but his shirt and hose. He looked as if he had spent the night in a stable. Parrish clutched her hand, so tightly she almost cried out.

"You are Edmund Faulkner, of Deadman's Place in the borough of Southwark?" the magistrate asked, not looking up from his papers.

Ned swallowed visibly. "I am," he said, his voice dry and barely audible even in the silence.

The coroners questioned Ned about the events of Tuesday morning. Only yesterday? It felt like an age since Master Parrish had first approached her for help.

The jurors and the Queen's coroner gathered round the bodies. Coby could not see nor hear exactly what they were doing, but the coroner appeared to be raising each sheet and pointing out the fatal wounds. The sickly-sweet scent of decay wafted across the courtroom. After a few minutes the jurors returned to their seats, some of them looking a little green. Ned was pale as death himself, and kept his eyes averted from the bier.

"I now call upon the first witness, Master William Watkins."

The thin man stood up and walked to the magistrate's bench, watched by his wife, who wrung a kerchief in her reddened hands and looked about to break down in tears. With much prompting from the coroner, he told his side of events, though there was not much to tell since the couple had remained in their own lodgings throughout.

Watkins returned to his seat, and the parish priest was called to give witness. He confirmed the time of delivery of the letter and vouched for Ned's good character. All seemed to be going smoothly, until the priest added that Ned had missed church the previous Sunday.

The coroners exchanged looks.

"Master Faulkner, can you explain your whereabouts on the Sunday in question?"

Ned flushed and mumbled something.

"Speak up, Faulkner."

"I was at home, your worship."

"You did not go to church at all?"

"No, sir."

The jurors murmured in consternation. The church imposed heavy fines on all recusants, and repeated offences drew the suspicion of being a Roman Catholic.

"Why not?"

"I was... unwell, your worship."

"Can anyone vouch for your sickness?"

"No, sir. No one saw me that day, except my mam."

Parrish let out a slow breath, and Coby realised Ned could have named him as witness to his whereabouts on Sunday. She withdrew her hand. Bad enough that they sinned together in such an abominable way, but on the Lord's Day...

The magistrate asked the priest to sit down, and called for the next witness. Master Parrish stood shakily and made his way to the front of the courtroom. Ned glanced up at his lover, a look of desperation in his eyes, then he returned his gaze to the floor.

"You are Gabriel Parrish, a player…" the magistrate's voice dripped with contempt, "of Bermondsey Street in the borough of Southwark?"

"Yes, your worship."

"And you are acquainted with the accused?"

"We are… old friends."

"Did you deliver the aforesaid letter to Father Nicholls, as related before this court?"

"I did, your worship."

"When did you first see the accused, on the morning in question?"

"The bells had just tolled nine, your worship."

"Nine?" Derrick looked at Ned. "Some three hours after the murder took place."

"I was minded to flee, your worship." Ned replied slowly. "But my conscience pricked me at last, and I made my way back to Southwark."

"Where were you, those three hours?"

"I can't remember, your worship. I wandered out of Southwark, past St George's and down to Newington, and thence along lanes and paths unknown to me."

"Did anyone see you?"

Ned shrugged.

"But you did in time return," Danby put in. "And at three o'clock yesterday afternoon, you came to this very courthouse and confessed to your crime."

"Yes, your worship."

"I think we have heard everything we need to hear," the Queen's coroner said. "The accused admits to having killed the aforesaid Thomas Armitage, in defence of his own person, and to have found his mother dead by the hand of the same

Thomas Armitage. I put it to you that the said Edmund Faulkner has hitherto been a lawful citizen of this parish, and ask you to judge this case accordingly. Gentlemen of the jury, you may withdraw to consider your verdict. The witness may stand down."

Parrish made his way through the departing jurors and took his seat next to Coby. A servant came in with goblets of wine for the magistrate and coroners. Somewhere a bell chimed the hour, followed by twelve strokes.

"Damn that priest," Parrish muttered. "Why could he not have kept silent about Ned's absence from church? It was only once, I swear, and then only out of fear of that bastard Kemp."

The officer called the court to order, and the magistrate asked the foreman of the jury to deliver the verdict. The man cleared his throat.

"We, the aforesaid jurors of this case, do agree that the defendant Edmund Faulkner killed and slew Thomas Armitage, in defence of his life and property, and that having fled in shame at his deed, did willingly return and surrender his person to the law, within that same day. We likewise agree that the aforesaid Armitage slew, or did cause to die, Mistress Margaret Faulkner, in the commission of said crime of robbery."

Coby sighed with relief, and squeezed Parrish's hand.

"He's not out of the woods yet," the actor muttered.

Coroner Danby got to his feet.

"On behalf of Her Majesty the Queen, I hereby grant bail of five pounds to the defendant, pending further proceedings. Master Faulkner, you are free to go about this city and not to leave its bounds, upon your own recognisance and the payment of said sum."

A murmur of surprise passed around the court. Such swift and clement dealings were almost unheard-of, and yet five pounds was an enormous sum to a man of Ned Faulkner's

ANNE LYLE   331

means. Coby glanced at Master Parrish and knew he was
thinking the same thing. Who, if anyone, would pay the bail?

The jurors and other witnesses filed out, and the clerk of the
court began gathering up his notes. Coroner Danby beckoned
Ned to approach the bench, and said something to him. Ned
nodded and signed the document he was given, and one of the
guards who had brought him in removed his chains.

Ned turned towards them, blinking as if awaking from a bad
dream, and Parrish rushed forward to embrace him. Coby followed more slowly. As she drew near, she heard Ned ask:

"How can I ever repay you?"

"For coming here, and bearing witness? It was the least I
could do."

"No, for putting up the bail money."

"I?" Parrish held him at arm's length. "I would gladly have
raised ten times that, had I known, but…"

"Then who?"

Parrish shrugged, and they both looked at Coby.

"This was Mal's doing, wasn't it?" Ned asked wonderingly.

"I suppose so," she replied, then added, in harsher tones
than she intended, "He must care about you very much."

She turned on her heel and walked out of the courtroom,
tears pricking in her eyes. She wiped them away with her cuff
and cursed her selfish jealousy. If Master Catlyn wanted to use
his influence to save a friend from the gallows, it was no more
than she ought to expect of any Christian. She walked back to
the Tower in an ill humour with herself, wishing she could return straight away to Thames Street and forget about everything
except the performance tomorrow.

CHAPTER XXV

Mal spent an anxious morning criss-crossing the city on real and imagined errands for the ambassador. At no point was he hit over the head and dragged into an alley by his brother's captors, somewhat to his disappointment.

He had been in a siege or two in his career, but this waiting was worse than any he had endured. What he needed was a distraction, a bodily exertion to ease his tortured mind. He was tempted to head up to Bishopsgate and beat seven shades of Hell out of that whoreson Cooke. He could not risk it, however; if he went anywhere near Bedlam, the villains might learn they were found out and then all would be lost. No, he had no choice but to feign ignorance and wait for them to make their move.

At the very least he could fortify his defences. To that end he made his way westwards to Thames Street and asked for directions to the house of Henry Naismith of Suffolk's Men.

The door was opened by a girl of about fifteen who looked him up and down with a cynical air.

"Maliverny Catlyn, to see your master," Mal said. "On the Queen's business."

The girl's mouth fell open, then she remembered herself,

bobbed a curtsey and ushered him down a dark hall and through a half-open door.

"A Master–"

"Catlyn!" Naismith exclaimed, getting to his feet. He waved the girl out. "Not bad news, I hope, sir?"

"Not at all," Mal replied. "I merely have some additional instructions for the morrow."

"Of course, of course, only too happy to oblige. Will you join us for dinner?"

"I… Yes, thank you."

"Excellent." Naismith went to the door. "Betsy! Tell your mistress we have another to dinner."

He returned to his desk, where a fat ledger sat open, and shook sand over the page.

"Please, sit down," he told Mal, tidying away his pens and ink.

Mal closed the door, then sat down gingerly on an ancient stool on the near side of the desk. How to begin, without betraying Hendricks' confidence?

"As I am sure you are aware, sir," he said at last, "the skraylings are not universally loved."

Naismith grunted, and shut the ledger with a thud.

"Tell me something I do not know," the actor-manager said. "I have had men spit on me in the street for going into business with one."

Mal frowned. He knew feelings against aliens in the city sometimes ran high, but having avoided the skraylings as much as he could, he had seldom witnessed it at first hand.

"You've had problems at the theatre?" Mal asked.

"Nothing serious," Naismith said. "One troublemaker who was dismissed as soon as he was found out. My other men are trustworthy, I can assure you, sir."

Mal nodded. "I fear the general populace are not."

"All too true, alas."

"I therefore think it unwise to put the ambassador within easy reach of anyone with a grudge against the skraylings."

Naismith sighed. "You wish us to perform at one of the royal palaces," he said.

"No."

"Oh?"

"I do not want any… conspirators to feel they have the better of us," Mal said. "The play will still be put on at the Mirror, but with utmost care for the ambassador's safety."

The actor-manager looked relieved, and patted his ledger absentmindedly. "Of course, we will do whatever is necessary."

"Can you show me around the theatre this afternoon?"

"It would be my pleasure, sir."

At that moment a bell rang, and Naismith got to his feet.

"That will be dinner," he said. "Please, come this way."

He led Mal into the front room of the house, a small dining-parlour with smoke-darkened panelling. A worn oak table took up most of the space, with a chair at the head and benches either side. Hendricks, who had been standing behind the nearer bench with head bowed, turned and looked up as they entered, and gave Mal an almost imperceptible nod. So, the hearing was over already.

"Please." Naismith gestured to the place at his right hand, opposite Hendricks.

A few moments later Mistress Naismith joined them, and Betsy brought in a large pie with steam rising from the slashes in the pastry. A fishy aroma filled the parlour.

"Eel pie," Naismith said with a broad smile, and tapped the side of his nose. "My wife's mother's secret recipe."

They said grace and sat down to eat. After serving the pie, Mistress Naismith kept up a steady stream of small talk whilst they ate. In the course of the next half-hour, Mal learnt far more than he ever wanted to know about the comings and goings on Thames Street.

"Are you not hungry, Master Catlyn?" she asked as she re-filled her husband's goblet. "You've hardly touched your pie."

"It is delicious, truly, fit for the ambassador's table. My thoughts were... elsewhere."

"Ah, what it is to be young and in love," she replied.

"Sorry?"

"When a young man is so distracted, there can be but one cause. A girl."

Hendricks' knife skidded on his plate, making a hideous screeching noise and splashing gravy across the table.

"Where are your manners, boy?" Naismith barked, leaning across and giving him a clip around the ear.

Hendricks flushed scarlet and muttered an apology. The rest of the meal passed in near-silence, and though Mal tried once or twice to catch Hendricks' eye, the boy remained intent on his own dinner. In any case, an open discussion of the morning's events would have to wait until Mal could catch him alone.

After the plates were cleared away and Mistress Naismith had taken her leave of them, Naismith pushed back his chair and belched contentedly.

"A fine wife, that," he said. "Very fine."

Mal murmured an acknowledgment. The pie had been very good, though it might as well have been bread and water for all that he could taste it in his present mood.

"God a' mercy." Naismith belched again. "Alas, I cannot walk all the way to Bankside in this heat. Hendricks, be a good lad and take Master Catlyn to look about the theatre."

"Yes, sir."

He flashed Mal a grin that went unnoticed by his master. They made their farewells and set off towards London Bridge.

"How did it go?" Mal said at last.

"Master Faulkner was freed on bail." Hendricks described the hearing in brief. "Do you think," he added in a low voice, "Kemp will take the bait, sir?"

"We can but hope," Mal replied.

They walked on in silence, Mal running over the few known facts for the thousandth time and wishing they would miraculously fall into a pattern, like a winning hand of cards. They did not. He let out an involuntary grunt of frustration.

"Sir?"

"Nothing," Mal replied.

The city drowsed in the midday heat, its air heavy with the stink of sweating humanity and their refuse. A few citizens made their way listlessly across London Bridge: porters pushing handcarts laden with goods, bored matrons drifting from shop to shop with even more bored maidservants in tow. In a narrow gap between the buildings that lined the bridge, a cloud of blowflies buzzed around a beggar who might have been dead or merely asleep, though either way he would not be allowed to remain there long.

Mal hoped they would not bump into Ned in Southwark, though no doubt he was lying low with Parrish. Tomorrow, when the actor would perforce be at the theatre – that was when Kemp would strike, if he had any wits. And there was nothing Mal could do about it.

They arrived at the theatre at last, and Hendricks led the way around to the back door.

"This will have to be locked during the performance," Mal said, eyeing the door. "We want no one creeping in unnoticed."

"Of course, sir."

They went through the tiring room, now made ready for the performance tomorrow. Trestle tables had been set out under the back window with wig stands and hand mirrors ready for the actors to apply their makeup, and some of the props and less-valuable items of costume hung from pegs on either wall. They walked out onto the stage and Mal surveyed the galleries. After a moment's consideration he vaulted down into the yard, took the stairs two at a time and went along the lower gallery to the lords' room.

It was much like the Rose, with a simple latched door between it and the rest of the gallery. Even if that were bolted, someone could lean or climb around the dividing wall, or simply take a shot from the yard. Not protection enough, not by a long way.

He glanced over at the minstrels' gallery above the stage. The central section was some four or five yards from the main galleries on each side, and cut off from them by solid walls of wattle and daub. Enough to deter or delay an assault, at least in public.

"How do you get up there?" he shouted down to Hendricks.

The boy beckoned him back to the stage, and led him through the tiring room to a stair leading upwards.

"This was where you were sleeping when Wheeler came in," Mal said, as they emerged into the office.

"Yes, sir. Through here is the gallery."

He opened a pair of folding doors, and Mal walked out onto the narrow space overlooking the stage. It was common enough for the richest patrons to buy seats up here, where they could be seen by all, but the ambassador had insisted he should have the same view as the rest of the audience. This time Mal would overrule him. More than one life was at stake now.

As they walked back through the box-office, he noticed the two practice staves propped up in a corner. Perhaps there was another way to work off his anxiety.

"Care for a fight, Hendricks?"

• • • •

They sparred on the stage, and for a while it was as if the last few weeks had never happened. Coby realised how much she had missed their time together, back when there was nothing more urgent to think about than the next fighting move.

"You have not forgotten your lessons, then," Master Catlyn said when they stopped for breath.

"No, sir. I've practised them alone, and run through them in my head when I could not practise." And imagined much more. If she were not already red-faced from the exertion, she would surely be blushing now.

"Very good," he said, leaning back against one of the pillars and mopping his brow with a handkerchief. "Any more of that beer?"

"Sorry, sir," she replied. "I think Master Rudd took the last of it home with him, and the supplies for the audience won't be delivered until tomorrow."

He grimaced at the news and pushed himself upright in one fluid movement. A ray of sunlight flashed on the silver pommel of his dagger, bright against the black livery.

"Sir?"

"Mmm?"

"I'd like to learn how to fight with one of those," she said, pointing to the dagger.

Master Catlyn blinked against the bright light. "Why? I warned you, did I not, that the best thing to do in a knife fight is run away?"

"I know, sir, but–" she looked around the empty theatre "– we are up against desperate men. Men who nearly killed Master Faulkner, and might try to kill anyone else who stands in their way."

"All the more reason to run."

"And what if I cannot?"

"All right," he sighed.

She stared at him. "You aren't going to try to dissuade me?"

"You've made up your mind. Now you get to live with your decision." He gestured to the knife on her belt. "Hand it over."

It was an ordinary ballock knife, a nine-inch single-edged blade, suitable for use at table as well as in a fight. He examined it carefully, then handed it back. The familiar tool felt strange in her hand, a friend turned foe.

Master Catlyn smiled thinly. "Changed your mind yet?"

"No."

"All right then." He drew his own dagger, then to her surprise laid it on the floor at the foot of the pillar. "Come at me."

"Sir?"

"Do it."

She advanced, blade held overhand at chest height.

"Level with the floor, dammit," Master Catlyn growled. "Elbow out. You want to gut your enemy, not yourself!"

She adjusted her stance. The knife was heavy in her hand, its wooden grip slick with sweat. She struck, but in an instant he caught her right wrist in a reverse grip, grasped her elbow with his other hand and twisted her arm behind her back.

They repeated the move several times, and each time he disarmed her. On the final pass, he kept the knife.

"Right, now you try."

She took a deep breath and held her ground, letting him advance. She went for his wrist but her arms were too short, the blade came too close to her body and she faltered.

"Again. This is a fight, not a courtly dance."

They tried again, but her right arm ached from being twisted behind her back and her movements were too slow.

"Again."

On the third attempt she managed to grab his wrist and tried to twist his arm, but he was far too strong for her. Eyes locked, they contended for the knife for several heartbeats before he glanced sideways. Without thinking she followed his gaze. Almost casually he twisted his arm from her grasp, leaving her off-balance. She stumbled against him, and hot pain bloomed across her belly.

"Careful, you idiot," he growled, pushing her away.

Then he looked down at the blade, and at the stain spreading outwards from the slash in her clothing.

"Let me see that."

"It's naught but a scratch, I assure you, sir." She pressed her hand to her left side, praying she would not faint. She could not let him see…

"Nonsense, it bleeds too fast. Here, take off your doublet."

Coby stepped back, shaking her head.

"If you want to learn to fight with steel, you have to learn to deal with the consequences," he said. "Now take off your doublet."

She did so, fingers trembling. Master Catlyn pulled up her shirt and frowned when he saw the corset. The blade had sliced into it after nicking her skin, and the bottom edge was already red with blood.

"What is this?" he asked with a laugh. "Are you such an old man you need hold your stomach in with this?"

"Not my stomach," she muttered.

His eyes travelled upwards, paused at her breasts, then examined her face for several moments. She returned his gaze with a strange feeling of detachment. She had imagined being found out in so many different ways – including being injured – that it was almost as if it had already happened.

"You are a girl," he said at last.

She nodded.

"Well, maid or man, that cut needs stitching. Do you have needles and thread here?"

"In the tiring house," she said, trying to breathe slowly.

"Good." He glanced around. "I will also need clean linen. And a candle." He set off for the stage door. "And some wine or brandy, if you have it."

"The candles are in the office, in a box under the table," she rasped. "And if you look behind the stack of new seat-cushions, you'll find a small glass bottle wrapped in a bit of sacking."

"All right." He looked back at her, concern in his eyes. "Take that damned thing off and sit down."

She leant against one of the two pillars and unlaced the corset, listening to Master Catlyn clattering about in the tiring house. He had taken the revelation so calmly, like it was nothing out of the ordinary. She didn't know whether to be relieved or disappointed. Mostly she felt like she was going to be sick.

By the time he returned, she was sitting against the base of the pillar, clutching the front of her shirt against her breasts and feeling horribly naked. He knelt at her side, set down his armful of supplies and pulled up the shirt just high enough to expose the wound.

"Hmm, not too long or deep, but a stitch or three will help it heal cleanly," he said.

He rummaged in the sewing basket and produced a skein of silk thread and the curved needle she used for mending props and padded costumes. She winced at the thought of it being stuck into her own flesh.

"Is this the right stuff?" he asked, holding up a bottle. The blue-green glass had a knobbly texture, like cobblestones.

"Yes. Master Naismith bought it from a skrayling apothecary. It is accounted a sovereign remedy for stage nerves."

Master Catlyn uncorked the bottle and sniffed. His eyebrows went up, and he began to cough.

"That should do the job very well," he said faintly.

He took one of the squares of linen and upended the bottle against it. The sharp scents of juniper, mint and distilled spirits filled the air.

"This will sting somewhat," he said, bending closer.

"I thought you wanted me to drink– *owww!*"

"I did warn you."

He cleaned the wound, probing gently around it with rough-tipped fingers. She had been looking away, staring up at the empty galleries, but now she turned her gaze to his head, which was level with her breasts as he bent over to examine the wound. Her heart felt like it would break free of her chest, it was pounding so hard. Surely he must be able to hear it?

"Right," he said, straightening up. "Now to get down to business."

He began to unstrap his sword-belt. She swallowed hard and clutched the shirt tighter. She was alone with a man, a man who knew her sex and had touched her naked flesh...

"What, you think I would ravish you, and you in such a sorry state?"

Coby looked away, afraid he would see willingness in her eyes. Would it be ravishment if she wanted him?

He slid the dagger scabbard from his belt and put it aside, then folded the belt, right sides together.

"You'll want to bite down on that, if you've never been stitched before," he said. "Your master won't thank me if you bite through your tongue."

He lit the candle with a flint and tinder, then held the point of the needle in the flame.

"W-what are you doing?"

He looked up, smiling. "You're not the only one with a skrayling trick or two up your sleeve. I learnt this one on campaign." He turned his attention back to the needle.

"Burning off the grease and dirt helps prevent the wound from festering."

"You're going to stitch me up with a hot needle?" she squeaked, shuffling around the pillar.

"It will cool very quickly," he replied, shaking it in the air. "Here, I'll quench it in your tincture, just to be certain."

The needle hissed as it came into contact with the liquid. Coby shuddered.

"Come now," Master Catlyn said, threading the needle. "If you want to be a man, you'll have to learn a man's courage."

"That's easy for you to say," she muttered. He seemed not to hear.

She placed the folded leather in her mouth as instructed. The needle pierced her skin and she fought back a whimper, biting down on the leather strap until she feared she would leave permanent marks in it.

"Breathe," he murmured. "That's right. One more."

One more turned into two more, several more. She began to wish he had let her drink from the bottle. Instead she prayed silently for courage and, above all, chastity. *The pain is punishment for my sins. The sin of lust. And pride, to think I could learn to fight like a man.*

When it was finally over, he cleaned the skin around the wound once more then bandaged her ribs. He helped her to her feet and held out her doublet so she could put it back on, but she shook her head.

"I will have to soak everything straight away to get the blood out," she said, bending awkwardly to pick up the corset. "My Sunday best, too."

"You are better with a needle than I," he said. "I dare say they will soon be mended."

"But I will not," she whispered. Now her secret was out, how soon before everyone knew?

"I knew there was something amiss," he went on, "that first afternoon in Paris Gardens. But I confess I didn't suspect… this. How long–?"

"Five years," she said. "At first it was just a travel disguise to keep me safe from the soldiers, but then when I lost my family… I had no other choice, apart from whoring. And that I will not do."

He nodded in approval. "I suppose your name is not Jacob, either. What shall I call you?"

"I think you should address me the same as ever, sir," she said after a moment's consideration, "otherwise you may make a slip of the tongue."

"Does no one else know?"

"No. It was never the right time, somehow."

"And now?"

She shook her head. "I must ask you not to tell anyone. I am still not ready to face the world in my true guise."

He fixed her with his dark, intense gaze. "Your secret is safe with me."

"Thank you, sir."

"I would do no less for any good friend," he said. "Stay here. I'll fetch you a bucket of water from the mill-stream to wash your bloodied clothes, then I must get back to the Tower."

She crouched to blow out the candle and put away the needles and thread. Why did men never tidy up after themselves?

She paused, basket and candle forgotten for a moment. A good friend, he had called her. Well, it was a place to start – if only she could be sure she could trust him. He was an intelligencer, an informant upon other men. What would he not say, or do, in the service of that spider, Walsingham?

CHAPTER XXVI

So, Hendricks was a girl. It made a strange kind of sense: the beardless chin, the unbroken voice, the refusal to go swimming… If he did not see through the disguise before now, it was hardly surprising. Despite her coyness this afternoon, he had seen enough to guess she scarce needed a corset to conceal her figure. He wondered what she would look like in a gown. Probably no more convincing a woman than any other lad who minced across a stage.

He walked back to the Tower deep in thought. Was there anyone within the world of the theatre whom he could take at face value? Not Hendricks, certainly not Ned; who was next? Naismith seemed too indolent a man to go to the effort of deceit, but he could not say the same about Thomas Lodge. The playwright had the kind of overweening pride that often led men astray. Then there was Wheeler: was he acting alone, or did he have allies?

At least he was now certain Hendricks would keep her mouth shut. He had been careless to confide so much in her, though women had a knack for worming men's secrets out of them without giving anything away in return. Damn her for making a fool of him, and damn himself for being so blind!

As he walked through the outer ward towards the ambassador's quarters, he heard the splash of oars echoing in the tunnel under St Thomas's Tower. Moments later an uncomfortably familiar tableau came into view: a skiff rowed by red-cloaked guardsmen, with a manacled prisoner sitting on the thwarts, head bowed.

"Who is that?" he asked Captain Monkton as the prisoner was led, struggling like a wild animal, up the stairs.

"Some actor suspected of distributing seditious pamphlets." Monkton laughed unpleasantly. "Topcliffe will soon have him speechifying."

The prisoner screamed and redoubled his efforts to break free. The name of Richard Topcliffe was enough to loosen any man's bowels. It was said the Queen's interrogator had been granted permission to set up a torture chamber in his own house in London, the better to develop his own methods of extracting confessions.

As for the identity of the struggling man, he must be Wheeler, the fellow who had tried to steal the play scripts. What was he doing here, unless... Perhaps Hendricks had been right about Wheeler being the author of the scurrilous poem. The city authorities were as edgy as new recruits on the eve of battle, ever since that business with the Guildhall libel back in May.

Wheeler stared wild-eyed at Mal as he was dragged towards the gateway under the Bloody Tower.

"I know you!" he shouted. "You're one of them!"

Monkton looked at Mal, his eyes narrow with suspicion. Mal shrugged, trying to keep his rising fear in check.

"I've never seen him before in my life," he said, and walked briskly up the stairs of St Thomas's Tower before his face could betray him.

One of what? The Huntsmen? If Wheeler somehow knew about that, and said so under torture, Mal's tenure as the ambassador's bodyguard would be over in the snap of a finger. Perhaps literally.

When he entered the Tower, one of the skrayling guards asked for the watchword.

"*Shakholaat*," Mal replied, hoping he had pronounced it correctly.

The guard inclined his head in acknowledgment and told him the ambassador wanted to see him right away. Mal went up the steps and knocked on the door. There was no reply.

"Your Excellency?"

Still no answer. He unlatched the door and went in.

Kiiren was staring out of the window, hands clasped behind him, spine taut as a bowstring. Mal unstrapped his sword belt and laid the rapier and dagger on the bed. What he wouldn't give for a good clean fight against the bastard behind all this, instead of creeping around the city like a thief in the night.

"Where have you been all day?" Kiiren asked without turning round.

"Out on your business," Mal replied, unbuttoning his doublet. It was the truth, more or less. "I visited Naismith and had a look round his new theatre. I'm concerned about your safety tomorrow—"

"My safety?" Kiiren turned, and Mal saw with shock there were tears in his eyes. "What about your safety? I wait here all afternoon, I do not know if you are alive or dead."

"I am sorry—"

Kiiren all but flew across the room and hugged him tightly, then held him at arm's length.

"I thought I had lost you again, *amayi*."

"You don't get rid of me that easily," Mal replied with a laugh.

"We will call off this foolish contest," Kiiren said, "and leave here. Someone else can take my place."

"Sir, you cannot." Walsingham would have his head on a pike if he let the ambassador snub the princes like this. "We must catch the men who are plotting against you."

"Why do you care so much for these people? Are you not one of us any more?" He stared at Mal. "Have others turned you against me?"

What others, Mal wanted to ask, but felt it was best not to reveal his ignorance.

"Of course not," he said.

The skrayling's expression softened. "No, I do not think they would ever convince you." He released Mal and walked away. "But I cannot allow you to put your life before mine. You will give up this guarding of body and remain here, where you are safe."

"No."

"Please, *amayi*. For me."

"No," he said more firmly. "Do not ask this of me."

"Why?"

"Because they will kill the man whom they plot to replace me with." Play along with this superstition of theirs, for Sandy's sake. "These Christians are not reborn, and they believe their souls go to a terrible place if they die without a priest's blessing. If that is true, I cannot bring such a fate upon even one of them."

"You were always gentle one, *amayi*. Very well, I trust you in this."

"Only in this?" Mal took off his doublet and threw it on the bed.

"In all things."

When Mal turned back round to face Kiiren, the skrayling's eyes widened.

"You are hurt, *amayi*!"

Mal looked down at his shirt. It was spotted with the girl's blood, as if he had done as she feared and taken her maidenhead. Perhaps he had in a way. He smiled to himself. She was not so very plain, to tell the truth. A little too skinny for his tastes but quick-witted, and lively enough to be promising.

"It's nothing," he said. "Just pig's blood, from a careless butcher's boy in the market."

He stripped off the filthy linen, scrubbed it under his armpits, then rummaged around in the chest at the foot of the bed for a clean shirt. After a moment's thought he pulled off the bandages as well, salved the tattoo, and allowed Kiiren to help him with clean dressings. Whilst he was tended, he rehearsed in his head what he was going to tell the ambassador.

Kiiren tied the last of the bandages and planted a moth-wing kiss on his bare shoulder. Mal shrugged him off and pulled on his shirt. Best to get this over with, before Wheeler started naming names in an attempt to stop the agony.

"There is something more I must tell you, sir, though it pains me to do so. Something I would not have you hear from others." He drew a deep breath. "You know there are enemies of the skraylings in England, calling themselves Huntsmen."

"Of course."

"Did you also know there are many of these Huntsmen in the lands where I grew up?"

"It has been reported to me, yes. How else you think I find you?"

"Then you know my elder brother Charles is – or, I should say, was – one of them?"

"Yes."

"Did your informants also tell you that... that I am one too?"

"You?" Kiiren stared at him. "How can this be? To kill your own kind..."

He backed away, the blotched pattern on his face more pronounced than usual.

"I killed no one," Mal assured him. "When I was sixteen, they forced me to join against my will, took me on one of their rides. I... I saw Erishen murdered."

Kiiren muttered something in the skrayling tongue in a venomous tone Mal had never heard from the mild-mannered ambassador before. He looked up.

"Liar," Kiiren spat.

"Sir?"

"If you are Erishen, you cannot have seen his death with living eyes. We are reborn only into bodies of unborn children. If you saw, you are not him."

"I–" Now he was totally confused. If Sandy had not been possessed that night, why...? The murder had been horrible, but surely not so horrible as to make a man lose his wits.

"Why do you lie to me?"

The young skrayling stood toe to toe with Mal, staring up into his face with inhuman amber eyes. Mal could think of nothing to say that would not further incriminate him at this point.

Kiiren turned paler still, if that were possible.

"You are in their pay," he said slowly. "They have taught you our tongue, that you may deceive me better."

"No–"

"Get out."

"Sir!" Mal had to force himself not to grab the ambassador by the front of his silken robes. "I swear to you I am not in the pay of your enemies. Now let me do my job and protect you from them."

He snatched up his sword belt and wrapped it about his waist, adjusting the buckles with military precision until both blades rested in the perfect position for combat. By the time he finished the familiar ritual, Kiiren had calmed down, at least a little.

"Very well," the ambassador said. "Now go. I do not wish to look upon you."

Mal snapped a formal bow and walked out. In the antechamber he halted, the reality of what had just happened finally hitting home, like a wound that goes unnoticed in the heat of battle.

He had come within a hair's breadth of dismissal, endangered Sandy's life and probably lost Kiiren's trust forever. As soon as the ambassador's visit was over, his job would be done and he would never see the skrayling again. The thought should have been comforting.

He paced the antechamber, cursing his stupid mouth. Wheeler probably knew nothing; it was his word against Mal's, and with the ambassador as his ally and protector, Monkton would have been hard pressed to make anything of it. Well, it was too late now.

A pity he had not managed to get more information out of the ambassador whilst the ruse lasted, but he had a few crumbs to go on, not least the confirmation that Kiiren had enemies amongst the skraylings as well as in the city. He would report to Walsingham tomorrow, after the play. All that mattered now was that he was still able to protect the ambassador and, with any luck, find Sandy and bring him back. Best to forget about the skraylings and their heresies, and focus on the here and now. Starting with a good night's sleep.

Coby spent a restless night trying to find a sleeping position that did not feel like she was being stabbed again. The knife wound had not bled through the bandages, thank the Lord, but it was still tender to the touch. She consoled herself with pleasant memories of Master Catlyn's closeness, wishing there was more to remember.

Perhaps the accident had been the hand of Fate, nudging her towards her true destiny. She was bound to be found out eventually, and who better to do that than the man she loved? Of course he might not return her feelings. He had made no move to take advantage of her, though that might simply be because he was a gentleman, not a Bankside ruffian. At least he would not speak of her as the apprentices did of their conquests, or so she hoped. The names they called the poor girls who gave in to their charms made her ashamed to call them friends.

It was all moot anyway. Now he knew her secret, there would be no more fighting lessons, no more running hotfoot across the city with urgent news, no quiet moments of comradeship. He would start treating her like a helpless girl – had done so already, fussing over her and bringing her water to wash her bloodied clothes. Sooner or later someone would notice, and then her five-year adventure would be over. Best to forget she had ever met him.

Lying awake and miserable in the watery light of dawn, she realised with horror there was still much to do before the performance, including delivering the trunks of costumes to the theatre. In the past it had been one of her tasks to help the draymen, but that was out of the question now; she could barely walk without wincing, never mind lift a heavy leather box. There had to be a way out that wouldn't draw Master Naismith's suspicion, something less strenuous that could occupy her time.

As she washed and dressed she ran through everything she could think of. All the arrangements had been made well in advance, even without Master Dunfell's further help: the makeup and wigs were at the theatre, a spare plot-board written out, the costumes checked and re-checked… That was it. There had been a dress rehearsal on Monday, and only she and Master Parrish had stayed behind to put away the costumes. What if they had missed some damage that needed a last-minute repair? And if none existed, it could be made…

Tiptoeing down the stairs in stockinged feet, she took Master Naismith's bunch of keys from their hook by the front door. She put on her shoes, slipped out of the door and round to the barn. Sunlight flooded in as she pushed back the door, catching motes of dust in a glittering whirl and making her sneeze.

Leaving the door ajar to let in some light, she mounted the steps at the back of the wagon. Inside, three large storage trunks awaited her. She unlocked the nearest and went through the folded layers of fabric. It had to be something important, so she could justify being freed from other duties to mend it. And the damage must be obvious and plausible but easy to repair. To ruin the play after all their hard work was unthinkable.

Nothing in the first one fitted the bill, being mainly soldiers' uniforms, shoes and belts. The second was more promising, however. In here were the faerie queen's gown and the doublets belonging to the three princes. The doublets had silver buttons down the front and silver-tipped points at the waist. A lost button or broken cord would be believable, but would take only minutes to replace from the spares in her sewing basket.

She turned her attention to the queen's gown of sapphire-blue silk brocade. The outer skirt bore a matching strip of velvet all round the hem, to guard the more fragile silk from damage. It was already worn a little flat where it dragged on the floor, but not enough to be noticeable. And yet what was more natural than for a misstep by young Philip to catch on it and tear a section loose?

Hardly daring to breathe, she took out her knife and cut the velvet guard near the back of the skirt, then began to pull it away from the brocade. She cut the more reluctant stitches as well, to prevent tearing, and soon had a very convincing "accident" on her hands. It would take a good hour to sew it up again, even working quickly – and she was not minded to be too quick.

Ned picked up a Venetian lace ruff, and let it fall. No point in trying to tidy this place; Gabe would hate it, and in any case there was nowhere to put everything. He contented himself with straightening the bed and gathering their dirty linens in a basket to take to the laundress.

He was just peeling an embroidered stocking from its sticking-place on the headboard, when a knock came at the door. He froze. Who could it be at this hour? Gabe would be at the theatre by now, applying makeup and fussing over his costume, and Mal was on duty at the Tower. He cat-footed it over to the door. The rain-soaked, sun-dried wood had warped in its frame, leaving cracks wide enough to see through. A dark eye stared back at him.

"Faulkner?" the visitor asked.

"Who wants to know?"

Ned hoped he sounded more confident than he felt. The ancient timbers would not keep the stranger out for long, not if he were determined to come in. Ned could only hope that, if it came to a break-in, the draper in the shop below would send someone up to investigate the noise.

"I'm a friend of your friend Catlyn," the voice behind the eye said. "Now are you going to let me in or not?"

Ned recalled his jibe at Mal. *You don't have any friends.* So who was this man? If he was telling the truth, he was at least not one of Kemp's allies. Mal would not conspire to kidnap his own brother, of that he was certain.

"I'll let you in," Ned shouted, "if you can tell me the maker's mark on the blade of Mal's rapier."

"Christ's balls! This isn't a game."

"There are men out there who want me dead. You could be one of 'em."

"All right, all right. It says 'Me fecit Solingen' down the fuller. Not that you won't find that on half the rapiers in London."

"And?"

"There's a triple cross after the inscription, and the initials JM as well. Satisfied?"

Ned made an affirmative noise and shot back the bolts. The man entered the room, glancing round with disinterest.

"I need you to come with me." He picked up a broad-brimmed hat, considered it for a moment, then tossed it back on the pile. "Better if you're not recognised."

"By whom?"

"Now, that's the question."

Ned folded his arms. "You still haven't answered my question. Who are you?"

"Name's Baines. More than that, you don't need to know. Don't want to know, if you get my drift."

"You're one of Walsingham's lot."

Baines inclined his head.

"So what are you doing here?" Ned asked.

"You have intelligence that's of use to my masters."

Ned swallowed. He had feared all along it would come to this. As if reading his mind, Baines grinned.

"No need to shit your breeches." He held up a striped djellaba, a gift from a Moorish admirer of Gabriel's, and threw it at Ned. "No one's going to lay a finger on you. Not as long as you do what you're told."

Wrapped in the concealing garment, Ned followed Baines down Bermondsey Street and thence westwards through Southwark. Just before Battle Bridge they turned aside, down a narrow alley that led to the river. Before they reached the turbid waters of the Thames, however, Baines halted in front of a battered door.

"What is this place?" Ned asked in a low voice.

"A place."

Baines opened the door and went inside. Ned followed, the horrible feeling he was being watched growing despite their being out of public view.

"This place stinks like a charnel house," Ned complained,

lifting a fold of the djellaba to his face. He thought he was used to the city's many foul odours, but the smell of death brought back too many memories.

Baines led him down a short passageway and opened another door. The room beyond was dimly lit by ripples of sunlight reflecting off the river and through the uneven shutters. Blowflies rose in a cloud as they entered, circling the men's heads in irritation at the disturbance of their feast. On a rough pine table in the centre of the room lay a corpse, bloated and greenish-grey, like a week-old oyster from the bottom of the barrel.

"Fished him out of the river," Baines said. "Know him?"

Ned stepped a little closer, trying not to gag.

"Kemp," he muttered.

The villain might have been much the worse for his sojourn in the river, but Ned would have known that face anywhere. He had seen it often enough in his dreams. And his fantasies of revenge.

Baines grunted. "Thought as much. But you're the only man left alive to testify – the only one apart from Kemp's employer, at any rate – and we had to be sure."

"Drowned?" Ned asked.

"Hardly." Baines pushed the corpse's head to one side, revealing a jagged bloodless gash. "Messy, if you ask me. Not the work of a man accustomed to such business."

"And that's supposed to make me feel better, is it?"

"We're not here for your benefit. But if you don't want to be next, you'll do exactly as I tell you."

CHAPTER XXVII

Coby sat in the box-office, mending the gown she had ripped earlier that morning.

"What's going on here?"

She started, almost stabbing the needle into her thumb. Looking up she saw Master Dunfell standing over her. Behind him two servants were manhandling a padded bench up the stairs.

"Just some last-minute repairs, sir." She held up the hem of the gown. "See, good as new."

Dunfell sniffed. "I hope so."

The servants carried the bench out onto the gallery and traipsed back through the box-office. Coby bent her head to her task. Just another couple of inches and she was done.

The servants returned with another bench, followed by other liveried men laden with baskets of food, wine and silver tableware. The banquet was set out on a table at one end of the gallery, whilst Dunfell fussed over the disposition of every item.

As the servants departed with empty baskets, Philip came running up the stairs.

"Oi, Jakes, where's my gown?"

She snipped the end of the thread and held it out to him.

"Here you go."

He gathered the thick folds in his arms and wandered out onto the balcony to examine her work in better light. Coby followed him, curious to see what delicacies were eaten by dukes. Plates of pastries ringed a silver stand piled with peaches and grapes. Flagons of pale wine were chilling in a porcelain cistern that stood on three gilded lions' feet.

"Where do they get this stuff in summer?" Philip asked, dipping his hand into the cistern and pulling out a chunk of ice.

"Get your filthy paws out of there, knave!" Master Dunfell flapped his hand towards Philip's wrist.

"I am also curious, sir," Coby put in. "Surely it cannot have been kept since winter."

"Some houses have deep cold cellars filled with great blocks of ice, it is true," Dunfell said. "But that is rarely possible in London. No, His Grace owns an ice-making engine."

"An engine just for making ice?" What she wouldn't give to know how such a thing worked.

Dunfell nodded. "A secret alchemical process, invented by the skraylings. It is the only one in England, I believe."

Not the only one, Coby thought. But perhaps the only one owned by an Englishman. She bowed to the duke's secretary and took her leave. There was still plenty to do, even though it was a good hour until the theatre opened.

The tiring room was empty for the nonce, and she took advantage of the quiet to make one last check of all her preparations. She took down the plot board from its hook and ran down the list. The props had all been set out on a table by the stage door in order of use: a scroll with tasselled ends, a basket of apples, a lute, three lanterns, a match-cord in a brass holder and a fake severed head in a sack. The only thing missing was the cage containing a live popinjay, which Master Eaton was bringing with him.

A hand grabbed her collar and something icy cold and wet slithered down her back. She yelped and sprang up, reaching behind her back and trying to get the ice cube out. Philip was standing a few feet away, arms folded, a malicious smirk belying his girlish features.

"That's for ratting on me to Master Parrish," he said.

"I did nothing of the sort."

"Says you. Little Master Ne'er-Do-Ill. Where were you the other night, anyway? With Catlyn again?" The boy leered. "Bet you squeal like a girl when he fucks you."

Coby's fist flew up of its own accord, hitting Philip's face with a satisfying crunch. The young actor fell on his backside with a wail, clutching his nose.

"What's all this?" Master Naismith appeared from nowhere and hauled Philip to his feet. "God's teeth, lad! Here, let me have a look."

Philip removed his hand from his nose. A thin stream of blood ran down from one nostril, and his lip was already starting to swell. Naismith cuffed Coby round the head.

"What in God's holy name did you think you were doing, boy?"

"He said–"

"I don't care what he said, you don't punch one of my actors in the face the morning of a performance. Now go and get some ice from his lordship's table, and be quick about it!"

She did so, thankful that Master Dunfell had already left. By the time she returned, Master Parrish had arrived and was fussing over his apprentice like a broody hen. Master Naismith hauled her away by the ear.

"What am I going to do with you boys?" he said, shaking his head. "Go on, get on with your work. I'll deal with you later, when the play is over."

They left the Tower later than planned, after a long and fruitless argument about seating arrangements. Kiiren had not been happy about the decision to sit in the gallery above the stage, but Mal had overruled him. Once the young ambassador might have tried to cajole him into changing his mind; now he was distant and imperious in demeanour.

As the ambassador's coach rattled along Bankside, a trumpet rang out in the distance, announcing the opening of the theatre doors. Mal shook the reins of his borrowed gelding and urged the beast into a trot, passing the coach and gesturing for the driver to speed up. The man shrugged, pointing to the crowd that blocked the turn into Gravel Lane. Mal turned his mount back towards the skrayling guards, beckoning them to ride forward and clear the way. Their leader hesitated, stooped to confer with the ambassador, then waved his men forward. Mal sighed. This was going to be a very long day.

The crowd parted like the Red Sea as the skrayling guards rode ahead of the coach, baring their teeth in friendly warning. Soon the coach was through the gates and heading for the back of the theatre, watched with idle curiosity by many on the fringes of the crowd.

Mal dismounted and knocked on the back door. It was opened by a boy in a corset and farthingales, his face covered in white makeup. The boy took in Mal's royal livery with a shrewd glance, then his eyes widened as he saw the skraylings.

"Come in, sirs," he replied in a piping voice quite unlike Hendricks' husky alto. "My lord Suffolk is already within."

Mal turned to Kiiren, who gestured curtly for him to go ahead. As they stepped into the darkened hallway at the foot of the stairs, Henry Naismith emerged from the tiring room.

"Welcome, sirs, to our humble theatre–"

Mal touched a finger to his lips.

"Please do not address the ambassador, either now or after the performance," he said, pitching his voice to carry into the tiring room. "It is against skrayling protocol, and might disqualify you from the contest."

"Of course, of course," Naismith told him. "Please assure His Excellency we respect his people's customs."

Mal thanked him, and escorted Kiiren up to the box-office. As they emerged onto the gallery, Suffolk and his party got to their feet in a rustle of silk and lace. The handsome fair-haired woman must be Lady Grey, from her likeness to her eldest son; others were cousins and hangers-on of the sort that surrounded every man of influence. Mal was surprised to see Blaise amongst their number, however. Either father and son were reconciled, or they were putting on at least as good a show up here as on the stage.

It crossed his mind that Grey would make the perfect Huntsman assassin, able to get close to the ambassador then hide behind his father's considerable influence. On the other hand he would have to be foolish or desperate to try such a gambit, and Grey did not have the look of either. On the contrary, he appeared at ease, and greeted Mal warmly.

"Catlyn!" He embraced Mal, murmuring in his ear, "I see you did the right thing after all."

Before Mal could react to this unexpected statement, he found himself being introduced to the duke.

"Father," Blaise said, "I'd like you to meet Maliverny Catlyn, an old friend of mine from Cambridge."

"Your Grace." Mal bowed low. "It is an honour to meet you."

Suffolk inclined his head in acknowledgment.

"I am always glad to know more of the company my son keeps. Did you enjoy your time at Cambridge?"

"Y-yes, sir. I took a great interest in music and astronomy, though my father urged me to study the law."

"Very wise of him."

Throughout this brief exchange the duke's eyes scanned Mal's face without pause. Did Suffolk know, or suspect, that Blaise had acquaintances amongst the Huntsmen? Given his son's erstwhile antipathy towards the skraylings, he must surely be on the lookout for anyone who might prove an enemy.

"The play is about to start, my dear," the duchess said, gesturing towards the stage with her fan. "Do sit down."

Mal stepped back into the shadows of the gallery. Should he be guarding the door against enemies from within the company, or watch the audience for signs of armed assassins? He decided to stand to one side of the gallery door, where he had a good view over the head of the ambassador into the crowd below.

The door opened a crack, making him start.

"Is everything to the ambassador's satisfaction?" Hendricks asked in a low voice.

Mal nodded. "Shouldn't you be downstairs, dressing the actors?"

"All done," she replied. "Master Parrish likes to do Pip's makeup, so I'm not needed now until the end of the first scene."

Mal glanced towards the duke's party, but everyone's attention was fixed on the stage, where Henry Naismith was reciting the introduction to the play.

"How are you?" he asked Hendricks. "Does my... tailoring pass muster?"

"It is sore," she conceded. "But it does not burn or fester."

"Good."

An awkward silence.

"I should get back to work," Mal said.

"And I too."

"Right."

She reached out a hand and touched his arm, turned scarlet with embarrassment, mumbled something incomprehensible and slipped away into the tiring house. Mal caught himself grinning, and immediately felt a pang of guilt. The poor child had entrusted him with a secret as delicate as his own; only a dishonourable varlet would take advantage of her innocence. He rubbed a hand across his face, wishing he could soothe his distemper with some of the ice-chilled Rhenish the duke's guests were enjoying, and resumed his vigil.

At the start of Act Three, the cannon was raised up onto the stage via the trapdoor, to add spectacle to the scene in which the pompous second prince lay siege to the gates of Elfhame. Coby had checked the mechanism earlier by lamplight, but now with the cannon primed with the flash powder provided by Master Cutsnail, she had to keep all flames well away.

She picked up the keg and made her way back through the cramped space as fast as she could; she didn't need to be told that standing under a firing cannon was a bad idea, even if the stuff was perfectly safe as long as it wasn't mixed with gunpowder...

Gunpowder. She recalled Wheeler's empty pistol. Heart pounding, she scurried past the wave engines and other stage machinery, and up the short flight of stairs. The tiring room was full of actors preparing to head out onto the stage. Should she warn them now? No, best to make certain, or Master Naismith would have her hide for ruining the performance with a false alarm.

She pushed through the crowd of actors to the back of the room, where the row of makeup tables stood under the windows, and tore open the keg. Hands trembling, she shook out some of its contents onto a clean rag and held it up to the light. Her eyes widened in horror. Black specks marred the red-brown powder.

Even as she turned to warn the actors, they began to march onto the stage through the curtained exits. She elbowed her way through the stragglers, heedless of the pain in her side.

"Master Naismith?"

The actor-manager stopped and looked round. He was dressed in antique armour, with a plumed helm that sat on the back of his head and gilded buskins on his feet.

"Not now, lad! This is my big scene."

"Please." She grabbed hold of his sleeve. "Sir, I think Wheeler put gunpowder in the skrayling fireworks."

He frowned at her, the garish stage makeup exaggerating his expression. "And that's bad, is it?"

"Yes, yes, really bad. Please, sir, we have to stop Master Rudd from lighting that fuse."

Ambassador Kiiren was most intrigued by the appearance on stage of the little cannon, but Mal was glad the muzzle was pointing well away from the minstrels' gallery. He had been in enough battles to respect the indiscriminate power of artillery.

A group of actors emerged from the tiring house below them, dressed in white cloaks and bronze helms. Their leader struck a heroic pose, brandishing a smouldering match-cord at the end of a brass rod.

"He'll put that out if he's not careful," Mal murmured to himself.

He stepped nearer the front of the gallery, battle instincts roused. The actor cleared his throat and began his speech.

"My brother's cause is lost; a cooling card
Lies at his feet. Thus ends his ardent suit.
But I, who on his heels did ever follow hard,
Run now ahead, unwavering in pursuit.
This queen I'll woo with actions, not with words,
With cannon's loud report and clash of swords."

He lowered the match towards the cannon's powder hole.

"Stop!" someone shouted.

Mal caught a brief glimpse of another man in armour bursting onto the stage, then he threw himself at Kiiren, knocking them both to the floor of the gallery. An instant later the fretted balustrade exploded into tinder, followed by a wave of screams from the theatre yard below. He pulled himself closer to Kiiren.

"Are you hurt, Your Excellency?"

The ambassador groaned and rolled over. His dark hair was full of dust and he had a scrape on his cheek where he had hit the floorboards, but there was no blood staining his cerulean robes. And for the first time since last night, he looked pleased to see Mal.

"What happen?" he rasped, spitting out a mouthful of sawdust.

"The cannon exploded, I think. An accident."

At least, Mal hoped so. A poorly cast barrel, the wrong mix of powder; anything could go wrong with such powerful weapons, and frequently did.

He got to his feet, shielding his eyes against the dust and smoke. Someone pushed past him, heading for the tiring house. The crackle of flames grew louder as the fire reached the faux-marble pillars with their thick layers of oil paint.

"Help us!"

He turned to see Grey kneeling a few yards away, cradling his father in his arms. The duke sprawled on the gallery floor amongst the ruins of their seating, face white as paper. His left hand pawed at a metal splinter the size of a tent-peg embedded in his thigh.

"Help me up," Kiiren said, coughing. "I will tend him."

"No, sir, you must lie low. This could be a diversion to scatter our forces and make you more vulnerable."

"Lord Suffolk is our greatest advocate amongst English. I do not wish him to die."

Mal looked around.

"Where are your retainers?" he shouted at Grey.

"Gone, the craven varlets. Please, Catlyn–"

Another, smaller explosion rocked the gallery, this time accompanied by a blinding flash of light. Mal froze, torn between obeying the ambassador and holding to his commission. Whatever he did next, someone was going to die.

Master Naismith staggered backwards through the curtain and collapsed at Coby's feet, his face a bloody ruin. She opened her mouth to scream, but only a thin animal sound came out.

"Come, we can do nothing for him," Parrish shouted, ushering her towards the back door. The exit was surrounded by panicking actors.

"Where are the bloody keys?" someone yelled.

"Here!" Coby fumbled at her belt for the heavy iron ring.

As they wrenched it open, she remembered why the door had been locked in the first place.

"Master Catlyn!"

She ran towards the stairs. Parrish grabbed her arm and tried to hold her back.

"Don't be a fool!" he shouted over the din. "We have to get out!"

She shook him off and ran up the stairs, pressing herself against the wall as the richly clad nobles streamed down to safety. Even in the near dark, she was certain none of them was Mal.

"Master Catlyn!"

By the time she reached the gallery, it was almost empty. The refreshment table had been knocked over and the floor was a mess of broken porcelain, fruit pulp and half-melted ice.

"Hendricks!"

Her heart leapt as she saw Master Catlyn crouching near the ruined balustrade.

"Hendricks, get the ambassador downstairs. I need to help carry His Grace to safety – he is sorely wounded."

"Of course, sir."

She glanced at Suffolk and paled, then returned her attention to the ambassador.

"If you please, Your Excellency...?"

The skrayling was a good six inches shorter than her, so even with her injury it took little effort to support him as they made their way downstairs. The tiring room was thick with smoke now, and she had to put out one hand to feel the way to the back door. At last they emerged coughing into daylight, and she led the ambassador a safe distance from the burning building.

The escaping audience, emerging from the main gates on the far side of the theatre, poured out into Gravel Lane or across the bridges to Paris Gardens. A few stragglers turned back to gaze at the spectacle, but most Londoners were too well aware of the danger of fire in a city built mostly of wood.

"Hendricks, yes? We meet again," the ambassador said, smiling at her.

She could not return his greeting. A vision of Master Naismith's ruined face rose in her memory. What was there to smile about?

A taller skrayling ran up, his whorled face creased with concern, and questioned the ambassador in his own tongue. Coby stared at the theatre as if in a dream, her hair curling in the waves of heat that rolled across the seared grass. Suddenly she recalled that the powder keg with its deadly contents was still in the tiring room. And Master Catlyn was in there with it.

With a cry of despair she ran back towards the burning building, but halted when the shapes of two men appeared through the smoke billowing from the door. They were carrying something between them. The duke.

"Master Catlyn!" she shouted hoarsely, beckoning to them. "Get away from there!"

The rescuers stumbled towards her. Not fast enough.

"Everyone, get away from here as quick as you can!" She gestured to the skraylings, but they just stared at her. She pointed to the theatre. "Great firework. Kill all."

Lord Kiiren barked an order to his guards, who ran to help carry the duke. Within moments the injured man was settled on one bench of the coach, and Coby found herself bundled inside, squeezed between the ambassador and Master Catlyn. Lord Grey crouched awkwardly on the edge of the bench opposite, steadying the duke as the coach lurched across the field. Coby tried not to stare at the spike of gunmetal still protruding from the duke's leg, but it drew her eye as if daring her to blench.

The coach turned left towards Newington to avoid the crowds heading towards the river. They had barely gone fifty yards when a dull explosion rocked the coach. The horses whinnied in terror and broke into a canter, causing the coach to bounce along the rutted road and Lord Grey to curse loudly. When the driver finally brought the beasts back under control, Coby dared to twist round in her seat. Through the small back window she could see a pall of black smoke rising from the ruins, and flames devouring what little remained. The theatre was destroyed, and Suffolk's Men with it.

CHAPTER XXVIII

Baines halted outside a glover's shop opposite the Bull's Head, pretending to admire the rich hues of the leather samples nailed to a board. Ned hunched inside the djellaba, convinced the foreign garment would only attract the attention he was desperately trying to avoid.

"That the place?" Baines asked him, jerking his head discreetly in the direction of the tavern.

"Yes, but it'll be empty today. Everyone who can spare the time and money will be at the Mirror." *Like I would be, if there wasn't a murderous throat-slitting bastard after me.*

"Good. Better chance of our man spotting you."

"You're going to use me as bait?"

In the fraction of a second before Ned's feet could obey him and break into a run, Baines caught his arm in a pincer grip and drew his dagger, keeping it at waist height.

"Going somewhere?" Baines growled.

"No, no. Just for a drink." *God knows I need one.*

"Good. Now, here's the plan–"

A low boom sounded in the distance.

"What was that?" Ned asked, looking around. Then he remembered; Gabriel had told him a cannon was to be fired during the play. He hoped it was going well.

"Oi, pay attention," Baines said, flicking the dagger blade towards Ned's belly. "Now, in a minute we're going to stroll into that next alley, where you'll take that thing off. Next, you stroll back out, go straight across the street to the tavern and order your usual drink. If you see anyone you know, greet them as you would any other day, talk to them, play a game of shove ha'penny–"

"You'll have to lend me an ha'penny, then. And money for beer."

Baines rolled his eyes, but counted out fourpence into Ned's waiting palm.

"Right, now, if you see anyone watching you, make some excuse and leave your friends, all right? Make out you're drunk, and leave the tavern…"

He proceeded to describe the route Ned should take.

"That's a dead end!" Ned squeaked. "What if this fellow follows me in and murders me?"

"Then he'll hang for it. After he's confessed to everything else."

"That's not much of a comfort," Ned muttered, glancing towards the tavern. He desperately needed a piss now, as well as a beer.

At that moment Southwark's church bells began to toll, first one then many together.

"What's going on?" Ned asked. "Surely it's not four o'clock already?"

"Can't be." Baines said, his head cocked on one side in concentration. "That gunfire came from the west, so did the first bells. St Mary Overie, by the sounds of 'em."

"But why–?"

A ripple of screams passed down the street, going west to east.

"Fire!" a man shouted. "Fire in Bankside!"

The moment Baines released his grip Ned was off, muttering desperate prayers as he ran westwards toward the Mirror.

Those fleeing the fire stopped for a moment to stare at the young man as he ran past, djellaba billowing in his wake, then they remembered their peril and moved on. The wind was in the west; all Southwark was in danger of burning.

Coby leant back into the padded seat, taking comfort from the warmth of Master Catlyn's leg pressed against her own. She longed to lay her head on his shoulder and… But not here, in front of strangers. Instead she thought back to the afternoon's events, wondering where, how she could have done things better. Something else bothered her, though. Something about their escape from the theatre–

At the end of Gravel Lane the coach turned left, skirting the southern edge of the suburb.

"Where are we going?" Lord Grey asked, craning his neck to look out of the window.

"To our camp," the ambassador replied. "Your father needs best care."

Grey frowned. "Not by your kind. Turn the coach around."

"I do not advise it–"

"Take us to Lambeth," Grey said, his tone brooking no argument. "We can get a wherry to Suffolk House from there."

The duke beckoned to his son and mumbled something in his ear. Grey shook his head.

"It's too far, Father." He looked back at the ambassador. "Lambeth. Now."

The skrayling's eyes narrowed, but he rapped on the roof of the coach and shouted an order in his own tongue. The coach lurched across the road and traced a semicircle through an open field, turning back the way they had come.

No one spoke for a long while. Coby glanced from the ambassador to the duke's son and back. Master Catlyn had told her Grey disliked the skraylings, but surely not enough to risk his father's life, or to disobey his command? She remembered Wheeler. Men could be driven to do desperate things out of fear and hatred.

Grey bent over his father, coughing, and her own throat itched in sympathy. Her lungs felt like the inside of a chimney, scorched and soot-blackened. As if anticipating her need, the ambassador drew a bottle from under his seat, uncorked it and passed it around. It was *aniig*, lukewarm now but as welcome as cold beer on a summer's day. She took a long gulp then passed the bottle to Master Catlyn, who did likewise before offering it to Grey in turn. The duke's son shook his head, but at a gesture from his father he relented and took the bottle, lifting it to the injured man's lips, though he did not drink any himself.

The road to Lambeth ran across the marsh of the same name towards the Canterbury Arms tavern and, beyond it, the pale tower of St Mary-at-Lambeth next to the bishop's palace. Pollarded willows lined the road, their blunt heads shorn of withies to build the now-ruined theatre. Brown cattle dotted the water meadows, grazing placidly, unaware of the chaos downwind of their pasture. The damp, sunken landscape seemed to echo Coby's misery, and she rubbed her treacherous eyes with a sooty cuff.

At last the coach slowed down, and Master Catlyn leapt out before it had even come to a stop. Leaning out of the window, Coby could see few wherries on this stretch of the river; most of them would have rowed downstream in anticipation of the end of the play and found themselves busy earlier than expected, ferrying the fleeing theatregoers to the north bank. She climbed out of the coach stiffly, glad to have her feet on the ground again.

Master Catlyn hallooed again, and at last one of the small craft turned in their direction.

"Where to, good sir?" the wherryman called up.

"Suffolk House, as quick as you may!"

Master Catlyn returned to the coach and helped Lord Grey to carry the duke down the weed-slick steps to the wherry. Coby watched them, hand to her mouth, fearing they would slip at any moment. At last the duke was safely aboard, and his son joined him.

"I should go home too," she told Master Catlyn as he came back up the stairs. The full enormity of what had happened struck her, and tears started in her eyes. "It's all my fault. I should have been more watchful, and now M-M-Master Naismith is... is..."

Dead. The word stuck in her throat.

"You must be brave, lad," Master Catlyn said, and clapped her on the shoulder. She nodded, pressing her lips together to stop them trembling. "But if your mistress can spare you, come to the Tower before curfew. I want to know everything that happened this afternoon."

"Yes, sir."

He turned back to the waiting ambassador, and they boarded the coach. As it rattled away eastwards, she suddenly realised what had felt so wrong, back in the theatre field. The horses, which should have been made frantic by the mere proximity of the fire, had stood placidly in their traces whilst one of the skrayling guards sat on the driver's seat, eyes closed. Only when the powder keg blew had they panicked. Bewitchment. It was the only explanation. Her hand strayed to her chest, to the comforting contours of the wooden cross tucked inside her shirt. Perhaps her countrymen were right after all to shun the skraylings. Fireworks and ice engines were one thing, but this smacked of devilry.

She patted her pockets, realising she had left her purse on the makeup table. The pennies were a puddle of molten silver by now, she supposed. Well, there was nothing for it but to walk back to London Bridge. Perhaps by the time she got there, the crowds would have thinned a little. Not that she was anxious to go back to Thames Street. The thought of facing Mistress Naismith, knowing she was in part responsible for making her a widow, turned her insides to lead.

Ned reached the end of St Olave's Street and skidded to a halt on the muddy cobbles. Over the rooftops he could see a column of black smoke rising to the heavens. Judging by the direction and distance, it could have only one source. The Mirror.

"Oh, Angel," he whispered.

Eyes swimming with tears, he crossed Long Southwark and headed west towards Bankside, making slow progress against the torrent of people fleeing towards London Bridge. He scanned every face as they passed, but though a few were familiar, none was the man he sought.

As he neared the Rose, he caught a glimpse of what appeared to be a pair of richly dressed whores, their blonde wigs and silken finery singed and soot-besmirched. One was weeping into a filthy handkerchief. The illusion was spoilt, however, when the other 'woman' pulled off her wig and threw it on the ground in disgust. Even through the thick makeup, Ned recognised the boy apprentice from Suffolk's Men.

"Hey, you! Philip, isn't it?" Ned ran over to the boys. "Have you seen Gabriel Parrish?"

Philip looked him up and down and sneered. "He's dead. Not that I care."

Ned stared at him in horror. No, not dead. Not Gabe.

The other boy looked up from his handkerchief and seemed about to say something, but Philip silenced him with a glare.

"Come on, Noll, show's over. Let's go home."

Philip pushed past Ned, tattered skirts held high. The younger boy trailed after him, still sniffing into his handkerchief.

Ned walked on, numb with grief. The crowds were thinning a little, and he made his way through them towards the field behind Paris Gardens. A trail of discarded shoes, beer bottles and trampled bodies led back to the gate. The hawthorn hedges were smouldering, too wet to burn after the recent rains. Wisps of burning thatch rained down towards him. The field was deserted, a waste of churned mud and ash. No, not quite deserted. Ned blinked, unable to believe his eyes.

Gabriel was still wearing his costume of gold brocade, though his stockings were filthy with soot and his golden hair stood up in sweat-soaked spikes. In the ruddy light of the burning theatre he was a boyish Lucifer, dazed by his sudden fall into Hell.

With a cry of joy Ned ran towards him. Gabriel stared back blankly.

"Gabe?" Ned halted, hesitant, just within arm's reach.

Gabriel drew a deep breath and his eyes focused again. "Ned?"

Ned flung his arms about his lover, pressing cheek to grimy cheek. "God in Heaven, Gabe, they told me you were dead!"

Gabriel returned the embrace. "I thought I was, but now I live again." His breath was hot in Ned's ear, sparking memories of their nights together. Ned kissed him, heedless of who might be watching.

"Come on," he murmured at last, echoing Philip's words. "Let's go home."

He led Gabriel down Gravel Lane to the outskirts of South-wark. Cautious householders, torn between fleeing the fire and leaving their homes vulnerable to looters, lingered in their gardens with bundles of valuables, staring at the pillar of smoke that loomed over the borough like a sign from God. Ned remembered he had left some of his own belongings behind at his mother's house when he went to stay with Gabriel, as well as the rosary Mal gave him for safekeeping. He supposed he had better go back home and collect them. There was nothing else to keep him there, except the rent from his mother's tenants. And if the house burned down, he would not have even that.

As they walked along the road towards Deadman's Place, they were passed by a coach accompanied by a dozen skraylings on horseback. The vehicle drew to a halt just ahead of them, and Mal climbed out.

"Ned?" He paused, hand on sword hilt.

Ned's knees gave way, and he dropped to the ground, head bowed. A pair of black leather boots, smeared with mud, appeared on the edge of his vision and halted before him.

"I'm so sorry, Mal," he mumbled. "I never meant–"

"Get up." A hand grasped his arm and hauled him to his feet. "I thought you were with Baines," Mal said in a low voice, drawing him aside.

"You knew about that?" Ned eyed his friend, trying to judge his mood. Mal's features were flushed from the fire, but he looked calm enough.

"Would you rather have been hanged for murder?"

Ned swallowed, and stared at the ground. "I deserve no less."

Mal made a derisive noise. "The Ned Faulkner I know never wallowed in self-pity."

"Perhaps you don't know me as well as you think."

"Enough!" Mal sighed. "We've both lost loved ones to these bastards. Don't let them force us apart too."

He held out his hand, and Ned grasped it, then embraced his friend. Mal stank of smoke, even worse than Gabriel. Not surprising: he must have been in the thick of it. Ned released him and craned his neck to get a better look at the coach. The skrayling guards were gazing in all directions, as if expecting an attack at any moment.

"What's going on, Mal? Is someone trying to kill the ambassador? Did–" His blood ran cold. "Your brother…"

"I didn't see him. I don't think this attack was part of their plot."

"If not, then who?"

Mal shrugged. "Plenty of people hate the skraylings."

"I remember a time when you were not so fond of them yourself," Ned replied.

Mal stiffened, and Ned cursed his stupid mouth. Not a wise thing to say within earshot of a dozen of them.

"What would you have me do to help?" Ned said. "Go back to Baines?"

Mal glanced at Gabriel. "Take him home first. I'll deal with Baines. If I need you, I'll send word."

"Thank you."

Mal nodded curtly and returned to the coach. After a moment the vehicle lurched into motion and continued on its way.

"What was all that about?" Gabriel asked, staring after the retreating cavalcade.

"I think…" Ned bit his lip. "I think I might be forgiven."

Coby unlatched the front door of the Naismiths' house and slipped inside. The murmur of women's voices came from the front parlour. One of them, surely Mistress Naismith, was sobbing inconsolably. Coby crept past the door towards the stairs, but before she could reach the bottom step, Betsy emerged from the kitchen, her face pale and streaked with tears.

"Oh, Jacob!" she cried, and ran up to hug Coby. "We thought you were dead too!"

She burst into tears, burying her face in Coby's chest. The parlour fell silent for a moment, then a group of middle-aged women poured out, exclaiming over Coby in mingled tones of relief and disapprobation.

"My dear boy," one of the women crooned, stroking Coby's singed hair. "Your mistress has been so worried about you."

Coby glanced at Mistress Naismith, but her master's widow was already returning to the parlour.

"Don't mind her," another of the neighbours said. "We all thought it was Naismith come home after all."

"You, girl," the first woman said to Betsy. "Go and fetch hot water for Master Hendricks here."

Betsy released Coby, much to her relief, and went back to the kitchen, though with many a smiling, tearful glance backwards.

"So," a third woman asked Coby in a low voice, "is it true? Is Naismith dead?"

She nodded. "I saw it with my own eyes."

The women burst into exclamations of grief, though to Coby's eyes their performance seemed well rehearsed.

"He died almost instantly," she added. "I am certain his suffering was very brief."

Leaving the women with this crumb of comfort, she headed upstairs to her room. She wanted to strip off her filthy clothes straight away, but decided it was wiser to wait for Betsy to bring the water. Instead she paced the small chamber, wondering how soon she could ask to be excused. Mistress Naismith was too wrapped up in mourning her husband to care about a mere apprentice. Coby was a little surprised at that. Her master had often praised his wife, but received little but complaints in return. Although, Coby reflected, if she had been stuck at home whilst the menfolk toured the country or caroused at the taverns, she would have been jealous and frustrated too.

She wandered about the room, unable to settle. Her eyes fell upon the sheets of paper pinned to the wall above her bed: her earliest sketches of the trapdoor mechanism. She pulled them down and tore them into little pieces, fighting back tears. If she started crying now, she feared she would never stop.

A knock on the door made her start. She opened it to find Betsy waiting with a bucket of warm water in one hand and clean towels under her arm. The girl bobbed a curtsey, and Coby showed her in, shoving the wad of torn paper into her pocket.

"Have you seen the boys?" Coby asked, as Betsy set the towels down and poured some of the water into the bowl on the washstand.

"No, we–" The girl put her hand to her mouth. "You don't think…?"

Coby shook her head.

"I'm sure they were in the first rush of people to escape the tiring house," she said. "Perhaps they went home to their own families, to reassure them?"

She didn't think Philip would do such a thing out of concern for his parents, so much as from a desire to avoid Mistress Naismith's wailings.

"Yes, yes, I'm sure that's it," Betsy said, nodding a little too hard, as if trying to convince herself. "You're so clever, Jacob, I would never have thought of that."

Coby turned away and unbuckled her belt, hoping Betsy would take the hint and leave. She did not. An involuntary hiss of frustration escaped Coby's lips.

"You're not hurt, are you?" Betsy asked, coming closer.

"No, not at all. Just tired."

"Only… Only I don't know what I would have done if you… if you–"

She flung herself at Coby, sobbing. Coby caught her by the arms and steered her gently but firmly towards the door.

"Perhaps," she said, "you could run along to the Johnsons' and ask if they've seen Pip. That would set your mistress's mind at rest."

Betsy looked up at her, face puffy and streaked with tears.

"But… what if Mistress Naismith needs me?"

"She has her gossips for company. She will not miss you if you are swift, and you will be doing her a great kindness. And it would set my mind at rest, too."

"It would?" Betsy blew her nose on her apron.

"Most certainly," Coby lied. She could not wish ill upon Philip, not after today, but she would not be sorry either if she never saw him again.

"Then I will go straight away," Betsy said. She gave Coby a watery smile. "I'm so glad *you* came home safe."

"So am I," Coby murmured to the door as it closed behind the girl.

She slid the bolt home, then took off her doublet and hose and hung them up to air, brushing off the worst of the soot. A pity: it had been the best suit she ever owned. With a sigh of relief she stripped off her filthy linens and dropped them in the laundry basket, then washed herself all over with a flannel and a sliver of soap and sluiced the soot from her hair. By the time she had finished, the water was tepid and filthy. She rubbed her hair with a towel and then dressed in a clean corset, breeches, shirt and stockings, and put her old suit on. Mistress Naismith had no need of her here, that was certain. Best to slip away before Betsy returned.

Closing the door quietly behind her, she ventured out onto the landing. The house below her was silent. She padded downstairs in her stocking feet, put on her shoes, and was out in the street in moments.

CHAPTER XXIX

Mal strode along the wall-walk until he reached the Martin Tower. He had insisted on doing this himself: if Ambassador Kiiren had been shocked at Mal's flogging, the sight of one of Topcliffe's victims would distress him beyond measure. He knocked and a yeoman warder let him in, closing the door behind him with an ominous thud.

The warder led Mal down a narrow stair to the lower chamber. It was not unlike the one in the Salt Tower where Mal had stayed on his first visit to the Tower, but with arrow slits instead of glazed windows. In the gloom Mal could just make out the shape of the actor, huddled on a simple cot bed. The stink of fresh urine hung in the air.

Mal waited until the gaoler had left, then walked over to the bed.

"Wheeler?"

The man mumbled something. Mal touched his shoulder and he flinched, whimpering like a whipped dog. Mal took a candlestick from the table and held it up, surveying Topcliffe's handiwork. There was little to be seen, no blood or broken bones, but he could read the story of the actor's torment in the shaking of his limbs and the taut lines of his face. He had been put on the rack and questioned for some considerable time, until his sinews were fit to snap. The warders would have had to carry him here, and still he was in too much pain to even get off the bed to piss in a pot. Mal sat down on the edge of the bed, causing the actor to whimper again as the mattress shifted beneath him.

"Who are your confederates, Wheeler? Where will they attack next?"

"Go to the Devil."

Gritting his teeth, Mal put his hand on the man's shoulder again and pressed down. Wheeler screamed, the cry echoing from the stone walls like the ghosts of all the prisoners kept here over the centuries.

"Who are they?" Mal asked, when Wheeler was quiet again.

The actor rattled off a list of names between sobs of agony. None of them were familiar to Mal.

"Who wrote the poem?"

"I– I don't know. H-H-H-Harris gave it to me, I d-didn't ask."

"Was it your intention to kill the Ambassador of Vinland, by burning the theatre with him inside it?"

"How… How else do you think you kill a demon?" Wheeler tried to laugh but broke off, gasping against the fresh agony it caused him.

"You think the skraylings are demons?"

Wheeler looked up at him with bloodshot eyes. "Don't you?"

"You said the other day you had seen me before," Mal replied. "Are you sure it was me, or someone who just looked like me?"

"How should I know? Demons can look however they want. Perhaps it was one of them masquerading as you."

"You've seen a man who looked like me but was not me?" Hope rose in his breast. Could Hendricks have been right, and these diverse plots were all one?

"You tell me," the actor whispered. "Was it you I saw in the Bull's Head, conspiring with Suffolk's Men?"

"What is your quarrel with Suffolk's Men?"

"They consort with demons. They deserve to die."

The memory of a boyish face, white with terror beneath a layer of ash, came vividly to mind. Mal leant on Wheeler's shoulder again, and this time he took satisfaction in the man's screams.

"No one deserves to die like that," Mal growled. "Not even you."

He got to his feet and went over to the door to summon the gaoler. Behind him, Wheeler's cries turned to manic laughter.

"I die in God's grace," the actor cackled. "Can you say the same? Can you?"

Mal walked back to the ambassador's quarters the long way round, more shaken by the encounter with Wheeler than he cared to admit. Try as he might to deny it, there was something unholy going on here, and he could not say for certain that his own soul was not destined for damnation.

Coby sat at table in the ambassador's quarters, staring sightlessly at the congealing supper on her plate. She knew Master Catlyn's anger over the day's events were not directed at her, but that had not made their discussion any pleasanter. Now he had gone to question Wheeler. She did not envy the man, though she could not pity him either.

She looked round sharply as the front door opened. Master Catlyn stepped through the tiny vestibule into the dining chamber, his face hard as stone. He shook his head in response to her enquiring look, then sat down, poured a goblet of wine and drained it.

"Wheeler knows nothing," he said at last.

"But I thought–"

"Oh, he was behind the attacks on the theatre. But the other business... no."

She reached out a hand, placed it over his.

"You should tell the ambassador," she said. "About your brother, I mean."

"No." He glanced about the dining room. The skrayling guards had finished eating and were gathered round the other end of the table, watching four of their fellows play Five Beans. He refilled his goblet then stood up. "Come."

They went through into the small parlour between the dining room and the ambassador's bedchamber. The door of the latter was closed. He gestured for her to sit down on the bench set against the panelled wall, and sat down next to her.

"He is very afraid," Coby said, inclining her head towards the door.

"It is one thing to know you are going into danger," Master Catlyn said. "Quite another to look Death in the face."

She saw again Master Naismith lying bloody at her feet, and her throat tightened.

"They won," she whispered. "I tried to stop them, but they, they destroyed everything–"

He put an arm around her shoulder. Her last defences melted away and she began to weep, great sobs that tore at her throat and wounded side. He held her, saying nothing. At last she could cry no more, her ribs ached too much. She groped in her pocket for a handkerchief and found the handful of torn paper. The trapdoor. The cannon. Fresh tears welled in her eyes and she gasped for breath.

"Here."

Something hard and metallic was pressed into her hand. A pewter goblet. She sipped the wine, wiped her nose on her cuff, and drank again. The sweet spiced liquid burned a path to her stomach and out into her veins.

"Better?"

She nodded and handed the wine back to him, found the handkerchief in her other pocket and blew her nose. She dared not look up at him, not with her face all swollen and blotchy from crying, as she knew it must be. She picked at the hem on her handkerchief and wished she had brought her sewing basket with her.

"You should sleep," he said. "It's been a long day."

She began to protest, but he was right. The day's exertions had turned her limbs to lead, and her head ached from weeping. He led her through into the small bedchamber where she had slept before. A greenish-blue lamp stood on a chest against the right hand wall, casting a sickly corpse-light over the room. The square panes of the window glowed deep violet in the gathering dusk, and shadows thickened in the corners of the room and under the curtained canopy of the bed. Coby shivered, wishing she were back home in Thames Street.

"Wheeler and his friends may have won their battle," Master Catlyn said softly, staring out across the river, "but the war is not over."

She joined him at the window. The sun was sinking, somewhere to their right, gilding the dark waters of the Thames. Wherries hung with lanterns plied their way between the city and Southwark, taking revellers home. The skraylings' encampment was dark for once, a huddled mass of domed tents silhouetted against the fading sky. Had they doused their magical lamps out of respect for the dead?

"You have to tell him," she said again.

He made no reply. Coby wondered what had passed between the ambassador and his bodyguard whilst she was in Thames Street. Did Lord Kiiren blame Master Catlyn for seating them so near the cannon? None of them could have known. If it was anyone's fault, it was her own for not check-ing the flash-powder in daylight before using it.

"Did you know," he said at last, "the skraylings believe they are reborn into new bodies when they die?"

"No. I... I always wondered if they had a faith of their own, though. They resist the message of Christ so strongly."

"But none of them has spoken to you about it."

"No." She lifted her hand towards the cross hidden under her doublet, uncomfortable with this heretical turn of the con-versation. "It's not something that comes up in business dealings. Anyway, what has that to do with your brother?"

"It's not only skrayling bodies they can take."

She stared at him. "No. That's..."

"Possession?" He turned towards her, dark eyes glinting in his shadowed face. "How else do you explain my brother's madness?"

"No."

"He – the ambassador – sought me out." His voice was low, urgent. "Why? Because he knew one of his kinfolk had been murdered near my father's lands, and a boy born there soon afterwards. What he does not, I think, know is that there were two of us."

"Sandy is possessed by a skrayling."

"Yes."

"And those men who stole him away?"

He sighed. "I don't know. Perhaps hired by the Huntsmen."

She recalled his reluctant confession. "Do the Huntsmen know about the skraylings, about what they can do?"

"It would explain why they hate and fear them so much. But I cannot say for sure. After that night, I did not hide my distaste for their methods, and Charles did not confide in me again." He laughed bitterly. "I would be far more use to Wals-ingham if he had."

"If the Huntsmen have him and know what he is…" She felt sick at the thought. Possessed or no, he was Master Catlyn's brother.

"We should both get some rest; there is much to do on the morrow." He turned to leave.

"Don't go!" she cried out. The thought of being left alone in the dark, in a building full of demonic creatures that were willing and able to violate her very soul, terrified her. "Please, stay with me."

His jaw tightened. "Do not tempt me. I am in no humour to be gentle."

"I…" Shame turned to indignation. "I was not offering my body."

"No?"

"No." She sat down on the edge of the bed and pulled off a shoe. "Faith, you men think of but one thing."

"One *thing*, aye." He leant on the door jamb, grinning at the double entendre.

She mimed throwing the shoe at him, then let it fall to the floor. She had not the spirit for this game, not tonight. She swallowed past a lump in her throat, afraid she would break down in tears again if he made another jest at her expense.

"Forgive me." He dropped to one knee at her feet and took her hands in his. "This business has put us both out of sorts. I presumed too much."

And I too little, she thought, but dared not say it. She could not meet his eye. His touch, his closeness already threatened her resolve. She had not offered, but she was not sure she could resist if he chose to take.

"Go to sleep," he said. "I will keep vigil, if you wish."

"Thank you, sir."

"Please, call me Mal."

"Thank you. Mal." He was still holding her hands; she could

feel her palms and fingertips beginning to sweat. "And... and you can call me Jacomina."

"I think it would be better if I stick to 'Hendricks'," he said with a smile. "Unless you are ready to tell the world?"

She shook her head. "Not just yet."

"Come then, *boy*, into bed with you."

He released her hands and pulled off her other shoe. She shuffled back on the bed and lay down, still fully clothed. He pulled off his own boots and sat down next to her. After a moment he sprang up and disappeared into the next room, returning soon afterwards with his lute. She smiled, recalling that first meeting at Goody Watson's. Half a lifetime ago, it seemed.

He settled himself against the headboard and began to play – a slow, melancholy tune she had never heard before. The ghostly lamplight picked out the planes of his face, throwing them into sharp relief against the dusky night. Black lashes caught the light now and again as he blinked, and his left hand moved along the neck of the instrument, only inches from her face. She sighed and closed her eyes. Now she might sleep.

Mal glanced down at the sleeping girl, lying on her side with her head pillowed on a fold of the counterpane. The bluish light stole all the colour from her face; she might have been dead but for the slow rise and fall of her shoulder. Too exhausted to dream tonight, by the looks of it. Thank the saints. Nightmares enough awaited her, faces of dead friends, screams, gunfire... At least she had not killed anyone, even if misplaced guilt told her otherwise.

He carefully lowered the lute to the floor and slid down the bed until he was lying next to her. He ought to go back to the ambassador's chamber, but he did not like to think of her waking alone, perhaps from death-haunted dreams, her cries summoning the skraylings to investigate. He lay back on the bolster, laced his hands across his chest like a stone effigy and closed his eyes, letting the now-familiar sounds of the Tower lull him to sleep.

He opened them again to a bright spring day, the air full of white petals blowing in a stiff breeze off the hills. Rows of es-paliered apples and pears, as tall as his head, stretched into the distance. He was in the walled garden tucked into the slope behind Rushdale Hall, playing with Sandy whilst Maman and the other grownups fussed over Charlie. All because their brother was getting betrothed, whatever that meant.

Sandy had a new bow and a quiver of blunt-tipped arrows, and was pretending to be one of the New World savages from the illustrated book in their father's library. Mal could see him, creeping along on the far side of the espalier, a pheasant's tail feather sticking up from his bonnet like a pennant. Mal had a wooden sword slung at his hip, but right now he was bran-dishing a crooked length of apple branch, pretending it was one of Charlie's guns.

"Bang, bang! You're dead!"

"No I'm not!"

Sandy ran to the end of the espalier and fired an arrow that missed Mal completely.

"Yes you are," Mal said. "I shot you through the branches."

"You can't do that, it's cheating." Sandy threw down his bow and arrows and launched himself at Mal.

"Is not." Mal rolled over, pinning his brother to the ground. "I killed you fair and square."

Sandy went limp underneath him, and the sky darkened.

"Sandy? Oh Sweet Jesu, no!"

Mal looked about him, but the woods were empty. They had been abandoned here, cast out by the Huntsmen for their cow-ardice. The stink of woodsmoke and burnt flesh drifted on the night breeze. Mal felt something tug at him, deep inside: an instinct like that of a homing pigeon.

"Come on, Sandy, get up!"

He shook his brother, who moaned but did not wake. Mal felt dampness on his cheeks and tried to wipe it away. Not tears. Blood. He scrambled to his feet and heaved his brother up and over his shoulder.

At first the going wasn't too difficult. Deer tracks led through the bracken, in roughly the direction Mal wanted to go. He stumbled along, bent under Sandy's dead weight. Sweat dripped into his eyes and trickled down his back. His limbs were heavy and sluggish, as if he were wading through water. It was as much as he could do to put one foot in front of the other. Then another. And another.

After a while he felt, rather than saw, the trees give way to open moorland, wreathed in mist. Far above, the sky swirled with silver and lead and palest gold. Not a creature moved across that dead landscape, nor any bird sang.

The inner call tugged at him again, and he staggered onward. The earth was lumpen here, bound together in tussocks of dry, slippery grass, impossible to walk across without turning an ankle, even unburdened. And the creatures were circling, just on the fringes of his vision. He wanted to drop Sandy and run, but then they would both be dead. He wished Kiiren would come, with his bright light that drove away the nightmares.

Nightmares. This was just another dream. He stopped and looked about him, and the creatures faded away into the dark. And Sandy... Sandy was gone too. They had taken him and they were going to kill him. Mal broke into a run, leaping from tussock to tussock and then into the air, running across the roiling mist as if it were solid ground.

There. A glow in the mist below him, warm and welcoming, like candlelight. He dived towards it, but at the last moment pulled back. This must be done gently, instinct told him. His feet touched earth once more. No, not earth, nor grass, but an uneven pavement of small stone blocks with weeds growing in the cracks. A wall of pale golden light, shot through with rainbow colours like a soap bubble, shimmered just beyond the reach of his fingertips. Smiling, he stepped through it–

Coby woke from a dream in which she had been sewing pieces of red and gold silk onto the walls of the theatre whilst Master Naismith tried to distract her with readings from Marlowe's *The Massacre at Paris*. Then she remembered, and her heart contracted with grief.

On the bed beside her, Master Catlyn smiled in his sleep. She smiled back, then to her surprise he sat up, eyes wide and unseeing. Moving slowly he got to his feet, pulled on his boots and began to walk towards the night-black window. She opened her mouth to call out his name, but the words died on her lips. As she watched, the window melted away, becoming a tunnel through trees whose branches laced overhead, shimmering green in the sunlight. She glanced away for a moment, back towards the darkened room. The faint glow of the skrayling lamp illuminated the walls and floor, cold as Thames water. It was still night. She turned to the window again. In the tunnel it was daylight. She clutched the cross about her neck and whispered a prayer.

As he moved towards the mouth of the tunnel, another figure appeared at its far end, his mirror image in all but dress: another Master Catlyn, thin-faced and shabby but unmistakable. The missing twin. Sandy raised his arms in greeting and Mal stepped into the tunnel. Coby sprang up from the bed with a cry – but the sunlight flared and she was thrown back, blinded.

When she opened her eyes again, Mal – and the tunnel – were gone.

CHAPTER XXX

Mal staggered and fell against the edge of the bed.

"Hendricks?"

He blinked, trying to make out the pale shape in the darkness. The figure on the bed stirred and sat up.

"*Rehi?*"

The voice was familiar, even as the word itself hovered on the brink of meaning. *Brother*.

"Sandy?" Mal scrambled onto the bed, grasping his brother's shoulders. "What are you doing here?"

He looked about the room. This was not the Tower. Two arched windows, rather than a rectangular one, and on the wrong side of the bed to boot.

"Where am I?"

His eyes were adjusting to the darkness now. The room was about the same size as the one he had been in moments ago, but with bare stone walls instead of panels and plaster. The windows were glazed on the inside; on the outside, thick iron bars set into pale, fresh mortar spanned each narrow opening. Through them Mal could make out a lawn running down to the dark moonlight-flecked surface of a river, and on the opposite bank, a vast dark shape, all high crenellated walls and towers. A faint gleam of candlelight revealed windows here and there, some far above the ground. A palace or castle by the river. Was he in Southwark, looking north towards the Tower, or somewhere else entirely? Only daylight would tell.

Sandy came over to stand at the other window. He began to sing softly, this time in English.

"Then woe is me, poor child for Thee!
And every mourn and say,
For thy parting neither say nor sing,
Bye, bye, lully, lullay."

"Sandy?"

His brother did not respond, only stared out into the darkness. He was dressed in a fine woollen doublet and hose, a little worn around the seams like a rich man's cast-offs, and a crisp new linen shirt. His hair had been cut short and he was clean-shaven. Only the manacles around his wrists, and the fetters on his ankles, betrayed the fact he was no guest here.

"O brothers too, how may we do,
For to preserve this day
This poor youngling for whom we do sing
Bye, bye, lully, lullay."

Mal stepped closer, wondering why Sandy had chosen that particular song. The change of words, from "sisters" to "brothers", was no slip of the tongue, of that he was certain. He laid a hand on his shoulder.

"Sandy? It's a bit soon for Christmas carols, eh?"

Sandy turned to look at him, and his eyes widened. He cocked his head to one side, studying Mal's face.

"Who are you?" he asked. The chains clinked as he lifted his hands to grasp Mal's chin.

"I'm your brother," Mal replied.

"Who are you? What is your name?"

"Mal. Maliverny Catlyn. Your brother."

Sandy relaxed his grip, then slapped Mal so hard his teeth rattled.

"Wrong answer!"

"Sandy! What is wrong with you?"

"Who are you? What did you find out?" He seized Mal by the shoulders. "Tell me! You can't hide in there forever, you know."

Mal placed his hands either side of his brother's head. "Alexander, listen to me. We have to get out of here–"

Sandy let out an ear-splitting shriek and clapped his hands to his head.

"Oh God, make them stop! Please, Mal, make them stop…"

Mal took his brother in his arms, and Sandy immediately went limp, almost falling to the floor before Mal could catch him. Mal carried him over to the curtained bed and laid him down. Sandy curled into a ball, making a thin keening sound. Mal had never seen him this bad before, not since–

"Maggots," Sandy muttered. "They eat you from the inside, gnawing, gnawing…"

God's teeth, what had they been doing to him? Though it was too dark to see much, Mal gently probed his brother's head and limbs for bruises, cuts or any other signs of torture. Nothing. What, then, had they done to bring him to such a state of torment? Who were their captors, and how in the name of all that was holy had he been brought here? Drugged and abducted from the Tower? Was Kiiren somehow behind all this?

He stumbled over to the door. It was locked, of course. He pounded on it, demanding that their captor show himself.

There was no response. He went back to the bed and lay down beside Sandy, stroking his brother's hair. Best to conserve his strength and wait until morning. Perhaps daylight would show him a way out of here.

Ambassador Kiiren burst into the room dressed only in his underlinens, his short hair dishevelled.

"Where is Catlyn-*tuur*?"

Coby shrugged helplessly and gestured to the window. "I... I thought I saw him disappear into a tunnel of light."

It sounded so ridiculous, and yet the skrayling did not seem surprised. Instead he picked up the lamp and swirled its contents so that it glowed a little more brightly, then set it back on the chest. Coby wrapped her arms about her knees, unsure of how one ought to behave in the presence of a foreign ambassador in his night attire.

"Did he wear his earring, last night?" Kiiren asked.

Coby stared at him. "His earring? You mean the black pearl?"

"Yes. Please, try to remember. It is important."

She cast her mind back over the evening's events.

"I was lying on the bed, here, and he was playing his lute," she said. "I remember looking up at him and noticing that his earlobe was bloody. I thought perhaps he'd hurt himself, during the..."

Kiiren looked grave. "Please, tell me everything," he said, sitting down on the end of the bed. "Go back to beginning, from moment you arrived here."

She recounted all she could remember of the evening's events, wondering as she did so how the ambassador had known Mal was gone.

"Stop," he said when she started describing the tunnel. "You say there was another Catlyn-*tuur*?"

"Yes, his brother Sandy." She paused, knowing she was

going against Mal's wishes. But the ambassador needed to know what was going on. "His twin."

Kiiren stared at her for a moment, his face sickly pale in the lamplight, then he buried his face in his hands, murmuring something in his own tongue.

"Your Excellency? Are you unwell? Shall I fetch your servants?"

He looked up. "No. No, that is not necessary." He got to his feet and went over to the window.

"Where is he?" Coby asked.

"West of here, beyond city. Not very far, but not near."

"How can you be sure?"

"When you close your eyes, how can you be sure where your hand is?"

She shrugged. "I just know. I feel it."

"Just so." He smiled, and sat down again.

"The thing I saw: the tunnel. It was real, wasn't it?"

"Yes, of course."

"But how...?"

"It is gift of our people, to walk from our dreams into those of others. When bond is strong or need very great, mind can bridge worlds. Dreams can pass into waking world, and things of waking world into dream."

"Magic," Coby whispered.

"If you wish to call it so." He cocked his head on one side. "You are afraid now?"

"No! Well, perhaps a little."

He smiled. "Without fear we are fools, yes?"

"So Mal – Master Catlyn – has gone into the dream world?"

"And back again into your world, but not here."

"He is with Sandy?"

"Yes."

"Can... Can humans possessed by skraylings do that?"

Kiiren stared at her. "Possessed?"

"Last night…" She swallowed, afraid she was betraying a confidence. "Master Catlyn told me he believed his brother is possessed by the spirit of a skrayling."

"That is not quite truth, but close enough."

"So, what do we do?" she asked. "To get them back."

"We must find them first." He sat cross-legged on the end of the bed and folded his hands in his lap.

"More magic?"

Kiiren held up his hand. "No speaking, please."

The skrayling sat motionless, his eyes closed. Coby hugged her knees tighter, expecting another uncanny apparition to materialise at any moment. Long minutes passed. Surely there ought to be something by now, mysterious glowing lights or a wind out of nowhere to blow out the candles? Not that there were any candles, only the strange blue lamp fading into darkness. Coby laid her cheek against her knees and closed her eyes, imagining Mal waiting for her at the end of a tunnel of light, arms held out to embrace her–

She jerked awake.

"It is done," the ambassador said, clapping his hands together.

He climbed stiffly off the bed. The lamp had gone out, replaced by the pale light of dawn.

"Do you know where they are?" Coby cried, scrambling after him.

"I saw great house by river. Where might that be?"

Coby's heart sank. "There are dozens of great houses along the Thames, sir."

"As great as Nonsuch?"

"They are in one of the royal palaces?" That made no sense. Why would Prince Robert hire ruffians to abduct Sandy, when he could have the Privy Council order the arrest of anyone he pleased?

"In, or near." Kiiren shook his head. "*Amayi*, what have you done?"

"Excellency?"

"My apologies, I did not mean you."

He swept out of the chamber, still muttering imprecations under his breath.

"Your Excellency, should I alert Sir Francis Walsingham?" she called out after him.

Kiiren stopped dead in his tracks. "No. We can trust no one with this."

"But–"

He fixed her with cold yellow eyes and she shrank back a little.

"We will say Catlyn-*tuur* is sick after fire and I tend him," the ambassador said. "No one, not even Leland-*tuur*, will risk anger of Queen Elizabeth by doubting my word."

"There must be something I can do."

"This is not human business. Please, go back to your friends and leave this to me."

He strode up the steps to his chamber and disappeared inside. Coby bit back tears of fury. How could the ambassador be so kind one moment, and so cold and arrogant the next? He was just like other skraylings after all. She sat on the edge of the bed and pulled on her shoes. Master Catlyn was out there, and she was going to find him if it was the last thing she did. On impulse she picked up his sword belt, rapier and dagger, and wrapped them in a cloak. They were no use to him here, and if she did find him, he might be glad of some cold steel between him and his enemies.

With a last glance back at the closed bedchamber door, she made her way out of the ambassador's apartments and through the outer ward to the gates of the castle, which stood open in the cold light of early morning. Torches still burned in the gateway, casting a warm yellow glow against the mist rolling in off the river. Coby stepped aside into the shadow of a tower, strapped the sword belt around her waist and then wrapped the cloak around her for warmth. The rapier was heavy, and so long that its tip scraped on the ground unless she kept her left hand pressed against the hilt. She began to walk more quickly, praying the guards would not notice.

The ambassador was right about one thing: she still had friends, and they owed Master Catlyn a debt of honour. She would show the skraylings this was human business after all.

Mal jerked awake to the sound of keys rattling. He got to his feet, groping for his rapier hilt. Too late he recalled he had removed his weapons before settling down next to Hendricks.

The door opened, and a heavily built man wearing blue and white livery and armed with a quarterstaff came into the room, looking around warily as if expecting an attack. He eyed Mal with puzzlement, then stepped aside to let his companion past: a plump-faced, pretty girl of about sixteen, carrying a plate of bread and a flagon. As she came into the room, Sandy stirred and sat up. The girl screamed and dropped the plate.

"Oi, what's this?" the retainer shouted, swinging the staff in an arc before him.

Mal ran at him, but the man was too fast. He jabbed the end of the staff at Mal's breastbone, knocking the wind out of him, and backed out of the room with an oath. The door slammed shut before Mal could reach it, and a key scraped in the lock.

Mal pounded on the door, more out of frustration than any hope that it would be opened again. He turned and leant back against it, breathing gingerly against the ache in the centre of his chest. Sandy was kneeling on the floor, gnawing at a hunk of fallen bread like a starving man.

"I don't suppose they brought enough for two," Mal joked, then realised it was the truth. The girl had screamed because she had not been expecting two prisoners. Which suggested he had not been brought here by Sandy's captors.

He squatted next to his brother and examined the thick metal bands about his wrists. Bronze, not iron. Strange, to make gyves of the stuff, unless... Kiiren had said that lodestone protected against evil spirits, and anchored the soul to the body. Did iron do something similar? Mal stared at his brother and made the sign of the cross. That... thing inside him had reached out across the bond between them and used witchcraft to twist Mal's dreams to its own ends.

He went back to the window. The palace on the far riverbank was silhouetted against the rising sun, and Mal had to shield his eyes from the reflections off its many gilded onion domes. A pale stone building with dozens of slender towers and chimneys: not the sprawling red-brick complex that was Hampton Court; nor was it Greenwich, which faced north and stood at the foot of a steep hill. Richmond, then. So whose house was this? Who was so powerful that he would dare traffic with demons under the very nose of Prince Robert?

Ned was dozing in a tangle of warm sheets when the knock came at the door. Not Baines again, surely?

"Master Parrish?" a high voice piped. "Master Faulkner? Are you in there?"

Damn. Hendricks.

"Hang on!" he shouted, scrambling out of bed and pulling on his drawers.

He opened the door and ushered the boy inside. Hendricks took one look at Ned and turned away, blushing, to gaze fixedly at a playbill nailed to the inside of the door. The paper was yellowed with age and torn around the edges, and the ink blurred from damp, but the title was still clear: "The Tragedy of Dido, Queen of Carthage, written by Christopher Marlowe".

"Is Master Parrish…" The boy hesitated. "Did he get out safely?"

Ned rummaged in the laundry basket for a not-too-filthy shirt, sniffed one, threw it on the floor, and eventually settled for yesterday's. It smelt faintly of the charnel house, but it would have to do.

"He's well. Gone to buy–" He looked up and froze, shirt forgotten. "Why are you wearing Mal's sword? What's happened?"

"Master Catlyn has been spirited away," the boy replied, hugging his ribs and looking as if he was about to burst into tears.

"What? I thought he went back to the Tower with the ambassador."

"He did. And I… He asked me to go there, to tell him about the fire."

"You were there when it happened?" Ned asked. "Who was it? And how in Christ's name did they conjure him out under the noses of the beefeaters?"

"Conjure is the right word," Hendricks replied. "He was stolen away by magic. Skrayling magic."

"God's teeth!" Ned crossed himself. "You're not jesting, are you?"

Hendricks shook his head. He seemed about to say more, but footsteps sounded on the stairs outside. Before Ned could stop him, Hendricks had thrown the door open.

"Master Parrish!"

Hendricks flung his arms around the startled actor, who tossed a warm loaf in Ned's direction then returned the embrace.

"Faith, what's all this?" Gabriel murmured, looking askance at Ned over the boy's shoulder.

Ned shrugged in reply. Voice shaking, Hendricks repeated the story he'd told Ned.

"Ambassador Kiiren says they are both away west of London," he added, "in one of the royal palaces or perhaps near it."

"Why should we believe that?" Ned replied. "If skrayling magic stole Mal away, the ambassador could be in on it."

"I don't think so," Hendricks said. "He seemed very upset."

"Upset at having his schemes discovered, more like."

"Enough!" Gabriel glared at him. "Come, let's break our fast and decide what to do about this."

Ned finished dressing and they gathered around the small table, perched on an assortment of stools and chests. After a couple of abortive attempts to sit down whilst wearing the rapier, Hendricks eventually unbuckled the sword belt and laid it on the bed.

"Near one of the palaces, eh?" Gabriel said, pouring three tankards of small ale. "Doesn't narrow it down a lot."

Hendricks made no reply, only picked at his bread. Ned smiled to himself. So, it was as he had suspected. Mal might deny any interest in boys, but there was something between those two, if only on Hendricks' side. God knew Mal's ambivalence had never stopped Ned from dreaming.

"Could be Molesey Prior, near Hampton Court," Gabriel went on. "Or Syon House. Essex is a friend of Northumberland, and we all know what they say about the Percys."

"You think the wizard earl has discovered the secret of skrayling magic?" Ned asked.

"Could be."

"My lord Suffolk might know," Hendricks said in a small voice.

"Suffolk? Yes. Ferrymead Park borders the Syon estate. If not the duke himself, then perhaps his servants know some gossip."

Gabriel got to his feet, brushed crumbs from his doublet and put on a soft velvet cap that covered most of his singed hair.

"Going somewhere?" Ned asked.

"I think we should pay our respects to our patron, don't you, Hendricks?"

The boy obediently rose and went to open the door, though not without a longing glance back at the rapier on the bed. Ned drained his tankard and made ready to join them.

"Not you," Gabriel said.

Ned opened his mouth to protest, but Gabriel silenced him with a kiss.

"I need you to make yourself useful, love," he murmured, and produced a purse from his pocket. "We'll need transport upriver, and perhaps the means to break a man out of bondage."

Ned took the money and weighed it thoughtfully in his palm.

"I reckon I know just the man."

Mal sat down on the end of the bed. Sandy was sleeping again, his features relaxed for the first time since Mal's arrival. Trying to move silently so as not to disturb his brother, Mal examined every inch of the room. There had to be some way out of this trap.

They had not yet shackled him, which was his main advantage. Perhaps they were counting on the fact that he would not try to escape alone, and with Sandy in tow he would have little chance against their enemy's henchmen. A quarterstaff might be a good weapon to subdue a madman, but he didn't doubt they had other more deadly arms beside. His own life doubtless meant nothing to them, whatever their plans for Sandy.

He mentally inventoried the contents of the room and each item's possible uses. It did not take him long. Their accommodation had deliberately been stripped of most of its furniture and all of its bedding, probably to prevent Sandy from taking his own life.

The most promising weapon was the piss-pot, which could be used to hit the guard over the head, should he turn his back, or its contents could be thrown in his face to blind him.

The bed and its mattress could be pushed up against the door to prevent anyone entering. That would not be much use unless he could find another way out. He examined the windows carefully. They hinged outwards, blocked by bars set into fresh mortar. If he had a knife or even a belt buckle, he might be able to poke it through the gap and dislodge them eventually, but he had neither. Not that time was likely to be on his side. The servants must have reported to their master by now; indeed he had expected Sandy's captors to come straight up here and demand to know how Mal had got in. Unless no one in authority was here right now.

A country house in Richmond, an absent master, and a manservant in blue-and-white livery. The cards fell into a pattern, though it was not one he had expected. Walsingham had it right: Blaise Grey was the rotten fruit to draw in the wasps, whilst the father stayed aloof and loyal to the Crown. But were they working with the Huntsmen, or against them? Either the father was a hypocrite, or the son; and Mal could not decide which of them he trusted least.

CHAPTER XXXI

Mercifully Southwark had been spared a conflagration. A couple of cottages at the end of Gravel Lane had burnt down, and several trees in Paris Gardens were no more than charcoal skeletons, but the rest of the suburb had escaped with only minor damage. Even so, Bankside was unnaturally quiet, even the bear-baiters' mastiffs cowering silent in their kennels.

"Perhaps everyone is at church, giving thanks for their escape," Coby said.

She and Master Parrish were leaning on the gate at the entrance to the theatre field, unwilling to approach closer to the smouldering ruins. Either side of where the theatre entrance had been, blackened timbers thrust up from the earth at odd angles, the only remnants of the staircase towers. The tiring house was a heap of silver ashes, stirred into ghostly life by the breeze.

"The bodies must have burnt to nothing," she said. "Poor Master Naismith."

"A pyre fit for Athenian princes. Come, there is naught we can do here."

At Master Parrish's suggestion they stopped by the Naismiths' house in Thames Street to enquire after the apprentices. Betsy told them Philip had paid a brief visit yesterday evening, with

Oliver trailing in his wake as ever. Coby exchanged knowing glances with Master Parrish. They both knew only one thing would tempt Philip back here so soon: the hoard of jewels under the floorboards. Mistress Naismith had rallied somewhat and wanted to know all about the previous day's events, so they accepted her offer of breakfast before setting off for Suffolk House.

Coby found little to say on the journey; the walk up the hill to St Paul's and then westwards along the Strand brought back too many memories of her visit with Master Naismith. By the time they arrived the great house was only just beginning to stir, and a single retainer in blue-and-white livery stood on duty at the gate.

"Gabriel Parrish and Jacob Hendricks of Suffolk's Men, come to report to His Grace on the condition of his servants and their theatre," the actor said.

The retainer looked down his nose at them.

"His Grace is indisposed."

"We know that," Coby put in. "I helped rescue him from the fire."

The retainer hesitated, and Master Parrish leant closer.

"Perhaps we could speak to his secretary, Master Dunfell? He had supervision of the theatre business until recently."

"Wait here. I'll send word to Master Secretary."

The retainer ducked into the gatehouse for a moment, then resumed his station, gazing impassively out into the street. Coby looked about the empty yard. Blank windows stared back at her, their leaded panes dull as old pewter despite the sun overhead. She started as a pale-faced man in riding leathers emerged from one of the doors, but he headed straight for the archway leading to the stable yard with only the briefest of curious glances towards the visitors.

"Anyone would think the duke was dead," she whispered to Master Parrish.

After several more minutes another retainer arrived: the same man who had greeted Master Naismith on their previous visit.

"Master Dunfell is absent on His Grace's business," the man said, leading them across the yard. "However Lady Katherine would like to see you." His tone of voice suggested he was as surprised by this turn of events as themselves.

They followed him into the great hall, along a passageway and out into a second courtyard. A marble fountain stood in the centre, its waters still as a mirror, ringed by fruit trees in tubs. Grand apartments were ranged around the other three sides. The retainer showed them through a studded door, past a marble staircase and into an antechamber lined with gilded panelling, its ceiling painted with scenes of Greek goddesses and nymphs. Enormous vases of blue and white porcelain stood on tables inlaid with marquetry of precious woods, one in each corner of the room, and coloured glass glowed like jewels in the windows, displaying the Suffolk coat of arms and their red unicorn crest. Coby stared about in open-mouthed awe. The theatre's tawdry glamour paled in comparison to the real thing.

Voices echoed down the stairs, magnified by the high ceilings and marble floors. A woman's voice, and a man's.

"... stop him, Dunfell, you know he's far too weak to be moved."

"I, Your Grace? I am but a humble servant, and do only as my lord commands."

"And what does Doctor Renardi have to say about the matter? I cannot imagine he is happy with this... adventure."

"Doctor Renardi agrees with His Grace. He says the evil airs of the city are not beneficial to my lord's condition."

"Hmph. Evil airs indeed. Tell him I will have his head if my husband dies."

"Yes, Your Grace."

Rapid footsteps descended the stairs and crossed the entrance hall, fading as their owner went out into the courtyard. A few moments later the Duchess of Suffolk swept into the room, followed by two ladies-in-waiting. Coby and Master Parrish both leapt to their feet and bowed low.

"Your Grace."

The duchess smiled graciously at them both, though Coby thought she looked tired and worried. Hardly surprising, when both she and her husband had come so close to death.

"You are the young man who helped everyone escape from the theatre," the duchess said to Master Parrish.

"Not I, Your Grace," he replied, gesturing to Coby. "That was all Hendricks' work."

"Really? And so young." She beckoned to one of her ladies, who handed over a velvet pouch. "For your pains."

Coby bowed again. "R-really, Your Grace, it was not I. Master Catlyn rescued your husband. Him and Lord Grey. I just helped the ambassador down the stairs."

"Oh. Well, perhaps you could give this to Master…"

"Catlyn."

"Indeed." She dropped the purse into Coby's palm, as if reluctant to touch an underling's flesh.

"I will," Coby replied. She forced out the words. "When I see him again."

"Splendid." The duchess gathered her skirts about her. "Come Nan, come, Jane."

She swept out of the room in a rustle of silk brocade, the ladies-in-waiting scurrying after her like lapdogs. Master Parrish let out a soft whistle.

"A formidable woman," he said.

"She's terrified," Coby said quietly.

"What?"

"She might be dressed as if for a visit to court, but she wears no makeup or jewels. And something is wrong. You heard what she said on the stairs."

"They were talking about the duke."

"Yes. And... and now I remember." Yes, that was it.

"Remember what?"

Footsteps sounded in the hall.

"I'll tell you when we're well out of here."

They were shown back out to the gatehouse where, at Master Parrish's prompting, Coby tipped the porter for his troubles. She felt rather guilty for spending Master Catlyn's money without his say-so, but it might come in useful later to have a friendly ear in the duke's household.

When they were well out of sight of Suffolk House, she seized Master Parrish's arm and dragged him into a doorway. "Yesterday, in the carriage after the fire, the duke said something to his son, and *he* said it was too far."

"What was too far?"

She lowered her voice, afraid they were already attracting too much attention from passers-by. "Somewhere the duke wanted to go, instead of his house in London."

"Such as...?"

"Ferrymead Park."

"Ferrymead?" Master Parrish stared at her. "But why there?"

Coby grinned in triumph. "Because that's where they've been keeping Sandy. And that's where Master Catlyn is now."

"That's – It's madness. Why would the duke abduct Mal and his brother?"

"I don't know," Coby replied. "But why else would His Grace be so anxious to travel in his wounded state, unless there was something there, something more important than his own life? And is it not a marvellous coincidence that he owns a house so close to one of the palaces, just as Ambassador Kiiren saw?"

Master Parrish shrugged. "It does look very odd, I'll grant you that. All right, let's go and find Ned. It's as good a trail to follow as any."

"Where do you think you're going?"

A shape detached itself from the shadows under the stairway and blocked his path. Ned groaned. Not him again!

"I don't have time for this," he told Baines. "I've got business to attend to."

"What sort of business?"

"None of yours."

The next thing he knew, Baines had twisted one arm up behind his back and was using his other hand to grind Ned's face into the rough-cast wall of the shop.

"None of my business, eh?"

Ned willed himself not to struggle. That would only encourage a bully like Baines.

"Still, it's a bit early in the morning to set you loose in the taverns," the intelligencer growled in his ear. "So how about you tell me what's so urgent?"

"No."

"No?"

The pressure increased until Ned yelped in pain.

"No," he whispered to the wall. Not this time. He would not betray Mal again.

"Do you serve your Queen or not?"

"All right, all right!" His mind raced, trying to come up with something that would satisfy the intelligencer. "I was going to the Tower to see Mal. Thought he might know what was happening with the contest, what with the Mirror burning down and everything. I owe Henslowe some money."

Baines released him with a grunt of disgust. Ned raised a hand gingerly to his cheek, and hissed as his fingers brushed raw flesh. This was going to be a beauty of a bruise, and maybe a scar to boot.

"Well then," Baines said, "in that case we can go together."

"What?"

"Walsingham wants to know what happened yesterday. Seems your friend Catlyn was in the thick of the action."

"No!"

"What do you mean, no? He was there, wasn't he?"

"Yes. Yes he was," Ned sighed. This was all going to come out soon enough. "But you'll be wasting your time. He's not at the Tower."

Baines drew his knife. "If you're lying to me again, Faulkner–"

"It's the truth. Mal was taken from the Tower last night."

"Who by?"

"How should I know? All I know is, he's gone."

"So that's what Naismith's whelp was doing here. And here's me thinking you boys were just getting together for a game of Hoodman Blind." He smirked. "I think you'd better come with me anyway."

"No, I–"

Baines seized him by the arm.

"You can come quietly and with all your guts on the inside, or not. Up to you."

He marched Ned down to the river and they caught a wherry across the Thames, disembarking on the quayside under the shadow of the Tower's outer walls. Ned fully expected to be dragged inside and thrown into the darkest dungeon, but they carried on past and turned left at the top of Tower Hill.

"Where are you taking me?" Ned asked, trying to keep his voice from quavering.

Baines made no answer. After a few yards they turned right

into a narrow street lined with tall timber-framed houses. Baines stopped at one of the doors near the far end, knocked, and they were let in.

"This is Walsingham's house," Ned hissed, when the servant had left them to wait in the black-and-white panelled atrium.

Baines nodded curtly. Ned stared down at his cracked and scuffed shoes, feeling very shabby in the starkly elegant surroundings of the spymaster's home. The servant returned a few moments later, saying Sir Francis wanted to speak to Baines, and the intelligencer disappeared through a doorway set into the panelling. Ned was left in the atrium to ponder his fate. Should he run now? There didn't seem much point; Baines would just hunt him down and bring him back here again. In pieces.

Eventually the servant reappeared and conducted Ned through the same door, down a passageway and out into the garden. Baines stood, hands folded behind his back, on the far side of a small lawn. Beyond him, the Queen's private secretary was a blot of inky darkness against the jewellery-box colours of the flower bed. Ned pulled the cap from his head and clutched it nervously in both hands as he approached them.

"Baines tells me Maliverny Catlyn has gone missing," Walsingham said, clipping a long drooping stem from a honeysuckle and dropping it into a basket at his feet.

"Yes, m'lord." Ned swallowed, then added, "Spirited away by magic, m'lord."

The shears clicked loudly, then were silent. Walsingham turned to face him, his dark eyes burning like embers in his parchment complexion. Ned clutched his cap tighter.

"Magic," Walsingham said. "Do you mean to say witchcraft?"

"I– I don't know, m'lord."

"I am no lord. 'Sir' will suffice."

"Aye, m'lord – I mean, Sir Francis."

"Why was this not reported to me sooner?" Walsingham asked Baines.

"I didn't know nothing about it, sir, not until Faulkner opened his mouth just now."

"Then perhaps," Walsingham said, "you would be so good as to find out."

"Yes, sir. Right away, sir." Baines snapped a bow and went back into the house.

Ned gazed after him, wondering what he was supposed to do now.

"So you are Edmund Faulkner, the one survivor of a certain little conspiracy," the spymaster said.

Ned couldn't think of an answer that wouldn't incriminate him further, so he merely ducked his head in obeisance. Walsingham tossed the shears into the basket with a clatter that made Ned jump.

"Nervous as a cat on a kennel roof," Walsingham said with a smile. "So, what have you not told me yet?"

"Nothing, sir."

"Come now, there must be something more. There is always more to a story than first seems." He gestured for Ned to walk with him back to the house. "This is no simple plot to replace a bodyguard with his double, is it?"

"I wouldn't know, sir."

"You wouldn't know. But I do. If these men have witchcraft at their disposal, why not attack the ambassador directly? Unless it is not the ambassador who is the target."

"They were after Mal all along," Ned breathed. "But why?"

"That is what I would like to know. And that is why I must know everything you know, or suspect."

Ned bit his lip, uncertain how much to tell Walsingham. Was it betraying his friend, or helping him?

"Mal and his brother are in or near one of the royal palaces, west of London," he said at last.

Walsingham halted on the threshold and turned to stare at Ned, squinting against the sunlight. "How do you know this?"

"Hendricks told us, sir."

"Us?"

"Me and Gabe, sir. Gabriel Parrish the actor, I mean."

"I know who Parrish is. How did Hendricks find out?"

"Don't know, sir," Ned replied. He wasn't about to tell Walsingham that Mal was consorting with underage boys. It had nothing to do with the disappearances, and would only get Mal into serious trouble when they did find him. "I suppose he went to see the ambassador on some errand, what with the theatre burning down."

"Hmm." He ushered Ned into a parlour that overlooked the garden. A fire burned in the grate, but it was still shadowed and chilly. "What *were* you up to this morning, Faulkner?"

"Sir?"

Walsingham sat down in a chair by the hearth with a sigh.

"From what Baines told me, it sounds dangerously like another conspiracy. Hendricks running back and forth on mysterious errands when he should be mourning the loss of his master, Parrish no better, and you just happen to be right there in the middle..."

"We were going to find Mal and Sandy," Ned blurted out. "Take a boat upriver, and look for them."

"But you don't know where they are."

"Well, no, sir, not exactly where. But we have a rough idea."

"A rough idea. So, you plan to go blundering around the Thames valley in search of two men who have been locked away where no one can find them."

Ned hung his head. Put like that, it did sound stupid.

"Still, it might prove fruitful," Walsingham added.

"Sir?"

"There is a chance you may alarm the conspirators into showing their hand too early."

Ned grinned. Now he was on surer ground. "Like a bluff at cards."

"Precisely." Walsingham picked up a small bell that stood on a table at his elbow, and rang it briefly. "Very well, continue with your scheme, and tell Baines to supply you with whatever you need. We wouldn't want you to walk into a trap unarmed, would we now?"

"No, sir. Thank you, sir."

The manservant appeared, and Ned followed him back to the atrium. A trap? He didn't like the sound of Walsingham's plan one bit, but on the other hand, what choice did they have?

Before the sun had climbed halfway to its zenith Mal had exhausted all his ideas on how to get them out of their cell. He had hoped that if Sandy could magic him here, Sandy could magic him back, perhaps even magic them both back, but his brother had lapsed into a silence as profound as any Mal had seen before. No amount of pleading or cajoling raised so much as a flicker of recognition. At least he was not screaming or twitching in one of his terrible seizures, for which Mal thanked God at least once an hour.

His other hope was that he might attract attention by waving something from the window. With an entire palace and its dozens of windows only a hundred yards away, someone must surely see him and wonder what was going on in Suffolk's country mansion. However, the bars prevented the window from being opened more than a finger's breadth, and the small thick panes were impossible to break.

At around noon, footsteps sounded in the corridor outside. Dinner, perhaps? Mal went over to the door to listen, but could hear no voices. A key grated in the lock. Mal flattened himself against the wall, and as the door opened he kicked it wide and launched himself at the armed retainer, sending them both careening out into the corridor. They struggled for a moment, then Mal heard a familiar voice say:

"I wouldn't do that if I were you."

He whirled, and the retainer's staff hit him in the ribs from behind. Mal staggered and caught himself against the door frame – and froze when he saw a crossbow pointed straight at Sandy.

Blaise was dressed for riding in a doublet and hose of buff leather trimmed with brown velvet, and his face was flushed with exertion. The crossbow, a heavy German hunting model inset with mother-of-pearl, was tucked casually under his arm.

"I must say, Goddard," he remarked to the retainer in idle tones, "When I heard your report, I thought you'd been drinking my father's best sack. But here he is, as large as life. How are you, Catlyn?"

Mal straightened up, and the butt of the quarterstaff prodded him in the back. He reluctantly stepped back into the room. Sandy stared at Blaise, wide-eyed, and began to mutter under his breath. The retainer moved towards him, quarterstaff at the ready.

"Don't distress yourself, Alexander," Blaise said. "I'll get to you later."

He gestured for Mal to move to the opposite end of the room.

"What are you going to do with us?" Mal asked.

"I? Nothing." Blaise cocked his head on one side, looked back at Sandy and then at Mal. "How did you get here?"

Mal folded his arms. "I don't know."

"Wrong answer." Blaise aimed his crossbow at Mal's foot.

Mal weighed up his options. Blaise had not resorted to violence when he had questioned Sandy – assuming it was his words Sandy had echoed – but he probably had no such qualms with Mal himself. Injured, Mal was of no use to his brother, but if he revealed Sandy's magic, would that do Blaise's work for him? What would the Huntsmen do with that power once they had it under their control?

"I used witchcraft," Mal said.

"You?"

Mal nodded, praying Blaise would believe him.

"How?" Blaise asked.

"I flew here on wings of night, drawn by my brother's need." As he said the words he knew they were true, in a fashion; his dreams had led him to Sandy, even if the magic had not been his.

"A pity you couldn't just fly out again," Blaise sneered.

"Perhaps I choose not to," Mal replied.

"Brave words." He called over his shoulder. "Ivett!"

A young man in livery entered the room, carrying two sets of gyves joined by chains. These were plain iron, not bronze. With many a nervous glance at his master, Ivett placed the irons around Mal's wrists and ankles, securing them with simple padlocks.

"Now you have no choice," Blaise said, when the man was done. He backed towards the door, the servants preceding him out of the room.

Mal yanked the chain between his wrists, but it was well forged and solid. Blaise was right; he had no choice now but to stay here and wait out whatever plan the Greys had in mind.

Ned climbed the outside stair to Gabriel's lodgings and let himself in.

"What took you so long?" Gabriel asked, eyeing the heavy satchel that hung at Ned's side. His gaze flicked to Ned's face and he leapt to his feet. "God in Heaven, what happened?"

"Nothing."

"Doesn't look like nothing to me," Gabriel said, putting his hand under Ned's chin and tipping his head to one side to get a better look at the scrape.

"A run-in with that whoreson Baines, if you must know," Ned grunted. Seeing the concern in his lover's eyes, he added, "Don't fret, it's all sorted out between us."

"Well. Good." Gabriel turned to Hendricks. "Ready?"

The boy nodded.

"Right. You two head upriver, I'll report to the ambassador. I think someone should keep an eye on Suffolk House."

"You think Ambassador Kiiren was talking about Whitehall Palace after all?" Hendricks asked.

Gabriel shrugged. "You say he said 'not close', didn't you? But we can't be too sure. Skraylings may measure things differently."

Ned took Gabriel's face in his hands.

"I won't be parted from you again," he whispered.

"Don't be a fool, love," Gabriel replied, catching hold of his wrists. He glanced significantly towards the boy. "Hendricks needs your help. What good would I be in a fight?"

"I've seen you with a sword. Not nearly as good as Mal, mind–"

"Play-acting, and well practised as any courtly dance. In a real duel I would be minced meat, and you know it."

"All right," Ned sighed, and brought one of Gabriel's hands to his lips for a tender kiss. "My lady must do as she pleases."

The look Gabriel gave him from under lowered lids almost made Ned send Hendricks on his way, and to hell with Mal.

"Right," he said, releasing Gabriel. "We'd better be off."

"Tyrell's is the best livery stable in Southwark," Gabriel said. "Tell Tom the stable lad I sent you, and you'll get a good price."

Ned looked at Hendricks. "Can you ride?"

The boy shrugged in apology. That would be a no, then.

"We'll hire a boat," Ned told Gabriel. "Neither of us will be any use to Mal with a broken neck."

"Be careful, sweet," Gabriel murmured, hugging him.

"Don't worry about me. I have the Devil's own luck."

CHAPTER XXXII

Coby leant on the gunwales of the little boat, scanning the Middlesex bank for a good landing place. They were about a mile downstream from Ferrymead House, and the golden pinnacles of Richmond Palace glinted above the trees to the west. They had seen no sign of the duke's barge, though this was not surprising since it had a head start on them of at least an hour.

"There," she cried, pointing to a level stretch of grass beside a willow. Faulkner steered the boat towards it, and soon their prow bumped against the bank. The little craft spun like a leaf in the current, coming to rest with its stern amongst the willow roots that stretched down into the water.

"Christ's balls," Faulkner muttered, shaking his arms and flexing his fingers. "Why in God's name didn't we hire a man to row this thing?"

"The thing about secret missions is–" Coby paused for effect "–they're secret."

Faulkner looked away, suddenly unwilling to meet her eye, like a schoolboy caught truanting. Coby's heart sank. She knew he was hiding something, but how was she to get to the truth? She could hardly beat the information out of him.

"Half the Tower probably knows where we've gone by now," Ned replied with forced casualness, then paled. "You don't think they'd torture Gabe for information, do you?"

Coby was tempted to say yes, but she thought how she would feel in Faulkner's place.

"No," she replied, scrambling ashore and tying the painter to a low branch. "He'll be quite safe, I'm certain of it."

Faulkner grunted as he threw her Mal's bundled-up weapons. "So what do we do when we get there?"

"How should I know? You're older than me, and wiser in the ways of the world. Don't you have a plan?"

"I did, but it rather involved Gabriel coming with us."

"If you could get your thoughts out of the gutter for five minutes together, Ned Faulkner–"

"You're the one chasing halfway across the country because you're smitten with a man who doesn't even notice you."

Coby folded her arms, refusing to rise to the bait. It was none of Faulkner's business what Mal thought of her, or she of him.

"Why do you hate me so much?" she asked him.

"I don't hate you."

"You don't like me."

"Well what do you expect, when you're such a hypocrite?"

"A hypocrite? Me?"

"Yes, you. Acting all holier-than-thou over me and Gabriel" he pulled a prissy face in imitation "when you earn your living dressing boys up as women, so they can act out love scenes with men. In public."

Coby swallowed. "I hadn't thought of it like that before."

Faulkner said nothing. He didn't need to.

"I'm sorry," she said in a small voice, and set off across the water meadow, tears pricking her eyes.

Talk about looking for the mote in the other man's eye! She had heard many sermons about the abomination of boys playing women's roles, but since the preachers in question did not approve of women acting on stage either, Coby had thought it surely the lesser of two evils. That her own role made her complicit in encouraging masculine love had never occurred to her. No wonder Faulkner disliked her so much. Well, she could at least do better from now on. Starting with looking to her own faults first.

She wiped her eyes and headed for a stile in the hedge. The last of the summer's flowers stirred at her passing and grasshoppers fled in all directions. A group of cattle watched her warily, flicking their tails at the thistledown drifting in the breeze. Leaden clouds massed in the west. She hoped they would reach Ferrymead before it rained.

Ned jogged to catch her up, the satchel over his shoulder clanking slightly as he ran.

"What's in the bag?" she asked.

"Lock picks." Ned flashed her a smug grin.

"Lock picks? How…?"

"Borrowed them from Baines," Ned replied, then looked sheepish.

She stopped dead. "You've told Walsingham's man where we're going?"

"How do you know Baines works for Walsingham?"

Coby hesitated. How much did Faulkner know about Mal's business? Not as much as he thought, she suspected.

"You told me he was an intelligencer," she replied. "That means Walsingham, doesn't it?"

"Uh, Hendricks!"

"What?"

"Run!"

Coby glanced over her shoulder and saw the bullocks lumbering towards them. Pressing a hand to her side, she loped towards the hedge, but Faulkner soon overtook her. He vaulted the stile with enviable grace and stretched out his hand to-wards her.

"Come on, Hendricks, move your arse!"

She staggered the last few yards and was hauled painfully over the stile. The hilt of the rapier dug into her ribs, trapped against the wooden beam, and for a second she feared it would pull free and slice her in two. Then she was over, the beasts snorting and pawing the ground impotently as the two of them collapsed on the dusty road. Coby looked at Faulkner, and they both burst out laughing.

"Some rescuers we are," she wheezed.

Faulkner got to his feet and dusted himself down.

"Come on," he said. "We've got work to do."

"Damn!"

"What?"

Ned pointed due west to where creamy-white battlements rose above the trees.

"Syon House," he said. "Belongs to the Earl of Essex. And we're on his land."

He looked about, expecting to be accosted by servants at any moment.

"Essex lives here?"

"His sister does, since she was widowed last year. Rumour has it Northumberland is betrothed to her already."

He scuttled over to a group of elder trees heavy with wine-dark berries, and beckoned for Hendricks to join him.

"How come you know so much about the doings of great men?" Hendricks asked, her brow furrowing in suspicion.

"I've got friends in high places," he replied with a wink. In truth it was mostly Bull's Head gossip, but he wasn't about to admit that. "Been to Whitehall Palace, me."

The boy looked sceptical.

"All right, only once," Ned admitted. "But I did see Prince Arthur, as close to me as you are now."

Speaking of the prince reminded Ned of the tennis match, and of Grey's cold eyes that so belied his friendly demeanour towards Mal. He should have known the fellow was up to some wickedness.

"So how do we get to Ferrymead House now?" Hendricks asked, peering through the leaves.

"The London road surely passes close by here. Didn't you never come this way before, when Suffolk's Men were on tour?"

"No. I think we played at Suffolk House once, when I first came to London, but I was so mazed by everything I could scarce tell one great mansion from the next."

Ned scanned the park. London born and bred, he was out of his element here. Over to the right the trees thickened into dense oak woodland, its shadowed depths more dangerous to his eyes than a Southwark alley. A rich man's private hunting ground. Ned prayed they would not end up as the ones hunted.

Footsteps sounded in the corridor, then a key turned in the lock. Blaise entered, accompanied by Goddard and two other men, both of the latter armed with stout cudgels tucked into their belts. Sandy whimpered and pressed himself into the farthest corner of the bedstead. Blaise beckoned to Mal, who looked back at his brother.

"Touch him again," he told Blaise, "and you'll wish you'd never been born."

Blaise said nothing, only gestured for him to leave.

They left Goddard stationed outside the room, and Mal was taken downstairs and through a door into the great hall. The night's chill still clung to the stone walls, though the morning light reached in through the tall windows to caress the terracotta tiles with pale fingers. The high table was strewn with books and papers and the remains of breakfast.

At one end of the dais an archway opened onto a straight wooden stair running up to the lord's private apartments. Mal was ushered through the empty solar into the bedchamber beyond, where Suffolk sat propped up in bed. A black-gowned doctor was washing his hands in a porcelain basin, but looked round as the visitors entered.

"His Grace is not to be troubled for long, *signore*," he told Blaise, wiping his fingers fastidiously on a towel.

"I think my father is fit to decide for himself," Blaise replied.

The physician gave a curt bow, little more than a bob of the head, and stumped out of the room, followed by a servant carrying the basin. As they passed, Mal could not help but glance into it: the contents swirled red and black with clotted blood.

The duke was almost as pale as his linen nightshirt and his eyes were bright with pain. He gestured to his men, who seized Mal by the arms. Blaise stepped in front of Mal and gazed down at him with a mixture of disgust and fascination. Slowly he unbuttoned Mal's doublet, gentle as a lover. He unlocked one manacle and slipped Mal's arm out of the sleeve on that side before replacing the iron band around his wrist, then repeated the process on the other side. Mal made no attempt to resist; he was outnumbered three to one, and he had no intention of giving Blaise one iota more pleasure than he had to.

Blaise drew his dagger and held it up before Mal's eyes, daring him to flinch. Mal stared right back. Blaise smiled and went round behind him. After a long moment, Blaise seized the back of Mal's shirt and slit it from neck to hem. Mal stiffened, recalling the last time he had been in this position. Blaise began to unwind the bandages.

"One would think the skraylings inured to brutality," Blaise said in conversational tones, "considering the customs of the

New World's savages. Did you know they cut out the hearts of living men as sacrifices to their gods?"

"The skraylings, or the savages?" Mal replied, matching Blaise's nonchalant air.

Blaise only laughed softly. "And yet they almost broke their alliance with us over a mere flogging. You must be very important to them. Or at least to the ambassador."

"He has been... gracious," Mal said.

"So I see." Blaise threw the last of the bandages aside. "These wounds are healing well."

Mal watched out of the corner of his eye as Blaise went over to the table where the doctor had washed his hands. A large medicine cabinet decorated with scenes of Christ's healing miracles stood against the wall. Blaise turned the key in the lock and opened the doors wide.

"Of course they would heal a lot faster with stronger medicine." He returned with a small glass bottle and a swab on a stick. "I'm afraid this may be a little painful."

Mal steeled himself for the sting of *ashaarr*. The swab touched the edge of a welt, cold at first then – He bucked in his captors' grasp, barely feeling their hands tighten on his arms as a thousand white-hot needles pierced his raw flesh. The pain echoed through the halls of his body like a gunshot, leaving him breathless and shaking.

The duke spoke for the first time since Mal had entered the room, in a voice faint but steady.

"Who are you?"

"Maliverny Catlyn, of Rushdale."

The duke glanced over Mal's shoulder. Another touch, another searing wave of pain.

"Not your Christian name. The creature inside you."

Mal shook his head, then ground his teeth together as Blaise applied the swab once more. Was this how they tortured

Sandy? There had been no outward sign of harm, but now Mal's imagination was conjuring the effect of this tincture on a man's innards. Bile rose in his throat.

"No matter," the duke said. "I know already. You are Erishen. Both of you."

Mal stared at him. How could that be? And yet he knew it for the truth. He remembered dying at the hands of the Huntsmen, because he *was* Erishen. A sob escaped his lips.

The duke chuckled drily, a spasm that soon turned to wheezing coughs. Blaise left off tormenting Mal for a moment and handed his father a goblet.

"Damned fire," the duke gasped, when he had his breath back. "So, Erishen, what were you up to in Derbyshire? Looking for old friends?"

Mal squinted at him, distantly aware that he had bitten through his own lip and blood was running down his chin. "Friends?"

Blaise applied the swab. When Mal's vision cleared, the duke was leaning forward in bed, his eyes fever-bright.

"What did you find out?"

"Nothing," Mal hissed.

After that, time dissolved into a series of fractured moments strung together with a thread of agony. Questions repeated over and over, for which he had no answer nor explanation. Was Suffolk a Huntsman, trying to find out if his comrades' secrets had been breached? Or an agent of the Crown, attempting to ferret out the skraylings' true purpose? It scarcely mattered. He tried to pray, but the words would not come. A lullaby ran round and round in his head and, underneath the alien words, a soft voice calling him *amayi*. Beloved. He clung to the memory like a drowning man.

His torment was interrupted by a new voice and a stir of motion around him. Lifting his head Mal saw the young retainer

Ivett, his face pale and eyes carefully averted from the scene before him.

"Letters for you, Your Grace," Ivett said. "By separate couriers from London."

The duke beckoned the man over and held out his hand, then waved him away absentmindedly as he perused the contents.

"Another pompous missive from Northumberland," he said after a few moments. "He wishes to commiserate with me on the loss of the theatre. Hypocrite. And a note from my wife, enquiring into my health. I am afraid I shall have to disappoint her." He tossed them onto the counterpane. "Now, where were we?"

Mal drew himself up to his full height and spat blood in Suffolk's direction. Blaise leaned in close, his breath hot in Mal's ear.

"You're probably thinking," he murmured, "that sooner or later I'm going to run out of welts. And you're right. Fortunately you have a great deal more skin. And if you think this stings on half-healed wounds, just imagine what it feels like on newly flayed flesh."

"Enough, Blaise," the duke said with a peremptory gesture at his son. "Take Master Catlyn downstairs, and his brother also. I fear that more drastic measures are needed."

By the time they reached the London road, the sun was at its zenith. Ned sighed with relief to be out in the open again, on well-ordered terrain under the dominion of Man.

"I swear you led us thrice in a circle," Hendricks muttered, picking burrs out of his stockings.

"Well we're here now," Ned replied. "Come on."

He took the remains of their breakfast loaf from his satchel and tore it in two, suddenly aware of how hungry he was after his exertions. And how sore. Muscles ached in parts of his body he didn't know had muscles. What he wouldn't give for Gabe's gentle ministrations right now...

They set off westwards down the dusty road. He hoped this turned out to be a wild goose chase, a misunderstanding by a foolish besotted boy. If Hendricks was right and Suffolk had both Mal and Sandy captive as part of some insane conspiracy, things were going to get difficult. What did the boy expect them to do, against the duke and all his wealth and power?

"Do you not think it odd," Hendricks said around a mouthful of bread, "that Northumberland is Suffolk's close neighbour on the Strand, and now he looks set to do the same here?"

Ned shrugged. "Rich men flock around the Prince of Wales, and build their houses close to the royal palaces. Northumberland and Suffolk are two of the richest, so of course you find them together."

The road passed some three-quarters of a mile north of Syon House, running along the edge of its fine parkland. Despite Ned's fears they were not stopped nor even taken much notice of. This close to London there was always plenty of traffic on the roads in fine weather, and two servants going about their masters' business were nothing remarkable.

After about half a mile they came to a crossroads. A new-looking milestone marked 'London xi miles Winchester lviii miles' jutted out of a patch of raw earth. They turned left towards Twickenham, following a farmer's wagon laden with straw. Ned glanced at his companion, who grinned back. Breaking into a run they caught up with the wagon and scrambled aboard.

"How far is it now?" Ned asked, leaning over the side of the wagon and staring southwards.

"Master Dunfell told me it was right across the river from Richmond Palace, so it can't be far." Hendricks pointed south-eastwards. "Look, are those not the palace towers?"

The wagon lumbered onwards. At last it drew level with the palace, and the two of them slipped down from their perches and into a dry ditch by the roadside. The traffic here was thinner; less chance of being seen, but more chance of being stopped if they were. A flash of blue and white in the distance alerted Ned in time, and he pulled Hendricks into the hedgerow.

"One of Suffolk's retainers," he hissed.

They crouched in their hiding place, watching the road ahead. A few moments later a mounted courier rode past at a steady trot, a satchel flapping against his hip.

"Suffolk's household must be in uproar," Ned whispered, "wondering why his lordship has come all the way out here with such a great wound."

When the road was clear again, they made their way cautiously southwards. Soon they came to a pair of tall wrought-iron gates surmounted by gilded unicorns. An avenue lined by slender elms curved into the distance, drawing the eye and tempting the feet to follow.

"Not that way!" He grabbed Hendricks' arm. "Let's see if we can get closer without being seen."

He led the boy further down the road, and soon they came to a much smaller track leading to a cluster of farm buildings. They slipped from one to the other, keeping a wary eye out for farmhands. Probably they were all sitting in the sun, enjoying a jug of ale and digesting their dinners before getting back to work. Ned licked his dry lips. A pint would go down perfectly right now.

He stopped and peered around the corner of a barn towards the distant manor-house, waiting for Hendricks to catch up.

"This would be much easier if Gabriel were here," Ned grumbled.

"Why?" Hendricks asked, leaning back against the wall. He looked as though he was going to throw up.

"He could dress up as a maidservant," Ned replied, pointing towards some bushes where laundry was drying, "and get into the house unnoticed."

Hendricks rolled his eyes. "That's rank folly. He would never pass."

"Gabriel was the finest actor of women's roles in London, in his youth."

"And now stubble gilds his cheeks and his voice has dropped an octave. Besides, how many servant girls talk like queens or goddesses?"

Ned stared into the distance, lost for a moment in memory. "I first saw him as Venus, you know, when he was with the Admiral's Men. 'For Dido's sake I take thee in my arms, and stick these spangled feathers in thy hat. Eat comfits in mine arms, and I will sing–'"

"Hush!" Hendricks elbowed him in the ribs.

"You have a better idea?"

"I shall just walk up to the house and present myself," Hendricks replied. "I am still one of Suffolk's Men, and therefore the duke's servant. Since our company is now in sad need of a master, surely it is not so strange that I should seek him out here?"

"That is a very dull plan."

"At the very least I can look about the house, as much as I dare. We still have no proof Master Catlyn and his brother are here. If they are not, we can return to London and no harm done."

"And if they are?" Ned asked.

"Then…" Hendricks looked glum. "Then we need a real plan."

CHAPTER XXXIII

Coby walked along the avenue towards Ferrymead House, her heart pounding. If Master Catlyn's guess was right, she was about to step into a den of villains and traitors who would stop at nothing to conceal their plot. Still, she could not back out now, not with his life riding on the success of their mission.

After a few minutes the house came into view. Red brick wings extended from an older stone building, joining in front to form an elegant modern gatehouse with a stucco panel depicting the Suffolk coat of arms. Above the gatehouse blue-and-white pennants stirred listlessly in the breeze.

She drew a deep breath and walked towards the gates, which stood half-open. A man in Suffolk livery emerged from the darkness within, a loaded crossbow aimed at the ground. Coby froze, praying her face did not betray her.

"Who goes there?"

"J-J-Jacob Hendricks, of Suffolk's Men, with an urgent message for His Grace."

"My lord Suffolk is too unwell to see anyone."

Her heart sank. Was their plan to be thwarted so quickly?

"Wait," the man said. "Is this about the playhouse, the one that burnt down?"

"Yes," she replied. "I bring grave news that his lordship will want to hear as soon as possible."

"You'd better come in."

He led her across the courtyard and into a dark-panelled entrance porch. Coby's footsteps whispered on the terracotta floor-tiles as she followed the man through the passageway beyond and into the great hall. The bare stone walls and elaborate hammerbeam roof belonged to a bygone age, as did the crossed polearms of antique design that were its walls' only decoration. A modern marble fireplace had been added along one side, but it remained a cold, gloomy space, even on a bright summer's day.

On the dais at the far end of the hall, Blaise Grey sat at a long table, flicking rapidly through the pages of a small fat book bound in red leather. He showed no sign of awareness of her presence, even when the retainer announced her in a voice that echoed from the high ceiling. Grey dipped his pen in his inkwell, appearing to copy something from the book onto a sheet of paper. Coby approached slowly, wondering what task could be so absorbing.

At last Grey put the pen down, sanded the sheet he had been working on, and looked up. His face was drawn, as if he had not slept in many hours, and stubble darkened his cheeks above a gold-bronze beard. Eyes grey as the river in winter raked her features.

"You are the boy from the theatre."

"Yes, my lord."

Grey beckoned her over. "I was told you have urgent news for my father. About the fire?"

She approached the dais. The surface of the table was a few inches below her eye-level, and she stared at it rather than endure that cold gaze any longer. Grey swiftly gathered up the papers he had been working on and closed the book, as if not wanting her to catch even a glimpse of their contents. Curiosity roused, she mounted the steps at the end of the dais and swept a low bow.

"Yes, my lord." She clasped her hands behind her back to stop them shaking. "Master Naismith is – is dead, my lord, and Master Rudd, and the theatre burnt to the ground. We are ruined."

She could not help glancing sidelong at a sheet of paper protruding from underneath the book. It was covered in strange symbols like nothing she had ever seen before. A cipher? Mathematics? Or just nonsense, like the fanciful glyphs on magicians' robes?

Grey said nothing for a long moment. Coby looked up, half-expecting him to be pleased at this reversal to his father's continued alliance with the skraylings. He was not.

"How did this happen? Who was responsible for loading the cannon?"

"I– I was, my lord–"

Though she anticipated the blow, it still sent her reeling. She landed hard on both knees and the heels of her palms. Her side felt like it would gape open and spill her guts over the polished boards. Breath caught in her throat. Tears would only make it hurt more – and perhaps anger Grey further.

"Addle-pated cull! My father is dying in agony–" Grey swept his arm across the desk, sending books and papers cascading to the floor. "I should have you flogged all the way back to London for this."

"I am most truly sorry, my lord," she whispered.

A booted foot caught her on the shoulder and she tumbled from the dais. In the long moment before she hit the floor, she managed to tuck her arms about her ribs and keep her head high enough to avoid cracking it on the tiles.

As she lay there praying for Grey's wrath to subside, a pale metallic gleam caught her attention. A silver and niello button in the form of a Tudor rose, just like the ones on Master Catlyn's livery doublet. She closed her hand over it, hoping Grey hadn't noticed.

"Get up." Grey sighed. "What's done is done. Besides, only a fool would stay in the theatre knowing the cannon was about to explode."

"It was John Wheeler." The words came out unbidden.

"Who?"

"He was a hireling, a malcontent. Master Naismith dismissed him, but it seems the mischief was already done."

Grey nodded, his expression thoughtful.

"Stay a while, boy. Get yourself to the kitchens and ask the cook for dinner. My father will no doubt want to hear about this."

She thanked him profusely and backed out, bowing low. A narrow escape, but worth a bruising. If Master Catlyn were still here, she now had an opportunity to find him.

The same armed retainer showed her back out into the courtyard and thence into the kitchen in the north wing. The large room was empty of servants, though stacks of used dishes and plates suggested a meal had recently been consumed. He gestured to the leftovers laid out on the table then departed without another word. This was her chance. She looked around for another exit, since she could hardly go back out into the courtyard.

One side of the kitchen was almost completely occupied by a brick fireplace, furnished with spits of various sizes and an oven at the side. A range stood under the window at the far end, iron bars set into more brickwork with charcoal pans beneath. The wall nearest the house was pierced by two low doors with a dresser between. Deciding that the right side was likely to be more conspicuous, since its rooms looked onto the courtyard, she padded towards the door on the left.

• • • •

After Hendricks had disappeared down the drive, Ned considered what he should do next. Even if the boy were right and Mal and Sandy were being held prisoner here, they still had to snatch the two captives from under the noses of who knew how many armed men and make their escape – in a boat moored over a mile away, on the edge of the Syon House estate.

"Shit! Shit! Thrice-damned shit and buggery!"

There was only one choice left. Horses. Mal could ride, and so presumably could Sandy if he put his addled mind to it. And if there was one thing a noble house had no lack of, it was horses.

Ned had seldom had a chance to try his hand at riding. Few people of his acquaintance could afford to keep a horse, and though there were livery stables aplenty from which to hire a nag for the day, where would you take it? Everything a man could ever want lay within the bounds of the capital, or so Ned had always believed. Now he cursed his narrow horizons. There was a whole world out there – and a new world across the Atlantic – just waiting to be explored.

Perhaps this was his day to start. He had been unwilling to ride here, but to ride back at Mal's side, triumphant, now that was a dream to be savoured. He slipped through the doors of the nearest barn. No horses here, just a lot of hay. Stables, that was where horses were kept. Or paddocks. There must be some horses out in the open in this fine weather.

He was making his way back towards the road, thinking it a safer place to be caught than on the duke's property, when a mounted courier came thundering up the drive, heading in the same direction as the one they had seen earlier. Another so soon? His gut clenched in sudden fear. Had Hendricks been caught already?

• • • •

"Sandy, are you awake?"

Mal squeezed his brother's hand, but got no response. They stood back-to-back around one of the pillars supporting the roof of a cellar beneath the great hall, the right wrist of each bound with thin cord to the other's left and a single length of iron chain cinched around both their throats, secured with a padlock. The weals on Mal's exposed back itched where they rubbed against the rough brickwork but thankfully the pain of his earlier torment had subsided. Blaise had been telling the truth when he said the tincture enhanced the rate of healing, though the price was not one Mal would wish to pay again.

He looked around the cellar, his eyes now adjusted to the darkness. Faint shapes of sacks and barrels, such as could be seen in the storerooms of any great house. A flicker of movement that might be a rat. How long were they going to be left down here? Was that the "more drastic measure" Suffolk spoke of? A slow death by starvation, or to be eaten by rats? But the duke didn't look like he was in any condition to take his time over this interrogation. He wanted answers, fast. But what answers?

Sandy stirred and moaned. "Mal?"

"I'm here," Mal replied. His words echoed loudly from the cellar walls, and he lowered his voice. "Did they hurt you again?"

"No. What happened? How did I get here?"

Mal whispered his thanks to Our Lady. His brother was unharmed and lucid, at least for the moment.

"Suffolk has us both captive," Mal replied. "He seems to think we are both possessed by a skrayling called Erishen."

"He is right, in a sense."

"How so?" Mal wasn't sure he wanted to know, but he needed every advantage he could lay his hands on if he was going to get them out of here.

"You remember Erishen's death," Sandy went on, "at the hands of the Huntsmen?"

"Yes," Mal replied, wishing he didn't.

"And the flight into darkness?"

"A little."

"Erishen should have sought refuge in the nearest unborn child, but he panicked and followed the trail of the lodestone necklace stolen by his murderer. That led him to our mother. He was careless enough to seek rebirth in a woman bearing twins."

"Careless?"

"When skraylings are taught about rebirth," Sandy said, "they are told to avoid twins. When two bodies share the same womb, the migrating soul can lose its way, be damaged, even broken in two…"

Two babes in one womb. It could have been him locked up in Bedlam, and Sandy free to study at Cambridge. Perhaps it would have been better that way. Sandy would have worked hard, instead of running about town with a head full of beer and dreams. But would Sandy the scholar have had an opportunity to meet Kiiren? Would he have been too poor and unworldly to pay the hospital bills? It was useless to speculate. They were both in God's hands, and He would do with them as He wished.

"A fragment of Erishen's soul and memories lodged in you," Sandy went on, "but most are in me."

"How do you know all this?" Mal asked. "Why didn't you tell me sooner?"

"It was Jathekkil's doing. By freeing me from my iron shackles, he let Erishen loose again. At first I was lost in nightmares—" His fingers tightened on Mal's. After a moment he drew a shuddering breath and went on. "Terrible visions I would rather forget. But at last I learnt the truth."

"Yath-il–?"

"The man you call Suffolk. He is another like me. A skrayling in human flesh."

"But he's not mad." At least, no more than any other wicked man.

"He did not take a human body by accident. And he's not the only one."

"What are you saying? There are other skraylings masquerading as humans? Who are they?"

"I don't know. I shared Erishen's memories for only a few days, and what I saw was garbled. Perhaps given time I could tell you more, but…"

Mal felt his brother shrug.

"And now you are sane?"

Sandy laughed softly. "What is sanity? Am I sane for knowing I am possessed, and by whom?"

"I will get us both out of here, I swear," Mal said. "And if there is any cure amongst men or skraylings, I will find it."

Coby pressed her ear to the door, and immediately leapt back like a scalded cat. Someone, a girl by the sounds of it, was just the other side, singing quietly and slightly out of tune. A clatter of dishes followed, and the singing stopped.

Coby returned quickly to the scrubbed oak table and began piling a slice of bread with chunks of cold mutton. She had just poured herself a cup of ale when a girl of about her own age came through the left-hand door with an armful of clean dishes. The girl paused, bobbed an uncertain curtsey and then set about putting the dishes back in their places on the dresser. She glanced curiously at Coby once or twice as she began collecting another stack of dirty tableware. Her hands were red and coarse, and still damp from her work, and her dark curls escaped from her linen cap and stuck to her forehead.

"Haven't seen you here before," the girl said eventually.

"I'm with Suffolk's Men," Coby replied indistinctly, chewing on a particularly gristly bit of mutton. "The theatre company."

"You're an actor?"

"I'm Master Naismith's – the late Master Naismith's – apprentice. Was, I suppose."

It was not a lie; she had not said she was an actor, but the girl would no doubt assume. The girl looked her up and down, perhaps wondering what she looked like in women's clothing. A mistake. Coby quickly changed the subject.

"You must have heard about the fire?" she asked.

The girl nodded, wide-eyed. "Were you there?"

"I was. I–" She was not about to confess her role in it to this wench. But if she gained her confidence, she might learn something more about Master Catlyn.

"I had to rescue the Ambassador of Vinland from the flames," she said, congratulating herself on the girl's suitably awed expression.

"That must have been so dangerous." The scullery maid put down the pile of plates and wiped her hands on her apron. "I'm Margaret, by the way. Only everyone calls me Meg."

"A pleasure to meet you, Margaret," Coby replied, getting up from her seat and sweeping her best courtly bow. "I'm Jacob. Jacob Hendricks."

Meg giggled and blushed. Coby sat down again, and began relating a version of the previous day's events that cast herself in the lead role. Years of listening to the actors' boasting had not been for naught. Meg listened in rapt attention, her dishes forgotten.

"You are so brave," she sighed, when Coby finished, then added coyly, "I wish I had a man's heart."

"You have," Coby assured her, meaning any woman could do as much. Too late she realised how it must have sounded to the impressionable girl. "I– I meant that you are braver than you know."

"I wish it were so." Meg came and sat next to her on the bench. "There is a madman in this house. The screaming and moaning – it would chill the blood of the very Devil."

"Really? Who is he?"

"I don't know, nor care to. He was brought here a few days ago. Mistress Sheldon says he's a distant cousin of my lord Grey, but I cannot see the likeness. And then last night another arrived out of the blue, and him the very image of the first. Though if he is mad also, I have not seen it."

"You have seen both of them?"

Meg nodded. "I have to take them their meals three times a day. Fair turns my bowels to water, the mad one does."

Coby hid her triumphant grin by taking a gulp of ale. "How would it be if I came with you? That would soothe your fears, surely?"

"Oh yes!" Meg cried. "I could not be afraid with such a bold hero at my side."

"It must be almost two o'clock," Coby said. "When do you take their dinner?"

"By my troth, I had quite forgotten the time," Meg said. "Mistress Sheldon is taken to her bed with one of her megrims, and I have had so much to do–"

"Come then, let's get it done, then perhaps I can help you with your work." She shook her head sadly. "I have no master now, and know not what I am to do."

Meg scraped debris off two of the plates and set about ladling them with more of the leftovers. Coby took a pitcher and drew ale from a barrel by the door, smiling to herself. This was all going even more smoothly than she could have hoped.

The girl led Coby back into the main house via the right-hand door, through a dining hall where an elderly steward dozed over his tankard, down a gloomy corridor and into a small parlour overlooking the river. To Coby's surprise, Meg put the plates down on the table, took the pitcher from her and caught her by the hand.

"Come, kiss me," she murmured, slipping her arms around Coby's waist.

Coby hesitated. She needed to keep this girl sweet if she was to help Master Catlyn, and after all, what harm could one kiss do? She bent her head and nuzzled Meg's neck, unsure of how to proceed. She had seen men and women kiss often enough, but how to go about it?

Meg sighed and turned her head, brushing her lips against Coby's. After a moment's awkwardness their mouths found one another and worked together in languorous, instinctive pleasure. So, this was what kissing felt like. But now what? Should she break off, or was it too soon?

She thought about how she would want Master Catlyn to kiss her. Hooking the girl about the waist she pulled her closer and caressed the nape of her neck with her free hand. Meg moaned in the back of her throat and slipped her tongue between Coby's lips. Coby stifled a squeak of surprise then hesitantly returned the favour, tracing the girl's sharp, uneven teeth with her own tongue. Meg pressed her belly against Coby's hips – and stopped as she encountered the hardness of the pigskin prick in Coby's breeches.

Coby released her with a muttered apology. Unabashed, Meg wriggled back into her embrace and whispered in her ear.

"Would you die for me, hero?"

Coby winced at the innuendo, but it gave her an idea.

"Not here," she replied. "There is perhaps some more private place where we may… converse undisturbed?"

Meg grinned. "Now?"

"Go now, and wait for me. I will deal with your madman, then come to you."

She felt guilty about duping the girl, but it was for her own good. Better to weep over being cruelly deceived than be punished for helping the prisoners to escape. Besides, the little strumpet had been the one to start this.

"I mustn't," Meg said. "Mistress Sheldon will have my hide–"

"I will take the blame," Coby told her. "I did seduce you, did I not?"

Coby kissed her again, giving one soft buttock a squeeze for good measure. It always seemed to work for Master Eaton.

"I'll be in the middle stable," Meg breathed in her ear, "in the loft over the bay mare's stall. The madman is in the chamber above this one, he and his twin both. Do not tarry, my love, I beg you."

Coby waited for her to leave, then with some difficulty picked up both plates and the pitcher and carried them out into the passageway. The pewter-ware rattled together in her grasp, and she took a deep breath to steady her nerves.

CHAPTER XXXIV

Footsteps and voices sounded at the far end of the cellar, and warm lantern-light sent shadows lurching across the walls. The rats scattered in panic. Craning his neck around the pillar, Mal could see Blaise and at least three of Suffolk's retainers. Two of them were carrying a heavy iron brazier and another, whom Mal recognised as the man Ivett, had a small sack. Mal gave Sandy's hands a reassuring squeeze. Their palms were damp from long contact, but now fresh sweat pricked in his armpits. He didn't like to think what uses Blaise might find for hot irons.

The brazier was placed next to the pillar, about a yard from Mal's bound right hand. Ivett half-filled it with charcoal from the sack and struck flame with flint and steel. Whilst the man worked, Blaise walked round the pillar, scanning each captive's face in turn.

"To think I once called you friend," Blaise said, when he had completed his circuit and stood in front of Mal again.

"I was just thinking the same," Mal replied. "You are not the man I thought you were."

"That is ironic, coming from a man possessed."

Ivett carefully placed more pieces of charcoal over his burning tinder. The scent of smoke reminded Mal of the burning theatre. Of a fragment of iron embedded in the duke's leg, the magic-dampening metal intimately mingled with blood. That was the moment Suffolk's plans had unravelled, blown apart by those who hated the skraylings, aptly enough.

"Your father is a monster," he said, looking to Suffolk's retainers for a reaction. "A skrayling in a man's body, just like me."

Blaise snorted a laugh. "And they say your brother is mad."

The men joined in his laughter, though Mal thought he saw doubt in Ivett's eyes. No doubt the young servant had seen too little of the world to be hardened to the brutality of his so-called betters. Still, it might be enough to drive a wedge between man and master. Mal recalled a brief moment of clarity on his ignominious march down to the cellar, when he had stumbled against the table on the dais and landed face down amid Blaise's notes. Peculiar script, like no code he had ever seen.

"That was skrayling writing I saw on those papers, was it not?" he said to Blaise.

A wild guess, but it struck home.

"How else does your father know so much about the skraylings?" Mal continued. "Unless he is one of them."

"Why should I believe you over my own father? You are the monster, you and your brother. I will purge the demons from your flesh, and your immortal souls will thank me for it when we meet in Heaven."

Mal realised Blaise was telling the truth as he saw it, as the Church taught its flock. Once Mal might have agreed, but there was too much human cruelty in Blaise's countenance. Surely a merciful God would not act through such a man.

Blaise bent and blew gently on the coals, the red glow turning his features into a demonic mask. With a last smile at Mal he departed, taking his father's silent, grim-eyed men with him. Mal and Sandy were left alone with the hellish glow of the brazier, and the returning rats.

Coby stared at the empty room in dismay. This was the one Meg had described, was it not? And it looked bare enough to serve as a cell. Yet the door stood wide open, its occupants gone.

She went back out into the passageway and put the plates and pitcher down on a chest that stood under a window. The captives could not have been gone long, and perhaps had been moved in haste since no one had thought to tell the servants yet. She ventured further into the north wing. The next two doors were unlocked, the rooms equally empty of people though properly furnished. The third was also unlocked, but its shutters were tightly closed so that she could see little in the gloom.

"Meg? Is that you?"

Coby jumped at the sound of the woman's voice, then recalled Meg's account of the cook, Mistress Sheldon, being unwell.

"Sorry, m'm," Coby said softly, trying to mimic the maidservant's country accent. "I thought you might want some dinner."

"I told yer to leave me be, clot-brained wench!" Mistress Sheldon shifted on her bed and fell back with a groan. "Now get out."

"Yes, m'm." She backed out and gently closed the door.

Master Catlyn and his brother surely could not be anywhere up here. Where else might they have been taken? She looked out of the window into the courtyard. Opposite was the stable-block, and at its left-hand end the upper storey of the older building jutted out on all sides, a modern timber-framed structure extending the lord's accommodation for greater comfort. Investigating the solar was out of the question unless she wanted another beating from Lord Grey. She sighed, aware that she had set herself an impossible task. How she had ever thought she could rescue Master Catlyn, she did not know.

Her attention was drawn downwards to the courtyard by movement in the shadows of the entrance porch. Blaise Grey emerged from the house, leading a strange little procession towards a low door in the corner of the courtyard. The Duke of Suffolk had his arms around the shoulders of two retainers, doing his best to walk upright despite his evident pain. What were they doing, going down to the cellars? Unless…

Heart pounding, Coby crept down the stairs and along the passageway past the great hall, then made her way outside and crossed quickly to the cellar door. She dared not go in, and yet she could not stay here. Any moment someone might spot her lurking in the courtyard where she had no right to be. The dilemma was solved for her when she heard booted footsteps approaching from within. No chance of crossing the courtyard without being seen. She darted towards the open stable door.

Ned approached the house cautiously, keeping out of sight of the gatehouse. The outer wall on the right looked like his best bet, only a few narrow unglazed windows piercing the red brick surface. Not the gentry's quarters then; most likely a stable block. The brickwork was old enough to be weathered in places. And one thing this city boy knew was how to get in and out of buildings by unconventional routes. Often with another man's outraged wife in hot pursuit.

The wall was not the easiest he'd climbed, and his ascent was not helped by the fear that any moment he would hear shouts, or worse still feel the sting of a musket ball. He reached his chosen window unchallenged, however, and a glance over the sill revealed no movement inside.

Wriggling sideways through the narrow embrasure, he fell onto a pile of hay. The loft was dark and dusty, no sound but the occasional stamp of a hoof from the stalls below. He began to feel his way on hands and knees towards the trapdoor.

A hand grabbed his wrist, and he stifled a yelp.

"Is that you, Jacob?" a female voice murmured invitingly.

Jacob? Was young Hendricks making trysts instead of rescuing his beloved Mal? It seemed very unlikely, and yet Jacob was scarcely a common name in England.

The girl moved closer to get a better look at him.

"Who are y–"

Ned launched himself at her, clapping a hand over her mouth and pushing her down in the hay.

"Not a word," he growled. "Scream, and I'll slit your throat. Understand?"

The girl nodded, on the verge of tears. Then she closed her eyes and went limp beneath him. She thinks I'm going to rape her, poor little bitch. He sighed and relaxed his grip.

"Stay here," he told her, "stay silent and thank Christ and all his apostles I have not the slightest interest in your... thing."

The trapdoor rattled and Ned leapt up, the girl forgotten. As it opened, Ned took one moment to assure himself the emerging figure was not Hendricks, then lashed out with a foot. The man's head snapped back and hit the trapdoor with a dull thud, then he slithered down through the opening, limp as a sack of flour. The girl clapped her hand to her mouth, stifling a scream.

Ned peered down into the stable. Horses stirred and stamped their feet at the disturbance, but no one had raised the alarm. The man – a groom by the looks of him – lay on the stable floor, his head and limbs at unnatural angles. Ned swallowed, the bile rising in the back of his throat. Another death on his hands. Had he turned killer so easily? With a last warning glance back at the girl, he slid down the ladder to the stable below, closing the hatch behind him.

He started as the stable door swung open and a familiar figure slipped inside.

"Hendricks! What are you doing here?" Ned hissed. Not that he needed to ask, after his encounter in the loft.

The boy pressed a finger to his lips and motioned to the courtyard. Ned peered over his shoulder and saw two liveried servants crossing the courtyard.

"Are you sure Mal is here?" Ned whispered in the boy's ear.

Hendricks took a button from his pocket and showed it to Ned.

"All right," he said. "What do we do now?"

Shadows danced across the walls of the cellar and Mal was instantly alert, ears pricked to catch the voices of his tormentors. He saw them first, however: Blaise with a manic smile etched into his face by the brazier's infernal glow, and behind him Suffolk, grey-faced and sweating as he leant on his menservants' shoulders. Shaking the men off, the duke limped over to a barrel and perched on the edge, his wounded leg stuck out before him.

Blaise took out a bunch of keys and removed the padlock holding the chain in place. He caught the chain as it slithered free, gathered it up and threw it to one of the men.

"Leave us," he said.

The servants made their obeisances and left, though not without a few backward glances. Were they afraid for their lord's safety, with only Blaise between him and two dangerous prisoners? Or did they have their own doubts, having thought on Mal's earlier words? If they did, it was not enough to sway them from their lord. The cellar door thudded shut behind them with dreadful finality.

He struggled against his bonds, until the cords cut into both their wrists and Sandy cried out in pain. Blaise laughed softly.

"This will all be over soon, and your souls will be free," he said, smiling down at Mal.

His dark blond curls almost brushed the low ceiling. Mal longed for a sword in his hand; Blaise's greater height would be a disadvantage in a fight here, and the thought of wiping that sanctimonious smile off his enemy's face made Mal's heart sing. As if guessing Mal's thought, Blaise only smiled the more. The battle was already over, and Mal had lost.

Mal swallowed against the soreness where the chain had pressed just below his Adam's apple.

"You're going to kill us both."

"If necessary, yes. But my father would prefer one of you to live. I can't imagine why."

I can. He thinks Erishen knows about him, and he wants to know how much. Truth is, I'd like to know myself.

He tried to marshal his thoughts into an argument that could convince Blaise of his father's perfidy, but could conjure nothing he had not already said.

"Why this farce?" he asked Blaise at last. "Why not just slit our throats?"

"You must have a chance to repent. And it would be such a messy death, don't you think?"

Blaise produced a small linen pouch, and from it sprinkled powder onto the brazier. After a moment the acrid scent of the skraylings' dream-herb rose into the damp air. Hope bloomed in Mal's breast. If Suffolk – or rather Jathekkil – was invoking the same dream-magic as Kiiren had done, what was to stop Sandy from spiriting them both out of here?

As the smoke drifted up around the captives, a delicious feeling of lassitude washed over Mal and he slumped back against the pillar, watching the delicate play of light on the curved brick wall opposite. His brother's fingertips were hot as coals against his own, pulsing in time with Mal's heartbeat. Their

flesh melded together, like two steel bars beaten into a single
sword blade.

He shook his head, trying to clear it of the drug's befud-
dlement.

"*Dë itorro, pahi saca.*" It was Sandy's voice, but Mal knew it
was Erishen speaking. *The dream herb will not be enough.*

"Silence, demon!"

A snap of flesh on flesh.

"I told you not to touch him," Mal said.

Blaise came round to the other side of the pillar.

"I am the son of a duke," he purred. "I do not take orders
from commoners."

Blaise glanced at his father, and nodded. He produced a small
bottle from his pocket and uncorked it, then seized Mal's chin
with his free hand and forced his head back. His eyes were glittering shards of amethyst and topaz, filling Mal's vision.

"Thou hast the devil," Blaise recited from the gospels. "Who
goeth about to kill thee?"

He dug his fingers into the corners of Mal's jaw, forcing his
mouth open, and tipped the bottle so that a little of the liquid
poured between Mal's lips. Mal tried to spit it out, but Blaise
pressed his jaw shut again, tilting his head back as far as it
would go until he had no choice but to swallow or breathe the
stuff in. The bitterness of the potion left his mouth dry as
paper, but at least it didn't burn like the healing tincture.

The iron hand released him, and he sagged forwards, barely
able to hear Sandy's cries of protest over the roaring in his ears.
The walls of the cellar spun about him, as if he were blind
drunk. He sucked in a deep breath, desperate to clear his head.

Blaise stood in front of him once more, holding a dagger, if
such it could be called. The blade was a sliver of obsidian, its
edge so sharp as to be translucent. Blaise held it motionless a
few inches from Mal's heart.

"If you're going to kill me," Mal rasped, "for Christ's sake get on with it."

"Not until it's time."

"Time for what?"

But Blaise was gone.

Rain sluiced down the windows of the long gallery at Rush-dale Hall. The house was empty but for the two boys, its many chambers cold and silently watchful. They were playing a favourite game, standing face to face, hands raised and finger-tips touching. The aim was to mimic the other's movements so closely as to be a perfect mirror image.

Sandy withdrew his left hand and Mal pulled back his right, a fraction of a second too slowly. Sandy smiled in tri-umph, and Mal remembered just in time to do the same. He fixed Sandy's eyes with his own, watching for any sign of his twin's next move. Something told him there was more at stake here than bragging rights. A trickle of sweat ran down his back.

"Which of you is real?" a distant voice taunted them. "And which only the reflection in the mirror?"

Mal tried to take control of the game, but Sandy was too quick for him, had always been too quick. Sandy was real, and Mal only the counterfeit, the shadow, his brother's needs al-ways taking precedence over his own.

"You are nothing without him," the voice went on. "A ci-pher, a nobody, dispossessed and friendless."

No. He dared not even speak aloud lest he lose the game, but he knew the voice could hear his thoughts. I have friends. Ned and Hendricks and...

"Kiiren? I think not. He is using you. He only wants to find Erishen."

"We are both Erishen," Sandy said, his voice loud in Mal's ears.

Too late, Mal opened his mouth to echo the words.

ANNE LYLE   453

"Yes, you are both Erishen," the voice whispered in Mal's ear. "In this crucible of dreams I shall distil your two souls into one body, remake you as you were."

"No," they said in unison.

"You have no choice. When the night-blade severs Erishen's spirit from your body, you must join with your brother once more. Or take your chances in the dark."

As one the twins turned their heads. Jathekkil was circling them, a trail of light following him like a serpent's tail, wrapping them about. Mal looked down at himself: his ethereal body glowed a deep molten yellow, whilst Sandy was a brilliant violet, almost too bright to look at. Beyond the circle of light, coal-black shapes lurked in the corner of his vision. Whenever he turned his head, they slid away behind him. Not because they were afraid to be seen, but because they were toying with him, daring him to look and be sent mad by the sight.

Something else tugged at Mal's attention, something more important than the dark lurkers. A faint current like the undertow of a river, an eddy circling a void that begged to be filled. And he could fill it, start again, free of this body and the responsibilities that went with it.

"No!" Jathekkil screamed. "That one is mine. You shall not have him."

Mal focused all his attention on the current, seeing it swirl towards that tiny void. An unborn child, not far away. Richmond Palace. Princess Juliana in her confinement. Now he knew why the duke wanted to die here.

"Kill me," he told Jathekkil, "and I will end your scheme today. Traitor."

CHAPTER XXXV

"What have you done?" Coby said in horror, staring at the corpse at the foot of the loft ladder.

"It was an accident, all right?" Ned muttered.

"Is...?" She glanced up at the loft in horror. "You didn't kill the girl, did you?"

"Of course I didn't. What do you take me for?" Ned followed her gaze. "Put the fear of God into her, maybe, but she's safe and sound up there. What were you thinking anyway, arranging trysts with wenches?"

"I was trying to put her out of harm's way," Coby replied. "Come on, we'd better hide this body."

They carried the groom's corpse into one of the empty stalls. She had seen plenty of dead bodies in her short life, but never touched one before. This one was still warm, like a living man. Somehow that didn't make it any better.

When they were done, they hid in another empty stall where they had a good view of the courtyard through the open stable door. Coby told Ned everything she had seen: the empty room, the suspicious writings on the table, the duke and his son going down to the cellar.

"The cellar? What are they doing down there?"

Coby's throat tightened. "Where better to torture someone, if you don't want their screams to be heard?"

A noise overhead alerted them – too late. Ned staggered as a bale of hay dropped on him from a great height, and he blundered into Coby, who fell back into the stall, narrowly avoiding smashing her skull on the back wall. Meg scurried down the ladder and out into the stable yard.

"Help! Help! Murder!"

Cursing, the two of them leapt to their feet, but Suffolk's retainers were already converging on the stable. The porter levelled his crossbow at them.

"Come on out."

Ned flashed Coby an accusatory glance, then stepped forward, hands raised to show he was unarmed. Within moments they were surrounded, Ned's satchel and the bundle of Mal's weapons confiscated, along with both of their belt knives.

"What do we do with them, sir?" the porter asked another man, a sergeant-at-arms judging by his gilded Suffolk badge and heavy but muscular build.

The sergeant examined the confiscated belongings, raising an eyebrow when he unwrapped the silver-hilted rapier.

"Take them to His Grace," he said.

"With respect, Master Goddard," a younger servant put in, "my lord Suffolk asked not to be interrupted in his work."

"Did I ask your opinion, Ivett?"

"No, sir."

Goddard took hold of Ned, and another liveried retainer seized Coby. The porter kept his crossbow at the ready whilst the two captives were marched to the cellar steps. The young manservant Ivett fumbled with the door latch, trying to juggle the unwieldy armful of weapons. At last the door swung open, and the men shoved Coby and Ned down the steps.

"Better bring those along to show His Grace," Goddard told Ivett.

Coby ducked under the lintel, focusing all her attention on not losing her footing. The stone steps down into the cellar were dished from long use and slick with damp. Ahead of them, a warm glow of lanterns beckoned. A peculiar smell hung in the air, a bitter herbal scent overlaying the earthy, dusty odour common to cellars.

"My lord?" Goddard called out.

They emerged into the main body of the cellar and stumbled to a halt. The tableau arranged before them defied explanation. Four men, living and breathing but motionless as statues, as if posed for the painter's art.

"My lord!"

Ivett dropped his burdens and rushed over to the duke, who lay on the floor, his face deathly pale and twisted in fury. The man holding Coby loosened his grip, but she was too appalled by what she saw to think of escape. The smoke rising from the nearby brazier caught in her throat, making her cough. Rainbow trails swirled as she looked about the cellar. The man holding her screamed and let her go, batting the air around him blindly. Coby thought she saw a smoky blackness whirling about his head, a blur of flying shapes like monstrous bats, before the man stumbled away through the shadows towards the cellar steps. She crossed herself and muttered a prayer.

Goddard swore and drew his sword. For a moment Coby thought he was going to cut down the captives, but he began walking slowly towards the duke like a man in a dream. Ivett screamed as the sergeant raised his sword, and tried to shield his fallen master with his own body. Coby looked away as the blade fell again and again, thudding into flesh like a butcher's cleaver.

Pushing past a confused Ned, she ran to the nearest of the two figures bound to the pillar and looked up into his face. Not

Master Catlyn, or at least, not her Master Catlyn. This one was gaunt and pale from too many years in a dark cell: Sandy. She went round to the other side of the pillar, and found Mal, stripped to the waist, eyes tight shut and a frown of concentration creasing his dark brow. Blaise Grey, his expression blank, held a glassy night-black blade to Mal's chest. Neither of them seemed aware of her presence.

She shot a glance back at Ned, who smiled grimly and launched himself at Blaise. The blade flew from the taller man's hand, shattering against the bricks. Blaise's eyes snapped open and he fought back, seizing Ned in a stranglehold. Coby snatched up the bundled weapons and drew the rapier, wondering what on earth she was going to do with it.

As Ivett's screams died away, she realised someone was speaking in a language she had never heard before. It was Sandy.

"*Icorrowe amayi'a. Dë sasayíhami onapama.*"

A brilliant light flared around him and when Coby's vision cleared, he was gone.

Sandy – or was it Erishen? – flew upwards like a hawk released, into the nacreous grey sky. Jathekkil howled in frustration and threw himself at Mal, but his hands passed through him. The eternal darkness of the dream realm was replaced by the subterranean gloom of the cellar, lantern-light gilding the brickwork. Mal staggered, no longer bound to his brother, and collided with two struggling figures, sending the three of them crashing to the ground.

A hand caught him under the elbow and pulled him to his feet. A pale face, worried eyes. Hendricks. She pressed the rapier hilt into his right hand. Cold steel. Yes. He placed his left thumb against the ricasso and slid it downwards onto the blade, wincing as the metal sliced his flesh. Blood flowed over steel, and the last of the fog cleared from his mind.

Ned lay sprawled at his feet. Blaise ran over to his father, seized the sword from Goddard's hand and ran the sergeant through in one powerful stroke. Goddard collapsed to his knees, weeping in realisation of what he had done, then pitched forward on his face. Blaise heaved Ivett's corpse off the duke's prone body.

"Father!"

"Grey." Mal's voice was hoarse, but it carried across the low-vaulted space. "Get up. You can mourn him later."

Blaise got to his feet. His face was pale, his eyes red and unfocused from the drugged smoke. "He's not dead."

"Something we can both be grateful for," Mal said. "Now let my friends take your father to the good doctor."

"Why should I trust you, demon?"

"Because there are three of us and only one of you."

"You shall not touch him."

"Then he'll die."

Blaise's mouth tightened in frustration, but he stepped away from his father. Ned lifted the duke's shoulders and Hendricks took his feet, her eyes never leaving Blaise.

"I could call my men," Blaise said.

"What men?" Hendricks put in. "Two, no, three are dead. One has been driven mad with fear, which leaves an elderly steward, a doctor and your porter. Unless there are others I haven't seen."

Blaise advanced on her, white with fury.

"Who do you think you are, whelp, to speak to me like that?"

She smiled. "Ned, drop your end."

"No!" Blaise halted, trembling with the effort at self-control.

Hendricks inclined her head in acknowledgment and began to back away towards the cellar steps. Mal waited until they had left.

"So, will you let us go freely?" he asked Blaise.

"You know I can't do that."

"Then we are at an impasse." Mal hefted his blade.

"You won't get far," Blaise said. "There's a palace full of royal guards just over the river."

"And your family," Mal said, "how far will they get? A prince and his most trusted advisor, repeated through the generations?"

"I can only aspire to my father's level of power and influence."

"You still don't see what he is, do you? You think he is merely the Duke of Suffolk, loyal servant of the Crown and mentor to the Prince of Wales."

"Merely? What more is there?"

"The throne itself," Mal replied.

"I desire no such thing, and I will cut dead the man who even whispers such treason in my presence."

Mal stooped and drew his dagger from its scabbard. Grey picked up the cloak in which Mal's blades had been wrapped and flipped it around his hand for protection. Goddard's weapon was shorter and heavier than a rapier, and therefore slower, but no less effective. Mal had borne such a sword himself in times of war, and seen what it could do to an unarmoured man.

Both adopted the *seconda guardia* position – sword held horizontally and waist-high – with left hands held out to one side, ready to catch an incoming blade on dagger or cloak. Mal watched and waited, allowing Grey's impatience to do most of his work for him. No flurry of blows here, like actors on a stage – a real duel was a mind game, out-thinking your opponent in order to get in that one deadly blow.

After a few more moments of watching and pacing, Mal made his move, a swift thrust to his opponent's right side, well away from the entangling cloak. Grey sidestepped and parried down and outwards. A rapid disengage and counter-thrust almost skewered Mal in the guts, but he turned sideways at the last moment and the blade passed a hair's breadth from his flesh. Grey withdrew, and they resumed their guard positions.

"How did your brother escape?"

"How should I know?" Mal replied. "I was tied up and drugged. One of my friends must have cut him free."

Grey lunged, his sword point aimed straight for Mal's heart. Mal parried with his dagger whilst his own blade snaked upwards in a counter-thrust towards his opponent's face. Grey swirled the cloak, enveloping the rapier and deflecting it past his ear. Mal leapt backwards, withdrawing his blade before the weight of the cloak could wrench it from his grasp.

The edge of the cloak swept across the brazier and caught fire. Grey dodged behind the pillar, shaking off the burning fabric. That left his off-side vulnerable. Mal manoeuvred around the pillar to his own right. A thrust through the guts would finish off his opponent for good. He recalled Leland's instructions. *Don't let it happen again.*

"We can stop this any time you like," Mal said, stepping back a pace.

"I'll stop when you're dead at my feet, demon."

To Hell with Leland's instructions. He thrust towards Grey's vulnerable side. Grey tried to bring his blade around in time to parry but the pillar blocked his way. The point of the rapier pierced doublet, shirt, and slid between his ribs.

Grey's eyes widened as Mal withdrew the blade. He clutched the wound, trying to draw breath, and staggered against the pillar. The sword fell from his hand. Grey looked up, eyes hard as flint. His mouth worked but no words came out.

"I've wasted enough time on you already," Mal told him.

Never taking his eyes off his opponent, Mal retrieved his sword belt and backed away. When Grey made no move to follow, Mal turned and bounded up the stairs to the courtyard. Somewhere out there, Sandy was waiting for him.

The porter strode across the courtyard towards them, crossbow raised. He halted when he saw what they were carrying.

"Put his lordship down gently, or I shoot."

"If you shoot me, I'll drop him," Coby replied. "Help us, if you want your master to live."

With the porter's aid they carried the duke up to his bed-chamber, where his doctor fussed over him and scolded them all in broken English and what Coby guessed was obscene Italian.

"Now then, you two, come with me," the porter said.

"No," the duke gasped. "Let them go. It is too late now."

The porter looked dumbfounded, but he could hardly contradict his master so he left them with a curt bow. On the table nearby, next to a large medicine cabinet, Coby spotted a white porcelain dish contained the missing pearl earring. How had that ended up here? She scooped it up and dropped it in her pocket.

"Where is my son?" Suffolk asked.

"In the cellar with Mal," Ned said. "Settling an old score."

The duke nodded. "He had his chance. He cannot stop me now."

Coby exchanged glances with Ned, who shrugged.

"What have you done with Sandy?" she asked Suffolk.

"I? Nothing." The duke smiled bitterly. "I underestimated Erishen. It has been too long since any of us tried such a ma-noeuvre."

"He's raving," Ned said, picking up the black doublet that lay draped over a chair. "Come on, let's find Mal."

"Yes, go, go," the doctor said, shooing them out of the door. "His Grace must rest."

Back in the courtyard they were met by Mal. In the leaden light of a cold September afternoon he looked almost as haggard as his brother, his pale flesh slick with sweat. Coby handed him the doublet and he put it on gratefully.

Then they heard the hoofbeats. Looking through the open gate Coby could see a lone rider cantering down the drive, but by the sounds of it there were a dozen or so others behind him. There was no sign of the porter.

"The river," Mal said to her as they ran back into the house.

"We have a boat," she gasped, "but it's some distance off."

"How do we get out?"

"I saw a door at the far end of the passage–"

"Locked," Ned told them as they reached him.

"Don't you have lock-picks?"

"Yes, but…" He looked sheepish. "I have no idea how to use them."

"Here, give them to me."

She shook out the canvas roll and selected a probe. All those hours spent dawdling over her broom in the workshop, so she could eavesdrop on her father instructing his apprentices, would not be for naught.

"Do you know what you're doing?" Ned asked.

"Hush."

She felt around inside the lock. Typical symmetrical design, three wards. She probed the furthest for depth and width, then chose a skeleton key from the roll. It turned in the lock, but did not engage with the mechanism. She withdrew it and selected another.

"Hurry up!"

"I told you to be quiet," she replied. "Damn, too wide."

She tried one after another, searching the roll in vain for another key of the right size. Longer and narrower. Ah! She seized the key and slid it into the lock, whispering a prayer. It turned, and the bolt snicked back.

"Well done!" Master Catlyn helped her to her feet whilst Ned rolled the lock-pick set up and stuffed it in his satchel. "Now, let's get out of here."

The door emerged between two buttresses onto a narrow strip of level ground. Beyond, a grassy slope was all that lay between them and the river. Several boats were still moored at the jetty. Mal paused. They still didn't know where Sandy was, though as long as he was away from here, that had to be a good thing. Or so he hoped. He scanned the façade of the palace opposite. Its windows gleamed dull gold in the afternoon sun. Was Prince Robert there now, staring back?

"At least we don't have to run all the way to Syon House," Ned said with a grin. "All we have to do is row across to the palace–"

"No."

"What do you mean, no?" Ned gestured towards the palace. "Where better to take sanctuary?"

"What would we tell the prince's household?"

"That you and Sandy were abducted and held prisoner–"

"By the prince's own mentor? And that I attacked the duke's son and left him for dead?"

"Good point."

A low rumble to the east made Mal look up. Leaden clouds massed overhead – another thunderstorm? Reaching the jetty, he found Hendricks had untied all but one of the boats and was pushing them out into the river.

"Well played!" He patted her on the shoulder. "Now, everyone aboard!"

Hendricks and Ned got in, taking the fore and aft oars respectively. Mal cast off, leaping into the little craft as it started to move downstream. He gestured for Hendricks to surrender her oars; the girl was already white, her face taut with pain.

She smiled in thanks and moved to sit in the narrow space between the two rowers.

On the slope above them, armed men were issuing from the house. Men in royal livery. And behind them, a tall figure in black and gold. Mal swore under his breath and bent to his oars. Hendricks craned her neck to see past Ned.

"Is that–?"

"Prince Robert, yes."

The royal guards ran down the slope and raised their crossbows. Mal pulled harder on the oars, expecting to feel the thud of a bolt any moment, but the missiles plopped harmlessly into the river around them.

"With any luck we'll be out of range before they can reload," Ned grunted.

Across the water more guards, this time carrying arquebuses, were running out of the palace.

"Say your prayers, lads," Mal muttered.

A second round of crossbow bolts whined through the air, and Ned yelped.

"Are you all right?" Hendricks asked him.

"Near miss," he grunted, pulling a bolt out of the woodwork beside him and tossing it in the river. "Told you I had the Devil's own luck."

Hendricks crouched in the thwarts, looking from bank to bank in horror. The arquebusiers lined up, primed their weapons hurriedly and raised them to their shoulders. Like a string of firecrackers the arquebuses erupted in noise and smoke – and something hit Mal's left shoulder like a sledgehammer. As the force of the impact ripped through his body, he let go of his oar. It bounced in the rowlocks and began to slip, very slowly, into the river.

"Christ and His Holy Mother!"

"Sir?"

"Get the oar," he told Hendricks through gritted teeth.

He glanced at his shoulder, which burned as if thrust through with a hot poker just above the collarbone. The black fabric of his doublet was torn and wet, the ragged hole scarlet around the edges, but the blood was not spurting from some vital conduit. That at least was a relief.

Ned continued to row, but with Mal incapacitated they were making slow progress. The arquebusiers began to reload. Mal used his uninjured arm to pull Hendricks towards him, turning her back to his belly so they could ply the oars as one. So small, she fitted into him like a lover... For a moment he rested his cheek against her hair, letting the pain melt into the distance, then they bent to the oars and pulled, and he ground his teeth against the fire in his shoulder.

The rumble sounded again from downstream, echoing across the water. Not thunder, nor, thank the Lord, more gun-fire. Drums.

"*Rehi!*"

Mal spared a glance backwards. Sandy was waving to him from the prow of a large craft heading in their direction. The ambassador's barge.

The royal guards halted, looking to their captains, who motioned for them to lower their weapons. Prince Robert stood on the jetty, arms folded, watching the oncoming barge. Hendricks twisted round with a grin of relief, but her smile faded on seeing Mal's expression.

"The ambassador will save us, won't he?" she whispered.

The drumbeat changed and the rowers on one side shipped their oars. The barge began to turn in a wide arc.

"Come on, Mal!" Ned shouted, hauling on the oars.

The wash from the barge pushed against them, even as their efforts drove them on. Mal's vision began to go dark around the edges, until all he could see was the bright patch of his own blood on the girl's doublet in front of him, accusing him of failure. He turned towards the barge. The vessel's dark bulk loomed over them for a moment, and Mal felt sure its oars would rake the little skiff out of the water and tip it over like a child's toy. Then the barge was past, lurching side-on to the current as it turned back for London.

"Sandy!"

His brother looked round for a moment from where he stood in the barge's prow, arms wrapped about the diminutive skrayling. He gazed at Mal with dark eyes that seemed to look right through him, sparking a jolt of some buried memory that strove to reach the surface of Mal's mind but floundered like a drowning man and was gone. The barge swung round and Sandy disappeared from view behind its central canopy.

Dammit, now they really were on their own. Kiiren had what he came for, and he was leaving the rest of them to the wolves.

CHAPTER XXXVI

Coby turned to look at Mal. He was deathly pale, his eyes un-focused. Had he lost so much blood already? It was hard to tell against the blackness of his livery doublet. Without thinking she let go of both oars and put her palms to his face.

"Don't die on me," she whispered.

He coughed and managed a weak grin. "I'm in no fit state."

Over his shoulder she glimpsed a pale-haired figure in the stern of the barge, swinging a coil of rope. Gabriel Parrish. Moments later the rope sailed overhead and she flailed for it.

"Careful!" Faulkner shouted at her. "Here, take this and wrap it round the cleat."

He passed her a loop of rope. When she looked blank, he pointed to the two-pronged metal thing on the prow, where the painter was still tied. She clambered past Mal and wrapped the line around it as best she could before the retreating barge pulled the rope taut. Faulkner threaded the loose end under the thwarts and secured it, just to be certain.

"They could have bloody stopped to pick us up," Faulkner muttered. "Here, let me see him."

"I'm fine," Mal replied, waving him away.

Coby slid onto the thwart on his good side.

"You don't look fine," she told him.

"S'not the first time I've been shot at." He peered at the wound. "Closest, though."

"We're going to have to get nearer to the barge," Ned said, pointing to the next bend in the river. "We're going to be all over the place at this rate."

Fortunately Parrish had had the same idea, and had enlisted one of the skraylings to help him haul the skiff in. They picked up speed, slowly edging closer to the barge's stern. Mal seemed to be rallying now they were getting away, though his face was still pale and drawn. She clutched his good hand and talked to him in a low voice.

"We did it, sir. We found you both and got away. See, we're nearly to the barge."

"And then what?" he rasped. "What happens when we get back to London?"

"Don't worry about it. Your brother is safe. That's all that matters, right?"

He nodded. "Aye."

She looked back upstream. The prince and his men were already leaving the jetty, heading back into Ferrymead House.

"What will they do?" she asked Mal.

"Ride ahead," he replied. "There are no bridges between here and London, so unless they commandeer a vessel..."

"You think they would try to stop us?"

"I don't know. A diversion to Bartholomew Fair is one thing; assaulting the Prince of Wales' mentor is a touch more serious."

He started to laugh, but it turned into a grimace. Just then the skiff's prow bumped against the stern of the barge, knocking them all aftwards. Strong hands reached down to haul them aboard, and for a moment all was a confusion of greetings in English and Vinlandic.

"Catlyn-*tuur*!" the ambassador cried, rushing to his former bodyguard's side. "Come, sit down and let me tend your hurt."

"That's all you seem to do," Mal muttered, but allowed himself to be led away.

Faulkner and Parrish were likewise reunited, entangled in a passion embrace in a corner of the barge's stern. Coby found herself alone once more. No, not alone. Sandy was staring at her, his brow furrowed. Then to her surprise he bowed in the skrayling fashion.

"*Hësea.*"

It sounded more like a sneeze than a greeting, but she bowed politely in return.

"I don't think we've been properly introduced, sir," she said. She sounded idiotic in her own ears, but what else was one to say? "I am Jacob Hendricks, of Suffolk's Men."

"*Erishen.*"

"That's your name? Erishen?"

He nodded. Well, if the madman wanted to pretend he was a skrayling, Coby was not going to argue.

"Come on," she said. "Let's go and see how your brother is doing."

Mal drained the cup Kiiren handed him, grimacing at the bitter taste.

"What the hell do you put in this brew?"

"Many herbs," the ambassador replied. "I shall not bore you with names."

He had stripped off his robes and wore a plain brown tunic like a skrayling servant. By his side was a multi-tiered wooden box full of glass bottles and strange implements. Mal unbuttoned his doublet and shrugged out of it, gritting his teeth against the pain.

"*Tsh*, let me do that," Kiiren said. "You will make bleed worse."

"How did you come to be here?" Mal asked as Kiiren examined the bullet wound with professional detachment.

"Your friend Gabriel came to me and told me your friends had gone to house of Lord Suffolk near palace. I think perhaps you might need my help, so I tell Leland-*tuur* Lord Suffolk sends for me."

"And he believed you?"

Kiiren smiled. "Lie down now. You will soon feel... strange."

"I feel fine," Mal lied. Either the boat had started to fly through the air, or something was very wrong with his sense of balance.

As he began to sway on his feet, Kiiren eased him onto the bench and propped him up on pillows.

"Close eyes and sleep," the skrayling said. "When you wake, all will be mended and we will be back in London."

Mal opened his mouth to protest, but he couldn't feel his tongue any more.

"Nnnnh..."

Coby knelt at Mal's side, clutching his cold hand. Ambassador Kiiren had said the coldness was normal, but that she could warm Mal's hand with her own if she wished. She scanned Mal's pale features, wondering what torments he had been through during his brief captivity. Apart from the clotted blood on his lower lip, there was no sign of outward hurt. Ambassador Kiiren had cleaned up Mal's left earlobe and reinserted the pearl earring; he seemed to think it important, though she couldn't for the life of her imagine why.

She was vaguely aware of the ambassador and Sandy sitting on cushions nearby, murmuring together in the strange language. All this magic made her uncomfortable, now she had seen it up close. She would never forget that scene in the cellar, everyone frozen as if time itself had stopped. And yet if she and Ned had not intruded, perhaps Blaise would have killed both brothers. Why was Suffolk behind all this, anyway? Surely he did not want to see the ambassador harmed? It made no sense for him to sponsor a theatre company and then conspire against the judge of the contest. Too exhausted to think straight any more, she retreated into the memory of Mal pulling her close in the little boat and half-dozed, half-daydreamed most of the way back to London.

She roused when his hand tightened on hers and she realised he was awake. He opened his eyes, squinted up at her, mumbled something, then coughed.

"Drink," he wheezed.

Coby passed him the cup Ambassador Kiiren had left with her for just this purpose. She held it to his lips and he sipped.

"Water?" he asked with a grimace.

"The ambassador assured me it's clean," she replied.

He drank the rest obediently, then tried to sit up. He turned pale, leant over the side of the bench and retched thin sticky fluid onto the deck. She wondered when he had last eaten.

"Lie back," she sighed, and went to fetch a bucket of river water.

"Where are we?" he asked when she returned.

"Nearing Westminster."

"No one's tried to stop us?"

"Not yet."

He rubbed his brow with the heel of his right hand. "It's only a matter of time."

"Will... will they arrest you?"

He nodded, not looking at her. "How can they not? I cut Blaise down and left him for dead."

She recoiled a little. Knowing that Mal had once been a soldier was one thing; hearing him speak so casually about killing a man... Recalling their fighting lessons together, she realised how much he must have been holding back. Lucky, then, she had only fading bruises and one accidental cut to show for it.

He appeared not to notice her reaction.

"I thought I'd seen the last of the Tower," he said with a grimace.

"Sir Francis will vouch for you," she assured him. "Ned got the lock-picks from Baines, so I'm sure Walsingham must know of our mission."

"What? God's teeth, can he not keep a secret for five minutes together? I swear I will knock some sense into him one day. If I ever get the chance."

She stared at him, realising with horror they might have only minutes together before he was taken from her forever. Minutes she did not want to spend discussing Ned Faulkner.

"Sir, I–"

Gunfire sounded from downstream.

"I think we've arrived," he said.

Ned stood in the bows of the barge, watching for the first sight of London. As they rounded the last bend before Westminster the view opened up, revealing the broad green expanse of Lambeth Marshes to their right and the palace of Whitehall to their left. Beyond Lambeth the city was a dark stain on the Middlesex bank of the Thames, covering the gently rising slopes almost as far as Islington.

He instinctively ducked as the shots rang out. Gabriel crouched next to him, peering over the gunwales, his delicate profile taut with apprehension.

"What was that?" Ned asked him, not daring to rise. He'd been shot at enough for one day.

"There's a line of skiffs across the river, between the palace and Lambeth Stairs. Royal guards by the look of it."

"Christ! And here was me thinking we'd got away with it."

The oarsmen slowed their pace, and the ambassador picked his way past them to the bow, Sandy trailing in his wake. It was uncanny how much he looked like Mal now, though he had not spoken an intelligible word to Ned since they had escaped Ferrymead. Ned resisted the urge to cross himself. Out of his wits Sandy might be, but this was something different. Something... wrong.

Kiiren spoke to Sandy in the strange language, and the tall man ducked into the covered bower.

"They try to stop us?" the ambassador asked Gabriel.

"It looks that way," Gabriel replied.

Kiiren nodded, and shouted something to the oarsmen. They continued to row ever more slowly, until the barge was drifting along mostly by force of the current. As they drew within an easy bowshot of the blockade, the central skiff rowed forward a few yards.

"If it please Your Excellency," the officer in the bow shouted, "His Royal Highness the Prince of Wales demands that you hand over the man named Maliverny Catlyn. Immediately."

"And if I do not?" Kiiren replied.

"Then my lord prince regrets that measures will be taken, to the great dismay of your people."

Kiiren drew himself up to his full height.

"Dismay will be his, if alliance between our people is broken."

"Is that a threat, sir?"

"No. I wish to... negotiate."

"I will convey your request to His Highness."

The skiff turned towards the western bank and soon reached Westminster Stairs, a long jetty projecting into the river. The remaining vessels manoeuvred to close the gap, their weapons still trained on the barge.

"Will the prince negotiate?" Gabriel asked the ambassador.

"I hope so," Kiiren replied softly.

"We could give them Sandy instead," Ned jested.

The ambassador turned a blotched grey and white, and Gabriel kicked Ned with the side of his foot, glaring at him and mouthing imprecations.

"Sorry," Ned muttered. "It was just a thought."

"So what do we do, Your Excellency?" Gabriel said.

"We wait. And hope your prince's mind has not been poisoned against us by Suffolk."

Mal swung his legs round and eased himself into a sitting position. He was damned if he was going to lie here like an invalid any longer, even if he wasn't ready to get to his feet and fight his way out. Hendricks watched him with concern, poised to leap to his aid should he falter. He smiled, hoping to reassure her he wasn't about to throw up again, and was rewarded with a softening of expression, though her grey eyes remained bright with anxiety.

He looked through the curtains towards the river. Crowds lined the banks, perhaps expecting some sudden and dramatic conflict between skraylings and royal guards. With any luck they would be disappointed. The shouted exchange had ended better than he feared, but he was not out of the woods yet. Kiiren's negotiations might fail. No, best not to invite defeat by thinking about it. He glanced across at his brother. Sandy sat cross-legged on the cushions, his expression as inscrutable as any skrayling. Had Erishen taken him over completely?

He was about to ask Hendricks to fetch the ambassador when Kiiren appeared in the curtained doorway.

"I have done my best," the skrayling said. "Now we wait."

"You have a plan?" Mal asked.

"I am hoping you have one," Kiiren replied. "I have negotiated many trade treaties, with my own people and with humans of lands beyond ours, but you Christians think very strangely. I do not know what will sway your prince to our cause."

Mal pondered for a moment. "He is his father's son, and his mother's also. Ambitious, yes, but cautious. He will not easily set aside this alliance, not if Walsingham has anything to do with it."

"Ah yes, your friend Walsingham. But he is only one man. How many sit on Privy Council? Six? Seven?"

"Eight at least, including the prince. But Effingham may be on our side. Without the skraylings on Sark, the Narrow Sea will no longer be safe for our ships, nor the Atlantic. The Lord High Admiral could lose many vessels to the Spanish."

"Even so, that is only two. And your prince cannot set aside the law. If you killed a man–"

"Begging your pardons, sirs," Hendricks put in. "Are we certain that is true?"

They both looked at her.

"You wounded Grey," she went on. "But Suffolk's physician is very good, by your own account. He may not be dead yet, nor his father neither."

"There is still the assault to answer," Mal countered.

"But not, perhaps, murder. Not yet."

"Your friend sees truly," Kiiren said. "If Suffolk and his son both live, perhaps prince will be merciful."

Mal shook his head. "I like not these odds."

"But it is worth a try, sir, is it not?" Hendricks gazed up at him earnestly.

"I will send message to our best physicians, to attend upon Suffolk," Kiiren said.

"No."

They both looked at Mal.

"Why not?" Hendricks asked.

"Because if either of them dies under the skraylings' care, all is lost. They will say the ambassador sent them to finish what we started."

"So what do we do?"

"We must trust to the skills of Doctor Renardi," Mal said. "And pray."

Kiiren clicked his tongue. "Pray if you wish, but I will talk to prince."

"No, there is no time, not if we wish to move whilst the Greys still live." If they live. "You must hand me over now, and I will take my chances."

Hendricks turned pale and opened her mouth to protest, but he squeezed her hand in reassurance and warning.

"Tell them," he went on, "tell them you will release me into the custody of Sir Francis Walsingham and none other."

"You trust Walsingham?" Kiiren asked.

"As much as any man. If he is an ally of Suffolk, he dissembles very well, and plays a game of deceits that would put a Southwark card shark to shame."

"Very well." Kiiren lowered his voice. "I must take your brother to our camp. It is time to reveal what is done here."

"You were very keen to keep it a secret, once," Mal said.

Kiiren nodded. "It is forbidden for us to take human form. But now I know Erishen did not do this willingly, I think perhaps he may be forgiven."

"And my friends?"

"They must go home. I cannot allow them into camp." Seeing Mal's frown, he added, "I can have them escorted to guild house, if you wish, and guarded by my own men."

"Thank you, sir. It would ease my mind greatly." He smiled at Hendricks, and she attempted to smile back, not very successfully.

Kiiren went out onto the deck to await the captain's return.

Hendricks lifted Mal's hand and pressed his knuckles to her cheek, closing her eyes against the tears beginning to form.

"Sssh," he murmured, and pulled her closer with his good arm.

He kissed the top of her head chastely. Her hair smelt of smoke. Was it only yesterday that they had escaped the fire together? And now they had outrun death a second time, only to part after all. She would be much safer without him, that was for certain. Besides, what could he offer a woman? He had no property or fortune, no means to support a family. And to cap it all, he had made an enemy of the Prince of Wales. At this rate he would be lucky to get out of England alive.

Looking up he saw Ned standing at the curtained entrance, staring at them, and realised what this must look like. He almost pushed Hendricks away, but checked himself. He owed Ned nothing. Let the wretch think what he liked, at least for now. It was up to the girl to tell the others, if and when she was ready.

At last all was arranged, and there was nothing left but to make his farewells. He shook hands with Gabriel and Ned. The latter winked at him, irrepressible as always. Last of all he turned to Hendricks. After a moment's hesitation she slipped her arms around his waist and hugged him briefly, then retreated in embarrassment.

"God be with you, Catlyn," Gabriel said.

Mal inclined his head in thanks, pulled back the curtain and stepped out onto the open deck. The light was fading fast, and the crowds had dispersed to their homes. A wherry bobbed close to the barge's prow, with two royal guards in the stern, partisans held stiffly at attention. As Mal stepped aboard he recognised Baines at the oars. The intelligencer gave a slight shake of his head, and began to row.

Mal looked back towards the barge. He was glad that Ki-iren had found what he came here for, but his joy would be short-lived. As soon as it could be done, Mal would have that creature driven from Sandy's body, and all would be well again.

Mal was escorted through the maze of Whitehall Palace to a modestly furnished parlour far from the great chambers of state. Walsingham was seated at the head of a polished oak dining table, his gaunt features luminous as alabaster in the candlelight.

"Well, Master Catlyn," Walsingham said when the guards had left. "You have stirred up quite a hornet's nest this day."

"That was not my intent, sir."

"No?"

The spymaster gestured towards the door. Mal turned to see Baines shooting the bolts into place. His gut tightened in fear, and for an instant the dizziness brought on by Kiiren's sleeping draught seemed to have returned. Was Walsingham another guiser, a skrayling behind a mask of human flesh? He thought not, but there was no way to be sure.

"Sit down, Catlyn," Walsingham said, less gently this time.

Mal did so, though all his instincts bade him run. The spymaster's dark eyes scanned his face.

"I trust we have the right brother," he said at last.

"Shall I show you Monkton's handiwork?" Mal asked. "It's still fresh."

He realised at once he had said the wrong thing.

"What were you thinking?" Walsingham hissed, leaning forward. "Abandoning your post to chase off after your brother?"

He nodded to Baines, who came up behind Mal's chair, placed a hand on his left shoulder and squeezed. Mal gasped as spears of agony drove through his flesh, and ground his teeth together in an effort not to cry out.

"I was abducted."

"By witchcraft?" Walsingham's eyes gleamed with Puritan zeal.

"I don't know." Mal swallowed, throat tinder-dry. He had no proof of anything that had happened. After all, it had just been a dream, hadn't it? "All I know is, I went to sleep in the Tower and woke up in Ferrymead House, incarcerated with my brother."

"You think someone broke into the ambassador's quarters, drugged you and smuggled you out, all unnoticed?"

"St Thomas's Tower looks out over the river, sir. And I may have left the window open. The nights have been muggy of late."

Walsingham's eyes narrowed. "What happened after that?"

"I... I was taken before Suffolk and tortured for information."

"What information?"

"I don't know."

Baines squeezed again. Harder. The edges of Mal's vision darkened, and his left arm began to twitch uncontrollably.

"S-s-something to do with Derbyshire, and, and skraylings. I think they wanted to know what I knew about the Huntsmen."

Mal feigned breathlessness whilst his thoughts ran ahead. Well, half-feigned anyway. Walsingham gestured to Baines, who fetched a cup of wine from the table and pushed it into his good hand. Mal gulped at the sour liquid, but it was pulled away before he could manage more than a mouthful.

"Suffolk trying to curry favour with the skraylings, eh?" Walsingham said, steepling his hands.

"No, sir. I think Suffolk is one of them. A Huntsman, I mean."

It was a risky gambit, but if Walsingham did not already know who and what Suffolk was, he would not hear it from Mal. The spymaster's reaction to any talk of magic told him that such an accusation would not be welcome.

Walsingham shook his head. "I cannot believe it. He has always spoken out in support of our skrayling allies. If it were his son you accused, that would be another matter."

"Suffolk and his son have been working together all along, sir. It was Blaise who was my tormentor."

"So you attacked the father, and slew the son to boot."

"Blaise is dead?"

The spymaster glanced at Baines, but this time Mal was too quick. He leapt to his feet and put more than an arm's reach between himself and his captors. Just enough truth to be believable, that was what Baines had taught him.

"I swear to you, Sir Francis, upon my mother's soul, His Grace the Duke of Suffolk is a traitor working against our alliance with the skraylings. He plots to put another on the throne of England."

He stood there, panting, his every breath pulling at his shoulder wound until he thought it must bleed afresh. Baines crouched into a fighter's stance, but Walsingham waved him back.

"That is a very serious accusation, Catlyn," he said softly.

"I know, sir. I would not voice it if I did not believe it to be true."

"Do you have proof?"

Mal shook his head. "No, but the ambassador believes me. His people are... not unacquainted with the Huntsmen's handiwork. He will vouch for the fact that my brother suffered hideously at their hands."

"Ah, the ambassador. Then he remains our ally? You found no sign of collusion with our enemies?"

"None, sir."

Walsingham nodded. "Good. I do not think the prince wishes to offend the Vinlanders, and if Suffolk is in any way guilty..." He spread his hands.

Mal let out a long breath. Baines was still watching him suspiciously, but without Walsingham to back him up the intelligencer could do nothing.

"You will remain in custody–" Walsingham began.

Mal froze.

"–in my home, under house arrest," he went on, "until such time as this business with the skraylings can be smoothed over. Baines?"

"Thank you, sir," Mal said, relief washing over him. At least he wasn't being sent to the Tower.

Walsingham waved him away, and Baines drew back the bolts on the door, a sour look on his face.

"Nice move, college boy," the intelligencer said as they walked back through the palace.

"What do you mean?" Mal asked, trying to sound nonchalant.

"Throwing it back on the skraylings. Gets you off the hook, gives them a way to placate His Highness. You'll go far in this business."

"You think Walsingham will employ me again, after what I've done?"

Baines laughed. "He likes men with guts. Just don't get too big for your boots, all right?"

Mal nodded. He had not even considered a career as an intelligencer until now; there had been too much else to think of in the past couple of weeks. Secrets, lies and a blade in each hand: wasn't that what he'd excelled in, all these years?

CHAPTER XXXVII

Mal sat in the window of the guest chamber, picking out a melancholy galliard on his lute. Say what you like about Walsingham, he was gentleman enough to send for Mal's belongings from the Tower. No doubt Baines had pawed through them, but it was a small price to pay. At least the rosary was safely hidden at Ned's house.

A sudden knock at the door made Mal start, and his fingers slipped on the lute strings.

"Come in," he said.

Baines opened the door, but did not enter. "Walsingham wants to see you."

Mal went down to the parlour and found Walsingham seated at the table, poring over a map. Mal coughed politely, and waited. After several minutes Walsingham looked up and beckoned him over.

"Suffolk is dead," Walsingham said without preamble. "The doctor says it was blood fever, from the leg wound."

"Common enough," Mal replied, trying to keep his voice as calm and level as the spymaster's. Certain as he was that Suffolk had taken his own life, he could hardly tell Walsingham that. "I've seen men half his age succumb in less time."

"Indeed. Which means we have only His Grace's word for what happened."

"But – Ah. You mean Blaise. He lives?"

Walsingham inclined his head. "Doctor Renardi was able to save him, though he is sorely wounded and may not rise from his bed for many weeks. He was not too ill to speak of his own part in this, however."

Mal stiffened, wondering what was coming next.

"Grey is young and hot-headed," Walsingham went on, "but apparently not as wild as we were led to believe. He claims that only obedience to his father's wishes made him espouse views against the skraylings, and that he is loyal to Prince Robert and the Queen. In view of this filial loyalty, Her Majesty has been prevailed upon to spare him a decree of attainder."

The cunning devil. It was the truth, in so far as it ran. And Mal could not contradict it without revealing everything he knew about the late duke. Did Blaise still refuse to believe Mal's claims that his father was possessed by a skrayling? Almost certainly. Mal would never have believed them himself a month ago.

"Did he say anything else?" Mal asked.

"Only that one of the Catlyn brothers attacked him, but he confesses he cannot be certain which one. And since the Crown cannot bring a case without a suspect, that is an end to the matter."

Odd. Blaise must surely remember fighting Mal, unless the blood loss from his injury had weakened his mind. Or someone had persuaded him that he did not want Ambassador Kiiren as an enemy.

"Then I am free to go?" Mal asked.

"So it seems," Walsingham replied. He picked up a leather purse that lay on the table. "I think you will go far in Her Majesty's service."

"Sir?"

"Do not look so surprised. Your methods may have been un-orthodox, but by exposing Suffolk as the leader of the Huntsmen you have cut the heart out of a dreadful conspiracy."

Mal wished it were true. But if Suffolk were dead, he had failed after all. And the Huntsmen remained untouched.

"A pity we did not catch more of them," Walsingham added.

"Oh? I hoped–"

"That Wheeler and his confederates were Huntsmen? So did we all. Alas they knew nothing. A band of petty malcontents: failed actors, tradesmen whose crafts have been superseded by skrayling wares, those sorts of fellows. Naught they could tell us led back to known Huntsmen's crimes."

"A pity indeed," Mal said, hoping his relief did not show. Wheeler's hysterical ravings had meant nothing then. It was a small consolation. Very small.

Walsingham slid the purse across the table. "A reward for loyal service."

Mal loosened the strings and looked within. The purse contained at least five pounds in gold angels. Not a king's ransom, but more than he had seen in a good long while.

"Thank you, sir."

"Do not thank me. That is a gift from Her Majesty. As you say, your dealings with the ambassador have been very... cordial, to the great benefit of our realm."

Mal nodded. The Queen was notoriously miserly, but she regarded the defence of England as her highest duty.

"Tell me, Catlyn. When you were working for the ambassador, were you approached by anyone?"

"I–"

Walsingham held up a hand. "Do not lie to me. I know you were."

"The Spanish," Mal said after a moment. "And the French."

"Only those two?"

"So far."

"Hmm, I suppose your position was curtailed somewhat early." Walsingham folded his long hands together. "Did either of them make any offers that we could use to our advantage?"

Mal considered. The promptings of the Spanish ambassador, to convert the ambassador to Christianity – and Papism – cut too close to treason, but the French… "I was offered property in France, sir. Some legal fiction to do with my mother."

"Really? How interesting. What was your reply?"

"That if it were brought before an English court, I would be glad of it."

Walsingham laughed sharply. "You are your father's son after all. Well, I suggest you speak again to the ambassador's man, and tell him you have changed your mind."

"Sir?"

"Free passage into France, property, perhaps even entry to the French Court? How should we refuse such an opportunity?"

"You want me to spy on the French, sir?"

Walsingham only smiled. "I do not trust Henri of Navarre's convenient change of faith. A loyal Englishman of Catholic parentage would be of great use over there."

"As you wish, sir." Mal bowed deeply.

Walsingham returned his gaze to the map. Seeing himself dismissed, Mal bowed again and left. Spying on the French, eh? Well, it beat nights spent on guard outside dockside warehouses in the freezing cold and rain, or fighting pointless duels on behalf of overbred young noblemen. And an estate in France was better than none at all. Perhaps he could take Sandy there, and forget about spying altogether.

Suffolk's Men gathered one last time at the Bull's Head. Coby hunched over her ale, feeling the absence of her late master more keenly than ever, here in the place that had been as much his home as Thames Street. The other patrons gave them pitying glances and a wide berth, though whether out of respect for their grief or through satiation of their appetite for gossip, she could not be sure.

Master Eaton was on crutches and he wore a bandage around his head that covered one eye. Gabriel Parrish was there, his scorched hair cut unfashionably short, Ned Faulkner by his side. The two had been inseparable since their return to London. She supposed she ought to be glad some happiness had come out of this dreadful business. There was little enough to go around.

The apprentices had been sent home to their families, now that their master was no longer around to keep them. That was all of them. Master Rudd had of course been killed in the explosion, and both his and Master Naismith's bodies destroyed in the fire. A few pieces of bone had been raked from the ashes and placed in a shared grave, since none could tell whose they were.

"I suppose that is an end to the contest," Coby said, drawing circles in a puddle of spilt beer with one finger. "And I was sure we would win, too."

"Perhaps the Prince's Men will yet play," Eaton said. "I doubt the ambassador cares for our woes."

"They say the duke is dead," Parrish said. "Or dying. At any rate, with Naismith and Rudd both gone and Eaton here maimed, we are a sorry crew indeed. It is a sad end to Suffolk's Men."

"What is to become of their widows?" Master Eaton asked, of no one in particular.

"Master Cutsnail has agreed to cancel all Master Naismith's debts on the theatre," Coby said, "in return for the chest of play-books."

"That is very generous," Parrish said.

"Not really," Coby replied. "Those plays are worth a great deal amongst the skraylings. I think he will make a handsome profit in the end."

"And the skraylings wonder why folk hate them," Master Eaton said.

"What will you do?" Coby asked Parrish, anxious to change the subject.

"Burbage has asked me to join the Prince's Men."

"And will you accept?"

"How can I not? I must work somewhere, and I would rather it were not for Henslowe." He gave Ned a wry smile. "I cannot forgive him for setting that miscreant Wheeler upon us."

Coby forbore from explaining there was more to Wheeler's actions than petty Bankside rivalry. If Walsingham had suppressed news of the conspiracy, she was not going to speak out and risk attracting the spymaster's attention.

"I wish you well," Master Eaton said. "For my own part, I must look to other professions. There is not much call for one-eyed actors."

"You should write a ballad about the fire, and sell it in Paul's Yard," Ned told him.

"I would rather forget the damned fire altogether," he muttered, and rising from the table he limped off in the direction of the jakes.

"What about you?" Parrish asked Coby. "Will Mistress Naismith keep you on?"

She shook her head. "She cannot afford another servant, not now. And what would I do? Sew clothes for her? It is all I know how to do. That, and running around after actors."

"And lock picking," Ned added with a grin. "I know a few fellows who might take you on."

"I would prefer to earn my bread honestly, thank you very much."

"You never did tell us how you learnt the trick of it," Ned replied, unabashed.

"I'm just good with my hands," she said. She thought of the trapdoor again, but it only brought back pangs of guilt. "I think I'm better off plying my needle."

"Come to the Prince's Men," Parrish said, putting his hand on her wrist. "Burbage always has need of reliable tiremen. Most of them are quarrelsome drunks or thieves, by his account."

She shook him off.

"I do not think so. I have had enough of actors."

The truth was, she too wanted to forget about the fire. The thought of entering the Curtain, or any other theatre, filled her with dread. She heard again the roar of flames and felt the heat singeing her face.

"You are still in love with… *him*," Gabriel said softly.

She nodded, swallowing against the lump in her throat.

"Then go to him," he went on. "Tell him how you feel–"

"He knows," she said wretchedly. Faulkner was smirking, the vile whoreson. "How could he not, after…"

"And?"

"And nothing. I haven't seen him since we got back to London. What if–"

"Do not dwell on such things. The ambassador would not let that happen to his dear friend, the brother of his beloved."

"You really believe what the ambassador told us?" Ned put in. "That Sandy is his long lost love reborn?"

"I saw him appear out of thin air on that boat," Gabriel said, turning to Ned. "If the skraylings can do that…"

"Yes, but…" She sighed. "It is too much to take in."

"Trust me, it will all work out in the end. Catlyn loves you."

"He does?"

Her heart tightened, hardly daring to believe. Mal desired

her, he had made that plain, but she was not such a fool as to mistake that for love.

"I saw the look on his face when you embraced him," Parrish said. "It was the look of a man who loves in spite of his own misgivings." He laughed softly and tightened his arm around Ned. "I should know."

At that moment Master Eaton returned with more beer.

"Here you go," he said, sliding a tankard across the table.

Coby took a deep draught, hoping to calm her nerves.

"Think on my advice," Parrish said. He clapped his hands together. "So, who's for a game of skittles?"

Mal stood before the gates of the stockade. It seemed a lifetime since he had first come here and been half-affrighted out of his wits by the strange music from within. He waited patiently whilst the gate guard informed the ambassador of his arrival.

He was shown through the camp to the same small tent where he had stayed after Bartholomew Fair. Sandy was lying on a heap of cushions, eyes closed and one of the skrayling lodestone necklaces about his throat. The air was thick with the scent of *shakholaat*.

"How is he?" Mal asked, sitting down on the opposite side of the brazier.

"At peace. For now."

"He used magic to get away from the cellar, didn't he? If he could do that, why did he not try sooner?" It would have saved us all a lot of trouble.

"You are not strong enough to be his anchor."

"But you are?"

Kiiren nodded. "If you had told me about him more soon… Instead I hear it from your friend Hendricks."

Mal looked away. This was not his fault, how could it be?

He knew nothing of skrayling magic, wanted nothing to do with it.

"I have been looking at symbols your friend Hendricks drew," Kiiren said, reaching inside his robe.

"The ones from Grey's desk? Are they skrayling writings?"

Kiiren held them under the lamp-stand and stared at them for several moments. "Yes, I believe so. They look very like ancient script of my people. Added to your witnessing, it is enough proof that Suffolk is... Guiser, as you call them."

"Was. Suffolk is dead."

Kiiren looked aghast.

"No. Then where–?"

Mal told the ambassador of his fears, that Suffolk had chosen to be taken to Ferrymead House because of its closeness to the palace.

"If that is true," Kiiren said, "our enemies' reach is greater than we suspected."

"But surely he is no threat at the moment? He is not yet born. And even if the child is a boy, his father and elder brother inherit before him. He cannot come to the throne unless..."

"Unless they die. Yes."

They pondered a while in silence.

"What are we to do?" Mal asked at last.

"Now? Nothing. As you say, he is not yet born. And even with wits intact, he cannot be a threat to us for some years yet."

"Why are they doing this, these skraylings who become humans?"

Kiiren sighed. "Many thousands of years ago, my people were very few, fewer even than now. We were afraid we would die and disappear altogether, but then humans came and after much time became friends of us. But still there were not enough children for those who wished to be reborn. And so some took human form. Those that did grew proud, called themselves gods, and there was war..."

"I do not think that could happen here," Mal said. "We have a God in Heaven, and do not worship men."

"Perhaps not. But to rule in secret, that is wrong."

"They seek to rule us?"

"They think you will take our lands, and those of our friends."

Mal nodded. "They are probably right."

"They are very afraid of you, and will break our oldest laws to protect our land."

"How do we stop them?"

"I do not know," Kiiren said.

"What about Sandy? He was lucid for a while, down in the cellar, better than I had seen him in years, and yet now…"

"That was Jathekkil's doing."

"How? Why?"

"Your brother was kept in irons for long time, yes? This hurt Erishen, made your brother soul-sick. Freeing him, your brother suffered for short while but then recovered."

"But–"

"Touch of iron sends Erishen back into depths of mind. Sandy is sane. But this cannot last. Kept like this –" he gestured to the supine figure "– he will soon be unwell as before."

"But you can make him whole again," Mal said. "Can't you?"

Kiiren shook his head. "Can you mend cup that is smashed to pieces? Ship that founders on rocks?"

"Then you can drive Erishen out, so he may be reborn."

"There is only one way to make it happen. Body must die, as Jathekkil tried with you."

"No. There must be something–"

"There is not. For either of you."

Mal shuddered. "You're saying Suffolk – Jathekkil – was telling the truth? That I have part of Erishen's soul?"

"Did I not tell you you are touched by Erishen?" Kiiren placed two *shakholaat* cups side by side. "If I pour into one of these, and my aim is not true, will not some fall into second? So it was with Erishen."

"Get it out of me."

"I cannot. Do you not listen to what I say?"

"I don't believe you. You're just saying all this because you want to keep Sandy to yourself."

Kiiren hesitated, looked at Sandy, then back at Mal.

"No. You may have him, if that is your desire. Take him. Go."

"You mean that?"

"Do not ask second time."

Mal stared at his brother. "But... he is not cured."

"There is no 'cure'," Kiiren said wearily. "If he goes with you and wears iron, he remains as he was. If he stays... He will be Erishen."

"So I lose him either way."

Mal rubbed a hand across his face. Was this not what he had wanted all these years, what he had prayed for? An end to the fits, the ravings, the silences? But at what price? He looked once more at his brother's face, serene and so like his own.

"Do it," he said. "I will not see him suffer any longer."

Kiiren inclined his head, mumbling thanks in a garbled mixture of English and Vinlandic.

"Enough," Mal said. "I have to go, before I change my mind."

He got to his feet, pulled on his boots and walked out of the camp without looking back. Night was falling fast. He had better get back before curfew. But back where? Not the Faulkners' house. Gabriel had moved in with Ned, and Mal was not about to intrude on them.

Walsingham's money lay heavy in his pocket. Thirty pieces of silver. He had to wrap his arms about his chest to stop

himself from throwing the purse in the river. As he approached
the bridge at the near end of St Olave's Street, a slight, fair-
haired figure jumped down from the railing. Hendricks. Her
grin faded as she realised he was alone.

"Sir?"

He shook his head, and they walked into Southwark together, the darkness gathering around them like a cloak. He
glanced at her profile as they walked, recalling that first day
in Paris Gardens.

"What of your friends?" he asked, more to take his mind off
Sandy than out of real interest.

She told him about Parrish and Eaton, and the disbanding
of Suffolk's Men.

"And you?"

"With my master gone, I have no other employ."

He laughed bitterly. "That makes two of us. Unless you
count Walsingham, and he has not charged me with any duties. Yet."

It was not quite the truth, but he was too weary to explain.
Perhaps tomorrow. After he had drunk himself into oblivion,
and sobered up again.

"You're going to work for Walsingham?" she asked.

"I need something to occupy my days. And I must confess
that ciphers are intriguing."

"I could help," she said, glancing up at him shyly.

"You?"

"Why not? Did we not work well together?"

He stopped, and drew her aside into an alley, where none
could see.

"It is too dangerous for a woman," he said softly.

"Then you do think of me as a woman."

In the gloom he could barely make out the pale blur of her
features, but he could hear the smile in her voice. By way of a

reply, he put his arms around her and bent to kiss her. She placed her hands on his shoulders and rose on tiptoe; at the pressure he let out an involuntary hiss of pain. Muttering an apology she transferred her hands to his waist. Her lips burned against his, and he drank from them like a man parched. Or frozen.

As she pressed against him, he felt something... hard. In her breeches.

"What in God's name–?"

"Um, just part of my disguise," she said, pulling away slightly. "Got to have something in there for the look of it."

"Oh. Of course."

He kissed her again, partly to reassure her that it didn't bother him, but mostly because he needed to forget the past hour. He stroked her temples, her hair, the small of her back, the tight curve of her arse... She trembled. Damn, still a virgin, of course. He moved his hand back to her waist. She pressed against him, willing but tense as a deer under the hunter's gaze. After a few minutes they both realised she wasn't the only one with a bulge in her breeches.

"If you like me this way," she said with an embarrassed laugh, "I shall remain a boy. It is what I am used to."

He released her, abashed. It had been one thing to lie with Ned when he was lonely and in need, but a boy... Here in England they might be safe enough if they were discreet, but in France it would be a very different matter. Rumour had it Francis Bacon's brother was nearly burnt at the stake for molesting one of his pages, and had to flee home to England in disgrace.

"That cannot be," he said. "If you insist on remaining in this guise, then you and I cannot be lovers."

"No!" She bit her lip. "What... what about Ned and Gabriel? If they can be happy together, why cannot we?"

"They are grown men and, more importantly, men of little consequence. I have brought myself to the notice of those in power, and must therefore remain above the law. In the eyes of the world, at least."

"And where those eyes cannot pierce?" she said, glancing at the shadows about them.

She looked so hopeful – but he would have to dash those hopes, for both their sakes.

"You are a woman – and a child. You cannot understand."

She folded her arms, her eyes glittering with indignation.

"How like a man! You think because I am a woman I am weak and useless. Well, Master Maliverny Catlyn, next time you are taken captive and in peril of death, *I* shall not come to your rescue."

She marched back out into the street, head held high. He burst out laughing and followed her.

"You have me there." He weighed the purse in his pocket. A dozen angels; and more to come, if he took up Walsingham's suggestion. "Very well, I will take you into my service. I owe you that much at least."

She halted and turned back.

"Service? I will not be your doxy."

"Honest employment, I swear." Though it will be a sore trial of my honour, if I am to be chaste. "I am a man of substance now. I cannot do without a valet to look after my wardrobe. That is what you do, is it not, tireman?"

She grinned at him. "Yes. That is what I do."

"Then it is agreed." He held out his hand, and she grasped it firmly. "Come, let's find an inn for the night, and tomorrow, lodgings."

She fell in at his side and they walked down St Olave's Street in companionable silence, leaving the skrayling camp and guild house far behind. One day he would go back for Sandy.

One day. Until then, he had another young soul in his charge. Perhaps he would make a Catholic of her yet. Making an honest woman of her; now there was a challenge.

EPILOGUE

Prince Robert shaded his eyes against the setting sun as the cavalcade trotted westwards along the London road. Golden onion domes glinted to his left, stirring a hundred memories of homecomings, but first he had a visit to make. A prince who neglected his magnates stored up trouble for the future.

Both riders and horses were bone-weary, though they had gone scarcely a dozen miles today. The sucking clay mud of the Thames valley had frozen overnight into a treacherous surface of ice-slick ruts and hollows that had already claimed one animal's leg and left its rider bruised and winded. Robert pulled his furs around him and flexed his gloved fingers. Having taken over his mother's tradition of the royal summer progress, he was no stranger to hard travel, but in this weather men of good sense stayed at home. If they could.

They passed the ivory grandeur of Syon House and turned south towards Ferrymead. Behind him, Robert could hear William Bourchier, the Earl of Bath, congratulating young Josceline Percy on his eldest brother's great good fortune in acquiring both Syon House and the lovely Lady Dorothy, though the boy seemed little impressed by either. Other lesser courtiers joined in the envious chorus. Robert noted those who sounded most sycophantic; it did not do for a powerful and ancient family like the Percys to become too popular. Especially the Percys. They had not forgotten that Robert's grandfather had been made Duke of Northumberland whilst they were only earls of that county.

Wrapped in these thoughts, he paid little heed to the servants that ran to greet them as they rode into the courtyard at Ferrymead. The master of the house was not, of course, at his door to greet them, so Robert left his escort in the great hall and ascended the stair with only Bourchier and Percy in tow. He found Grey in the ancient solar, seated by the fire. The young duke was wrapped in a crumpled blue velvet robe and clutched a small, fat book as if it held the very secret of life eternal; a psalter or book of devotions, perhaps? It would be understandable, for a man who had come so near death.

"You will forgive me if I do not rise, sire," Grey said, bowing as best he could from his seated position.

Robert clapped him on the shoulder. "I cannot chastise a man for hurts gained in protecting his own father. Even if he was a traitor."

Grey winced and mumbled an apology, then rang a bell by his side. Whilst the servants hurried back and forth with flagons of hot spiced wine and currant cakes, Robert sat down opposite and took a moment to study the man he had diverted his journey to see. Grey's features were gaunt and sickly pale as from long illness, which was no more than Robert had expected, but there was an intensity in his gaze that had not been there before.

"Will you spend Christmas at Richmond, sire?" Grey asked, after the servants had left.

"That is my intent," Robert replied. "Juliana is well enough for merriment, and I am not sorry to leave the city behind for a while. You must join us, at least for the Christmas feast."

"Alas, my prince, I am..." Grey gestured helplessly at his body.

"Nonsense," Robert replied. "I'll have my men carry you across the river and all the way to the great hall if need be."

Grey inclined his head in submission. Robert picked up one of the silver cups and handed it to one of the servants to taste. After a moment's hesitation the man sipped the wine, nodded, and returned it to the prince with a bow.

"Your son is well?" Grey asked, pretending not to notice this breach of etiquette.

"Both of them," Robert replied. "There was some talk of a fever, but I dispatched a skrayling physician forthwith."

"You trust them with your son's life?"

"My second son," Robert pointed out. "Besides, they are so cowed after that business with your father–"

"I had nothing to do with that, sire, I swear!"

Grey began to tremble as if he had taken another fever.

"I believe you," Robert told him. "I loved your father, and I confess his betrayal cut me deeply. But I am willing to let by-gones be bygones. *If* you find me your father's lieutenants amongst the Huntsmen."

"Oh I shall, sire, I promise you."

"Topcliffe is at your disposal, should you need him."

Grey sniffed. "Topcliffe is a butcher. And the leaders of the Huntsmen are too clever to reveal themselves to their foot soldiers. No, more subtle means are needed." He tapped the book on the arm of his chair. "Leave it to me, sire. I will have all the information I need, soon enough."

"Hmm. Well, I must be going. Juliana will fret if I do not arrive before dark. She thinks this country full of brigands and rebels."

Grey smiled fixedly. "I am honoured by your notice, sire." He reached for the bell.

"No matter," Robert said with a wave of his hand. "I know my way out."

He left by the east door and went down the grassy slope to the riverside. The sun was nearly on the horizon, and an ice-edged wind cut through his cloak as they crossed in one of the little ferry boats.

Leaving his guards and companions behind entirely, Robert strode through the echoing halls of the palace and made his way up to his wife's private apartments. There was a familiar scent here now, a sourness that he associated with the arrival of a new babe. Though not pleasant in itself, it spoke of life and health, for which the Lord be praised.

Ladies-in-waiting bobbed curtsies as Robert passed, though some glanced up at him with mock coyness. He wondered if any of them had been praying for the princess's death in childbirth. Lady Dorothy, perhaps, hoping to escape marriage to that old goat Northumberland? Or Lady Alice, plump and doe-eyed and ripe for bedding? Perhaps he would send for her later.

"*Meu príncipe!*" Juliana cried, leaping up from the window seat. "How I have longed to see you again."

He kissed her on the mouth, then looked about the room.

"And where is this fine young princeling you have given me?" he asked.

Juliana beckoned to her serving women, who brought forth a bundle of creamy silks and linens with a red, wrinkled face beneath a lace-trimmed bonnet.

"My dear, this is your son, Prince Henry Vasco Dudley."

Robert reached out a hand to touch the soft pink skin. The babe opened its eyes, blinked, then its tiny fingers closed around one of his own.

"Ah, he knows his papa!" the nurse crooned.

Robert gazed fondly at his son. The smallness of these fragile creatures never ceased to astonish him, each perfectly formed fingernail a miniature counterpart of his own.

"Hail, Prince Henry," he murmured. "Mayhap one day, King Henry the Ninth of England."

The babe looked him straight in the eye. And smiled.

About *the* Author

Anne Lyle was born in what is known to the tourist industry as "Robin Hood Country", and grew up fascinated by English history, folklore, and swashbuckling heroes. Unfortunately there was little demand in 1970s Nottingham for diminutive female swordswomen, so she studied sensible subjects like science and languages instead.

It appears that although you can take the girl out of Sherwood Forest, you can't take Sherwood Forest out of the girl. She now spends every spare hour writing (or at least planning) fantasy fiction about spies, actors, outlaws and other folk on the fringes of society.

Anne lives in Cambridge, a city full of medieval and Tudor buildings where cattle graze on the common land much as they did in Shakespeare's London. She prides herself on being able to ride a horse (badly), sew a sampler and cut a quill pen, but hasn't the least idea how to drive one of those new-fangled automobile thingies.

annelyle.com

Author's Note

I first came across the name Maliverny Catlyn whilst researching Sir Francis Walsingham for an early draft of this book, and knew I had to use it. The historical Catlyn was an ex-soldier in Walsingham's employ, a man who "possessed the manners and bearing... to be able to circulate freely within the higher echelons of society"[*]; unfortunately he was also a little old to be my swashbuckling hero, and a theatre-hating Puritan to boot! However he is a very obscure historical figure, about whom little else is known beyond what is stated above, and I was writing an alternate history after all, so I decided to make a few changes.

I divided the historical Catlyn into two characters: a forty-ish Puritan forced to work with a theatre company against his personal wishes (John Dunfell, the Duke of Suffolk's secretary), and a twenty-five year-old ex-soldier recruited by Walsingham. For the rest of Mal's background, I started with his name.

Maliverny is a name from Provence in France, and from what little I could discover through Google, belonged to a minor family of aristocracy. In Elizabethan England, it was not unknown for the upper classes to name younger sons after their mother's family: the most famous example is probably

Guilford Dudley, husband of Lady Jane Grey and brother of Robert Dudley, named after his mother Jane Guilford. Hence I made Mal half-French, the son of a French heiress and an English diplomatic aide at the French Court.

From there, everything fell into place. Provence was predominantly Catholic during this period, so it seemed obvious to me that Mal would have Catholic sympathies, although I wanted him to be pragmatic enough not to be a zealot, so I decided that firsthand experience of war on the Continent had made him cynical and wary of any cause. Also, the atmosphere of paranoid xenophobia in late 16th century England means that anyone of non-English birth and/or appearance is suspect, regardless of their religion, which would help to explain why Mal's career has been patchy, and provides another source of conflict.

My Maliverny Catlyn may not be true to the historical facts, but I aim to make all my characters as true to the period as I can. It's part of the pleasure of writing the genre – and reading it.

* Robert Hutchinson, *Elizabeth's Spy Master*, Phoenix, 2007.

ACKNOWLEDGMENTS

Firstly, I have to credit my publisher, Marc Gascoigne of Angry Robot Books, for his great taste in fiction – not just my work, but that of the many brilliant authors whose novels he has unleashed upon an unsuspecting world. Marc is a great sounding board for ideas, and puts up with the Tigger-like enthusiasm and anxiety of debut authors like myself with heroic patience. Angry Robot lieutenant Lee Harris earns my gratitude for editing and general cheerleading, and my agent John Berlyne for being our go-between and doing the boring paperwork so that I get paid for this stuff.

These days, writers rarely work alone in freezing garrets. Between online communities and offline events, it's easier than ever to share your work with other writers and get advice and feedback. I'd therefore like to thank all the dozens, nay hundreds, of people who have helped me over the years, but in particular my writing group in Cambridge, who critiqued numerous early drafts of this book: Una McCormack, Alex Beecroft, Rebecca Payne and Naomi Clark. You girls are probably sick of the story by now, but I promise this is the final version.

Fantasy writer and teacher extraordinaire Holly Lisle (no relation!) earns my undying thanks for her online courses on writing and editing, without which the manuscript of this book might still be languishing in revision Hell. Finally, two other authors deserve special mention for putting me on the path to publication: Ian Whates, for introducing me to Marc Gascoigne late one night in the FantasyCon bar, and Juliet E McKenna, for prodding me into attending SFF conventions in the first place.

Behind nearly every successful author, there's a long-suffering loved one who puts up with our hours at the keyboard and inexplicable obsessions with people who don't exist. Thank you, Richard, for your infinite patience and endless cups of tea.

Anne Lyle,
Cambridge, 2011

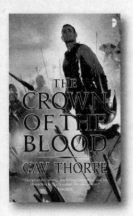

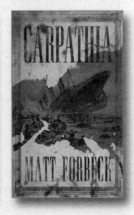

ANGRY ROBOT

TOO MUCH IS NOT ENOUGH
Collect the entire Angry Robot range

DAN ABNETT
- [ ] Embedded
- [ ] Triumff: Her Majesty's Hero

GUY ADAMS
- [ ] The World House
- [ ] Restoration

JO ANDERTON
- [ ] Debris

LAUREN BEUKES
- [ ] Moxyland
- [ ] Zoo City

THOMAS BLACKTHORNE
(aka John Meaney)
- [ ] Edge
- [ ] Point

MAURICE BROADDUS
- [ ] King Maker
- [ ] King's Justice
- [ ] King's War

ADAM CHRISTOPHER
- [ ] Empire State

PETER CROWTHER
- [ ] Darkness Falling

ALIETTE DE BODARD
- [ ] Servant of the Underworld
- [ ] Harbinger of the Storm
- [ ] Master of the House of Darts

MATT FORBECK
- [ ] Amortals
- [ ] Vegas Knights

JUSTIN GUSTAINIS
- [ ] Hard Spell

GUY HALEY
- [ ] Reality 36
- [ ] Omega Point

COLIN HARVEY
- [ ] Damage Time
- [ ] Winter Song

MATTHEW HUGHES
- [ ] The Damned Busters

TRENT JAMIESON
- [ ] Roil

K W JETER
- [ ] Infernal Devices
- [ ] Morlock Night

J ROBERT KING
- [ ] Angel of Death
- [ ] Death's Disciples

GARY McMAHON
- [ ] Pretty Little Dead Things
- [ ] Dead Bad Things

ANDY REMIC
- [ ] Kell's Legend
- [ ] Soul Stealers
- [ ] Vampire Warlords

CHRIS ROBERSON
- [ ] Book of Secrets

MIKE SHEVDON
- [ ] Sixty-One Nails
- [ ] The Road to Bedlam

DAVID TALLERMAN
- [ ] Giant Thief

GAV THORPE
- [ ] The Crown of the Blood
- [ ] The Crown of the Conqueror

LAVIE TIDHAR
- [ ] The Bookman
- [ ] Camera Obscura
- [ ] The Great Game

TIM WAGGONER
- [ ] Nekropolis
- [ ] Dead Streets
- [ ] Dark War

KAARON WARREN
- [ ] Mistification
- [ ] Slights
- [ ] Walking the Tree

IAN WHATES
- [ ] City of Dreams & Nightmare
- [ ] City of Hope & Despair
- [ ] City of Light & Shadow